Tutankhamun's Uncle

The Metamorphosis of Moses

A novel

Tutankhamun's Uncle

The Metamorphosis of Moses

A novel

Alan Bell

ZheeTanitH Press

For Hazel

**Part of an article published in *The Literary Digest*
20 January 1923**

'There were some remarkable wreaths, still looking evergreen,
and one of the boxes contained rolls of papyri, which are
expected to render a mass of information.'

During the euphoria following the discovery of Tutankhamun's
tomb many newspapers advised their readers that these scrolls,
historical documents of great significance, had gone missing.

* * *

On Tuesday, 28 November 1922, Lord Carnarvon wrote to
his friend, the great Egyptologist Sir Alan Gardiner: '…it is
Tutankhamun. There are beds, boxes and every conceivable
thing and there is a box with papyri in it.'

The papyri were never seen again. What happened to them?

This book is based on those papyri.

The Main Characters

The Royal Family

Amenhotep III	Pharaoh 1387 BC. Diplomat and skilled international statesman; ruler of the greatest empire in the known world
Queen Tiye	Wife of Amenhotep III. Zealot monotheist
Thutmoses	Crown Prince. First Son of Amenhotep and Tiye
Amenhotep IV, aka Akhenaten	Second son of Amenhotep and Tiye; Pharaoh 1350 BC
Nefertiti	Wife of Akhenaten
Tiye	Hittite princess. Lesser wife of Akhenaten. Mother of Thutankhaten
Meritaten	First daughter of Akhenaten and Nefertiti. Pharaoh 1335 BC
Smenkhkare	First son of Akhenaten with a lesser wife. Joint Pharaoh with Meritaten 1335 BC
Thutankhaten, aka Tutankhamun	Third son of Akhenaten and Tiye. Pharaoh 1328 BC

The Priests of Amun

Olamun	Chief Priest of Amun in Memphis
Ahpet	High Priest of Amun, residing in Thebes
Tinya	Successor to Ahpet. Distant cousin of Amenhotep III
Anen	Brother to Queen Tiye. To succeed Tinya as High Priest by order of Amenhotep III

| Aye | Son and successor to Anen. Cousin of Akhenaten and Thutmoses |

The Army

| Rebiu | General of Amenhotep III's army |
| Horemheb | Successor to Rebiu. Head of Akhenaten's army |

The Nobility

| Nanua | A noble distantly related to the pharaoh |

Foreign Kings and important characters

| Ikheny | Rebel Nubian king |
| Suppiluliumas | Hittite king, keen on expansion into Egypt |

Other Characters

Hapya	Priest of Aten. Tutor to Thutmoses
Kheruef	Amenhotep III's spy master
Miriam and Yuk	Royal servants
Sefu and Heru	Assassins

Gods

Amun	The head god of the state religion of many gods and spirits. His priests administer the empire
Mut, Nun, Atum, Tefmit, Shu	The gods of creation,
Tefnut, Nut, Geb, Osiris, Horus, Isis, Seth, Nephthys, Anubis	subservient to Amun
Aten	The god of the monotheists

Map of Egypt and Surrounding Powers c. 1375 BC

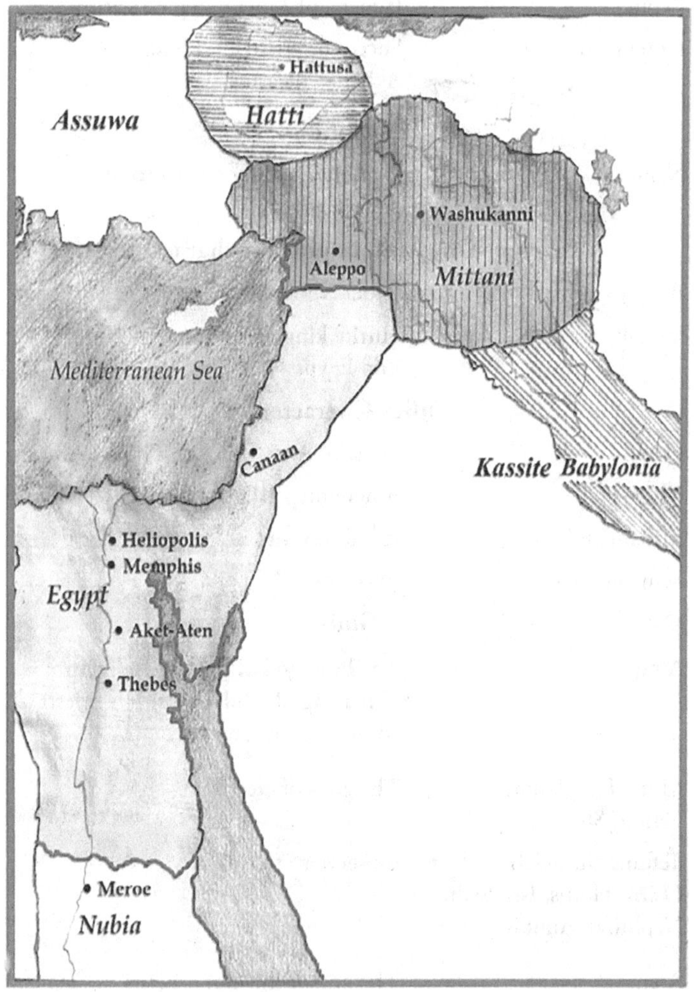

Genealogical Table

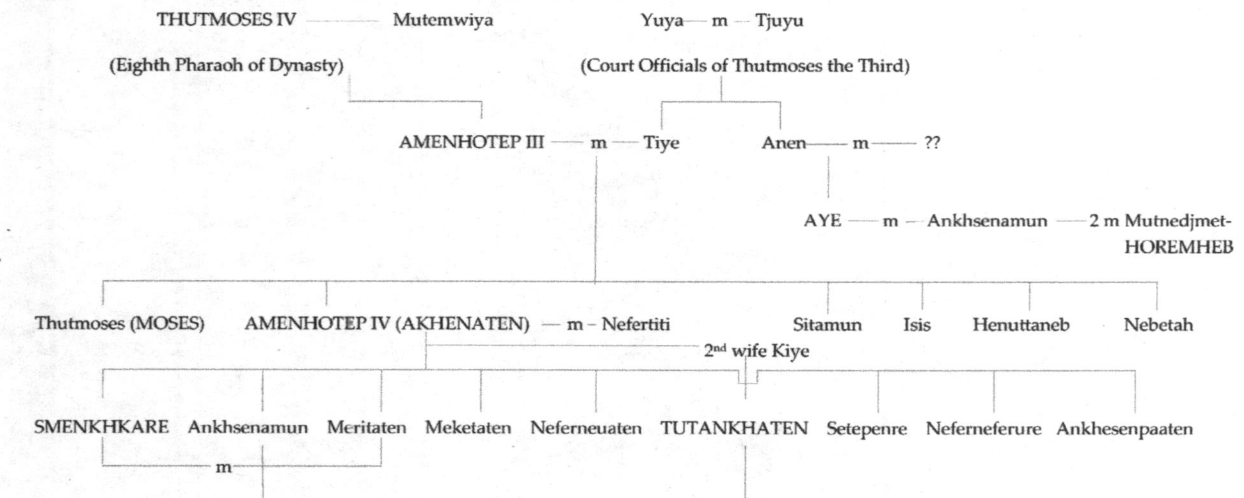

xi

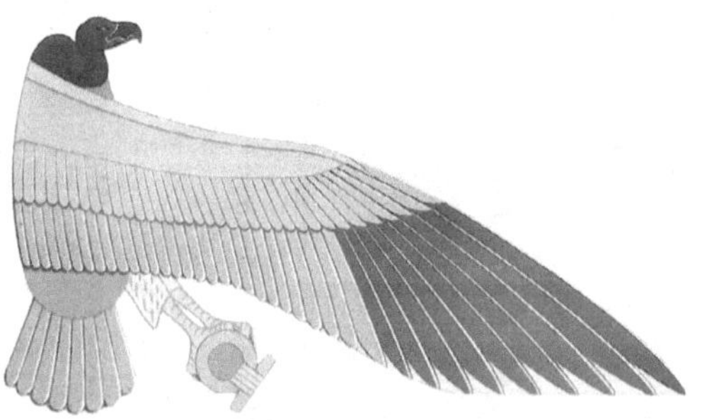

Prologue

The pharaoh looked at the bones she had cast. For a few moments, they rolled on her mat before they settled; he traced the inscribed runes with his fingertips. The marks on the bones were faded, and looked as if they had been there since the dawn of time, somehow older than the bones they were carved on. He looked, but he could not read them; that was why she was here.

The old woman did not seem keen to interpret the runes; she shifted in her chair and waited for the pharaoh to speak. She waited, and waited, but he didn't say a word. His head was bowed, and he seemed lost in the ineffable patterns spread on the leather mat.

'What is it you wish to see, majesty?' she asked, finally.

'I ... I don't actually know. I'm hoping the message is clear to you, and you can make it clear to me.'

She suppressed a sigh of irritation; so often the very people who dismissed her craft as superstition were the ones who wanted the most miraculous results. She looked down at the runes and an involuntary shiver passed through her; the message was clear, clear as day. But the pharaoh wouldn't like it. 'Majesty,' she said. 'You are hoping for a member of your family to come and help you?'

'I . . .' his resigned nod was enough.

The pattern the bones revealed was obvious and ominous. She could see the path that lay before him, and where it led. She was reluctant to tell him the full truth, sought for a way to break the news to him gently. Her life might depend on it.

'The omens are mixed, majesty. They speak of dissent among your people, of those who want to undermine you, defeat you. Of those who question your status as a god.'

'I am aware of that; everyone is aware of that, woman.'

The witch took a breath, calculated. She stretched out a withered hand, the skin loose and grey, liver spotted and heavily wrinkled; shifted one of the ancient bones so that it rolled onto its back. 'The one who is far away, who has fled. You believe he can help you in this struggle and bring peace and prosperity back to the land.'

'Yes. Well, I hope so. I'm not sure. I'm incapable of belief anymore.'

'Hope is blind, majesty; it is a delusion at best, food for the futile.'

'What do you mean, witch? What do you see?'

'He will not return. Be glad of this; if he returned, there would be strife such as you cannot imagine. You must forget him, and all that he stands for; only then can you regain the trust of those around you.'

'Then I am truly lost. I cannot rule without him.'

'It is as you say, majesty. You are lost; for now. But a time will come when your name will ring in the halls of history. All that you and your family have fought for will die here, but it will not disappear forever. One day your god will rule the world.'

'I don't understand. I'm doomed but I'm not. Do all witches speak in riddles?'

'The runes may not speak simply, majesty, but they do not lie. What I have told you is truth. What you choose to do with it? That is another matter. I have spoken, and I am done here.' The witch gathered up the bones and slipped them into her aegis; she rolled up the mat and slid it into a sheath hanging from her belt. With a perfunctory bow, she turned to leave.

The pharaoh gazed out to the sky, as if in a trance. He saw the shadow of an eagle owl transcend from the earth. It held prey in its talons, something still and lifeless. His trance broke. 'Wait. Please wait. I have more questions.'

But the witch was gone, the fragrance of stale herbs the only sign she had ever been there. The pharaoh leaned over the table, resting his chin on his hands. The disc of the sun settled on the horizon, lengthening the shadows in the chamber; darkness cloaked the lone figure at the ornate table. Dawn would find him there still, his brow furrowed, his knuckles white, ruminating on the impossible.

Fifty Years Earlier

1376 BC

Memphis, Egypt. In the reign of Amenhotep III

'Push, highness, push! You are nearly there.' Aoh wiped sweat from the queen's brow with a linen cloth while Queen Tiye stared, wild-eyed, back at her. For twelve hours the Queen had breathed, pushed, shuddered and suffered, mindlessly obeying the commands of the royal midwife; she had had enough, but her interminable labour refused to end.

The chamber where she lay was sparsely furnished. It was lit with dozens of candles and lamps which flickered in unison, a pulsing eddy of pale, cream light circling likes ocean waves around the chamber. A servant, a long-necked jug in her hand, scurried around the room refilling the lamps and replacing the candles as they burned out. Aoh turned to the girl; she needed her. 'Don't worry about the lamps now, girl; dawn will be here shortly.' She pointed to a corner of the room. 'Bring me those towels and a winding sheet.'

The room was all women, scurrying here and there to help as best they could, a hive of worker bees moving without thinking to service their queen.

The balcony was open to the elements, to try and pull in the coolness of the night. Luxurious veils of cream linen shivered softly as welcome air flowed across the balcony and suffused the room.

Tiye heard a feral scream rending the air of the chamber, realised that the voice was hers. *Please, let it be a boy.* She had given the pharaoh too many girls. Her jet-black hair matted against her forehead, she grimaced and pushed again.

Another rest.

She breathed a prayer towards the horizon. Suddenly, hope. She saw pale light heralding the dawn. Aoh, sensing her mistress' gaze, glanced up; fringes of pale grey crept across the horizon. A good omen.

Tiye loosened her grip on the side of the bed, and slumped back onto her pillows, exhausted. She conjured a little optimism; the approaching dawn rekindled her energy, at least a little. She could do this, with Aten's help.

'Change the clock!' Aoh shouted to an assistant.

The woman ran to the table and turned the sand clock upside down. 'There, it is done, the day begins.'

Aoh moved to the foot of the bed; it was nearly time. 'You,' she pointed and ordered, 'bring a cool cloth and comfort her highness.' She looked into Tiye's dark brown, almost black, cool eyes, 'Highness, breathe, and push, your child is here, nearly here.' Aoh stretched aching muscles and readied herself.

Suddenly, the bustle of activity was interrupted by the crack of a staff on the chamber's great cedar doors. Aoh snapped at the pale girl hovering behind her. 'You,' she said, her irritation clear, 'go and see who that is.' Before the diminutive servant could get to the door, a booming voice thundered out. 'Behold, the priests of Amun come. Make way for the servants of the gods.'

Aoh snorted in derision. 'Push, highness.' *Priests at a birthing; how useful.*

The tall cedar doors slid smoothly open and the procession shuffled in. Twelve acolytes, robed in black, heads shaved except for a tiny topknot, lined up before the door—six on the left, six on the right—to usher in the chief priest.

Tiye tried to ignore them; she had other things on her mind. The pain had peaked now, and the baby was ready to tear itself from her womb. It felt to her as if the priests had timed their arrival intentionally to create the maximum disruption. *They want me to fail; Olamun and his cronies have come to watch me die, or birth another girl. Damn them,* she thought, *and damn their blank stone gods.*

Olamun, the chief priest of the palace complex, approached the bed, but stopped when Aoh fixed him with a baleful eye. He might be a power in the royal household, but he was no match for the stout, pugnacious midwife. He took a couple of steps back, and looked for a way to retrieve his dignity.

He was tall, and thin, his face pinched and pale. Standing in the centre of the chamber, his acolytes ranged around him, he stretched out his meagre arms and began to chant. His voice was querulous and reedy, the sacred words unclear. He brought the tips of his fingers together; his acolytes moved to form a semicircle around him, casting wary glances at the midwives. They chanted with their high priest, a susurrating hum that filled the chamber, until the queen's scream silenced them. Olamun gestured resentfully to his entourage, his wand whipped up and down, and then up again; his acolytes resumed their prayer. The smell of incense filled the room, as Olamun's assistant swung a censor from the end of a long thin chain, a counterpoint to the acrid fragrance of the sour herbs Aoh had set to boil. Each of the acolytes held a censer in front of him, while Olamun held a wand, a sceptre of pure white, gilded with a golden tip. The crowd of priests did their best to look superior, but here in a chamber of working women they felt beleaguered and uncertain.

'Now, highness, breathe and push; I can see the head.' Aoh stepped deliberately in front of the chief priest, planting herself between him and Tiye, and turned to the servant on her right. 'You girl, pass me those cloths.' Aoh turned to her queen, 'We are nearly there, highness.' The servant turned to fetch more water, pre-empting Aoh's instruction.

Olamun paused in his chanting and sniffed regally. 'Make room, woman; I must witness the birth.' Aoh smiled menacingly and stood up. 'Certainly, Holiness; why don't you stand right here? The baby is about to emerge; the baby, and a certain amount of blood.'

Olamun stepped back at once. 'Erm, I can see well enough from here; get on with your work, mistress.'

The last of the lamps guttered and failed, but they were no longer needed. The first fingers of rosy light found their way into the chamber as Tiye's struggles reached a climax.

'Push, highness; push, and your work is done.'

'I am pushing, damn it!' Tiye shouted, her face contorted with effort and resentment.

The midwives redoubled their efforts; the acolytes chanted and tried not to look. Olamun cast a furtive glance towards the queen; Aoh sneered and crouched between the queen's legs, her hands working feverishly.

The lusty wail of a new-born drowned the pious chanting. 'It's a boy, highness; you have a son!' Aoh wrapped the child in fine linen swaddling and passed him to his mother.

Olamun's querulous voice rose in triumph. 'A boy! The pharaoh has an heir. The gods be praised.' He turned to his acolytes. 'Praise Amun. Give thanks to our great god for the gift of a prince.'

'Thanks be to Amun, praise be to Amun. Praise be to all the gods,' Olamun intoned, his acolytes repeating the mantra. 'They have bestowed their favour; they have given us a boy, he will be pharaoh, he will be ranked among the gods. Long live our Pharaoh Amenhotep and the fruit of his loins, our new prince.' *That the pharaoh's heir should come from the womb of a heretic*, he thought. *The shame of it.*

Aoh fixed him with a baleful stare; Tiye did likewise.

'And ... er, long live our queen.' *A shame you survived the birthing bed, you heretic bitch.*

Tiye breathed a prayer too, to a different god. 'Aten be praised! Thank you, my lord.' She held the tiny bundle in her outstretched palms and raised him to the light streaming in through the window. Her son formed a tiny silhouette against the disc of the sun as Aten finally cleared the horizon.

Amenhotep paced the floor of the small chamber. He clutched an old scroll in his right hand. The scroll gradually deformed under the pressure of his grip, and with an audible sigh, the end came off and dropped to the floor. Oblivious, he kicked it into the corner of the room, where the papyrus dissolved in a tiny tornado of dust. Catching the flicker of the tiny dust devil in the corner of his eye, Amenhotep looked down at his hand. *Damn,* he thought, *that scroll was a priceless relic, what am I doing?*

The distant clamour from the birthing suite was gone. The silence excited him. He breathed a prayer and walked out onto the balcony; the sun's disc was visible above the walls of the palace compound. *Aten*, he murmured, *let it be a boy*. He rested trembling hands on the parapet, trying to calm his nerves; he could do nothing but wait and pray.

In the hallway outside his chamber, the two guards exchanged a glance. 'What do you think, Shenti; worth a wager? Five shenas of copper it's a boy.'

'I'll take your metal, Umi; the pharaoh eats too much fish to make boys.'

A messenger hustled into view, his face flushed from running. Umi raised a quizzical eyebrow. The messenger winked, held his hand to his groin, middle finger extended. Shenti managed a wry grin; he might have lost money, but the news was good.

Umi smiled a smug smile. Five copper shenas would buy a few jugs of beer to wet the new prince's head, and he could brag about knowing about the new prince before the pharaoh. He reached for the great copper shield which protruded from the cedar door and stuck it three times with an easy swing of his hand. The guards on the other side slowly opened the heavy doors.

Umi turned to the opening, one hand behind his back gesturing the transfer of copper from his fellow guard. 'In you go, Mehy; wouldn't do for the pharaoh to be the last to know.'

Amenhotep dismissed the messenger with a cursory wave of his hand. He had shown no emotion while there were others in the room. He walked to the balcony and gazed out over the palace grounds, and further, to the Nile and beyond. The world bathed in the light of Aten; there was barely a cloud to trouble the cerulean blue. Amenhotep breathed out, as if he had held his breath all night. No matter. He was blessed; they were all blessed. His dynasty had a future now.

'I will name him after my father; Thut-Moses, the most beloved of Thut; a fitting name for a prince of the realm of the

gods.' For a moment, he was lost in his dreams: the prince leading an army into glorious battle; the prince marrying a beautiful
foreign princess; the prince leading a triumphal procession of
the gods at Karnak. Then he started awake, and shouted for his
chamber master.

'Dedu!'

Dedu hurried into the room, smiling. *The slaves knew before
I did,* thought Amenhotep. *No matter.*

'Dress me, Dedu; we will visit our son, the new prince.'

* * *

Ottah crept like the mouse that he was into the bedroom, already
cringing. He shuffled reluctantly towards the bed, gauging the
snores; hesitated for a moment, leant forward and gently touched
the High Priest's shoulder. No reaction. He gathered himself,
found a morsel of courage and prodded the sleeping priest. The
body in front of him shifted a little. A quiet growl told him the
great man was awake.

'What do you think you are doing, insolent fool?' The irate
priest's head emerged from a mess of tousled blankets.

'Messen —' Ottah managed two syllables before the flat of a
priestly hand landed a stinging blow on his cheek. 'Messenger,'
he said quickly, the priest's blow still ringing in his ear. 'From
the palace,' he added breathlessly.

Ahpet, the sleeping giant, rose to a sitting position. He was
approaching his sixtieth year and had been High Priest for five.
A handsome man, built like a soldier, he had been popular with
the ladies and his peers. All that had ceased, in theory, when he
became a celibate servant of the gods, a priest of Amun; a great
honour for his family. He smiled inwardly; priest or no, power

had its privileges, and unbridled power..., well his father had not realised what that would bring!

'Holiness, there is a messenger from Memphis, from the Pharaoh. He will not speak to anyone but you, Great One. He insisted that you be woken.'

Ahpet grunted. 'I am awake. Your clumsiness has seen to that.'

Ahpet shifted to the edge of the bed. *Marvellous. The queen must have given up the child at last, and the pharaoh wakes me in the middle of the night so I can congratulate his heretic wife on pushing out another princess for the royal coffers to feed.*

'Get me a piss pot and show him into the reception room while I ready myself.'

He looked around, spotting a blanket.

'And hand me that; I have no wish to expose myself to the likes of you.'

The servant placed the blanket around Ahpet, careful not to touch the flesh of the great priest. He took an involuntary step back, keeping out of range of the high priest's hands.

'Now go. No, stay and help me ready myself. Send someone to show the man to the reception chamber, and find me some food. Pharaoh's messenger can wait.'

Ten minutes later, Ahpet left his bedroom and made his way to his reception chamber, hastily wiping breadcrumbs from his robe. He swept into the chamber in a rustle of rich linen, and settled himself on the dais. He studied the familiar murals that adorned the walls, checked that his nails were clean, cleared his throat and finally acknowledged the messenger.

'What news is so important you must wake the high priest?'

He didn't look at the man, simply held out his hand and waited for him to place a scroll in it. Then he flicked his hand dismissively, indicating that the messenger should leave.

'Stop!' The messenger turned nervously in the doorway. 'I may need you to take back a message. Stand by the door.'

He unfurled the scroll and read. His eyes widened and a smile of genuine joy warmed his stern features.

'A boy!'

He looked up at the image of Amun on the chamber wall, addressing himself to his god. *You have increased your family, Lord Amun; it is well.* He returned to the scroll, and read the good news again.

She has done it, at last, the heretic. A boy. The dynasty is secured.

Ahpet roused himself; there was much to be done. He clapped his hands, and a slave appeared from the shadows.

'Quick, boy. Fetch my scribe. Then wake Qeb and tell him to gather the acolytes in the temple. Now!'

His eyes flitted to the rider, dishevelled and clearly exhausted.

'Go to the kitchen; you will be given refreshment. Be ready to ride back to Memphis when you are called. I will send a stable boy to find you a fresh horse.'

The rider hurried away, and the elderly, wizened scribe rose from the chair and made his way across the room, taking the rider's place in the doorway. Ahpet shouted through the open door. 'Forget the scribe; bring me a quill and papyrus. I must write this letter myself.' The scribe hesitated, fidgeting with his robe; the High Priest was not fond of writing letters himself; he spent much of his time rewriting half-formed letters that Ahpet threw at him in disgust.

'What are you waiting for?' shouted Ahpet toward the cowering scribe, his voice raised to a roar. 'Fetch!'

The scribe turned and shuffled away along the corridor.

'Run, damn you.'

'Thutmoses: a good name, an auspicious name,' Ahpet mused aloud. 'A name resonant with the power of the realm.' *We must wrest the poor infant from the toxic influence of his heretic mother before she has too much influence on his education.*

The scribe appeared at the doorway, flushed and panting. He gazed at his master, lounging on his high chair, legs wide open, displaying himself to the world. *What an old fool.* 'Here lord,' he said softly. 'Tools for writing, and papyrus of the best quality.'

'Bring them to my lap-table, fool.'

The scribe laid the tools of his trade on a cedar table, lap height for easy writing. Ahpet gazed to the heavens, seeking inspiration. Congratulations were in order, of course, and perhaps a subtle hint that heresy did not become a prince of the realm. He took the quill in his right hand and dismissed his scribe airily. He was so focused on the task at hand he forgot to offer the old man a slap.

'Now, how to begin?'

1364 BC

'Your son Thutmoses is a truly remarkable child, my lady Tiye, nurture him well. He has an extraordinary talent in absorbing knowledge and considering it logically as an older, wiser man might do. This is a rare gift, Tiye. Thutmoses is a child of destiny. Care well for him, my lady. He will be a wise and wonderful king.
Hapya, Priest of Aten.'

Tiye read the letter again and smiled. Things were going rather well. She set the scroll down on a small wicker table and settled back in her chair. The image of her son playing with blocks on a rug at her feet, chasing a cat across the courtyard of the royal compound, brought a hint of tears to her eyes. She missed him dreadfully, but giving him into Hapya's care would bear fruit in the long run. She sighed, and ran her finger along the rough edge of the papyrus. *I will see you soon enough, my little prince. And then we will do great things together.*

A polite cough interrupted her reverie. 'Your majesty, the pharaoh has received a messenger from Thebes.'

Yuk, her trusted servant, stood in the doorway, his broad shoulders almost filling the space; his genial expression, creased by a few worry lines, told her it was bad news, but not terrible. She picked up Hapya's letter, thought better of it, and set it down on the table again.

'And do we know what tidings the messenger brings?'

Yuk entered the room, and offered her a scroll; the papyrus was stained and damp—it had already passed through many hands. 'I have managed to *borrow* the letter, majesty. I thought you might wish to read it before it is placed in the archive.'

'You are my favourite thief, Yuk; what would I do without you?'

Yuk knew every servant, soldier and petty official in the palace, and they all owed him favours. Anything that reached the Pharaoh reached him, and everything that reached him reached her.

Tiye read the proffered scroll, her face darkening into a frown of irritation. Another request that Thutmoses attend the priests in Thebes, to continue his tutoring. The priests were missing the prince and worried about his lack of proper education. *As if the Theban vipers are the only ones with useful knowledge.*

'And what did my husband say in reply?'

'He said that Crown Prince Thutmoses was unavailable to visit them presently; he advised that the prince is rather busy with other royal business.'

'Hmm. A reasonable reply. And do you know when the Pharaoh intends for my son to visit Thebes?'

'He gave the impression that it would be soon, though my friend in the pharaoh's chambers tells me he did not sound overly enthusiastic. The Pharaoh said he values the work the priests do in the administration of the empire, and wants his son to learn from them. I gather he made it clear that was all he wanted his son to learn in Thebes.'

'If Thutmoses needs to learn how to count money, he can open a shop.' Tiye stood abruptly, and let a chain of onyx prayer beads fall from her hand. Yuk stifled a chuckle behind calloused fingers.

'Don't laugh at me, you scoundrel!' Tiye picked up the chain and threw it at him. Now they both laughed aloud.

'Fetch that dithering scribe, would you, Yuk? Those schemers in Thebes can twiddle their workshy fingers and wait for my son to grace them with a visit, but I need to answer this letter at once.'

Thutmoses looked up from the scroll he was reading, another question already on his lips. Hapya smiled indulgently, and raised his hands as if to ward off an attack. 'Peace, my young prince. Read it all the way through before you bombard me with fresh doubts. If you argue against monotheism as well as you argue for it, I will be hard put to give you answers.'

Twelve years old in body, the priest had told Tiye, *but twenty years of age in understanding.* Now he thought on it, he may have underestimated somewhat.

Old and grey, Thutmoses thought as he regarded the old man, *but spritely and sharp in mind.* He returned to his scroll, poring over the text, looking for holes in the argument, struggling to find them.

'All those little details, and the limitations of time,' he said. 'One god would not have time to look after every little thing on his own, even if he were omnipotent. He would need other gods to take a share of the work, to do the menial things. He would need help. Time would defeat him. Could it be that the priests of Amun in Thebes are correct in their thinking, just incorrect in their choice of gods? Could our state religion be right and you wrong, Hapya?'

'Ah, Thutmoses.' Hapya smiled. 'Let's go back to basic principles. If there is one god, and he is a universal god, who created himself from nothing, and created the universe from himself, then certain things follow logically: he is infinite, and eternal; he is omnipotent, and omniscient; he is in everything, and he is everything; he *is* time, and time cannot defeat itself. He is capable of all, and he has already done everything. Why would such a deity need helpers?'

'Maybe he would not *need* helpers, sir, but wouldn't it be better and easier if he had them? My father is pharaoh, and the Thebans say he is a living god, so he can do anything. Yet he has servants and soldiers and officials to do his bidding.'

'Mm,' said the priest, 'that is a good argument, my prince.' He stood, deep in thought, his brow wrinkled in thought, but an amused twinkle in his eyes. 'Thutmoses, let us look at this from another perspective. Does your father *need* helpers? Or does he rule in his own stead? Is he not like a god on earth that must be obeyed? If this is the case, then his helpers are ordinary people, servants to him; they are not pharaohs, are they?'

'No, they are simply mortals helping the god on earth.'

'Helping the representative of god on earth,' the priest corrected him.

'Representative?' said Thutmoses, catching the twinkle in Hapya's eyes. 'He *is* a god; that's what everyone says, that's what the priests of Amun say. Are you a dissenter, my priestly mentor?'

'But Thutmoses, how can he be god if there is only *one* god? He is simply god's representative in the overworld, doing what the god wants him to do.'

'You know,' Thutmoses said, acidly, 'you could be executed as a heretic for saying that.'

'As well I could, my prince, but we are discussing philosophy, are we not? It is merely a discussion, not a plan to take over the world.'

'Don't worry, Hapya; I will not tell the Thebans about your heresy,' he laughed, 'nor my father.'

'You are too kind, highness. You make an old sinner very happy.' *You trust me, and that's good; but I must trust you too, boy, my life depends upon it.*

Thutmoses, bored with arguing against a god he believed in with his every fibre, changed tack. 'If Aten is the one and only god, why is he treated as a minor deity by the Theban priests?'

'Thutmoses, there is more to consider here than theology. Politics plays a role too. The priests in Thebes derive their power from the pantheon of gods; if they acknowledge the sole rule of Aten, their worldly power is diminished. Their worldly power, and their wealth. Who in their right mind would give up such privileges for the sake of a philosophical argument? They will not accede so easily.'

'So, unless we remove the old priesthood, disprove their philosophy and reveal the lie behind their privileges, Aten's religion cannot flourish.'

'Unless we persuade them to see the error of their ways, you are right, they will not back down, and they will remain powerful, more powerful than we are. And that, my prince, will be a political struggle, if not a war. The gods may be the reason for the struggle, but the struggle itself will be between men, men of power.'

Thutmoses considered what he had learned. The grand narrative of religion told that in the beginning, before time existed, there was a spirit, Mut, who existed in chaotic darkness. He created Nun, and together they fashioned earth and water to rise out of the chaos, and, so, Egypt and the River Nile were created. A variety of descendants became gods of the air and moisture, the sky and the earth, eventually leading to the god Osiris, who married his sister Isis and became king, and Seth, who married his sister Nephthys. Both couples had sons; Osiris had Horus, and Seth had Anubis.

Eventually fraternal jealousy and led to Seth murdering Osiris; so Seth ruled the overworld and Osiris the underworld. But Horus, aggrieved at the murder of his father, fought Seth, defeated him, and to ensure no one entered his father's kingdom without having led a good life, forced Seth's son Anubis to be keeper of the underworld.

Horus was now the ruler of the world of the living, the god of the sky and the first pharaoh. This was where royal descent originated: all pharaohs were children of Horus; thus all pharaohs were gods. *And one day I will be pharaoh; do I really believe I will be a god?*

Thutmoses understood the old stories and, in a way, he loved them. It was a supernatural comfort to believe that the blood of the elder gods ran in one's veins. But under the influence of his mother and Hapya, he had imbibed the monotheistic religion of the Aten to the point where he could no longer accept the old stories as anything more than fairy tales to distract the ignorant.

He thought deeply about Hapya's words; the logic in them was overwhelming. He saw that he had a stark choice, one that he must resolve before he took the throne: he could accept the old religion, and revere the many gods of Egypt, a pantheon he was destined to join; or he could accept the religion of one god, the religion his mother urged on him, and that Hapya had taught him to understand. Either way, he faced a struggle; if he went with tradition, his mother would never forgive him; but if he accepted the rule of Aten, the priests would become his bitterest enemies. An apostate pharaoh would be too much for the Thebans to bear.

I am still a child, he thought, *and perhaps I am too young to make such a decision.* He looked at Hapya, busy cleaning a sheet of papyrus with a pumice stone. *And yet, I feel as if I have already made my choice.*

1362 BC

Thebes, Egypt. In the reign of Amenhotep III

Tinya cursed silently; the privileged station of high priest was turning out to be a poisoned chalice. And the fools carrying his litter seemed to be drunk, which wasn't helping his hangover.

He leaned his head out of the litter and bellowed at the nearest guard. 'You, there. Yes, you. If these idiots,' he indicated the six slaves struggling under the weight of the litter and the pitted surface of the road. 'If these idiots stumble again, kill one of them and find me a replacement.'

He thought better of it the moment he retracted his head. The litter was stifling, but out there it was torturous. Still, too late now; the High Priest couldn't be seen to be weak. The sneeze that rattled the litter sent the canopy swaying, just for a terrible moment letting the full heat of the sun in on him.

'Ottah, must you?' Tinya glared at his dishevelled servant. Gods knew what Ahpet had seen in him. But Ahpet was dead three years now, and he still hadn't got round to offloading the miserable mouse of a man.

'Are you ill, Ottah?'

'No, Great One, not ill. I think I may have an allergy to donkey…to donkey…Achoo!' Ottah stared glumly at his master, embarrassed. Tinya was easier to work for than that fat oaf Ahpet, thank the gods. But spraying the High Priest with saliva wasn't endearing him to the small, wizened man on the opposite bench. He felt painfully akin to the donkey turds that littered the road around them; the High Priest eyed his servant and the excrement with equal disdain.

Tinya was a good fit for the role, though, Ottah thought. He was distantly related to the royal family, but distant enough to carry a façade of independence. And where Ahpet was crude and loud, Tinya was subtle and discreet. A fox instead of an ox. 'Achoo!'

'Ottah, can you point that thing,' the priest indicated his servant's nose with a disgusted gesture, 'out the window? I really don't want to have to change my vestments before the ceremony. Talking of which, how long before we reach this noble's house? What was his name again?'

'Nanua, Great One. We should be there in an hour.'

'If our litter bearers don't melt first.' Tinya smirked, and Ottah allowed himself a companionable giggle, immediately regretting it as another sneeze threatened to erupt.

Tinya's stomach rumbled ominously; his fondness for wine did him no favours, sometimes. He sighed and gestured at his snivelling servant, who was busy ruining the cuff of his robe. 'Ottah, read me the notes on Nanua; I want to have a measure of the man before I meet him in person.'

Ottah rifled through the pile of scrolls on the bench beside him. 'Here we are, our court spy has given us quite a lot of information.' He cleared his throat and recited.

'Nanua, first son of Betuet, third cousin of the late pharaoh's second wife. Wait.' He peered at the scrawl in front of him.

'Our spy is good at snooping but his hieratic is abominable.
'Ah yes; second cousin of the late pharaoh's third wife. Holds
the franchise on date imports from Libya, which has made him
obscenely rich. General opinion is that he is something of a yes
man, but he has some powerful friends.'

'And his religious affiliations?'

'He has a shrine to Bat in his house at Memphis, and is
building one to Dedun in his new house; makes sense, given his
wealth. Rumour has it he is more lucky than astute, apparently.
No mention of Aten.'

'And do we know his opinions on our troublesome prince?'

'There's nothing here, Great One; it appears that Nanua plays
his cards close to his chest.'

'Well, he's not openly supportive, that's a positive. I shall
have to tease out his opinions at the feast.' Tinya pulled aside
the canopy on the shady side of the litter. The side of the road
up ahead was lined with crowds, holding baskets of petals. He
straightened in his seat and composed himself. 'Make ready,
Ottah; I believe we are nearly there.'

Tinya's retinue of priests, robed in white, began to chant as the
crowds came into view. A miasma of petals greeted them as they
neared the gate of Nanua's new mansion, and the people chanted
in unison; Tinya's mood lightened as he heard their supplications.
Good, he thought, *the people are with us, despite the ranting of that
heretic fool and his scorpion of a mother.*

The litter came to a halt, and a couple of slaves scurried over
with a podium for the High Priest to alight upon. Tinya waved
to the adoring crowd and then looked towards the massive,
gilded gates of the mansion. Nanua and his family were arrayed
in front of the gates, robed, like the priests, in white linen. Tinya

surveyed the portly aristocrat and his diminutive wife, and smiled to himself. His spy was correct, if appearances meant anything; Nanua acted with the ingenuous joviality of a born fool. His wife, on the other hand, looked shrewish and suspicious; Tinya made a mental note to steer clear of her.

The ceremony was brief and perfunctory; Tinya did his best to maintain an air of dignity as he showered blessings on the vulgar pretensions of his host, and he sighed with weary relief when it was over. A slave showed him to a huge, almost empty, room in the mansion where he could rest before the feast. He washed his face and hands in warm, lemon-scented water and considered the evening ahead.

The Egyptian nobility was, in theory, one of the four great power blocs of the empire. The royal family was pre-eminent, of course; but the priesthood, and the army, often dictated events and policy. The nobles were the wealthiest class and had real influence; but they tended to blow with the wind, relying on relatives among the priests or the military to gauge which bloc to support. More importantly, and more irritatingly, they were acutely aware that the pharaoh held total control over their position and wealth, and acted accordingly. *Which is to say*, Tinya thought, *they bow and scrape to the royal family like hounds to their master—unless the priests and the army can persuade them otherwise.*

Ottah knocked at the chamber door. 'Great One, the feast is ready; you are expected.'

'Yes, yes, I'm coming. You will stand behind my couch, Ottah, and keep your wits about you.'

'Great One.'

The feast was set out in a richly decorated hall. Nanua and his family, and the High Priest, were seated on a dais, served a constant procession of overly rich dishes by toiling slaves. Below them, minor nobles, army officers and priests from the local temple complex jostled for space and delicacies along a row of cedar wood benches, slaves dancing and swerving among the throng of competing appetites.

Tinya picked at his food, distracted. His stomach still rumbled and he eyed the heaving platters in front of him with queasy suspicion.

'Not hungry, Tinya? Or does our humble feast not meet your expectations?' Nanua's wife fixed a beady eye on the priest.

'Forgive me, Madame, I am not a man of great appetite. And on the contrary, the feast is very … impressive.' *Damn, I sound like I'm mocking her.*

'One should take one's pleasures with gusto, Tinya.' Nanua spoke around a mouthful of meat, half masticated. Tinya swallowed a shudder of disgust. 'You never know when they might be taken away, by a stroke of bad fortune, or a whim of the gods.'

'You are right, Nanua. Life is unpredictable; though I think the gods offer us a little more than mere whims.'

'Quite so, Tinya, quite so.' Nanua waved a dismissive hand, the other plunged into a dripping bowl of spiced olives. 'I am not one for underestimating the power of the gods. After all, they have seen fit to make me rich, and I am grateful, of course.'

'If only the crown prince shared your devotion, Nanua. I would feel more confident about the future of the empire if he did.'

'The prince is a boy, Tinya; he hardly knows his own mind yet.' Nanua smiled indulgently, the history of his meal decorating his teeth.

Tinya lowered his eyes to quell the threat of nausea, and thought back to his last encounter with Thutmoses. The boy had seemed very confident about his own mind, unfortunately.

'The logic of divinity leads, inevitably, to the concept of a single god, Tinya,' he'd said. 'Our fables about this or that god embodied in an animal or a rock, they are stories for children.'

'Stories they might be, highness, but they have real value. In time you will come to understand that religion is not simply a matter of relentless philosophical logic. It is the cord that binds a people together. If that cord is decorated with … stories … then what matter, if the people are one in their belief?'

'That sounds more like politics than theology to me,' said Thutmoses. 'And in any case, if what you say is true then soon I, too, will be a god. And even a high priest cannot argue with a god, can he?'

It took Tinya a moment to realise that Nanua was speaking again. He snapped out of his troubled reverie and faced his host.

'As I say, Tinya, you should not worry about the wanderings of a juvenile mind. And in any case, as I've told you, you have insurance if you need it.'

'Insurance?' Tinya was all ears now, wondering what he might have missed.

'Ah, well, that's another story, as they say.' Nanua stifled a laugh at his own joke, as the priest was clearly not joining in.

'And what is the story, exactly?'

'I have heard it whispered, in the shadowy corners of the corridors of power, that our prince is not what he seems.' Nanua tapped the side of his nose and attempted a conspiratorial wink; he managed a bemused blink instead.

Tinya didn't know whether to press him or laugh at him. *I doubt you spend much time in the corridors of power, dear Nanua; unless they are lined with food.* But there was no such thing as bad information, so he pressed. 'What do you mean, Nanua?'

'It is rumoured,' Nanua leaned a little closer, the waft of garlic and exotic spices making Tinya gag. The smiling noble looked around him, keen, it appeared, not to be overheard. *This must be good.*

'It is rumoured that the prince is a foundling, pulled from the river in a reed basket. The queen delivered a still-born boy, and the foundling replaced him.'

Tinya almost choked on a morsel of fish. 'But that's impossible. The birth was witnessed by the high priest and a dozen of his acolytes. They were there at the moment he … you know … emerged.'

'A deft midwife might be able to cover up what happened,' said Nanua. 'I don't suppose the high priest was keen to observe the gory details.'

'So … Forgive me, I don't mean to cast aspersions on your tale, but it is hard to accept. You are saying that the midwives somehow knew the child would be still born, and arranged for a substitute, a foundling, to be at hand so they could replace the dead child?'

'I am not saying this.' Nanua's eyes narrowed. 'And if word comes to me that you have even implied such a thing, I will see to it that your career ends rather abruptly.'

'So, what are you saying?'

'I'm saying that I have heard it said.' Nanua seemed inordinately pleased with his clumsy rhetorical flourish. 'Other may have spoken; I have merely passed the information on. Do with it what you will, but don't involve me.'

Tinya glanced at Ottah, standing behind his couch. His servant was slack-jawed with shock at the noble's revelation.

'And what would one do with such a story, do you think?'

Ottah made to speak; Tinya silenced him with a curt gesture.

'I suppose a person who suspected there was something in the rumour, not that I'm saying there is anything in it, might be inclined to find one of the midwives who attended the royal birth and ask a few . . . ah . . . pointed questions.' Nanua wrenched a wing off the carcass in front of him and proceeded to chew on it, noisily and with great gusto.

'I suppose they might,' Tinya said absently, his mind already working. 'I suppose they just might.'

'On the other hand,' Nanua continued as if he had not just spoken reason. 'This might all be a storm in a wine cup. The boy is too influenced by his mother, but he is young. When he grows a little, and enters the world of men, the real world of power, he will hear different opinions, and I have every confidence he will begin to see things in a different light.'

'I'm sure you are right, your excellence.' Tinya raised his goblet, salivating at the prospect of the rich red wine. 'He will come to his senses, in time, and with the right guidance.'

'And if not,' Nanua said smugly. 'Well, it is no harm to have a little insurance in hand.' He tapped his goblet's rim against Tinya's, and this time his conspiratorial wink was sly and accomplished. 'Not that you heard it from me.'

The feast petered out slowly. The drunkest of the guests were lifted gently from their benches and towed away safely by tired slaves. Mounds of leftover food were scooped up and carried away, the slaves eyeing their windfall with glee. A tidal wave of litter was swept up from the marble floor and carted off to gods knew where.

Tinya finally felt able to take his leave. He stood and offered fulsome thanks to his hosts. Nanua beamed, all smiles and idiot feature's again. His wife gave the high priest a last, withering stare as he departed.

Back in his chamber, he ordered Ottah to take notes. 'First, I want our court spy to listen out for this bizarre rumour. If he hears it, he must tell us immediately. Second, I want our minor priests and acolytes to spread it far and wide. True or not, it might serve as a weapon when the time is right. And third, I want to find one of the midwives who were there at the birth.'

'Do you think a midwife would confirm such a wild fantasy?' Ottah looked sceptical.

'It really doesn't matter. If she does, all well and good; we have our proof. If she doesn't, we can persuade her to spread the rumour on our behalf. If the people hear the story often enough, and from enough sources, they will believe it is true.'

'So, we are going to go with this story and use it to undermine the prince?'

'Not so fast, Ottah. We will collect what evidence we can, and we may, ah, assist the rumour in its circulation. But one step at a time. Like that oaf Nanua is so fond of saying, it won't hurt to have a little insurance to hand if things go awry.'

* * *

The Royal Palace, Memphis, Egypt

'Highness, the pharaoh approaches.'

Tiye acknowledged the messenger briefly and dismissed him. She didn't need his breathless announcement; she had heard the trumpets blaring in the courtyard. 'Children, come, gather around me. Your father is coming to visit.'

The seven children of the royal family arranged themselves around her; the boys beside her, Thutmoses still clutching his papyrus, Amenhotep the younger fidgeting, eager to get back to his toy soldiers. The royal daughters fanned out behind her in a loose semi-circle: Sitamun, the eldest, now a royal wife, and a rare beauty; Iset, soon to join her older sister as a royal wife despite her yearning to wed a foreign prince and have adventures in strange lands; Henuttaneb, child-like for all her seventeen years; Nebetah, thirteen going on twenty, holding herself like an adult; and Beketaten, the youngest, a boisterous toddler only dimly aware of her position in the greatest family in the world.

They stood as if posing for a group portrait, waiting for the sounds of tramping feet that would herald their father's arrival. The royal children were bursting with happy expectation; their father did not have time to visit them regularly, and this was a treat. Only Tiye felt apprehension; it was most unusual for Amenhotep to visit them like this, and she had a feeling it wasn't a strictly social call.

The sound of the pharaoh's retinue was close now. She clapped her hands and the room became silent.

'Your father is here. Show him you know how to greet the pharaoh.'

She waved a hand to dismiss the servants who had been trying to bring some semblance of order to the chaos of the chamber. They bowed in turn and scurried from the room.

The great doors slid smoothly open and guards streamed into the room. A pensive Pharaoh Amenhotep followed. The herald announced him.

'Amenhotep, Pharaoh of Egypt, lord of the two lands, god of the overworld. All bow before the pharaoh.'

Amenhotep wore no crown; that was for official duties. Here, in the palace, he preferred to remain as casual as tradition would allow. He stood tall and regal, his bronze, muscular body well-toned, but there was a problem, Tiye could see; his face showed the tell-tale signs of stress.

Tiye and the children bowed their heads and knelt before the god-king.

Amenhotep bowed his head to acknowledge them.

'Leave us,' he ordered the entourage that had followed him into the room. 'I will speak with my family.'

The room emptied; the children stood, waiting for one parent or other to tell them what they should do.

'Are you well today?' the Pharaoh asked his wife. He walked slowly to the balcony where Tiye sat, surrounded by their children.

'I am well, my beloved,' she replied with a smile.

'Children, please leave us; I need to talk to your mother.'

The royal children bowed their heads and left by a side door in one long file, their respectful silence giving way to a fluttering chorus of whispers and giggles.

Amenhotep and Tiye sat close together, in companionable silence. It didn't last; Tiye could see the words forming in her husband's mind. She took his hand and kissed it. 'Tell me, my love. I can see you need to speak.'

'Tiye, I have had a visit from Tinya, a most uncomfortable visit.'

Amenhotep continued. 'He came all the way from Thebes to reproach me—about you.' Amenhotep's voice was light but his face betrayed his anxiety.

She nodded in acknowledgement but said nothing; she knew her husband had more to say.

'The high priest burned my ears with his complaints. He worries that Thutmoses might be questioning the gods and the place of the priests of Thebes; he gave me the impression he was struggling to hold off a rebellion caused by your encouragement of our son's, what he described as heresy!'

'Husband, I have no interest in upsetting the priests of Thebes.' An impious grin spread across her face. 'Are they really talking about rebellion?'

Amenhotep didn't return her grin. 'He gave me the impression it was not just the priests who were concerned, but perhaps parts of the nobility too.'

'Lord, I ensure that our children get a balanced education, that is all. Our children will one day rule the world; there are things the need to know. I believe they understand the gods. Why would the priests be worried?'

'Tiye, you are my beloved, and I respect you as much as I love you. I also know when you dissemble. The priests are worried for good reason. When I was a child, most of my education was from them. I learned languages, mathematics, and history, all useful subjects. It has stood me well. But you insist on our Thutmoses' education being in your own sphere of influence. Then he argues with them, sometimes in public, denying their religion, the state's religion, and claiming Aten is a sole god.'

'He is just a child, Amenhotep.'

'He is not just any child, my love. His words have weight.'

'Let me speak with him. I will encourage him to keep his thoughts to himself.'

'See that you do. We must ensure that the priests see only what we want them to see.'

Tiye knew this was not the time to argue with him. Best to wait for a better opportunity. 'You are right, of course, lord.'

The pharaoh stood and left the balcony; he paced the spacious chamber. 'And Thutmoses?' Amenhotep asked. 'Does he understand our position?'

That worm from Thebes has got under his skin, Tiye thought. *I will not let him tear us apart with his subtle poisons.*

'My lord, you know as well as I that Thutmoses has a questioning mind. Is it so bad for the nation to have a crown prince who tests tradition and searches for the truth?'

'Tiye, to go against the priests in public is imprudent, and for one of our children to argue with them is a scandal; they are right in this. What we do in private is our concern, and Tinya and his acolytes will not interfere, I have his word on that. But in public, we must be seen to be in accord, the royal family and the priesthood. The people will not understand if they see strife. And we don't know which way the army will go if there is conflict between us.'

Tiye smiled thinly, but Amenhotep noted that the gesture did not quite reach her eyes.

'We rule the empire, but the priests administer it. They have power too. We rule the priests, but the priests rule the people's minds; and if the people's minds are turned against us, we are lost.' Amenhotep stopped pacing around, returned to the balcony, and sat beside Tiye; he took her hand in his. 'Let them think that they are important, Tiye. Let them think they rule you. Show the world what the world wants to see; as long as we are seen to be fair, we are free to do as we please. Teach Thutmoses what you want to teach him here, in the confines of our home, but out there he must be the Crown Prince and do and say what is expected of him.'

Amenhotep paused. Tiye sensed something important, and not to her liking, was coming.

'I am going to change the location of the capital. The administrative centre of our country will henceforth be in Thebes, not Memphis. I am going to build a new palace adjacent to my funerary temple at Malkata, and it will become our main residence. We will live opposite the great temple of Karnak, the place of Amun; we will of course be closer to the priests, and they will believe they have power over us because of it. But in reality, we will have more control over them.'

'You are taking the crown from its birthplace here in Memphis,' Tiye said.

'I am,' he agreed. 'But it is necessary.'

Tiye made to speak but Amenhotep lifted his hand to stop her.

'I have not finished,' he said, touching her lips with his fingertips.

'I am going to send Thutmoses on a royal trip. It will get him away from the court for a while. He is old enough now to be carrying out active duties as crown prince and to be seen doing so. I was Pharaoh at his age; it is reasonable to expect him to fulfil his royal role. He will tour the empire and our client lands. He can see for himself what a great and powerful nation we are, and meet our allies and those who rely on us. Great princes and kings will welcome him; he will have to deal with them and their descendants in the future, so it will be good for him to develop relationships with them now.'

'And how long will he be away?'

'As long as it takes. While Thutmoses is away I will impress on the priests that our family god is Aten, not as a lone god but as chief among the gods, for *us*. My new palace will be dedicated to him; not out of disrespect to Amun but respect for us. I will show the priests my respect for the gods; they will see the state and the gods brought together, the Pharaoh and Amun as one. Thutmoses will return to this new state of affairs. He will be part of the family and worship Aten; but he will also be part of our empire and worship Amun, with the people, through their priests. And all will be well.'

Tiye was impressed, despite herself. Her husband had outplayed her.

'Husband, I am yours to command, in this as in everything. I will do as you say, but understand this; my veneration of Aten will not take second place to anything in my life, except you, of course. There is sense in what you say, though, and I am not in a position to turn the world upside down, even for the sake of my god.'

Amenhotep breathed a visible sigh of relief. He had the response he needed. 'My beloved, you make my heart lighter,' he said at last. 'I know that you will do what must be done, and I trust you completely.' *But I will watch you like a hawk, my love, for the good of the kingdom.*

Tiye bowed her head, and kissed her husband's hand. *The priests have the upper hand for now,* she thought. *But my god will have his day.*

* * *

Thutmoses stepped on deck. The crew had already arranged the plank platform to the shore; now they stood at a respectful distance, as they had done for most of the interminable journey. His two personal bodyguards were already on shore, ready to escort him. The prince hurried down the gangplank and joined them. 'I am ready.' He said. The guards regarded him for a moment and then, with faces stoically set, trudged off across the arid landscape, raising devils of dust with every step. Thutmoses walked between them, looking around, trying to capture every detail in his mind.

He had been away from his family now for almost a year, and, with Numidia still to visit, was still months away from getting home. And home had changed; during his absence, the royal family had moved to Thebes. He did not feel comfortable at the thought of residing so close to the priests who, he knew, resented him and hated his mother. But that problem could wait; for now, he was content to travel and learn.

His grand tour had started in the early spring while the blazing sun was at its lowest. It had first taken him to Heliopolis. The primary temple of the city was known as the Great House of Atum-Ra, and its priests maintained that Atum-Ra was the first being, who rose self-created from the primeval waters; this interested Thutmoses, so he spoke for days with these priests, making notes and collecting artefacts.

His next stop was Avaris, the capital of Egypt under the Hyksos. Here, his ancestor Ahmoses had delivered the country from the foreign tyranny of these Canaanites, and had instituted Amun as the greatest of all the gods. The Hyksos had used Avaris as a trading centre for the eastern Mediterranean, and it remained rich from trade. It was now the administrative centre for Upper Egypt and welcomed its Crown Prince with great ceremony. The Hyksos interested Thutmoses greatly. It was rumoured that they were monotheists, though he found nothing to substantiate this interesting tale.

From Avaris he travelled along the coast to Gaza. And from Gaza he had visited Megido and Gebal, religious outposts of differing gods. He was learning a great deal about the religions of the empire; not quite what his father had intended, not quite the statesmanship his father required.

He then travelled over the empire's border to visit the Hittite King, Tudhaliya. The Hittites had been struggling to establish order for over a hundred years, and Tudhaliya had only recently brought his kingdom back to its former glory. In effect he had done what Thutmoses' ancestor, Ahmoses, had done and rid the land of unwanted intruders.

Tudhaliya had welcomed the young Crown Prince of Egypt with lavish gifts and promises of loyalty to his father, Amenhotep. The crown prince had spent an uncomfortable month feasting and being indulged, he wanted to study religion, not gluttony and excess. Tudhaliya promised his body and soul to the alliance with Egypt and asked Thutmoses if his father would give one of his daughters to one of Tudhaliya's sons in marriage; a marriage to cement the brotherly love between them and to further support the alliance of their countries. Thutmoses had left the Hittite kingdom unsure of the Hittite king's true feelings. Everything appeared too good for his liking, and he did not trust Tudhaliya, for all his loyal protestations.

His journey back to Memphis took him through Aleppo, Kadesh and Damascus; now, more than a year after he had left, he was at the bounds of Akhmim.

He had kept in touch with his father regularly during his travels. Amenhotep's own servants, his trusted aides, stayed close to his wayward son and sent constant updates on his progress, physically and philosophically, but most especially politically. The pharaoh was keen to hear Thutmoses' attitude to foreign leaders and how his statesmanship was developing. He hoped that his son's trip would prepare him to take on the mantle of a crown prince. Thutmoses had presented his father's men with what he wanted them to see. He kept his real mentor under wraps; for a year he had kept Hapya with him but away from prying eyes, spending his time as a crew member, assuming the disguise of a sailor. The priest, who had always been devoid of body hair, had become hirsute and unshaven. When Thutmoses was alone, the pair found time for reflection and philosophical discussion, well away from Amenhotep's men, discussion of the great god Aten.

A god in their midst! Akhmim was an excited place.

A fanfare rang out and drums rolled. The Overseer of the Land was waiting for him with his dignitaries and, behind him, crowds of people jostled, pushing and shoving, all wanting to see the spectacle.

The crown prince was brought to shore on a golden palanquin with gilded statues of lions on either side which he used as arm rests. Four giant Nubians at the front and a similar number at the back carried the litter along the wide plank, making their way to the river bank. There the crowd bowed in awe, dropping to their knees, noses touching the dirt of the dry riverbank.

The deacon, walking at the front of the procession, and followed by four sets of drums and four great trumpets, struck his wand three times on a bronze gong carried at his feet by a cowering boy, no older than six. Silence ensued. He looked around to ensure no one gazed upon the boy god, Thutmoses. He was satisfied. 'All rise and behold the Crown Prince of the Great Empire of Egypt. Thutmoses, son of Pharaoh Amenhotep, the third of that name, Overseer of the Priests of Upper and Lower Egypt, High Priest of Ptah,' he exclaimed.

Thutmoses grimaced at this last acclamation. *I am no high priest, any more than I am a god; but Ptah interests me.*

The standard bearer, with a flag so big it could have been seen in Thebes, dropped the tip of his flagstaff on to the shoulder of the Overseer, who was, like everyone else, on his knees, nose to the ground. The Overseer knew the meaning of the gesture and rose slowly, followed by others, officially in order of rank; but for most it was a race between the curious, all eager for a look at the prince. He was as much in awe as the merest peasant. A boy god on a golden throne, a crown prince in his district. He could tell his grandchildren about the day he was this close to a future pharaoh.

'You are welcome to our humble town, Your Majesty.'

The crowd burst into spontaneous applause as Thutmoses was led through the town and eventually to the Overseer's house for the official welcome.

The house was surprisingly spacious, and mercifully cool. His attention was drawn at once to a small knot of people gathered in the corner of the main parlour. He gestured to the Overseer. 'Who are these people?' he asked.

'They are your kin, Majesty. They are waiting to be introduced.'

'And while they are waiting, young prince, I will speak with my old friends.' Hapya appeared behind him, his face aglow. 'I'm sure the Lord Overseer will not keep you from your family for too long.'

They suffered the obsequious attentions of the Overseer for a full hour before they could slip away to his aunt's house to become properly acquainted. Thutmoses could finally relax, and enjoy the company of people he felt he had known forever.

At the end of a day of revelations, personal and religious, he crept into his bed, exhausted and happier than he had felt for a long time.

1358 BC

Thebes, Egypt. In the reign of Amenhotep III

'Every time you stir up the courtiers, I have to placate the priests. Don't you see the effect you're having?'

'I don't do it to upset the priests, father.'

Thutmoses looked out over the balcony at the rising sun; he had been dreading this conversation, he had known that it would have to take place. 'This is more important than the feelings of a few old men.'

'Those few old men could ruin us. A pharaoh with an apostate son is a man with a target on his back. Do you want to see us fall?' Amenhotep grabbed his son's arm and turned him away from the sun to face him. 'I hoped that showing you the duties of a pharaoh might give you a more realistic perspective. That you would realise this empire is bigger than you and your feelings. This empire that I strive to run while you undermine me.'

'I will do my duty as crown prince. But I cannot change my beliefs to suit the priests of Amun.'

'You, the crown prince, you are one of those gods you despise. How can you do your duty and ignore them?'

'Hapya says—'

'Hapya says!' Amenhotep's voice was thunderous. 'You still see that heretical old man against my express wishes. He is responsible for this; he and your mother. I should . . .' His voice trailed off. He was in a corner and he knew it. He could not punish Hapya without punishing Tiye, and he couldn't bring himself to do that. He tried a softer approach. 'Thutmoses, what the empire demands, is what your head knows, not what your heart wants. It demands leadership; and people won't accept a leader who makes them feel alien in their own land. You are the Crown Prince; will you leave the empire to rot while you pursue your own private salvation?'

Thutmoses listened, but his father's words faded in the light of the sun. *When I am pharaoh, I will bend the priests to my will. It's only a matter of time.*

'You are blind,' Amenhotep said. 'Blinded by zeal, like some mad prophet preaching in a public square, with no one listening.'

'I can see well enough to know the truth.'

'How can you be so sure? Listen well, Thutmoses; Aten is better served by a diplomat than a demagogue. Egypt will not prosper with a fanatic for a pharaoh.'

'Am I not a god, father? Am I not all-knowing? Your high priest says so, you have just said so. The state religion says so. Then how can I be wrong?'

Amenhotep raised his hand to strike, and Thutmoses flinched. Then the pharaoh pulled back his arm. He drew himself up and stood between Thutmoses and the sun, a giant, glowering shadow. In the four years since his tour, Thutmoses had grown, in stature and in confidence; he stood tall in his father's taller shadow. But he had to be cut down to size.

'You are not yet a god; you are hardly more than a boy You will obey me. You will stop talking about religion in public. You will stop insulting and tantalising the priests. You will act like a crown prince of Egypt and accept the world as it is, not how you want it to be. You will start acting like a man, not a spoiled child. Now leave my presence.'

Amenhotep remained on the balcony for a while, fuming. Where Thutmoses had stood there was only his father's shadow. He clapped his hands, and a servant materialised out of the shadows in the corner of the room. 'I wish to see the high priest. Send a messenger and ask him to join me in my apartments.'

The high priest arrived an hour later.

Amenhotep smiled the gracious smile of an approving monarch, a friend. Tinya smiled in return; but the eyes of both men were flinty and cold. The Pharaoh studied the man before him, looking for a weakness. He did not want to apologise for his son's behaviour. Instead he considered how he could undermine the high priest and still appear his ally. An idea took shape in his mind, and he held his hand in front of his face to conceal a slow grin.

'Tinya, my friend, you look weary. Are your duties weighing on you?'

'Serving the gods brings its burdens, your majesty.' The priest looked pointedly at a mural of the royal family. 'Every day brings its obstacles, and its rewards.'

'I would lighten your burden, Tinya. I would like to find a way to help you in your endeavours.'

Tinya saw his chance, but waited a moment too long. The pharaoh spoke again.

'My brother-in-law, Anen, is a good servant of my family and the empire. He is also a good servant of Amun, is he not?' Amenhotep leaned forward in his chair, his eyes fixed on the priest.

Tinya shifted uncomfortably on the stool he had been offered.

'Indeed, he is, Your Majesty. He visits the temple daily and leaves great gifts for Lord Amun. Amun smiles upon him.'

He realised his mistake and cursed himself for letting the pharaoh manoeuvre him so easily. He cursed the College too; they had pressured him into openly criticising the young prince, despite his warnings that the pharaoh would retaliate. Now Anen was to be forced upon them, a royal viper in the College. How could he get out of this?

'He would perhaps make a good acolyte for the god.' *Better to make the offer of a junior priest than have Anen forced on me.*

Amenhotep smiled a predator's smile. 'An acolyte, you say? I was thinking of something more…useful to you, Tinya. I am sure Anen would be only too happy to take a role as your assistant. It would ease my mind, to think you had such a useful shoulder to lean on. And it would strengthen the bonds between the royal household and the College, don't you think?'

Tinya's grimace was impossible to hide. But even as he nodded his reluctant acceptance of the royal gift, his mind was working. Perhaps this could yet be turned to his advantage.

'Your majesty honours us with this offer, and of course I humbly accept. Anen will make a perfect assistant and, as you say, the bond he creates will bring us all closer.' Now his smile was genuine. *It may be possible for me to turn your fool of a brother-in-law; then it is the College that will have the spy.* Tinya had heard rumours about family disagreements and jealousies. Perhaps he could use these to his advantage.

Amenhotep watched the wheels turning in the high priest's mind; he seemed too easy to persuade. Perhaps things had not turned out entirely as he had hoped. What was this wily old man thinking about?

Anen would be a pawn on the board between them, wrestled from greedy hand to greedy hand. But better a brother-in-law than a son. *Forgive me, brother; I am sacrificing you for the greater good of the family. And you may yet return the compliment, if this scheming priest has his way.*

'Then we are as one mind. I will speak to Anen at once. And you will make the necessary arrangements.'

'It will be as you command, your majesty.' The priest's voice dripped with honey; and the honey dripped with poison.

Tinya held up his hands in mock surrender. 'I had no choice. He had me in a corner. But I may yet turn things to our advantage. It may not be as dangerous as you think.' He smiled. 'I know Anen from old. We were friends as children. I suspect the Pharaoh is unaware of this. We have kept in touch, spoken as friends and allies of the gods.'

'That may be so,' observed Patenemheb, an ambitious young priest with the eyes of a cheetah, 'but what makes you think that friendship will triumph over family? Surely he'll just bend to the pharaoh's will?'

'No, I don't think so. Anen is not over-fond of his sister. He sees her as arrogant and zealous. He is also jealous of her position, although he does not admit it. He may well be just what we are looking for; if we play the game right, we can use him better than the pharaoh can. Anen may be the blade we need to cut out the heresy in our midst.'

'The Pharaoh will manipulate the situation, and Anen will be his pawn; perhaps we all will.'

'I think you are wrong, brother. I am sure he sees this as a great strategic move, but I see it as a tactical error.'

'Are you sure? What if he forces you to retire and installs his brother-in-law in your place? What if you simply do not wake up one morning, on the day the Pharaoh decides Anen will take your place?'

'You are too timid,' Tinya said. 'The Pharaoh would not dare assassinate the High Priest, and he cannot remove a high priest without good reason, that would cause him too many problems. He cannot afford to offend the gods; no, my position is safe.'

Another voice chimed in. In the chamber, set at the back of the Karnak temple, well away from prying eyes or unwelcome ears, sat a group of the most experienced and most trustworthy priests. It was a good place for the hierarchy of the Amun priests to discuss what only they should know. 'In families there are jealousies and rivalries; more so in a royal family. We can use that. Amenhotep may be astute, but when it comes to his immediate family, he is sometimes naive. And he knows we have the people in our pocket. He fears us.'

'But he is a god, the representative of all gods. Who are we to interfere with a god?' another priest interjected.

'Does that mean anything in this day, old man? Times have changed.' Patenemheb's voice was laced with scorn.

'Time may change, young man, but people don't. You would do well to remember that.'

Tinya interjected. 'If we argue amongst ourselves, we will get nowhere. It is the Crown Prince and the queen that we must focus on. We can mould him to our aims. With her it may be too difficult, but him? He is yet a boy, for all his swagger.'

The elderly priest had lived through several administrations. He spoke with authority.

'If he is only young, pliable and of no concern, then why are we so worried about him? And if his mother is as stupid as you all say, why does she make you all quake in your shoes? We have a crisis here. If not, why are we arguing over a young prince and his mother? The Crown Prince will one day be Pharaoh if we let him, and when that day comes, if he still holds these beliefs, we will be a forgotten sect, wandering in the desert and wailing about our glorious past.'

'If we let him? We have no choice. He will be the next Pharaoh.'

'But not for a while yet,' the man continued. 'Amenhotep rules over the greatest empire the world has ever seen, and rules it cleverly. How does he do that? He uses people. He senses their needs and soothes them with kind words, and his pretence of brotherly love and fatherly trust. He is master of the world because everyone loves him, and they love him because he makes them feel as if he will protect them. But he is human too, he is vulnerable. We must find his weakness and use it. Thutmoses will not change: I have seen this kind of zeal before, and there is no cure for it. If he is not stopped, then we will lose everything; you can say farewell to the wealth and power, the food and the wine. It will all disappear if you allow him to become Pharaoh.'

'*Allow* him to be Pharaoh? He is the first-born son of the Pharaoh. He will be the Pharaoh when Amenhotep dies. We can do nothing about that.' Patenemheb threw up his arms in frustration.

'You must not be afraid of the prince; simply understand the threat he poses to you. We should arrange to have him and his mother silenced. Engineer things so that Amenhotep is forced to disown his son and silence his wife.'

'Strip the prince of his title?' The priest who spoke was ashen with fear. 'That's treason; we could all die for this.'

'Technically, yes. But treason is only treason if you are caught in the act; otherwise it looks a lot like a heroic act to save the nation.'

He paused and looked at the faces around him, some frightened, some interested, some confused.

'The problem before us, the question we must ask and answer, is how do we do this? We must engineer his public disgrace; Anen may be our key to doing so. He can bring private vices into public view, if we give him the right incentive, or make the right threats. Let's at least pretend to welcome him until we find out what he knows, and if it's useful to us.'

Tinya hid a smile behind his hand. The old man had done his work for him. 'So, we will accept Anen into the fold, and see if we can use him to pry a chink in the prince's armour. Then we will force the pharaoh's hand. We have much to do, brothers; let's be about it.'

* * *

Tinya was back in the home of Nanua, his rich acquaintance now almost a friend. The heat was too much, even in the openness of the large room. Servants stood around in their shendyts, using their fans in an attempt to keep their masters cool, but the ostrich feathers were insufficient today.

'Come, let us walk in the garden.' Nanua said.

The two men walked out to the open space, which today had a linen awning stretched over it. It was a small space with a fountain in the middle. Normally Tinya's mind simply accepted his surroundings, but today the water feature and its constant peaceful dripping brought things to his mind; how things had changed since his childhood. Since the pharaoh's ancestors regained their land from the Hyksos there had been a boom in the economy. What a wonder this garden was, what a wonderful life they all had.

His thoughts were abruptly ended by Nanua. 'You need to be careful, my friend.'

Tinya turned to look straight into Nanua's eyes. 'I beg your pardon?'

'You need to be careful, Tinya. The pharaoh is impressed with your building of the new temple and everyone admires your work and closeness to Amenhotep, but . . .' he paused and looked around the garden; even in his own home Nanua seemed to be wary of others listening to what he had to say.

'Why, my friend? What do you know? What must I know?'

'I know nothing, I simply hear things, and I have the experience of a long life in the court. I would hate to see something happen to you, my friend. One has to be so careful these days.'

'I see, Nanua.' Tinya didn't see.

'It is so easy to miss the warning signs. They are always there, there is always someone there, just waiting to pounce when you least expect it. Take Anen, for instance. The pharaoh thinks he is on his side. He thinks by placing him in your college he will have access to your plans, your thinking. Amenhotep may come across as a caring diplomat who compromises on everything to keep everyone happy, but don't you believe it.'

This man is not as inept as I thought.

'Come, let us walk a little further.' Nanua took Tinya's arm and led him to the far corner of the garden. Once more he looked around, as if suspecting ears in the walls.

'The queen's family are provincial louts. Amenhotep's father employed her parents because he didn't trust our family. He wanted to have people around him that were loyal to him, and only him. He found outsiders that would owe everything to him, and so always be in his debt, forever his people. Her mother was the Aten high priest in their home town, so Tiye was bound to be endowed with her faith. Now, move forward fifty years and remember that Anen is her brother, of the same stock, shall we say. But, believe me, he is interested in himself rather than gods, he wants power.'

'Well,' said Tinya, 'he will have that when I am gone, the pharaoh has made that a reality.'

'When you are gone; exactly, Tinya. Remember those words and be wary, my friend. Trust no one, not even me.'

* * *

Kheruef, the royal spymaster, stood to the side of the window; moonlight spilled in and cut a blade of light on the marble floor, but none of it touched him. *A creature of shadows, even when he meets his king,* thought Amenhotep. He glanced at the man again. It was a strange thing; even if you spoke with him for an hour, afterwards you forgot his face in an instant. *The gods have fitted him perfectly for his role.* 'Speak, Kheruef. What brings you here like a thief in the night?' *But when do you come otherwise, my silent friend?*

'Highness, the men we posted in the College are here. They bring news, but I fear it will not be to your liking.'

'It rarely is.'

'I think you should hear them, highness. Bad news is better from the bearer.'

'Summon them.' Amenhotep considered his network of spies in the high priest's lair. They had brought him some useful information: Tinya's weakness for young boys; Intanye's addiction to the poppy. But he needed more; what was Tinya planning, and who were his spies in the royal household? That would be news worth having.

The spymaster glided from the room; it was as if he had never been there. A few moments later, he returned with two men in priestly garb; they prostrated themselves before their king.

'Speak,' he said, 'You are safe here.' Kheruef's attempt at a reassuring tone fooled no one.

'Your majesty, we have spent some days now watching Anen, as our master commanded.' Amenhotep glance at Kheruef; *I didn't order this.* Kheruef had taken a sudden interest in one of the murals.

'Go on.'

'Yesterday, Tinya and his closest advisers met in secret with a number of generals. Anen accompanied them to the meeting. This is as it should be, of course. But after the meeting, when the other priests had gone about their business, Anen stayed behind. He walked with the generals in the temple gardens; they were deep in conversation. I was not close enough to overhear what they were saying, but it seemed . . . suspicious.'

'Suspicious? Explain. Anen is a prince of the realm; he has known these men since he was a boy.' Amenhotep felt a tingle of worry tickle his spine. Something was wrong here.

'Their heads were bowed, highness. They spoke in whispers, and Anen passed a small bundle of papyrus to one of the generals. Then they left, and he went straight to Tinya's quarters. My colleague will speak now.'

The second spy had a nervous tic, a tiny flicker at the corner of his eye that irritated Amenhotep instantly. He rose to his feet without being invited to stand and began to speak, in a nasal whine which endeared him even less to his king.

'I work in Tinya's quarters, highness. I have access to a storage chamber from where I can overhear much of what happens in the high priest's rooms. Anen told the high priest he had done as commanded, and things were in motion. He did not say what things were in motion, but Tinya was pleased.'

'Leave us. You have done well, but you need to do more. Return at once to the college.' Amenhotep waved a regal hand and the two spies backed out of the chamber.

'What do you think, spymaster? I have not yet decided if your initiative is to my liking.'

'I crave your pardon, highness.' Kheruef did not look particularly contrite. 'The priests have gone beyond the stage of complaining. They are plotting something, and they don't have the crown prince's best interests at heart.'

'How far would they go?' Amenhotep didn't think the priests would stoop to assassination, but the meeting with the generals had the nasty smell of a coup.

'It is clear that they have put some kind of plan in motion. It is not my place, but...'

'But?' *If ever the gods invented a word to frighten a pharaoh, it's that one.*

'It might be wise to restrain the crown prince; perhaps even remove him from public life for a while.'

'You are right, Kheruef; it is not your place.'

'Highness.'

'Leave me. And bring me proof, Kheruef; I cannot act on rumours.'

'Highness.' A brief flurry of movement, and the spymaster was gone.

The Pharaoh clapped his hands for a servant. 'Bring lamps, plenty of them. I have had my fill of lurking in shadows. And send for my privy councillors. Tell them the matter is urgent.'

He slumped onto a cushioned couch and rubbed at his brow. There was too much to think about. Anen's venality had left him prey to Tinya's machinations; that much was clear. He could no longer trust the information his brother-in-law brought to him. Kheruef may have spoken out of turn, but his advice was good. How to put it into action; now, that was another matter.

The privy councillors looked dishevelled, like men who had been pulled hastily from their beds. *Theirs, or someone else's; no matter, they must earn their corn.* Some picked greedily at the refreshments laid out for them; a few stifled yawns behind aged hands.

'Gentlemen, there are two matters we must attend to at once.'

The councillors settled into a semblance of order and waited.

'First, my scouts bring news from our borders. It seems our neighbours grow audacious. We will send an army to tour the border garrisons, a show of force. The crown prince will lead them.'

There were muted murmurs of approval, and a few nervous whispers. Finally, Banefre, the most senior among them, said, 'This is wise, your majesty. The foreigners must learn respect; and you make an excellent choice of leader.' Something in the old man's expression told Amenhotep he had divined the reason for choosing Thutmoses.

'You mentioned that there are two matters, your majesty?'

'Yes, quite so. I mean to begin a programme of rebuilding and enhancement of shrines and temples to Amun.'

'That will incur considerable expense, your majesty.'

'When we honour the gods, we do not count coins. I have drawn up a list of works I wish to see completed. Make it so.'

The councillors shuffled back out of the chamber, leaving a trail of date stones and pastry crumbs behind them. Amenhotep's plan was not perfect, but perhaps it was enough. Let Tinya believe he was winning, that the pharaoh was acknowledging his power by offering a sumptuous gift to the gods. And sending

Thutmoses away might deflect the high priest's attention for a while, at least.

The rush of footsteps in the corridor brought Amenhotep to his feet, alert for danger. He heard raised voices; his steward, questioning a messenger.

'Highness, there is news from Nubia.' Djau's expression was grim. 'Out with it, man,' he snapped, almost dragging the terrified messenger into the chamber. 'Tell his majesty what you told me.'

'Highness, the Nubian king, Ikheny—'

'I know who he is, man; what of him?'

'He has declared independence, highness. He prepares for war.'

'Djau, summon the generals, now. And find me some maps.' *Well*, he thought. *It seems Thutmoses is going to war. Now he will learn what a pharaoh has to do. This may be what the world, and the gods, have been waiting for.*

1357 BC

Thebes, Egypt. In the reign of Amenhotep III.

'My lord,' he said to Amenhotep, 'I cannot find the crown prince in the palace grounds. I have sent guards everywhere but they fail to find him.'

Amenhotep had wanted to give Thutmoses a practical lesson on the battlefield, a lesson designed to show him how to lead an army and develop his potential as a great king; he wanted his heir to be likened to all his ancestors, the great and glorious warriors of their dynasty. However, once again, Thutmoses was missing.

'Find him.' Amenhotep quietly advised his chancellor.

The chancellor issued orders. 'Find the prince Thutmoses, his lord Amenhotep demands it of you.' Scribes, soldiers, nobles, courtiers, all rushed out to find the crown prince, all irritated with the wayward Thutmoses again.

After what seemed an interminable time a guard returned to the room, sweat pouring in rivers down the contours of his face, his heart pounding, his legs aching. He whispered into the lord chancellor's ear.

Amenhotep gazed into the distance through angry eyes. He turned to the chancellor. 'So, have you found him?'

'Yes majesty.'

'Then have him brought here—at once!'

'That is not possible highness.'

'Not possible!'

'It is impossible majesty...' he paused '...he is not in Thebes majesty. He is in Akhmim.'

'In Akhmim? What is he doing there?' Amenhotep could not believe that his son, the crown prince, had left the palace, and more, the capital, without advising him. Just what did he think he was doing?

It was Kheruef who spoke next.

'He is with his priest friend, majesty, Hapya. They say he is studying.'

Amenhotep's face became a dark shade of red. People around him took a step backwards. The anger could be seen to be brewing within him.

The great pharaoh controlled himself; he paused and thought long. The chamber was utterly silent. He slowly made a decision; his second son Amenhotep would go to war with him. Thutmoses would be ordered back to Thebes and put under house arrest in the palace awaiting him and his armies return; then his anger would return and the crown prince would take the full force of it. This time the young prince had gone too far, there was no way back for him, even Tiye would face his fury, they would both fear him in future, no more diplomacy, only autocracy dispensed with a whip.

* * *

'Who'd be a soldier, eh? Nine months in Nubia and all I've got to show for it is half a ton of sand up the crack in my rear. Any day now I'll go into labour and give birth to a dune.' Khui scratched his rear for the umpteenth time that day, and went back to leaning on his spear.

'Stop complaining, Khui.' Huya squinted into the glare of the desert morning. 'You could do a lot worse. My cousin's a clerk in the palace and he's bored out of his mind most days.'

'Yeah, well, you're probably right, but this feels like a complete waste of time. I haven't so much as waved a spear at anyone yet.'

'That's not the Pharaoh's fault, is it? This Ikheny character is trying to weasel his way out of a fight; talked himself into trouble and now he's trying to talk his way out. I've heard he's not quite right up here.' Huya tapped his temple. 'I've heard he talks to his cat.'

'Yeah, I had a cat like that once. Oops, look out, here comes the top brass.' They snapped to attention.

Amenhotep, accompanied by his younger son and a retinue of generals and aides, strode past, giving the soldiers barely a glance. The whole group disappeared into the huge tent Khui and Huya were guarding.

'He's a fine lad, Amenhotep the younger,' said Huya. 'Not like that other lunatic.'

'Yep, I'd have him for pharaoh any day over the god-botherer. The way I hear it, the priests at Thebes aren't exactly in love with him. Wouldn't surprise me if he "accidentally" fell into the Nile one day when the crocs were feeling peckish. See what his new god makes of Sobek.'

Huya's parched lips cracked into a grin. 'Well, seeing as he started off in the river, it would be kind of fitting, wouldn't it?'

'What do you mean, started off in a river?'

'Haven't you heard the rumour?'

'The only rumour I heard is that Thutmoses was playing truant and the pharaoh has locked him in his bedroom until he gets back from giving Ikheny a lesson.'

'Well, that one's true, far as I know. But there's more stories where that one came from. Let me explain.'

In the pharaoh's tent, maps and scouts' reports lay scattered across tables. They were camped on the shores of the sacred river on the borders of Kush; a good location for a camp but a poor position for battle. The pharaoh put his hand on his younger son's shoulder and pointed to a spot on the map. 'See here, Amenhotep,' he said. 'This is the town of Kerma. Just beyond its walls there is a wide plain, and the ground rises towards the north. If we place our main strength there, the Nubians will be hard pushed to shift us. Then, if they are needed, our cavalry and charioteers can swoop in from here,' he swept his hand over the western edge of the map. 'And decimate them. What do you think of our plan?'

Amenhotep had grown close to his younger son during the months campaigning in Nubia. The boy was much easier to like than Thutmoses, he thought. He would make a fine pharaoh.

'So, there will finally be a battle, father?' Young Amenhotep's eyes were wide with anticipation. 'Will we win?'

'Yes, my son, we will win. We'll show this upstart the cost of defying the Egyptian empire.' The pharaoh turned to his generals. 'Is all ready? When will our troops be in position?'

'Tomorrow at dawn, your majesty. The usurper's army is camped a few miles south of us. It seems they are ready to give battle at last. We will send skirmishers to entice them, and we'll be waiting for them.'

'No mercy on these rebels.' The pharaoh's voice was hard and sharp, like a sword blade. 'And capture Ikheny alive. I want to make an example of him.'

As dawn gave way to the mild heat of an autumn day, the Egyptian army stood ready on the plain of Kerma. In the centre, the Aten-tjehen division stood proud; they were the crack troops of the imperial army, and they would bear the brunt of the fighting that day. On the western flank, the charioteers and cavalry would be held in reserve in case of setbacks; on the eastern wing, Khui and Huya settled themselves into the second line of spearmen and archers.

'Well, here we are then. An actual battle. Wonder what old Ikheny's got for us?'

'From what I hear, they're basically a bunch of nomads wearing second-hand imperial armour. I doubt we'll be pushed too hard.'

'Yeah, that's all very well, but it only takes one arrow to kill a man. Even a gormless nomad can manage that.'

'Cheer up, Khui. It'll all be over by dinner time and we can go back to scratching our backsides outside the royal tent. Look sharp, here they come.'

A cloud of dust announced the arrival of the Nubian forces, preceded by Egyptian skirmishers who continued to goad them with sporadic flights of arrows and slingshot. Even from a distance, it was clear that the exiled Egyptian officers of Ikheny's command were struggling to keep good battle order. Amenhotep snapped an order to the aides and runners. 'Let's not give them time to come to order; tell General Bek to bring the Aten-tjehen to battle lines, slow advance.'

As the Nubians spread in a disorderly line across the plain, the pharaoh's troops began their slow, relentless advance. Their backs to the river, the Nubians had nowhere to go; with courage born of desperation, they threw themselves forwards, and broke upon the steel of the Aten-tjehen. War cries swiftly turned to screams, and the air was filled with the metallic tang of blood.

It was over in less than two hours. The reserves on the Egyptian flanks had not been needed; the pharaoh's favourites had crushed the enemy forces against the riverbank and destroyed them utterly. Those who had escaped the steel had given themselves to the Nile gods and drowned. As the dust and noise slowly settled, a small group of soldiers emerged from the throng, dragging the struggling form of Ikheny up to the Egyptian lines to face the pharaoh's justice.

'There you go. Job done, and I still haven't waved a spear in anger.' Khui took off his helmet and wiped his brow. Huya nodded, and took a drink of precious water from his flask.

'Those Aten-tjehen boys don't mess about, do they? Must remember never to make them angry.' The prisoner escort passed in front of the lines, Ikheny still wriggling and shouting futile curses at his captors, the Pharaoh, and the gods.

'Don't reckon he's getting off with a slap on the wrist and don't do it again, do you?'

Khui was right. Amenhotep had said he would make an example of the usurper, and he did. It took Ikheny three days to die.

* * *

'Behold, the pharaoh comes in victory! He has vanquished the enemies of the two kingdoms. He has brought peace to the empire. Praise him, he whom the gods have raised!'

Amenhotep reined in his horse and surveyed the welcome party. Returning to Thebes pleased him, and the sight of waving crowds calmed him. They still loved him, the masses, and he had brought them a victory to bolster their pride. The road ahead was thronged with cheering people; the flags atop the great temple flew high. At the front of the throng stood the priests in all their splendour, all lined in order, their white robes glimmering in the sun as the breeze shuffled the pleats of their gowns.

He turned to General Rebiu, who rode beside him. 'I see the priests have come out in force to greet us. Shouldn't they be busy preparing my jubilee festival, and finishing my funeral temple?'

Rebiu wiped the dust from his face and grinned. 'They are keen to show you their loyalty, highness. Or keen to look as if they are loyal.' The bluff general narrowed his eyes. 'His holiness the assistant high priest seems to have other things on his mind.'

Amenhotep followed his gaze. At the far end of the procession, Anen was deep in conversation with an old priest, his gestures suggesting he was issuing orders. The priest bowed stiffly and melted into the crowd. Amenhotep's brow furrowed for a moment; then he reassured himself. *I have been away too long.*

Now, he could see Tiye and Thutmoses, surrounded by courtiers, standing on a garlanded dais. Thutmoses stood and waved at his father. 'Well, at least someone is pleased to see us.'

Rebiu brought his thoughts back to the present. 'And someone's been busy.' Rebiu pointed away to their right. In front of Amenhotep's funerary temple, two giant statues of the pharaoh, each seventy feet tall, were slowly emerging from a forest of scaffolding. Amenhotep shuddered, despite the heat. Seeing a giant image of his face cast in cold stone was not a comfortable feeling. *Is that how I will look when I am dead?*

'Tinya has worked hard to finish your funerary temple, highness. He aims to please you.'

'No doubt he'd like to see the fruits of his labour used. Soon, I imagine.' The two men laughed heartily, and Amenhotep wished his comment had been a joke.

Eventually the pharaoh was able to meet his family on the balcony of the temple pylon. Amenhotep embraced Thutmoses, coldly, as Amenhotep the younger raced to hug his mother. 'The battle was amazing, mother!' he said. 'I want to be in the army when I am older. I will lead the Aten-tjehen. They crushed the rebels like cockroaches.' He chopped at the air with an imaginary sword. Tiye smiled indulgently. 'I think you need to grow a little before you go to war, Amenhotep. But I am glad to see you safely home.' She turned to her husband. 'And you, my lord. Aten be praised you are safe.'

'And Amun, and all the gods.' The words came from Tinya, who had weaselled his way through the crowd and now stood at the pharaoh's right hand, his jewelled sistrum limp in his hand. 'The people love you, highness.' He gestured to the crowds. 'The people, and the gods too; if you allow them. Your jubilee will affirm that.'

'I know my duty, priest. You have my thanks; the work on the temple is going well.' Amenhotep's voice was a potent mixture of gratitude and contempt; the high priest acknowledged the compliment with a cursory bow, and offered a smile, which failed somewhere south of his eyes.

'Anen, your brother-in-law, has been a great gift to the priesthood, highness. Much of this is his work. I thank the gods for him each and every day; and I thank your highness too for giving me such a wonderful assistant.'

'I am glad,' Amenhotep looked anything but. 'Where is my brother-in-law? I don't see him.'

'Oh, he is here, great one. I am sure you will see him in due course.'

Amenhotep briefly met the high priest's eyes; they were as cold as stone. *Careful, little man. That viper you are training may yet bite his master's hand.*

1354 BC

Thebes, Egypt. In the reign of Amenhotep III

The old priest fixed Anen with an icy stare. 'It is most unusual for a man to be well one day, and at death's door the next. You do not seem overly concerned.'

'He is an old man; old men fall ill. I am not his physician.' Anen shifted uncomfortably under the priest's scrutiny.

'Tinya was well yesterday. Today he struggles to breathe, and his tongue is purple. I do not think this is the effect of old age. And the physician you summoned is a clown in a doctor's hat. Where did you find him?'

'He is one of the royal physicians,' Anen blustered. 'He looks after my sister and her family. I am sure he knows what he is doing.'

The trouble with lying, he thought, *is that I'm really not very good at it; but a man can learn.*

'I will send for another physician, though I fear we are already too late. Perhaps you have something else to attend to?'

'I will not be spoken to like ...'

'And I will not be taken for a fool. There is something seriously amiss here, and I aim to find out what.'

Anen retreated from Tinya's chamber, leaving the sound of the high priest's laboured breathing behind. *Let him find another doctor; it is too late for Tinya, if my hireling has done his work well.*

Two hours later, the knock at his chamber door startled Anen out of his thoughts. He reached for a dagger, thought better of it. 'Who knocks?' he called out, trying to keep the tremor from his voice.

'It is Amenemhet. I bring terrible news. His Holiness, Tinya, is dead; he has gone to the gods.'

'I will come at once.'

The first part of his scheme had succeeded, though he worried about the troublesome priest who asked too many questions; he might be the next to meet Anubis. Now it was time to cement his position.

He had spent the last year spreading the seeds of doubt about Tinya: that he was too soft in his approach to the pharaoh, and especially to his troublesome son, the crown prince; that the College needed to be led by a stronger hand. No matter that Tinya's approaches had been blunted by Anen's machinations, or that he had regularly informed his brother-in-law about Tinya's schemes. Appearance was everything, and, as far as the fools in the College were concerned, Tinya was the weakling, and he was the strong hand, waiting to be unleashed, and now was the time. A year earlier, Anen had inducted his son, Aye, into the priesthood; in time, the ambitious young man would rise through the ranks, to join his father at the head of the College, if all went well. But first things first; now he had to call in some favours.

As he oversaw the preparations for Tinya's death rites (he pushed them to haste; surely the old man had died of some kind of plague, and the sooner they got rid of the body the better?) he sent Aye away with two messages: one for the pharaoh, humbly beseeching that he be allowed to take Tinya's place as the voice of the gods; and one for the man who had provided the poison and the poisoner, with the promise of further work.

The great hall of Amun was still garlanded in mourning cloth. Anen entered with a small entourage of acolytes, his most loyal men. The rest of the priests were still busy with Tinya's funeral rites. *Or they are not yet ready to declare their support for me, not openly.* He glanced peevishly at the huge space, and the little huddle of priest around him. 'Azibo, announce us; the pharaoh is waiting.'

Azibo approached the dais where Amenhotep sat. 'Highness,' he intoned, his voice ringing hollow in the vast empty space. 'His holiness, the chief priest of Amun, Anen, comes to receive the blessing of his Pharaoh, of his god.'

Anen stepped forward, aware that Tinya's ceremonial robes were far too small for him. *I look a fool, and my family are enjoying the sight.* He prostrated himself before the royal dais, conscious of bare shins trailing on the floor behind him, and waited for his brother-in-law to recite the ritual formula.

Amenhotep took his time, leaving Anen to grovel on the cold stone floor. When he made the ritual pronouncements, his distaste was evident in his voice. Tiye glared balefully at her brother throughout. Thutmoses seemed amused, if anything.

The little group of priests raised the ritual cheers, but they sounded tinny and insignificant in the huge chamber. As they chanted the final lines, 'The gods have spoken', a pigeon blundered through the skylight, crashed into a statue of Amun and fell dead at Anen's feet. He didn't need a diviner to tell him this was not an auspicious beginning.

A servant hastily cleaned up the carcass and sprinkled water to cleanse the chamber, and the pharaoh called the new high priest to his side.

'Brother-in-law, you are a power in the land now. But think on this; what the pharaoh gives, the pharaoh can take away. I would like to think your family ties mean something to you, and your loyalty to the throne.' Amenhotep's tone made it clear what he really thought. 'But just in case, I will be watching you like a hawk. Do we understand each other?'

'Only too well, your majesty. Rest assured . . .'

'I am not reassured, and I have no intention of resting. Bear that in mind.' The pharaoh turned abruptly on his heel and left the chamber, his retinue hurrying to catch up with him. As he reached the doors, the pharaoh clutched his side and leaned on his son for support. It was a long moment before he could move again.

* * *

Anen stood among his most trusted acolytes, triumph and resentment burning inside him. His mood was not helped by the appearance at the chamber entrance of the meddlesome old priest.

'Holiness.' The old priest's voice dripped with sarcasm.

'What do you want? I'm busy.'

'So, I see. I had a physician examine Tinya's body before you so hurriedly pushed him into the underworld, giving Anubis no time to prepare the scales. He thinks there is evidence of foul play. It is not conclusive, but there is reason to worry. May I suggest you are very careful about what you eat for the next while?' He fixed Anen with that baleful stare again and left as quietly as he had appeared.

Anen waved one of the young acolytes over. 'Go now, and send a message to general Rebiu. Tell him I need to speak to him as soon as is convenient for him. And remind me of that old priest's name.'

He met the general a few days later, in a cypress grove about half a mile upriver from the College. It was quiet among the trees, the only sounds the rush of the sacred river and the cries of the birds that patrolled its shores. Rebiu was tense, Anen could see it. He had already gone out on a limb for the new high priest, and he was not enthusiastic about being pushed to further misdeeds.

'Our pharaoh is ill, general, and there are enemies at the borders. I worry for the empire.'

'His majesty is ill, it is true. As for the enemies, they are really no more than bandits; the kings of our vassal states watch them with interest, but they are not about to strike. They value their heads too much.'

'It is as you say, general,' said Anen, testily. 'But it is a story that can be told in different ways.'

'What do you have in mind?'

'What if the pharaoh were to hear that the vassal kings were testing our strength in readiness for his death? That they anticipated our empire being severely weakened by the accession of Thutmoses?'

'His majesty is ill, Anen, but he has not lost his wits. And his scouts and spies bring him reports every day. It would go ill for anyone who chose to try and fool him.' Rebiu shrugged, settled himself against a cypress bough. 'I understand your aim, high priest, and I share it. The crown prince is trouble, and trouble we cannot afford, particularly if he becomes pharaoh. But what you propose merely exposes us to the pharaoh's wrath.'

'Then what do we do?'

'We would be wise to find a subtler path. One which may help the pharaoh understand the troubles of our times, and from where these troubles emanate.'

'We have been doing that for years and he doesn't listen. We need something more permanent, something which will permanently rid us of the crown prince, even if that means the pharaoh has to go also.'

'Are you a fool?' Rebiu hissed. If anyone overhears our words you will lose your head. Be sensible. Be realistic. We need to develop a plan to turn the pharaoh against his son which will give him no leeway, no way of return; a final and total reduction of Thutmoses to nothing. He is turning Anen, no matter what you think. I saw how he reacted to Thutmoses not being on the front line with us. Don't forget, I spent many months in Amenhotep's company on that campaign, and he needed someone to talk to confidentially at times. I know he wavers.'

'Go on, I'm listening. Tell me your plan.'

The general gave a brief, gruff laugh. 'Oh, I can't come up with a plan at the drop of a hat. This will need careful thought. But I think our efforts are best put to seeding doubts in the pharaoh's mind. Doubts about the crown prince. I don't think it will be impossible, if only because those doubts are already in his head. No, the trick will be to add the final straw, show him he must act against his son to save the empire.'

'You are a wise man, general, and more devious than I gave you credit for.'

Rebiu bowed his head in ironic acknowledgement. 'You are well placed to judge, high priest.'

'I propose we meet again soon. With the gods' help, some inspiration will come, or something may happen which will help our cause.'

'Keep your eyes and ears open, priest. Keep your spies at their work.'

* * *

It was dark, and the trek through the Theban mountains was hard and dangerous. The man stubbed his toes on a sharp rock and grimaced silently; he had no time for the luxury of rest. There was little light from the crescent moon, so he had to find his way by the stars.

He had begun his journey in Thebes three hours earlier, waiting for the sun to set before he took the barge across the river. He had found the donkey waiting for him, strapped to the pre-agreed post; his agent was proving useful. He had ridden the donkey around the back of the mountain, two hours providing his backside with some unwelcome bruising.

The sorceress was here, in the cave hidden to the left of the path; he had visited her many times.

He down a ravine that led to the desert sands at the end of the mountain range. He was close. He looked around and, when he decided all was safe, he dropped off the end of the ridge, and disappeared.

A short drop and he was there, a stone's throw from the entrance to the cave of Heka, god of sorcery. He pressed his back to the rock face and shuffled along the ridge. At times only his heels could find purchase.

The opening was small, barely large enough to crawl through. He slid his right foot along to the other side of the hollow while he slowly inched downwards. He could feel the opening now, right at the small of his back. He squeezed into the cave and rolled several times before coming to a halt against the cave side. He looked inside and saw the faintest light; a red light which occasionally changed to orange. He said the words *Heka totaro notada Heka* and waited for her reply.

A stone bounced off the floor to his right, then another to his left. He made his way slowly into the opening which, after a short distance, turned into a cavernous grotto with a small fire in the centre.

He crawled to the fire, looked into it, and waited.

She appeared out of the shadows, dressed in black robes and a black shawl. Her face was completely hidden. 'What do you ask of the god? Speak.'

'More of your potion, highness.'

She lifted the veil and looked into his eyes; fear wracked his spine. 'The god's medicine is rare and hard to come by. He does not make a gift of your whim.'

He knew she could read his mind. Truth mattered. 'Highness, Amun's priests beg you to help them. The request is not made lightly.'

'How do I know this to be true?'

'You know because you know. You are the high priestess of Heka; you know everything and everyone.'

She turned from him and looked into the flames. 'I see you come from evil who wishes but good. The god is not convinced.' She looked into his eyes and his fear grew.

'You are wise, lady.' He lowered his eyes. 'You know what is in my heart and in my mind. You know I am a disciple of Heka. I only ask you for help if it is truly necessary, and I am persuaded it is.'

She looked him up and down. She knew him and trusted him but he had to be afraid of her. Her magic could not work with those who were not afraid of her. She turned and walked into the shadows of the cavern. He could hear incantations and the crunch of bones being hammered in a pot. 'Lie back a while and rest. You will need your strength. It is dark out there and missing a step on the mountain paths would not be in your interests. I will be a while.'

He turned his eyes away so as not to have the gods look at him; *you never know what lurks in the shadows*, he thought. He slept.

'Wake; come now. Wake.' She had returned.

He had no idea how long he had slept. 'I am here.'

She presented him with a small phial. 'Do not return for more. If you do you will not leave this place again. There is enough here for your patrons' needs. It must be used sparingly, over time, or it will be discovered for what it is. Tell your client this and ensure that he understands it. A drop a day; no more, no less.'

He took the phial and placed it in a pocket deep inside his cloak. 'My client is grateful.' He proffered a jangling purse to the woman, who told him to place it on the floor. No one could touch her without feeling the approach of death. 'He hopes it will be enough for Heka.'

She knew who needed the potion and why. The gods were with the agent tonight, and his client.

'Go.' She turned and disappeared into the shadows.

He turned, made his way to the entrance and, placing himself on all fours, he crawled like a snake through to the ledge outside. He started to climb back to the path, back to the world. As he regained the pathway he looked at the stars, now merging into the dawning light, shortly to disappear without trace.

* * *

The man walked swiftly along the row of houses. He looked from side to side. He was sure he was being followed but there were so many people in the street. His hand gripped the pouch. The gold was safe. No one would take it from him. He had done as the priest had ordered; now he could enjoy his reward; starting with lots of high-end drinking.

He couldn't remember lying down, but the ground was hard against his back. He remembered the sharp, icy pain all too well. The warm liquid that bathed his chest had a familiar tang of iron. The hand that reached inside his tunic for the purse was not his own.

'Is he alright?' the voice seemed to come from miles away.

'Yes, he's fine; you know these country folks. Can't take a drink. He's had way too much. I'll take him back to his lodgings.'

I'm not fine, he wanted to say, but his tongue would not move, his mouth would not open.

'And my client will take back his gold.' This voice was much closer, a breath in his ear.

His last thought was to shout to Heka for her help, but Heka did not answer. Then — nothing.

1353 BC

Thebes, Egypt. In the reign of Amenhotep III

'The scholars are here, highness.' Thutmoses looked up from the scroll he was reading; a tingle of excitement coursed down his spine. 'Send them in.'

The two men were ushered into his chamber by a guard. Their clothes were dirty from the road, but made of fine cloth, and the smell of sweat was a little overpowering. Thutmoses placed a handkerchief over his mouth and nose and waved them forward. 'Come, gentlemen, sit and I will have refreshments brought. You look as if you have need of them.'

The two men moved forward to greet the prince, bowing as they made their way across the room. The older man spoke softly. 'You are too kind, highness. We apologise for our attire, but it has been a long journey and we believed you would want to see us as soon as possible.'

Thutmoses smiled and indicated the couches at the side of his grand chair of office. 'Then sit and tell me your news and why it is so urgent.'

The two men sat, clearly bemused. The prince had blithely invited them into his private quarters; if they had been assassins . . .

'I am Chisisi, highness,' the older man said, 'and my companion is Amenken. We buy and sell old documents and artefacts.'

'Who told you I am in the market for artefacts?'

Amenken inclined his head and flashed a glance at Chisisi. 'Your highness' interest in the religions of the empire is well known, and your devotion to Aten is legendary. What we have discovered may go to the truth of your beliefs.'

Chisisi took up the story. 'It appears that in the Land of Punt, near the Kingdom of Kush, there are texts written by ancient peoples, texts that speak of the one true god.'

'And why should these texts interest me?'

'The important thing about these texts, highness, is their age. If our source is correct, they are older by far than the stories of the Egyptian gods; if the word of their keepers is to be believed, they are from the dawn of time.'

'How did you come by this information?'

'That is a strange story. The incense that is used in your mother's village is brought there by merchants who travel from the south. Those merchants told us of a small, simple temple, hidden in a place of beauty to the north-east of the Land of Punt, where there are priests dedicated to the one true god. This is where the ancient texts are kept, and have been since time immemorial.'

Thutmoses digested the information, doubts struggling with eagerness to believe.

'And what makes you think this is anything more than a story told to fill a liar's pockets?'

'We spoke at length with the merchants, and we believe they are reliable. They also told us that they regularly travelled to a village in Punt, which is now called Coptos, but the inhabitants told them that the ancient name of the village was Atenakh—the city where the god was worshipped. There are ruins, outside the village, of a very great age. Perhaps they are the ruins of a temple.'

Chisisi paused to drink some water and eat a few of the dates laid out on the table in front of him.

'They told us that they obtained their incense from a small building on the edge of the village. It is a special place, a place that still venerates the origins of their one true god. It was here that they met the priests who told them about the ancient scrolls.'

'But do they call this god Aten?'

'They call their god Adon and they worship him as the only one god. They say he rises in the east in the morning and leaves the world in the west in the evening; his symbol is a shining disc. They do not know the true name of the god; it is lost in the mists of time, but they call him Adon, as the elders say that that is how the name sounds. Who else could it be but Aten, lord? We are planning to travel there ourselves, to verify what we have heard, and to discover if there is evidence in the texts that will give us more information.'

'Perhaps I should go there myself,' reflected Thutmoses. 'If there is proof to be found, I should be the one to find it.'

'As you say, highness. In this we are yours to command.'

'Leave me now. I will consider what you have told me, and make my decision. My thanks to you for journeying so far to bring me this news. It will not go unrewarded.'

The two men backed out of the chamber, bowing, and walked briskly to the palace entrance. There, they paused, and the older man spoke quietly. 'Go to the general, Amenken, and give him this message: the fish has taken the bait. I will find us an inn and await his instructions.'

* * *

The sun was low in the sky. From the balcony, Amenhotep and Thutmoses watched the farmers and labourers who had been toiling in the fields all day. They were making their way to their homes, weary but happy; the growing season was a time of hard work, but the rewards from the Nile flood were great. Thutmoses shaded his eyes with his hand and watched the peasants fade from view. 'If a person wanted to travel to the south, this would be a good time.'

'This is true, son. The sun is lower in the sky and the heat is more tolerable. If I were to travel south for any reason, now would be the time. Are you planning to travel to the south, Thutmoses, is this what this is all about?'

'I have had a visit from some travelling scholars. They have found some items of great interest in Kush, near the Nubian border. If what they say is true, these items come from our most ancient history. I want to go and see them for myself.'

Amenhotep hunched against the balcony rail; the pain was ever-present now, and his breathing was often laboured. 'I need to think about this, Thutmoses. There are larger issues at play. I am getting old, and sick, and my time here is limited. Even now, I can feel the pull of the underworld. You are a short step from the throne. Can we do without your presence in the capital? That is the question.' He stepped back from the balcony and slumped uncomfortably into a chair. 'I worry that your accession will not be easy. You need to keep your wits about you.'

'Aten will guide me, as he always has.'

'I don't think you understand the gravity of your situation. You will be virtually alone, Thutmoses; alone against the power of the college, and the will of the people. Is that what Aten wants for you?'

'Who are we to question what Aten wants, father?'

'I am a god, Thutmoses, as you will become; Aten speaks through me as all gods speak. If there are questions it is for me to ask them.'

'I apologise, father. I did not mean things to sound offensive, merely . . .'

Amenhotep placed a hand upon his son's mouth. 'Be quiet a little and listen. I do not question the will of Aten. I question your ability to play the political game that will ensue when I die. This is a game where the loser does not fare well. Your position, and perhaps your life, will be at risk.'

'I will accept the risk, and play the game, for the sake of my god. I will have faith in him to care of me and the family.'

Amenhotep took his hand and walked across the room. The pair sat away from the blazing sun.

'You saw those peasants going home after a hard day's work,' Amenhotep said. 'They rely on you. They have the gods, but most all they have us. They trust us to ensure their lives are worth living. This will be your responsibility and there are times when I worry about your ability to think enough about their welfare to ensure that the empire that our ancestors built will remain to provide for all of our needs. You need to think about that, my son.'

'I do, father.'

'You don't Thutmoses! Look at you. You want to go to the south because you have heard rumours about artefacts. You can see I am ill and heading quite swiftly towards the underworld. Now which should you be thinking of first? A fool's errand to the south, or building political clout here in the capital?'

'But . . .'

'But nothing, Thutmoses. You know there are those who listen and those who wait to speak. Many times, you are the latter when you should be the former. Please try to listen to others and understand their concerns. Listen to Amun's priests now and again. They administer the empire for us. They are our conduit to the people. They are the most important support that we possess. The empire is built on a political union that you must be aware of.' He noticed Thutmoses' face begin to drop. 'Come my son, hug me; let us show each other the love of father and son.'

Thutmoses readily agreed. Amenhotep smiled and felt warm. Thutmoses smiled and thought about the journey south.

'Do I have your permission to travel?'

Amenhotep sighed. 'Yes, you have my permission. But you will do your duty too. I will arrange for a state visit to Kush and Nubia, with you as my representative. You may dabble in antiquities as you like, but you will also conduct the necessary affairs of state. Is that understood?'

'Perfectly. I am happy to do both. But it is perhaps best if the king of Nubia is unaware of my other activities. The game is likely already afoot, and we should tread the narrow path.'

'Then we are agreed. Give me a few days to make the necessary arrangements. You should take a large military escort, to demonstrate our power as well as our good intentions. Where is this place you wish to visit?'

'It is a small village on the border of Kush and Nubia called Coptos. I will need to spend a few days there.'

'Then I suggest you do your private business on the journey home. The bulk of your escort can ride on ahead and bring me the news from your state visit.'

'I will do as you wish.' Thutmoses turned towards the door. 'I must go; I have much to prepare.'

Amenhotep watched him leave, and returned to the balcony. The sun was at the horizon now, its disc about to disappear over the world's rim, into the dark. He stretched stiff limbs, and called for a servant. 'Tell general Rebiu I need to speak with him. And send for my physician.'

The servant scurried off to do his bidding. Amenhotep let the waves of pain wash through him, and waited them out; when his mind cleared, he drank some minted water and began to sort out his thoughts. He would need to talk to Kheruef, and soon; as much as he regretted setting spies to watch his son, he could not afford more trouble now.

Rebiu was a curious character. Amenhotep liked his general and trusted him to some extent. He had been a good companion on the Nubian campaign, but there was something of the night about him which the pharaoh could not quite place, something which told Amenhotep not to trust him. There were reports of him being close to Anen; his spies were advising him to be cautious, because where Anen trod trouble lay.

Whatever the current circumstances, Rebiu was a good soldier, and was popular with the troops. He had the air of a man who would have your back in a bad situation, and Amenhotep needed that loyalty now.

'General,' he said when Rebiu appeared with Grand Chancellor Sennefer in tow. 'We have plans to make.' The chancellor was completely reliable, completely loyal to the throne, even if he was a miserable, unsympathetic wretch. 'Both of you, sit please.' The chancellor folded himself awkwardly into a chair; Rebiu preferred to stand. 'I wish for Thutmoses to visit Nubia,' he said. 'I have some official business for him to carry out, a state visit. I understand that he also wishes to conduct some personal business whilst he is there. He can do this during the return journey.'

'And what might the crown prince's business be, Highness?' Sennefer asked.

'It is nothing really, a personal matter. But it's a good opportunity to cement our ties with Nubia and Kush after the recent troubles.'

Rebiu spoke. 'We should send a full division of the army with him; it would . . . honour the King of Nubia.'

'No. Let's not make it look as if we are going to war with them again.'

Sennefer's laughter was polite; Rebiu's a wholehearted guffaw.

'Enough men to protect the prince, and make the visit look formal; I'd like to make a good impression on the king.'

'As your majesty commands.' Rebiu made to leave. 'I will arrange for a detachment of the household charioteers to accompany him.'

'Wait, general, and Chancellor. We have not yet decided on the official aim of the visit, have you any ideas?'

'The official birthday of your son, highness. We can advise the Nubians that on the occasion of the Crown Prince Thutmoses' birthday they will be honoured by a visit.'

'A good idea chancellor. Let it be done.'

Rebiu stood to attention, ready to leave. 'A regal visit,' he said, 'how wonderful. And the people can parade him from Thebes and celebrate with him on his way.'

Rebiu's smile was for himself. *Things are going very well indeed,* he thought.

1352/1351 BC

Thebes, Egypt. In the reign of Amenhotep III

The bed was not comfortable. The mattress felt as solid as the Lebanese Cedar its frame was made of. Even the feather down supporting his back seemed hard to his frail body. Amenhotep breathed in rasps and gasps. His physicians stood in the corner of the royal bedchamber, conferring in hushed voices.

The great Pharaoh opened his eyes. 'Water,' he whispered. A young Hyksos nurse hurried over with a goblet. She lifted his head gently to aid him; still he almost choked on the liquid.

'Highness, be well,' she whispered, tears in her dark eyes.

'My thanks, Miriam.' He managed a smile. He looked up to the ceiling and once more prayed to the gods that were painted in abundance there.

The chief physician came over to his bedside, checked his pulses—wrist, neck and heart—and intoned a prayer to Sekhmet. Prayer complete, he turned to the Pharaoh. 'Highness, we recommend a purge of your blood; it will clear your lungs and make your heart freer.'

Amenhotep was not convinced. 'Peace,' he whispered, 'give me peace, please. The purge can wait a while. Just let me rest.'

Outside, in the palace garden, Rebiu and Anen were conferring in hushed tones. 'Now is the time, Rebiu. The prince is where we want him, far away, and the pharaoh is at death's door, with a little help from our potion, too weak to argue; we must strike now. You are sure of the generals? They are with us?'

'Up to a point. They will tolerate the prince being deposed in favour of his brother; in fact most would prefer it. But don't abuse their trust. If they think you intend real harm to the royal family, they will spill your guts on the sand, you and all the priests.'

'I know what I'm about, Rebiu; just keep to your end of the deal and all will be well.' Anen sounded more confident than he felt. Now that the moment was here, fear clutched at his heart. The king was ill, and the poison was hastening his end, but it wouldn't require much strength to order an execution, should the Pharaoh discover the reason for his fate.

Rebiu turned and retired to the palace, where, in the anti-chamber, Rebiu's guards waited for their general, among a throng of nobles and courtesans. Anen was not far behind him.

Rebiu motioned to his chief officer and whispered in his ear. 'Fetch the prisoners, and keep them here until I give further orders.' His man nodded his head in obedience, turned, and drawing his arm across his body to indicate to his companion to join him, hurried from the room.

Rebiu turned to Anen. 'Five minutes.'

Rebiu's men joined them at the chamber entrance. He nodded to the guard on the right, who raised his sword and used its handle to knock on the door.

As the doors opened the throng in the ante-room came into view. Nobles smiling and bowing, courtesans showing faces filled with grief; and Rebiu and Anen, two steps away from the opening, waiting to be admitted.

The grand chancellor struck the ground with his wand and the High Priest of Amun and the High General of the Army entered the room.

Amenhotep lifted his head and took in their appearance. Anen looked terrified; Rebiu shifted uneasily from foot to foot, like his boots were too tight. *What is my brother-in-law so scared of? And why is the general with him?* Miriam propped him up on his pillows.

'Well, gentlemen. What brings you to my deathbed?'

'Your majesty, we would not intrude if the news were not so grave. As your majesty is aware, the College has spies in the courts of our vassal kings.'

'I am aware of your spies, Anen.' The pharaoh's gaze was cold.

'Quite so. We have been receiving reports for some time now, suggesting that our neighbours are preparing an attack on our borders. A concerted attack. They are waiting ...'

'They are waiting for me to die.'

'In a manner of speaking, your majesty ...'

'There is more that you are not telling me.' Amenhotep took a sip of water from the goblet Miriam proffered. 'Come on, spit it out. Now is not the time for reticence.'

'Rebiu's border patrols have been plagued by small skirmishes. Bandits, really, testing our strength. But, erm ...'

Amenhotep grew tired of Anen's dithering. 'Rebiu, will you tell me what's going on? If we leave it to my brother-in-law I will be dead before the tale ends.'

The general straightened up and swallowed. 'My men apprehended a pair of messengers, delivering scrolls to one of the bandit chiefs. The messages are from the Hittite king.' Rebiu took a deep breath; this was it. 'The messages say that the king and his allies are waiting for Thutmoses to take the throne. Then, when we are locked in strife over his imposition of the Aten cult, they will strike at predetermined points along our borders.'

'Do you have proof of this? Where are the messages?'

Rebiu walked to the bedside and handed Amenhotep a sheaf of papyrus.

As the pharaoh read, his face darkened to thunder. 'How do I know these are authentic? Any fool could have written these letters. Any fool, or any spy.' His gaze shifted to Anen, who shivered and looked away.

'There is more, your majesty. We have prisoners who will vouch for the documents, and the truth of what we say.'

'Where are they? Bring them to me and I will question them.'

Rebiu strode to the door and gestured impatiently to his officers stationed at the entrance. 'Bring the prisoners now.'

Two men, dressed in the clothes of Hittite merchants, were dragged into the chamber. They were clearly terrified. Their eyes widened when they saw the Pharaoh, and they fell to their knees.

'Mercy, oh great one. Have mercy on us.'

Rebiu stepped up to the taller of the two men and slapped him across the cheek. 'Stop grovelling, you dog, and tell the pharaoh what you told me.'

'We are emissaries of the lord of Kaska, who suffered the loss of grain to locusts. He joined with Hayasa-Azzi, Ishuwa and the Lukka, to find new lands to harvest. Our alliance attacked the Hittite city of Sapinuwa and in the archives we discovered their plans for attacking Egypt.'

The man subsided and slumped on his knees. Rebiu kicked him. 'Go on, dog; tell his majesty what you discovered.'

'Highness, the Hittites are sure that the crown prince, Thutmoses, will create division when he ascends the throne. They revel in his weakness, and wait only for word of his coronation to launch their attacks. They are as sure of success as they are of his inability to rule.'

There was a gleam of triumph in Anen's eyes; Amenhotep did not fail to notice it. 'This is proof, your majesty. This is the evidence that we are in mortal danger, and the crown prince is at the heart of it.'

Rebiu addressed his guards. 'Take these two wretches to the courtyard and execute them.'

The smaller man, who had remained silent, looked up. Anger replaced the fear in his eyes. 'But, you promised . . .'

Rebiu moved swiftly. He drew his sword and plunged it into the man's throat. With a brief shudder, he slumped to the floor, a pool of blood forming under him. The other man had hardly opened his mouth to speak when the point of a sword emerged from his chest, and he joined his comrade in death. Amenhotep looked suspiciously at the carnage on the floor.

Anen stepped forwards quickly to place himself between the soldiers removing the still twitching corpses and the Pharaoh. 'Your majesty, we must act, and act now.' Anen's voice wavered but he pressed on. 'If Thutmoses remains your heir, disaster will follow. You must set him aside in favour of Amenhotep the younger.'

'If I had the strength, Anen, I would kill you where you stand. But alas, my strength is gone, and so is my hope.' The cough wracked him and shook the bed. 'I will think on what you have said. Now leave; I cannot stand the sight of you. And Rebiu, have your men clear up this mess. I will go to my death on my own; I have no need of fresh corpses to accompany me.'

When the chamber was finally quiet, Amenhotep lay back on his pillows and heaved a great, shuddering sigh. They were right, and he knew it. *Save my family, and destroy the empire? Or save the empire and destroy my family. My last choices in the overworld will resonate beyond my death.* He was determined to preserve his son's birth right; but the walls were closing in.

* * *

Yuk settled into the niche at the corner of the corridor; with the drapes drawn, he was more or less invisible. Over the next hour, a procession of people came and went from the pharaoh's chamber: servants with fresh linen; physicians with jute bags of exotic medicines; kitchen slaves with platters of food that came back uneaten; and a furtive high priest with a general (Rebiu didn't do furtive; he was just too big) in tow.

Yuk's mind raced; this was the third visit in the past day; that was an unusual show of devotion for a dying monarch; more so, since the high priest hated the pharaoh with a vengeance. He slipped out of the niche, startling a nearby guard. Yuk held a finger to his lips and smiled; the guard winked and went back to his duties. *I'll make my way to the Pharaoh's ante-chamber and try to talk to sweet Miriam; she will know what's happening.*

Yuk glided through the corridors. As he moved through the palace, he stopped to exchange a word here and there with guards, servants and slaves; every brief conversation a snippet of intelligence.

He arrived at Amenhotep's ante-chamber, moving slowly through the assembled men of high class. They didn't question his presence there; he thought of himself as invisible. *Think yourself invisible and you will be invisible, the old witch had once told him.* He approached the doors to the bed-chamber and exchanged greetings with the guards.

He whispered in the ear of the guard closest to the door. 'Any chance you can let Miriam know I'm here? There is something I need to tell her, please?' The guard cast a casual glance around him and slipped through the door. A moment later he reappeared, Miriam by his side. *She looks exhausted*, thought Yuk.

Miriam settled into his arms. 'Oh, Yuk, thank the gods for a friendly face.'

'Come with me, my love.' Yuk led her along a narrow corridor. He found the bench he was looking for. 'Sit, Miriam, and tell me. What's happening? Everyone wants to know. There are so many rumours. Will the pharaoh die?'

'He will die, no one has any doubt. It could be soon but they really don't know. He is dreadfully weak, and nothing the physicians give him helps. I'm afraid, Yuk.' Yuk hugged her and smiled. Time to change the subject; lovers or not, his first duty was to his mistress.

'Tiye is only allowed to visit him in the evening. How can he just accept this?'

'It's a man's world Yuk, you know this. They have the business of state to take care of. Women and wives must come second; the Pharaoh is the Empire and Tiye is merely a wife.'

'But a special wife, nonetheless. They have been together since they were infants.' He frowned as another thought came to him. 'Do the priests not say prayers for him?'

'They do Yuk, many times a day.'

'But surely the high priest, Anen should be with him saying those prayers. Is he not?'

'Oh!' She showed anger for the first time. 'Him! He says little prayers. He and that big general constantly nag him, he can get no proper rest.'

Yuk's eyes narrowed, and he laid his hand on her arm. 'Anen and Rebiu? Tell me more, Miriam.'

An hour later, Yuk was heading to the queen's apartments, hardly noticing the servants and guards who greeted him on the way.

Tiye was waiting for him, her face a mask of worry. 'Speak, Yuk. What is happening to my husband?'

'Highness, it is as I suspected. The high priest is there more often than the physicians. Either the pharaoh is on the point of death, and requires prayer more than medicine, or Anen has more mischief up his sleeve. I'd wager a good jug of wine it's the latter.'

'How did we get to this position?'

'Miriam tells me your brother talks about only one thing to the pharaoh; he is trying to persuade Amenhotep to depose Thutmoses and raise the young Amenhotep in his place. He talks of nothing else, and Rebiu supports him, though I don't think the general trusts the priest any more than we do. I fear there is little to do but wait, highness.'

'I must send another message to Thutmoses and urge him to hurry home,' she said. 'If Amenhotep dies before he returns, who knows what my venomous brother will contrive?' She gestured to a slave for parchment and ink. 'How do you know all of this, Yuk?'

'All walls have ears, highness.' Yuk said confidently.

She finished writing the letter and handed it to Yuk. 'You will use a trusted envoy. Someone you know. Have the envoy hand this to the prince himself; no one else must see it, do you understand?'

'I understand, highness. It will be as you command.'

Yuk bowed and backed out of the chamber.

* * *

'This isn't working, Rebiu,' a tired Anen admitted.

'No, you are right; he will not disown the crown prince.'

'We have one last chance. The midwife. We must find the midwife.'

Rebiu looked blank. 'The midwife?'

'I have not told you before, my friend; I wanted to keep at least one last card to my chest. There was always a rumour that the Thutmoses baby had been swapped at birth.' Anen looked around, as if the midwife might be hiding in the garden. 'The rumour was that the real crown prince died at birth and was replaced with a foundling discovered close to the river. An old priest insisted this was the case, and he was one to be trusted. My people were tasked some time ago to investigate this rumour and they believe there might be some truth in it. They found one of the midwives who were present at the birth and, having confirmed it as truth, she suddenly disappeared. Whether she was lying or being truthful I don't know, but if I could find her, we could make her speak the truth ... as we see it. Let's hold off on the witch's brew for a while; keep the Pharaoh alive. Give me some time to find her again.'

* * *

'She is a fine dancer, highness, is she not? And a beautiful young woman.' Kashta, the Nubian king, laid a hand smeared with sauce on Thutmoses' arm. 'And Heira knows many other dances, highness. I am sure she would be pleased to show you ... privately.' The king's lascivious sneer made Thutmoses mildly nauseous.

'Your majesty is too kind. But I will travel far tomorrow, so tonight I must rest.'

'Ah yes, your private business.' Kashta's curiosity was written clearly on his face. 'You are searching for something, I think?'

'I am merely hunting some ancient artefacts, majesty.' Thutmoses had no intention of telling this devious wretch his plans. 'Nothing of importance.'

'As you say, highness.' Kashta made a small gesture to one of his attendants. The man slipped away into the darkness, to ready his horse.

The captain scanned the horizon for the sixth time that morning. Under the sparse shade of juniper and acacia bushes his troops sat around him, chewing on dried meat and casting him resentful glances. 'Not long now, lads,' he said cheerfully. 'Next meal will be at the barracks, and I'm sure the girls will look after you.'

A trooper caught the captain's eye. 'Dust, boss, lots of it, to the south-east.' He swivelled and looked where his scout was pointing. A low, dense cloud of desert dust swirled in the morning haze. 'This time we've got you, you thieving rats,' he whispered. 'Look sharp lads.' He turned to his lieutenant. 'Get the archers in position and we'll give our visitors a little surprise, then get the spear throwers up to the slope and wait for my word.'

The bandit troupe rode into the wadi with a jingle of harness and a chorus of raucous jokes; the jokes ceased abruptly when the first arrows found their target. As the bandits dismounted to find cover, three more fell, arrows protruding from inert forms. When the Egyptian infantry troops swooped over the brow of the hill, there was little left for them to do.

'Good work, lads. These cockroaches won't be bothering the borders any longer.' He pointed to a soldier standing next to the horses. 'You man, search their saddlebags. Keep an eye out for any papyrus; scrolls or maps. The top brass seem to think these bastards are working under orders, and we want to find out who's giving them. Wait, actually I'll search the bags; round up the horses for me.'

The leader's horse was an imposing stallion, almost pure white. *Too fine a mount for a ragged thief*, thought Asim. He rifled through the panniers; when he found the letter with the seal of Kashta, the Nubian king interposed with that of the high priest of Amun, he looked around. No one was watching. He folded the letter and slipped it into a pocket in his tunic. He knew people in Thebes who would pay good money to ensure the document didn't fall into the wrong hands; then again, there were people who would pay for precisely that. *Who wants to be rich?*

* * *

'Is this her?' Anen asked.

'Yes, your highness.'

'You're sure?'

'Yes.' A firm reply.

'Take the hood off her.'

The face that emerged was a study in fear. The woman before them had been kidnapped, bundled into a cart and brought to an abandoned house off the Memphis road. She stared in terror at the priest. The white of his robe dazzled her eyes. She was right to be afraid, she knew that.

'You are a midwife.' The white robe stated it, rather than ask.

'Yes lord.'

'How long?'

'More years than I care to remember, lord.'

'At the palace in Memphis?'

Now she knew, and a new fear overtook her mind.

'No master. Never at ...' A fist crashed across her cheek and her head rocked from side to side.

'Now, woman, we can do this in two ways. You can tell me the truth, or I hand you to people who will hurt you until you tell me what I want to know.' He grabbed her hair and swung back her head, brought his face down to meet hers. There was no way out.

'It was all a rumour, sir. The child was never exchanged. He was . . .' Another blow; she was sure that her jaw had been broken. It was difficult to talk. There was blood in her mouth; she could taste it. *Just tell them what they want to hear.* 'He was changed, sir. Yes, sir, the baby died and one was found by the river and changed so her majesty could have a healthy child.'

'Good. Get a message to the General. Tell him to be here quickly. We must go to the palace with this good lady.' He looked down at the ragged body beneath him. 'She smells. Clean her up.' He leered at the shivering wretch. 'We are going to see the great Pharaoh Amenhotep and you will tell him what you have just told me. Do you understand?'

She mumbled a yes. Soon she would be talking to a god, her lord Pharaoh Amenhotep. Could she really lie to him and condemn her soul to an eternity in hell? She had only been a young assistant at the birth, almost a bystander; if the rumours were true she really would not have known; it would have been hidden by the queen's own midwife, Aoh. There was little time left and she had to make a decision.

* * *

The village of Coptos did not look very promising, but Thutmoses pressed on. He had dismissed his main escort; they were on their way back to Thebes. Now he was dressed as a merchant, and his guards likewise.

After a few minutes questioning the villagers, Thutmoses knew he had been played. The village had no hidden secrets, except some closely guarded recipes for incense. The only temple he could find was a small, squat affair, a square mud-brick build-ing clearly dedicated to Amun.

'Are there no priests here?' he asked the village headman.

The wizened shepherd shook his head in reply. 'No, sir, we have no resident priests; on festival days they come from Apiket, a couple of hours north.'

'And have you heard tell of any ancient scrolls, or ruins in the area?'

'Again, no, sir. We are simple folk here; what would we be doing with ancient scrolls?'

Thutmoses had seen and heard enough. He remounted, and gestured to his guards. In a flurry of dust, they swept out of the village, and headed north.

A few minutes after they had left the village, another mer-chant came to quiz the locals. He did not stay long either, but took off in the direction that Thutmoses and his escort had taken. And after him, a shadowy figure in the brush on the brow of the hill overlooking the village quietly mounted his horse and headed south.

Thutmoses rested in the shade of a tall bank of reeds, his feet in the cool waters of the Nile. His escort was spread out along the royal road, ignoring him, as they had for most of the trip. He sighed, and threw a pebble into the water, watching the ripples spread and fade away. He needed to get home, find out how he had been tricked and by whom.

His mother's letter had increased his worry; he realised he was being played by more than one of his enemies. She said this was a second letter but he had no knowledge of a first. *What did that contain?* His father was dying, and he would inherit the throne of a kingdom divided.

The thunder of hooves interrupted his musing and he looked up. A rider approached them from the north, the capital, at a fast gallop. Was this another letter from his mother? This was not a good day.

Thutmoses stood to receive him but the rider went first to the officer in charge of his escort. They exchanged a few words, and the messenger passed him a papyrus scroll; even from a distance, Thutmoses recognised the royal seal. The officer, an aristocratic young man called Hapuneseb, adjusted the cuffs of his tunic and looked in his direction.

'I have brought word from the pharaoh.'

'Should you not address me correctly? Am I not your prince?'

'Well, that is something of an issue, sir. I think you should read this.'

He handed over the scroll. Thutmoses read with growing disbelief.

'I am deposed? My brother is the crown prince? What is the meaning of this?'

'I leave that for you to think on, Thutmoses; I thank the gods I am no politician. I have my orders; I must make for Thebes with all speed. We will leave you sufficient horses and a troop of guards.' Hapuneseb could not resist an aristocratic sneer. 'Otherwise, you are on your own, sir. I wish you luck.'

He snapped his heels together in an ironic salute and turned away to ready the escort for departure. A couple of reluctant soldiers ambled over with a small string of horses and waited as the rest of the escort thundered off up the road towards the capital.

Tiye stared at the papyri in stark disbelief. She looked at Miriam. 'And you saw his majesty sign this document with his own hand?'

Miriam nodded. 'Yes, highness, though the high priest had to steady his arm.'

She turned to Yuk. 'And you are sure this is genuine?

'I'm sure it is.'

Tiye held two documents. One contained evidence that Anen and others had lured Thutmoses away. It was not enough to have him arrested, but it was circumstantial evidence that he needed Thutmoses away from Thebes so that he could prey on the Pharaoh. It was obvious that Anen and others, Rebiu for one, had used Thutmoses' absence to persuade her husband to disown him. But why would the Pharaoh do such a thing? There was no precedent for it and, although they argued a lot, there was no lack of love between Amenhotep and Thutmoses. But here, in the other papyrus, was the evidence that it had worked, whatever it was they had used; proof of Amenhotep removing Thutmoses from the line of succession.

'Miriam, go to the pharaoh, and tell him I would speak with him.'

'Highness, the pharaoh ...' Miriam hesitated.

'Tell me. It can't be any worse than what is written here.'

'Highness, the pharaoh has made it clear he will not be swayed on this. He refuses to see you or Thutmoses. Something happened before the Pharaoh signed the document, when he was with the High Priest and the general, madam, and, of course, the old woman.'

An old woman? Why? Tiye's mind whirled. No, not her, no ... 'Did you recognise this old woman? Did she remind you of anyone?'

'No madam. I have never seen her before.'

'Why was she there?'

'I do not know, madam.'

'So, my son has been deposed and I can do nothing about it? I cannot speak to my husband?'

'I am afraid so, highness. When the chamber was quiet I asked his highness if there were any messages he wanted me to take. I made it clear I meant to you, highness; but his majesty said nothing, just looked at me. I swear there were tears in his eyes, but he said nothing.'

'Leave me. I need to think.'

The young nurse scurried out of the room, relieved to be gone. Tiye sighed; there was really not much to think about. She turned to Yuk; his expression was eloquent—eloquent and grim.

'You know Miriam well, don't you?'

'Yes my lady. She is my woman.'

'So, she can be trusted?'

'Without any doubt, majesty.'

Tiye paused. There was nothing she could do at the moment. She had trusty servants who would keep her informed. She would have to play things by ear until she could get Thutmoses home again. She turned to Yuk. 'I'd better let Thutmoses know, and quickly. Can you arrange it?'

'I'm afraid the pharaoh has already sent word to the prince; a friend in the stables told me a squadron of cavalry left early this morning. We won't outpace the cavalry.'

'But you can try.'

'We can try, your majesty. We will do everything possible to get to the prince first; if we don't, we will not be far behind, and he will have the benefit of your words to bring him home.'

'Then I will have my scribe write a scroll for my son. It will be ready when your horseman is ready to go. And, Yuk, may our lord Aten be with him all of the way.'

'I will ready the best rider in Thebes, majesty.'

'There is nothing we can do now but wait and pray. I'm going to the family chapel; I'm not to be disturbed unless … unless … '

'I understand, highness. If there is a change in the pharaoh's condition I will let you know.'

* * *

The gates of the palace came into view as the sun was setting. Thutmoses watched the disc of light sink towards the horizon and his heart sank with it. What had happened while he had been away? In the dim dusk, he saw a man he recognised, one of his mother's most trusted servants, sitting sloppily on a horse, waiting for what; the broken light of dusk? Thutmoses kicked his horse's flanks and rode forward at speed, pleased to see the outline of Yuk.

'Yuk; have you some good news for me?'

'Highness, your mother sent me to tell you to come first to her apartments. There is much to discuss.'

'Tell my mother I will first go to my father. I have to find out the truth of this business and have him change his mind.'

'As you wish, highness. I will tell her what you have said. But my advice to you is to do as your mother wishes. She is the one person whom you need to talk to. You need her counsel before you speak to your father.'

'I will see my father Yuk,' he said forcefully, 'I will change his mind. He cannot do this.' Yuk knew it was better to step aside and let the gods take over.

Thutmoses rode into the palace grounds and jumped from the back of his horse. A guard shouted for a stable boy and the horse was led away. Thutmoses brushed past every guard in every corridor, forcing his way to his father's chambers. Many a guard tried to arrest his movements, but many a guard sensed the thunder of his temper and stepped back. In no time at all he found himself at the entrance to the pharaoh's bedchamber. Guards brought their lances down in unison, barring him from the doors.

'Let me in!' he shouted. His voice echoed around the corridor.

'My lord, we cannot let you in. We have our orders. Please understand that the pharaoh's orders are for you not to enter.' The guard shifted uncomfortably; this was above his paygrade.

'How dare you?' Thutmoses shouted. 'I am the crown prince of this land. I am the future pharaoh of Egypt.'

'Forgive me lord, but we have our orders.'

One of the chamber doors opened slightly. His sister princess Sitamun's head appeared in the opening. She spoke to the first guard. 'My husband and father, your pharaoh, is happy that his son be admitted.' The guard bowed and both straightened their lances.

The smell that greeted him as he entered the chamber was the smell of senescence, of illness and approaching death; he knew this was the end. He turned to his sister, recently married to their father, a new queen of the land.

'Sitamun,' he said, 'what is happening? How is he?'

'He is dying, Thutmoses, there is no chance of recovery. He goes to join our ancestors in the underworld.'

'How, what happened? He was not this bad when I left. Yes, he had a few stomach pains and some discomfort, but from that to … this?'

'He has deteriorated quickly, brother, but when the gods decide we must obey. It is not his decision, it is that of Amun.'

He looked past his sister and made his way to the bedside. A foreign woman wiped herbed water over the pharaoh's brow. There was no sign of a physician in attendance. *So, he is beyond help.* He knew he should feel pity, but his anger trumped all other feelings.

'Father, what have you done?'

Amenhotep looked like a ghost. His skin was paper thin and had taken on a grey hue, the pallor of hopelessness. He stirred at his son's voice, and the servant propped a pillow under his head. 'Amenhotep, is that you?'

'No, father, it is I, Thutmoses. Why have you cast me aside? Have you lost your wits before your life?'

'It is too late, Thutmoses. I am sorry, I truly am, but there was nothing else to be done. You will understand in time.'

He is deluded, Thutmoses thought, *what have they said to him?*

'What on earth are you talking about, father? Has my uncle anything to do with this mess? Has Anen turned your head?'

Sitamun butted in. 'He is weak, brother. Please let him rest. Can you not see he is dying? He cannot answer your questions now, it is too late.'

The pharaoh made a gurgling noise, his right arm raised to touch his son.

'Thutmoses.' He was struggling to speak. 'Please . . . understand.' His voice trailed off and his arm dropped to the bedside.

Sitamun grabbed at her brother's arm. 'Thutmoses, now is not the time for this. Thutmoses?'

'Call me that name no longer. I was Thutmoses, beloved of Thut; now I am simply Moses, beloved of no-one.' He turned on his heel and left the bedchamber without a backward glance.

Thutmoses never saw his father again; he was dead by the time he reached the end of the corridor. And as he turned the corner he was arrested by the palace guards.

'You are to be taken to Memphis, lord. There you will be confined to the palace.'

* * *

They stood at the entrance to Amenhotep's tomb, as the priests chanted the ritual hymns, the instructions for his journey to the underworld and his appointment with Anubis and Maat. Amenhotep the younger, the pharaoh in waiting, stood at the front of his family's dais and watched, impassive.

'We waited seventy days for this, and now we are mere spectators at our father's funeral.' Sitamun' s voice was tight with anger and grief.

Before them, in clouds of incense, priests crowded the tomb entrance, bearing provisions for the pharaoh's journey through the underworld. Their chanting fell to a curious hum as they entered the tomb. One of the acolytes, a well-fed young man in expensive robes, tripped at the tomb entrance and spilled his basket of herbs and spices onto the dusty ground; Anen gave him the devil's eye.

'Marvellous,' snapped Tiye, wincing as the young priest scrabbled in the dust for his lost gifts. 'They mocked him in his final days, and now they mock him in death.'

The final notes died away, and the tomb door was sealed. Tiye stifled a sob, and gestured to her children. 'Come, let's leave the priests to their sport. We should attend the family shrine and offer prayers to Aten for your father's safe passing through the realms of darkness.'

Her daughters stood up and made ready to leave, but Amenhotep raised his hand. 'I will stay, mother. The rites are not complete, and it is my place to oversee them.'

'As you wish, my son. But I will stay no longer. Come, daughters, let's get to the barge. Will we see you later this evening?'

Amenhotep did not look at her. 'I don't know. It is possible that there are people who need to speak to me. To tell the truth,

I am not sure what I am supposed to do now, but I am sure someone will advise me.'

'No doubt, your majesty.' Tiye's voice was bitter with grief and anger.

1350 BC

Memphis, Egypt. Year 1, in the reign of Amenhotep IV.

'Behold, he rises to the throne of the two lands, he rises in the gaze of the gods. Amenhotep, fourth of his name, lord of the Nile, king of the two lands, emperor of the great lands. Behold, he rises.'

The priest's droning voice faded, and the small chamber succumbed to silence.

'Highness, the coronation will take place in three full moons. We have much to prepare. But see, highness, you are the pharaoh now. The world gazes on your magnificence. The priests of Amun await your command.' The supercilious expression on the priest's face made Amenhotep suspect he was rather more used to giving orders than obeying them.

'Leave us, priest, I need some time to think.'

'As you command, highness.' The priest slid out of the chamber in a whisper of white robes, a wisp of hair frolicking about his shaven crown.

Amenhotep IV, pharaoh of Egypt, monarch of the two lands, emperor of the many lands, stood on the balcony of the palace and looked out over the Nile. The disc of the sun rose over the horizon and spread its warmth and light; it was going to be a good day, warm and bountiful; the new pharaoh basked in the rays of Aten and forgot, for a moment, the troubles of his family and his new empire. There was plenty of time for that—later.

* * *

The sounds of festivities resonated everywhere, even here, in the forgotten corners of the palace complex at Memphis, a distance away from the centre of the empire, Thebes; they would go on until the official coronation, some weeks away.

In the dark of his apartment, Moses sat and tried to think of nothing at all. He should get up and light the lamps; the servants were probably celebrating like everyone else. *Almost everyone else*. He would have to stay here in the dark, and contemplate the future; light, now he considered it, would be wasted on that vista.

In the great College of Thebes, priests were no doubt patting each other on the back, congratulating each other for ridding the empire of this troublesome prince, this heretic. Moses almost smiled; they deserved their celebration, they had played a fine trick to get rid of him and his god. And somewhere, he hoped, his mother wept for him, even as she smiled for Amenhotep.

Small matter; here in Memphis, the heretic would become a hermit, and who would notice? Moses thought about praying but changed his mind. Just for now, he could do without gods, his or the others; he was truly alone. Tears burned his cheeks. 'Aten, Lord of light, guide my father's soul. Lead him safely through the trials of the underworld that he may join you forever in the light of the sun.' His voice faltered, and his prayer came to an end. *Why bother,* he thought. *My father is in Amun's hands now.*

Amun, and the priests who adore him. They who shape the empire, my empire, to their own desires.

* * *

Anen made his way crookedly across the floor of the chamber. He seemed to be fatally

hampered by the weight of his ceremonial robes. 'Highness,' he panted. 'The scrying is done. This is the most auspicious hour for the ceremony to begin. Are you ready, highness?'

More ready than you are, old man. Amenhotep rose from his throne and felt the weight of his own robes. *This is going to be torture,* he thought grimly.

They made their way down through the palace to the courtyard. The royal family, and a jostling crowd of nobles, were already there, waiting to be told which of the carriages were for them, or which of them would have to walk the ceremonial route.

Amenhotep exchanged a look with his mother. *She looks old,* he thought. *Old and defeated.* He smiled to reassure her, waved to his siblings and took his place in the lead carriage. A column of priests and soldiers formed up in front of them, the vanguard of the procession. Anen raised his head, and his reedy voice rang out. 'Open the gates! Let the coronation begin.'

The royal herald moved to the front of the procession as the great gates opened smoothly onto the street and the waiting crowds.

Miriam craned her neck and stretched on tiptoes, but she couldn't see over the throng in front of her. 'What's happening, Yuk? Have they opened the gates yet?'

103

'See for yourself, my love.' Yuk lifted her effortlessly and sat her on his broad shoulder. 'There, now you are the tallest person in the crowd.'

'The gates are still closed. What are they waiting for?'

'I expect the priests have another ritual to perform before they allow the new pharaoh into the light. They are not short of rituals, and this is a big day for them.'

He brought her back to earth gently and handed her a flatbread spread with honey. 'Here, eat; we will be standing here for a while.'

'Yuk, you old devil! Why aren't you hobnobbing with the royals, as usual?' Yuk looked to his left. An old friend was sipping wine from a leather gourd, grinning broadly.

'I might ask the same question of you, you old serpent,' Yuk said, laughing. 'Shouldn't you be guarding something or other?'

'They pensioned me off,' his friend replied. 'I think I heard too much from the old pharaoh's bedchamber and they don't want me spilling the beans.'

Yuk looked at him with a smirk. *Lying hound!*

His friend smirked back at him. 'These days I spend my time drinking cheap wine and looking over my shoulder. Doesn't do to be a loose end in a priest's plot.'

He is lying, isn't he? 'You're safe enough. You're too lowly for an assassin's fee.' *Has he seen or heard anything; anything my mistress should know?*

'I hope you're right, my old mate. But I'd wager one of us will be for it soon; whether it's me or the new pharaoh, now that's a question.'

Yuk wanted to take the conversation further, his friend had always had access to special knowledge in the palace, sometimes knowledge that he, himself, did not have, but Miriam broke the conversation as the palace gates began to open.

'The gates are opening. Finally.' Miriam beamed. 'Now we'll see everything. Help me, Yuk.'

'I will help and you will see.' Yuk lifted Miriam again to his shoulders, the folds of her tunic drifted across his face in the breeze. 'But you will have to describe it to me, I can't see myself now.'

A herald's voice cut through the murmur of the crowd but no one could hear a word that he said. Trumpets blared, and the first of the coronation procession spilled out onto the broad thoroughfare. Cheers erupted from every direction.

Miriam wasn't cheering; she was too engaged watching for family members as they paraded through the city gate. 'I can see the new pharaoh,' she said to a tiring Yuk. 'He looks very serious. And there's Tiye, your mistress; she just looks sad.'

'I wager the high priest is smiling, though,' Yuk said as he freed himself from the trailing cloth and looked at the procession. 'Everything has gone very nicely for him and his friends.'

The coronation had begun three weeks earlier, with a procession in Memphis, where the new pharaoh had made the traditional circumambulation of the city walls. Although Thebes was now the empire's capital, Memphis was still traditionally its heart. Three times Amenhotep had gone around the ancient capital's walls, before completing the ancient ceremony and heading down to the Nile and the next stage of the ritual. He had arrived in Thebes at the head of a flotilla of barges, which completely occluded the water of the great river and stretched as far as the eye could see. Small boats followed the ceremonial armada, personal boats for families and other crafts, whose owners made a small fortune carrying crowds of observers down to Thebes; those who could afford it wanted to see the spectacle, it was a once in a lifetime occasion.

Crowds of onlookers followed the entourage from the river as the pharaoh entered Thebes; they jostled for good positions along the sacred way. An occasional scream punctuated the good-natured competition as everyone pushed and shoved to see the pharaoh, a rare experience; they would have few chances to see him again, and probably less to view a coronation.

Amenhotep was carried high, in a golden litter, which was so heavy it needed eight great Nubians to carry it. The gold glinting from the pharaoh's costume drew the eyes of the onlookers and they loved the spectacle; cheers filled the skies.

Behind, Anen, in a smaller but just as impressive litter, made his exit from the second processional barge, allowing himself a smirk of approval. *He is no fool, our new pharaoh, smiling at the crowds.* He turned to one of his assistants. 'Tell some of our priests to go along the sacred way and distribute coin among the peasants. Make sure they proclaim it is the gift of Amun. They must not allow the throng to think it is from the royal family.' The assistant slipped away to do his bidding.

Miriam gazed in awe at the glittering jewels adorning the ranks of the nobles and courtiers following the royal carriage. She counted the headdresses of the priests; effigies of the gods in all their splendour. 'Sobek is there', she advised Yuk, 'and Bast, and there's Anubis and Hathor. I don't see anyone bearing the disc of Aten, though; do you think they forgot him, Yuk?'

'No, my love, I am sure they did not forget. More likely they purposefully decided that he would not be with us. They won, don't forget, Aten is a has-been.' Yuk sighed; his mistress would not be happy.

There was less pomp about this part of the ritual. As Miriam and Yuk watched from a distance, the royal party and the chief courtiers were led into the temple complex by an army of priests. 'See? The pharaoh wears only one crown; the red crown of the lower Nile. When he emerges from the temple, he will wear the white crown too, and then he will truly be lord of the two lands.'

'And then the rituals will be complete?' Miriam's voice was a little weary; it had already been a long day, and she didn't envy the great and the good, bedecked in weighty ceremonial garments.

'No, there is one more ritual to complete; the Sed. The new pharaoh must prove that he is fit to rule, that he is a warrior and a hunter, and worthy of the two crowns.'

'Where does that take place?'

'Here, in the great courtyard of the temple. They have prepared a course for the pharaoh, a trial of speed and strength. But we will see him, briefly, before then. He will come out so the nobles can acknowledge his possession of the second crown.'

Some thirty minutes later, the huge cedar doors of the temple of Amun opened and Amenhotep stepped out, now wearing the two crowns bound together; the white one of Upper Egypt now bound to the top of the red northern one. The assembled nobles and soldiers gave a roar of approval. Amenhotep inclined his head to them, and turned to his right, he walked into the courtyard where the Sed would take place. The gates closed behind him.

Amenhotep was handed a spear and a sword. He surveyed the course they had laid out for him; the sun beat down on the huge space, pitching sharp shadows among the hurdles and posts. 'Behold, he comes, the warrior king, the hunter king!' The herald stepped forward and indicated the starting line to Amenhotep. 'Highness, show us the prowess of the gods. Begin!'

Amenhotep breathed a silent prayer to Aten and began his sprint around the courtyard. His regal robes, and the weapons he now carried, threatened to trip him up at any moment. Sweat immediately beaded on his brow and his vision became blurred at the edges.

'Behold, the enemies of the crown. Behold the wicked armies of the usurpers.'

Amenhotep stopped by the martial effigies and drew his sword. He thrust the blade of star-iron into each of the figures around him.

'He is victorious; the warrior claims the spoils!' The herald's voice drove him on, to the next trial.

In the corner of the courtyard, partly in shadow, he could see the looming bulk of the panther. He readied his spear and approached. This was the most dangerous moment of the Sed ceremony, and Amenhotep was all too aware that something could yet go horribly wrong. The powerful creature hissed a warning at him, but the chains that bound it to a post stopped it from moving too far. Amenhotep thrust the long spear between the panther's shoulder blades, and it sank slowly into the welter of manacles.

'Behold, the hunter has killed. The hunter claims the spoils!'

The last part of the ritual was simple, on the face of it; Amenhotep had only to run up the steps onto the dais in the last corner of the courtyard and he was done. But it was scarily easy to trip, running up steps in full regalia. He steeled himself, took a deep breath, and sprinted for the steps. *Made it. I don't have to play this foolish game for another thirty years, until my jubilee—if I survive that long.*

Anen watched from the temple balcony as the young pharaoh completed the ritual and was led back to the temple. He was satisfied; the people had enjoyed the pomp, the nobles had had their day in the sun, and the pharaoh was in place. That was the end of the traditional rites; it was time to return to the present and the order of the day.

'Patenemheb,' he said, turning to a young priest. 'Fetch my son. Take him to the sanctum, and have my deputy prepare consecration robes for him.'

Patenemheb was a little taken aback. There had been rumours of Aye joining the priesthood, and in a high position, but so quickly and quietly at the time of the coronation? 'Holiness, you don't think it might be better to wait until the royal entourage is back in its palace?' Patenemheb's voice was solicitous, but Anen could feel unease radiating from him.

'Now, Patenemheb,' Anen insisted. 'And make haste. It is time for my son to take his place in the world, as his cousin Amenhotep has taken his. It is auspicious for him to be consecrated as the pharaoh is crowned.'

If pharaohs can found dynasties, then why not a high priest of royal blood?

1349 BC

Memphis, Egypt. Year 2, in the reign of Amenhotep IV

Yuk slipped out of the queen's apartment and found the two guards leaning on their spears. 'Look sharp, you two; can you not hear the fanfare?'

The guards shot him a resigned look and straightened up, spears upright at their shoulders. 'That's better; now the pharaoh won't think his mother is looked after by idiots.'

The royal commotion was drawing nearer; Yuk could hear the tramp of sandaled feet along the corridor. He hurried to the neighbouring room and settled himself by the window; from here, he could listen to everything that happened in the queen's chambers, and he suspected it might make for a lively encounter.

In her chamber, Tiye shifted uneasily in her seat. She had timed everything just about perfectly, but she worried that the pharaoh might not appreciate the surprise she had in store for him. *Too late for fear*, she thought. *I have done my part, now my god will do his. I hope.*

The herald tapped his staff on the door, three times, and his sonorous voice rang out along the corridor.

'His majesty, the Lord of the Empire, the god of the overworld, His greatness, Amenhotep, beloved of Amun, protector of the two lands, Pharaoh of Egypt, the fourth of that name. Behold, he comes, he comes, the living god.'

The doors to the queen's apartment rolled smoothly open, and the herald stepped to one side; his job was done. The Chancellor led the entourage into the royal chambers. Amenhotep fixed his eyes forwards and stepped into the chamber. Behind him, his wife, Nefertiti, took their daughter Meritaten by the hand and led her in. 'Come, my child. And remember to greet your grandmother the way I showed you.'

Meritaten looked around at the nobles and servants prostrate before her daddy and giggled. Nefertiti, clapped her hand across her daughter's mouth, pretending to be shocked and angry, but she was struggling to suppress a smile.

Tiye stood, a little stiffly, to greet her son, and bowed her head, also a little stiffly, to acknowledge her king.

Behind the royal presence the chancellor bowed and turned to the assembled entourage. He raised his staff, then banged the tip of it three times on the floor. There was a mass exodus back down the corridor, the courtiers returning the way they had come. The chancellor turned, bowed once more to Amenhotep, and indicated that he would wait on the other side of the door for his Pharaoh's return. He walked out and motioned to the guards. The great doors were closed quickly and silently.

Nefertiti was the first to greet Tiye. She bowed, acknowledging the queen, and then she took Tiye's hand and kissed it, acknowledging the mother. She radiated beauty, this new queen. She was considered by many to be the most perfect woman the gods had ever created. She seemed to glide into the room rather than merely walk, her jet-black hair hanging like a silk curtain behind her, a raven veil. Her face was symmetrical, her mouth wide and generous, her cheeks high and effortlessly sculpted, and her eyes were deep, dark pools, intelligent and kind.

Tiye acknowledged Nefertiti's greeting with a courteous smile and turned to her son. She bowed, as she was obliged to do.

'Good morning, mother.'

'Good morning, your highness. To what do we owe the pleasure of your presence in Memphis? Is it another god's celebration that brings you north?' Tiye tried and failed to hide the sarcasm in her voice. 'I am pleased and honoured you have given us your time. Please sit.'

Amenhotep seemed torn between formality and warmth. 'How are you, mother?'

'I am well, thank Aten. I understand that you have started to issue royal news bulletins to the people, Amenhotep; that is novel.'

'I want to be part of my people,' Amenhotep replied. 'You and father used to talk about being a part of the people, about making them feel that you were a part of their lives? Well I have taken that to heart.'

'That is wise and generous, my son, to show them that you care, and it is good that you include Nefertiti. It is only right that the importance of the queen is understood by all.' There was a brief, uncomfortable silence. Amenhotep knew where the conversation was going, and Tiye knew that he knew, so, she changed the subject.

'I hear that you have upset King Tushratta of Mitanni, Amenhotep.' She said. 'I well remember that it was he who helped your father in his struggles against the Hittites. Tushratta complained to me that you have sent him gold-plated statues, rather than statues made of solid gold. Pure gold was part of the payment

Tushratta is due for giving his daughter in marriage to your father, and for her marrying you now that your father is dead.' Tiye knew she was overstepping the mark. She might be the Pharaoh's mother, but there were limits.

'Why is Tushratta writing to you, mother?' The king's face had lost some of its kindness, and his brow creased.

'He and I are very close, Amenhotep. We often correspond.' There was a measured taunt in her reply.

'I would prefer that you don't discuss state business with people outside the family. The state's business is not your business now. Your concern is family.'

'Ah, family, Amenhotep; like brothers and sisters, you mean?'

'Mother, no.'

Amenhotep cursed himself for falling into the trap. Moses was always there, hidden behind Tiye's words and actions.

'Come now my son, meet your brother and bring him back into society.'

'I cannot mother, you know that.'

'Meet him then. Just talk to him. Now would be a good time.'

Amenhotep glanced towards the far corner of the room. Someone sat huddled in the corner trying to hide; someone who had been ordered to live alone.

Amenhotep cursed himself for finding himself embarrassed by this situation. He knew this might happen, especially on one of his visits to Memphis. It was forbidden for him to see Moses; his fathers' instructions were clear. Moses was in permanent exile from the world he was once on the brink of destroying; at least, that was how the priests told it.

Moses remained seated in the corner; his eyes downcast.

The uncomfortable silence resumed.

Amenhotep's eyes flicked from Moses to his mother. He knew she had arranged this moment, had plotted it; now the time had come, and he didn't know what to do. His anger at her spilled over onto his brother, much as he loved him; at that moment he could happily have struck them both down.

Tiye's face was a mask, but her heart was racing. The situation she had longed for and prayed for was finally here. Now she had to trust to her god, and her sons.

'Greetings, Moses.'

His wife echoed his greeting, a little more confidence in her voice.

'Greetings, Moses. I have always wanted to meet you. I am sorry that you have been locked away from us for so long. The law is the law, of course, but ... Oh, this is wonderful! Aten must have decreed it.'

Amenhotep had no idea what to do. His heart spoke louder than his head. He wanted so much to hold his brother in his arms, but he had to follow protocol.

'We should leave,' he said, his indecision obvious.

'Stay,' said Tiye. 'What harm can it do now, Amenhotep? Your brother has been in the shadows for so long now that the priests have all but forgotten him.'

Nefertiti turned to Amenhotep and whispered in his ear. 'Amenhotep, don't you think this nonsense has gone on for too long? You are the Pharaoh; you decide what happens, not the priests. Your brother has suffered enough, and, besides, he is no threat to anyone or anything now. He is simply Moses, the Pharaoh's disgraced brother.'

'Brother-in-law,' she said, 'it is well that we have met at last. And you should meet your niece, too. Here she is.' She put her arm around Meritaten and smiled at her brother-in-law. 'Isn't she a beautiful little girl? We have named her Meritaten, she who is beloved of Aten. The priests were a little shocked at first, but they acquiesced soon enough. We told them we had named her so to make your mother smile. They saw no threat in it. Perhaps there is a lesson here for you. Tread softly, and you may get what you desire.'

Moses looked at his niece, and his heart softened. His brother was more complex than he had thought; he had taken a real risk with his daughter's name.

'You have my crown, brother,' Moses said, 'but I do not envy you it. I am glad to be free of it, if I am honest. I am no one now, but I am your brother. You have nothing to fear from me.'

'These are generous words, Moses,' said Amenhotep. *But he is dangerous.* He could not escape the truth of it. His brother was a danger to his family, and ultimately a danger to the empire. Perhaps it was better for all of them if he stayed in the shadows, stayed in the past where he belonged. He needed time to think.

'Nefertiti, we must go.'

Tiye nodded to her daughter-in-law. She had planted the seed, and Nefertiti had helped her to nurture it. Now she must wait and see.

In the cramped, hidden chamber adjoining the room, Yuk smiled. His mistress was winning.

Nefertiti could see the tension etched in her husband's face. Her hands moved, caressing Amenhotep's head, reaching the long wisp of hair which hung loosely down the nape of his neck. She felt tense muscles beneath her fingers and worked at them gently to help him relax.

'Gods and priests: gods and priests and brothers,' he muttered. 'Thutmoses tried to be his own man but the priests defeated him, and forced my father to see things their way. So, the throne passed to me: power in a poisoned chalice. And there is Aten, the one god, the fly in the priestly ointment; I don't know how I can fix that.

'I am a god, apparently, I am infallible and omnipotent, but I do not feel like a god. Amun and his priests rule the empire, not me.'

'But you are one of their gods. You are pharaoh, and a living god.'

'I may be a god, but in many ways, they have more power than me. If only Thutmoses had been stronger and more diplomatic. I think he would have made a better pharaoh than me.'

Nefertiti felt the truth in his words. Amenhotep was a reluctant king, a reluctant god.

'You know,' Amenhotep continued, 'when we met him last month, it was not by chance. My mother would have led us back to each other eventually. And the fact is, she was right; we are not beholden to the priests, or we should not be. Why should I be ashamed of my only brother? Why should I keep him as a prisoner in Memphis? He should be Pharaoh, not me. I should be enjoying my simple life with my family, with you, my darling, and our beautiful daughter.'

'I wish things were so simple, Amenhotep. But the real world has a habit of ruining our dreams.'

'So is there no way out for me?'

'In the short term, no; but perhaps, if time is our friend, we may find a way. And I have a feeling that Moses, though you see him as part of the problem, may just turn out to be part of the solution.'

Amenhotep laughed, a short bark of wry amusement. 'It must be the fate of those named Amenhotep,' he said, 'to be loved and ruled by beautiful women.'

1348 BC

It was the festival of Sopdet. The time when the brightest star in the heavens rose with the sun, and the sacred river flooded. Amenhotep was in Memphis for the new-year festival. He had thought long and hard about Moses, and how he could resolve his quandary. One way or another, his trip to the city where his brother remained a virtual prisoner could be an opportunity. Now he was here, his courage almost failed him. *If I take this step,* he thought, *there is no turning back.* Letting Moses back into the world was like letting the family ghost out of the cellar. He took a deep breath and composed himself. There was only one way to find out what would happen. He tapped the bell on the table beside him, and a servant appeared out of nowhere.

'Send for the chancellor.'

The servant bowed and left the chamber.

Within ten minutes the chancellor, puffing as if out of breath, entered his master's room, genuflecting as far as an old man could; bow, stand, right hand to left shoulder and back to the right side, step, bow, arm ... until eventually, after ten steps, the final bow. 'Majesty,' he said and stood straight and firm, silently

117

thanking Amun for his help. He was not happy to be woken in the middle of the night, a fact he tried to hide. He had been busy until the early hours arranging the festival with the Sopdet priests, and they had drunk copious amounts of beer. He could feel tomorrow's hangover making an early start. 'You wished to see me?'

'I want to see my brother.'

The chancellor was too startled to hide his reaction. He tried opening and closing his mouth a few times, but nothing coherent seemed to emerge.

'You brother, majesty? Moses.'

'Yes, chancellor. Please bring him here this evening after the festival. I will see him privately. But let's keep this quiet, shall we? We don't want the world to see you do this, do we? It might not go so well for you.' The chancellor heard the implied threat loud and clear.

'No, sire.'

'Talk to him in the morning, and let him know of our plans. I don't want him thinking he's being dragged off to be executed.'

'I will do as you command, sire, and advise him of your wishes. And I will ensure that your meeting is confidential.'

The chancellor backed out of the room, bowing as he went. Outside, in the corridor, he composed himself. This was the last thing he had expected. Bringing him to the pharaoh, the god-king talking to him, this was unimaginable. Still, the pharaoh's wishes were not to be questioned, so he set off for his quarters, the pain of his hangover competing with the shock of his lord's instruction.

A little further down the corridor, a curtain twitched almost imperceptibly in a quiet niche. The figure that emerged a moment later smiled quietly, and turned to follow the chancellor's footsteps. Yuk knew someone else who would be pleased to hear this news.

Moses followed the Chancellor through the gardens and across the courtyard; his mind racing, he hardly noticed the revellers celebrating the new year. Nor was he noticed; with the cowl of his cloak pulled over his face he was anonymous.

'Chancellor, where are you taking me? I don't recognise this place.' The passage they walked along was unfamiliar, and less ornate than the main corridors of the palace, no images of gods on the ceiling, no painted columns.

'Forgive me for the indignity, high ... Moses. This is part of the servants' quarters. I thought this route might be more discreet.'

They turned a corner and Moses saw a door that he knew well; it led to a small apartment his father had used as his private office. Despite himself, he smiled; he had many memories of this place, good memories. The guards posted at the doors studiously ignored him. But they moved smartly enough when the Chancellor ordered them to step aside; he lifted his wand of office and tapped the door with its tip, three times. There were three answering taps from inside and then a servant opened the doors, and slipped away into the passage. He didn't look at Moses. *Perhaps I am invisible as well as anonymous.* Moses gazed through the dim light to see his brother sitting on a long divan, eating sweetmeats.

Amenhotep turned and smiled.

'Chancellor, you have done well. You may go now. I will summon you when you are needed.'

The Chancellor bowed and backed out. In the corridor, one of the guards smirked and raised a quizzical eyebrow; for one undignified moment, the chancellor thought the man was actually going to wink at him. 'Get on with your work,' he growled, and stalked off imperiously. The guard's smirk followed him.

Amenhotep smiled as he gazed at his brother; he couldn't help it. He wanted to reach out for him and take him in his arms. 'Thutmoses, you can take that ridiculous cloak off now. You look like a spy in a harem.' He laughed, and Moses, although wary of the situation and his surroundings, found himself laughing too.

'I feel like a beggar in a brothel.' Moses shrugged off the tattered cloak. 'That's better. I feel myself again. And, by the way, brother, that self is called Moses now; Thutmoses was destroyed by our father; he no longer exists.'

Amenhotep acquiesced to his brother's wishes. 'Moses, then.' The pharaoh took hold of his brother's arm and guided him to the far side of the chamber, away from prying ears. 'Sit, brother,' he said as they approached two jewelled chairs beside a golden table, 'and try the sweetmeats; they're good.'

'Why have you brought me here, Amenhotep? Is there a reason for us to meet?' Moses was used to being a prisoner in the palace, being ignored and left to while away days filled with monotony. He was not expecting his brother to call on him.

'There is.' Amenhotep placed his hand on Moses'. 'I am ready to reinstate you as a prince of the realm.'

Moses was stunned. 'You are … No, my brother, you cannot do that; father forbade it.'

'The new year is an auspicious time for new beginnings,' Amenhotep said, 'and what better new beginnings? I am Pharaoh now, and father is dead, so what I say is law. We are in the land of the living, not of the dead.'

Amenhotep leaned forward, his hands steepled. 'But there are things you need to hear, and understand.'

The sweetmeat turned to ashes in Moses' mouth. *He will free me and gag me at the same time. I should have known.*

'Do you remember the argument you had with our father, years ago, in his apartment? He almost struck you, he was so angry.'

'How do you know this? Who told you?'

'I was hiding on the balcony of a neighbouring room. I heard everything. Do you remember what he said? "Aten is better served by a diplomat than a demagogue." He was right, Moses, and you couldn't see it. He was trying to tell you what he was doing.'

Moses' mind reeled. If Amenhotep was right, then his father had been working to move the people of Egypt towards the worship of Aten all the time, and he had failed to understand his father's actions.

'If I reinstate you, I need to be sure that you understand the implications, Moses. That you understand we are all working towards the same goal. My methods, like our father's, are quieter, and probably slower, than yours. But they will not lead to the calamity of open war with the priests of the old gods.'

A sharp knock sounded on the chamber door. Amenhotep was expecting it. 'Come,' he shouted. A man Moses didn't recognise entered the room.

'This is Thethi, my spymaster. I think he has news that may interest you. Speak, Thethi; you are among friends here.'

'Highness, as you requested, I set a man to watch the chancellor. After he left these chambers, he hurried to the cloister by the main gate. My man says he met a priest there, a young man leading a horse. They exchanged a few words and the priest rode off in a hurry.'

'Then the die is cast. In a few hours, Anen and his friends will know that we have met. They will work out what's happening quickly enough. Thethi, leave us; thank you, you have done well.'

'Highness.'

Thethi slipped out of the room, and Amenhotep sat forward in his seat.

'So, Moses, this is my proposition. I will reinstate you as a prince, with real power. In return, you will act like a prince instead of a priest. Between us, we will try and bring a one god religion to fruition, without stirring the priests of Amun into open revolt. What do you say?'

Moses was too stunned to answer immediately. The revelation of his father's true ambitions made him feel guilty and foolish; he had shunned his father's love through blindness. Now his brother was offering him another chance; but he was not sure if he could play the role Amenhotep was proposing. It was resignation more than resolve that prompted his reply. He would do anything to escape the dismal monotony of internal exile.

'I will try, Amenhotep. I will try to do as you wish.'

'You must do more than try, brother. Aten must prevail, and we must see that he does. There is no other way. Don't let me down, Moses; and more importantly, don't let Aten down.'

* * *

The banks of the Nile were lush with crops for the coming year. Amenhotep watched barges pass by on their way to the sea. They carried goods for the delta: cloth, wheat and rice, and brought stone from the quarries at Swenett. The royal barge made good progress, helped by the southerly winds, and they arrived in Abydos after a couple of leisurely days. The new year festivities at the temple of Osiris were among the oldest in the Egyptian ritual calendar. As Amenhotep stepped off the boat he could hear the chanting and smell the vats of ritual beer.

He made his obeisance to the ancient deity, wearing the head-dress of Horus. The ritual drama was played out: the slaying of Osiris by Seth, Isis reclaiming the body parts of the dead god, the climactic battle between Seth and Horus, with Amenhotep playing the role of the ancestor of the pharaohs. The following morning, he re-embarked on the royal barge and resumed his journey down the Nile, heading for Thebes, for the final ceremonies.

Thebes was not pleasant at this time of year; the summer sun was sweltering and the night brought little respite from the heat, but in the great Amun temple at Karnak, with its funerary altars and enormous statues erected by numerous Pharaohs, the crowds were not in the least bothered by the conditions; they were there to enjoy themselves. Trumpets blared and ceremonial flags hung limp on their poles. There was a feeling of optimism in the stifling air.

In the palace, a cool breeze blew welcome fresh air through the corridors of power; a small miracle in the dog days of summer. Amenhotep relaxed in his chambers and considered his plans. The priests knew he was reinstating Moses, and he needed to reassure them. Now was as good a time as any. He sent for Anen.

There was no cool breeze in the high priest's chambers. Anen had to make do with the desultory comfort of a sleepy slave wafting an ostrich feather fan behind his head. When the messenger arrived, he brought an irritating draft of warm air into the chamber.

'Lord high priest,' the messenger advised, 'Amenhotep, the fourth of that name, lord of the . . .'

'Yes, yes, I am aware who the pharaoh is, man; get on with it.'

The messenger struggled to keep a straight face. 'My lord the pharaoh wishes your attendance at the palace immediately.'

'The pharaoh wants to see me? Now?'

'Yes, your holiness.'

Anen dismissed the messenger with a peeved gesture and an angry wave of his arm. He shouted for a servant.

'Get me a robe!' The servant turned on his heel and scurried away quickly to fetch a clean white linen robe.

Anen readied himself with the aid of his perspiring dresser. It was too hot for ceremonial robes today, but . . . He was hurried out of the temple and taken by sedan chair to the jetty, where a felucca waited. The moribund slave with the fan followed, flapping uselessly at the torpid air. Anen stepped out of his chair and walked regally along the hastily laid carpet to the boat. The cool water of the river soothed his irritation a little, but he was not looking forward to his audience with the pharaoh.

The chancellor struck the ground with his staff, three times, and bowed very low to the pharaoh. Anen genuflected on his left knee, as per tradition, but without enthusiasm

'His holiness the High Priest of Amun, Anen, beseeches audience with your majesty.'

Anen shifted irritably. Beseeching didn't suit him.

'You may leave us, Lord Chancellor,' Amenhotep said.

'Your majesty.'

Amenhotep appraised his uncle coolly. Rivulets of perspiration ran down his face, and his linen robe showed patches of sweat. *Excellent,* he thought. *He is too angry to play his games. We can get down to business.*

'Anen, I am going to reinstate my brother as a royal prince.'

Anen evinced surprise, but it wasn't very convincing. 'I'm not sure that I follow, highness.'

'You follow well enough, Anen. Your spies told you everything three days ago.'

Anen swallowed. It was an open secret that the priests spied on the pharaoh, and the pharaoh spied on the priests, but it was bad form to admit it.

'I want to know what you think, Anen. And what the College is planning to do in response. I am not about to change my mind.'

'The College will not be happy; you are breaking your father's word, to them and to the people. They will find it hard to accept an apostate as a prince of the realm. And I wonder what the generals will think.'

'You should know, uncle. You seem to spend a lot of time with them.'

'Erm, quite so. You will struggle to persuade them that this is a good idea.'

'I may struggle, uncle, but you have influence with them, clearly. Perhaps you could help to smooth the path.'

'I, er . . .'

'That's not actually a request, uncle. It's an order, from your pharaoh.'

'Then I have no choice.'

'Good, you understand me.'

'I do your highness.'

'Oh, and high priest,' Amenhotep said, 'can I also suggest that you at least wait a while before you start plotting against my brother? Give him a chance, Anen, he is a changed man. I don't think he will antagonise you as he did before.'

No, and Nile water isn't wet.

'Leave me now, and Anen . . .'

'Highness?'

'Think on what I've said. I will not take kindly to my brother being vilified by the College.'

'Highness.'

1347 BC

Thebes, Egypt. Year 4, in the reign of Amenhotep IV

'But I am the crown prince of Alalakh! Surely I should be seated closer to his highness the pharaoh than this camel herder from Amurru?'

Simaluk. the Director of Ceremonies, stitched a patient smile onto his face and tried again. 'Your majesty is a valued ally of Egypt, of course. But the seating plan is clear, and this, your majesty, is your place. His majesty the king of Amurru is closer to the pharaoh by no more than a cubit.'

'I am insulted. My father will hear of this.'

Your poor father will never hear the end of it, I'm sure. 'Your majesty, please be seated.' Simaluk's voice was reduced to a pleading whine. This hairy giant was holding up a queue of kings that stretched back almost to the Nile. He breathed a sigh of relief when the prince slumped resentfully into the gilded chair.

The royal audience chamber was a maelstrom of bickering potentates and harassed officials. The director's superior, Yuia, master of the audience chamber, presided over the madness with a resigned look on his face.

The third year of the reign of Amenhotep IV was at an end, the fourth beginning, and, by established custom, the kings of the region had come to Thebes to offer gifts, pledges of allegiance, and squabbles for the pharaoh to adjudicate. Slaves and servants carried bundles of rich fabric and chests of gold and jewels to and fro, waiting for the signal from their king or prince to present the gifts.

Yuia beckoned the director over. 'They are more or less in their places now; I think we can tell the herald to start announcing these barbarians in their turn, and see if we can get this over with without a war starting.' Simaluk hurried to the base of the royal dais, and signalled to the herald, who waited at the door of the hall. 'Get on with it, and blow hard. This is as good as it's going to get.'

Yuia tapped his staff on the chamber's wooden floor and began to declaim. 'Behold, the kings and princes of the earth are come; they offer praise and allegiance to the pharaoh, the king of the two lands, the lord of the many lands. Behold, the king of Amurru bears gifts for the pharaoh. Make way.'

The procession began. Kings, princes, chiefs and high priests came forward and presented their gifts, pledged their allegiance and prostrated themselves before Amenhotep. He acknowledged them one by one, thanked them for the gifts, pretended to believe their protestations of eternal loyalty.

The pile of treasure at the foot of the dais grew into an unwieldy heap. Yuia despatched a couple of royal guards to steady the tottering mountain of homage.

The king of Mitanni was seated quite close to the pharaoh's dais; only Tudhaliya, the arrogant ruler of the Hittites, sat between him and the Egyptian monarch. He rose, and approached the dais. When he had made his obeisance, he gestured to his vizier. The elderly courtier came forward timidly, leading a beautiful young woman.

'Your highness, I have brought no gold or fine fabrics. Instead I offer a gift from my heart. This is my daughter, Kiye. She is my eldest daughter, and she is the light of my heart. I ask that you take her as a royal wife, to cement the bond between our lands.'

Kiye stepped forward; if she was awed by the presence of the pharaoh, she didn't show it. Her features were regal and proud, and she was very beautiful.

Amenhotep inclined his head. 'Your majesty does me too much honour. I am pleased to accept your gift, and I acknowledge our bond.' He looked on the princess standing before the dais and admired her. She would grace the royal harem.

Amenhotep was not the only one looking at Kiye. As soon as she had stepped forward, Moses had felt his heart miss a beat. She was astonishing; a beauty to rival Nefertiti. But that wasn't what drew him to her. In her eyes he saw infinite patience and grace. In her figure he saw all that he had dreamed of in a woman. He felt a thrill of lust, and a frisson of shame. *She is my brother's wife; what am I thinking?* He willed himself to look elsewhere, but his eyes refused to leave her.

* * *

Moses swept his hand over the architectural drawing as he described the temple. 'And the portico here, facing the rising sun, can be opened out so the light of Aten can illuminate the interior.'

Amenhotep was impressed; his brother was an architect of real skill. But the location of the temple was a concern. 'It's beautiful, Moses, a gift to the lord Aten. But is Karnak the only place we can site it? The College will see it as an insult.'

'But all the gods are represented at Karnak. We can tell them that Aten is joining the fold. They may even believe us.' Moses' laughter was laced with venom. 'And if they don't, we still have a foot in the sanctum of the College. Aten can devour the old gods at his leisure.'

'Well, the priests are aware that I am obliged to build a temple to my personal god in the third year of my reign; in theory they can't complain if I choose to build at Karnak. And they are only too aware that Aten is the god of our family. But this may be a step too far, Moses. It may . . . '

Amenhotep swayed momentarily, and his eyes fell out of focus, as if he were staring into an infinite distance. Moses grasped his arm to steady him. 'Brother, are you well?'

'I'm well, I'm well, it's just . . . Sometimes, I think I can hear Aten's voice in my head; but I can never make out what he's saying. I'm sure he's just telling me this is the right thing to do. It's no matter; let's get on with our business.'

Dinner was a happy affair that evening. Moses joined his brother and his family, and Tiye, to celebrate the advances they had made. Amenhotep recounted his conversation with Anen. 'Anen just stood there, stupefied. What could he do? You could feel the heat from his anger ten cubits away. He hadn't a clue what to say.'

The laughter around the table was filled with the sound of victory. *But it's a small victory*, thought Moses. *We have to move on, to build on what we have achieved, but how?*

'When will you announce the change of name, brother?'

'Not before the Opet festival; I think we can hold fire until then at least.'

'I think there is something we can do in the meantime.' Moses leaned forward in his seat. 'The ancient sun god, Re, is associated with Amun in the ancient texts. We could have a friendly scholar "discover" this fact and spread the news. If we can hoodwink the priests into accepting Amun-Re as the central deity of Thebes, we are just a few steps away from installing Aten above the pantheon.'

Tiye arched a regal eyebrow. 'That would be good, Moses, really good. But the College will not jump to accept a new version of their precious god. How will we persuade them?'

'I think we can do something about that.' Amenhotep drummed his fingers on the table. 'If we can offer them something, a festival or a new temple complex, a fresh income stream, they will be easier to persuade.'

'Let's start more simply,' said Nefertiti. She rarely interfered in family plans, but when she did it was usually worth hearing. 'Let's invite them to celebrate the ascension of Amun-Re at the Opet festivities. Not as the chief of the gods, but as an exciting new addition. Then, when they think they have put the new god in his place, we can find some willing scholars to produce evidence of his eminence.'

'I like this plan.' Moses beamed. 'It puts us at an advantage even as the priests think they are winning. Let's do it.'

They raised their glasses and drank a toast: to their cleverness, and to the rise of the one true god.

* * *

'Anen, this is not a matter of choice. The pharaoh must build a temple to his personal god, and where better than Karnak? We can use this to our advantage.' Ijuju placed a wrinkled hand on the high priest's arm. Anen could see the liver spots peppering the leathery skin; Ijuju had been around forever.

'You are right, Ijuju, we have little choice. But there is more to this. My spies tell me the pharaoh has plans to change his name.'

'That's hardly a worry. Many pharaohs have added a name to their cartouche.'

In the corner Anen's latest introduction to the priesthood, his son Aye, had listened in silence for long enough. 'Oh, he's not adding a name.' His father shot him a disapproving look, but he ploughed on. 'What my father has neglected to tell you is the new name he has chosen: Akhenaten—the living spirit of Aten.'

Ijuju slumped back in his seat, and Anen glowered at his son. *You have overstepped the bounds of your position, boy. You need reining in.*

'That is … Well, that is simply outrageous.' Ijuju was struggling for words. 'He is practically declaring to everyone that he has left the service of Amun. Moses has infected him with his militant piety; no doubt he's behind the temple stunt too. I understand he fancies himself as something of an architect.'

'And what are we going to do about it?' Aye ignored his father's scowl and asked the question uppermost in all of their minds.

Anen leaned forwards, ready to scold him, but Ijuju held up a hand and smiled indulgently. 'Let the boy speak, Anen. You have trained him to this; perhaps he has something useful to say. What would you do, Aye?'

Now he had their attention, Aye realised he hadn't a clue how to respond. He shrugged apologetically, and looked down at the table. Ijuju's expression was a little more acidic now.

'It takes time, Aye, to learn the art of politics. Religious politics more than most. You are keen to contribute, and that's as it should be. But think on what has just happened. Until you are ready, and that means until you have gained sufficient knowledge and understanding of events, you may find it best to remember that you have twice as many ears as mouths.' Ijuju spoke softly but his eyes glinted like flint.

'Leave us, Aye, and attend to your duties. It's time for the acolytes to offer their oblations.' Anen could not resist a smirk as he dismissed his son.

'So, Ijuju, what do we do?'

'Well, we must accept the temple. We would look churlish if we did otherwise. And we can't stop a pharaoh from changing his name, however abhorrent we find it. But we need to see the larger scheme behind these insults.'

'And what is that larger scheme, do you think?'

'Amenhotep, egged on, no doubt, by his heretic brother, and his heretic mother too, has plans to make monotheists of us all. We need to gear up and keep our wits about us. War is on the horizon. And we must be ready when it comes.'

* * *

'This is excellent, Hekaib, just excellent. The scroll has almost all the elements we need. Almost.' Moses looked over the scroll again and scratched his head, deep in thought.

'Highness?'

'It's an amazing discovery, and it tells the story wonderfully, makes Amun-Re look like the chief of the gods. But it lacks something.'

Hekaib stared up at the prince from owlish eyes, and blinked in mild confusion. 'Highness?'

'Age.' Moses thoughts seemed to fill the air around him. 'It doesn't explicitly say that the story is ancient. For Amun-Re to be pre-eminent, he must predate the other gods of Thebes.'

'I may have a solution to that problem, highness.' Manuba, a second scribe, grinned and took a small leather pouch from his satchel.

'Tell me, Manuba.'

'See here, Highness, on the first page of the scroll. There is a gap here by the margin, enough for a few glyphs, I think.'

'And?'

'I could insert a phrase here indicating the great age of the story. No one need ever know, except us.'

'But fresh ink will give us away, Manuba.' Hekaib was nervous at the way the conversation was going. 'Everyone will know it's a forgery. And these are sacred texts. What right do we have to alter them?'

'We would not be the first,' Moses replied pointedly. He turned to Manuba. 'So, what can we do about the fresh ink?'

'Ah,' said Manuba. 'I believe I have something for that. My little toolkit here includes some powders that will make the ink look ancient, just like the rest of the scroll.'

'Manuba,' Moses said sternly. 'Why do I get the impression you have done this before?'

'Perish the thought, highness. But it's as well to be prepared, is it not?'

Moses smiled inwardly, even as he frowned at his mischievous scribe. Aten would hardly punish them for adding a little white lie to an ancient scroll; not if it brought Egypt closer to his worship.

'I'll have to turn a blind eye to your activities, Manuba; it wouldn't do for a prince of the realm to be involved in such goings on.'

1346 BC

Thebes, Egypt. Year 5, in the reign of Amenhotep IV

Kiye had had enough. 'Look, Nefret. It's not my fault I'm here, I didn't ask to be the thirty-fourth wife of a king who probably doesn't remember my name. And I didn't ask the gods to make me look this way. You don't need to be envious; look, your belly is swollen. When your child is born, you will rise in the ranks. I'm not your problem.'

Nefret's eyes flashed with triumphant anger. 'You are a spoiled bitch. You're all airs and graces. I swear your father only gave you to Amenhotep so he could be rid of you.'

Kiye's eyes filled with tears. She missed her father so much; her father, and her sisters, and her homeland. And these women in the harem seemed to blame her for everything. She wanted to get away; anywhere would do.

She stormed away from Nefret and her insults, and found herself at the great doors that marked the entrance to the harem. *Damn it*, she thought, *they won't kill me for taking a walk. And if they do, I'll probably be better off.*

She pulled at the tall, stately doors and found, to her surprise, that they were unlocked. She stepped out into the corridor and immediately felt the whoosh of air as two spears barred her way.

'How dare you?' she snapped, hoping she sounded like a queen in waiting. 'I'm a royal wife.'

'I know that, miss, and I also know that royal wives are supposed to stay in the harem unless there's a very good reason ...' He paused and let his eyes rove over her '...A very good reason to leave. Like a summons from the pharaoh.'

The regal act hadn't worked, so Kiye tried plaintive little girl. 'I just need to take a little walk; I want a change of air, just for a few minutes.'

'I don't think we can allow that, miss, much as I'd love to do you a favour.' The guard's gaze was openly lascivious now. Kiye's skin crawled.

'You are horrible,' she sobbed. 'Horrible. I should—'

'Guards!' Moses barked a command, but he had no idea if the guards would take any notice of him. He'd recognised the beautiful young woman at once, and that only added to his confusion. He did his best to look like a prince and strode forwards purposefully. 'Guards, what on earth do you think you are doing? This is a royal wife, the daughter of a king. Put your spears away. Now!'

To his complete surprise, the guards snapped to attention and pulled their weapons away. 'Highness!' they chorused in unison.

Moses turned to Kiye, and his heart leapt in his chest. He took a deep breath to calm himself and said, 'What ails you, mistress? Can I be of any service?'

One of the guards, a tall Nubian with an insolent air, made a gurgling sound in his throat. Moses fixed him with a steely glare. 'There are plenty of other duties in the palace. I could have you assigned to the gong farmers, if you prefer.'

The Nubian swallowed his laughter and lowered his eyes.

'Better. Now, I am going to take a short walk with the royal wife and, when we return, you two will have learned a little more respect. Do I make myself clear?'

'Highness.'

Moses took Kiye's arm and steered her away down the corridor, to a small recess that held a cushioned bench. He sat her down, and patted her arm. 'Tell me, mistress, what ails you. Can I help?'

The words poured out of Kiye in a torrent. How she missed her home; how the pharaoh had never so much as looked at her; how the other wives abused her. Moses could hardly keep up.

'Mistress, mistress . . .'

'Call me Kiye, highness.'

'Very well, Kiye. But please don't call me "highness"; I so hate that title. I'm no higher than anyone else.'

They talked for what seemed to Moses like a few seconds; but the bells from the palace yard told him it had been more than half an hour. He started; what was he doing?

'I must go, Kiye. But, if it helps, I have business that brings me to this part of the palace fairly regularly. We could talk again, if that would please you?'

'It would please me, Moses. If I don't have someone to talk to, I fear I will go mad.'

'Well, that's settled then. I'll talk to those idiots on the door and arrange for them to let you know when I am here.'

'Moses, thank you. I think you've saved my life.' The look in her dark eyes hinted at more than gratitude.

Perhaps, my lovely Kiye. And perhaps you have put my life in danger.

* * *

Ijuju led the scribe into Anen's chambers. The man didn't seem overawed to be in the presence of the high priest; in fact, he didn't seem to be all there. No matter.

'Holiness, this is the scribe I told you about. He has some interesting things to say about the scroll Moses sent us.' He ushered the man forwards. 'Tell his holiness what you told me.'

The man shuffled to the table in front of Anen and took the scroll from his satchel. He cleared his throat in the disagreeably loud way that old men do, and Anen noticed, with some distaste, that a few bubbles of phlegm had fallen onto the scroll covering. 'Holiness,' he said, his voice a rasping growl. 'I have been a temple scribe for some forty years. I have read most of the texts in the archives, at one time or another. I—'

'Get on with it, man,' Anen hissed. He didn't want to die of old age before this dirty wretch got to the point.

The old man unfurled the papyrus and smoothed it with an incredibly gnarled hand. 'See, here, and, ah, here. The text appears sound, but...'

'But?'

'What? Ah yes, it appears sound but there are two things. First, I am relatively familiar with this scroll. In fact, I may be the only person in the kingdom who is. I have read it on several occasions. And in my previous readings, this section,' he pointed to a row of glyphs near the margin, 'was not there.'

'Not there? What do you mean?'

'I mean, holiness, that this is a late insertion. Very late, actually. About eight hundred years late.' The man laughed, or at least, Anen assumed that's what the throaty gurgle followed by a hacking cough signified.

'So,' said Anen, 'you are saying that someone has inserted this passage into the text? But it looks as old and faded as the rest of it. How can you be sure?'

'Well, holiness, as I said, I am familiar with this text and I surely would have noticed this text before, if it had been there. There are ways of making fresh ink look ancient; it's frowned on, but it's not unknown. And there is another thing.'

'Go on.' Anen was intrigued, but the old scribe was sorely trying his patience.

'I cannot be absolutely sure, holiness, but I think ... I think I recognise the hand of the particular scribe.

Manuba liked this inn. It wasn't particularly sumptuous; in fact, it was pretty dirty, now he thought about it, and there were a few dodgy characters among the clientele, but no one threatened him here; he had used his forgery skills to help many of them at one time or another. And the beer was excellent, especially after the first jug had gone down.

He rose to leave. 'I'm off,' he called to the barman, setting his cup on the table. He felt a little unsteady as he made for the door. *Have I had one too many?* Outside, in the litter-strewn alley, he needed to relieve himself before he set off for home.

His first intimation that something was wrong was the hiss of a dagger being withdrawn from its sheath. The second was the hiss of a blade being drawn across his throat. He watched, faintly bemused, as a spray of blood appeared in front of him, and a gurgle escaped from his mouth.

The assassin held the little scribe under the chin until the spasms had subsided, and then let him down gently onto the urine-soaked sand. He looked up and down the alley; it was all clear. *I'm not happy about this,* he thought, *but orders are orders.* He knelt down and cut off the dead man's hands.

* * *

Nefertiti stirred, dragging herself slowly from sleep. She lifted her head and yawned.

'They make such a racket,' she said. 'Do they need to make so much noise so early in the day? The sun has barely risen.'

'It's the Opet festival, my love,' Amenhotep replied. 'And this year it falls during the harvest, and the harvest is good, so it's bigger than usual. Everyone will celebrate, even sleepy wives.'

Nefertiti watched her husband stretch lazily on the luxurious mattress. He didn't look like a man who wanted to take part in a ceremony. He yawned.

'The workers will get time off work and celebrate for days on end, all paid for by the priests, or so the priests will tell them.'

Amenhotep sat on the edge of the bed and stared vacantly across the room. Nefertiti, startled at his sudden change of mood, tried to snap him out of it.

'Husband.'

Amenhotep came back to himself with a small shudder and climbed off the bed. He set his feet on the cold marble floor and winced.

Nefertiti laughed at him and he growled good-naturedly in response.

'So, for the first time we will see Amun-Re at the head of the pantheon,' she said. 'The new spy in the court of Thebes.'

Amenhotep smiled wolfishly.

'I will enjoy seeing Amun-Re leading the procession. But not as much as I'll enjoy seeing Anen's face as he follows the god Moses imposed on him.'

He leaned over and kissed her.

'I love you,' he said. 'Now, on your feet, woman, and get ready to be a goddess.'

A few hours later Anwarapi, the director of ceremonies, a middle-ranking priest, had almost finished organising the procession. He was thoroughly enjoying himself despite the stress. He was the centre of attention, which was an unusual situation for him. Normally his duties were relatively menial, if not arduous; today, however, he felt good, he was the man of the moment, directing the elite of the country.

As he directed the celebrants to their positions, horses reared, men shouted, and chaos begged entrance; but he would keep them in order. He was determined to see to it that people remembered this occasion for the rest of their lives; for was this not his legacy, his gift to his children and their children?

Drawing himself up to his full height, which was not especially high, he checked that Amenhotep, Nefertiti and their family were ready to start. He bowed, and then held up his hand to the pharaoh. Amenhotep raised his hand in response, and the entourage departed.

In the crowd, Yuk applauded ironically. 'Well done, priest, you've managed to get something right for once in your life.' He paused and then laughed a great belly laugh. 'Or not, you stupid old fool.' He watched as the inept priest stepped back and trod on the foot of the Ani, the high priest of Nut as he made his way forward with the procession. Ani fell backwards into the dust of the road, which ruined his perfect white robes. A gaggle of young priests rushed around him to lift him to his feet and dust him down; they got him back in the procession quickly and silently. Meanwhile a couple of laughing soldiers watched his wand take a trajectory all of its own and land almost in the river, close to the mooring cable of the royal barge. The trumpeter standing next to him was caught off guard and ended up in the river, doing all he could to keep his instrument out of the murky waters.

Yuk recognised one of the soldiers helping the now dishevelled trumpeter, a grizzled veteran called Simayuf. He called out to his old friend. 'Simayuf, you old reprobate. Put that trumpeter down and come and say hello.'

The guard, waiting for the next part of the proceedings and the appearance of his master, made sure the Ani and all the necessary processors had recovered their composure before he took the few steps down to his friend. The pair shook hands and embraced with a huge hug.

'You know Miriam, don't you?' Yuk asked his friend.

Simayuf leaned on his spear and bowed his head in respect to Miriam. 'Of course, I know the young lady.' Simayuf said. His eyes met Miriam's. 'A lovely lady.' He gave her a swift salute. 'How are you, beautiful lady?' he asked.

'I am well, Simayuf, no thanks to this old man.' She prodded Yuk's ribs playfully. 'What brings you into the daylight with such a glum expression on your face?'

'I…Oh, I am sorry. I am just still reeling from the death of my chamber mate, Manuba…'

'What happened to Manuba?' Miriam was surprised. She looked up at Yuk; it seemed he already knew the answer.

Simayuf hawked and spat. 'Bad business, mistress. Caught in the street by a thief, and then…' he paused as if catching breath, 'Why the thief had to slit his throat, I don't know.' His head dropped.

'Yes, a bad business,' said Yuk; he put a huge hand on Simayuf's shoulder and gestured *leave it* to Miriam.

Miriam had no idea what they were talking about, save Simayuf's old friend and compatriot Manuba had died, perhaps had been murdered.

'It is, Yuk.' Simayuf sighed. 'I don't have Manuba to laugh with me anymore.' He smiled ruefully, and settled his spear on his shoulder. He looked back at the proceedings and the ridiculous priest. 'I suppose I'd better get back on duty and stop this fool of a priest from drowning in the Nile. We should share a jug of beer sometime, Yuk, and talk.'

Miriam prodded Yuk in the ribs, more forcefully this time. 'Good idea. It's hard to get this old fellow out of the house these days.'

'I'd like that, Simayuf. Maybe this evening? That disreputable beer house you and Manuba used to frequent?'

'You're on.' Simayuf turned and set off back to the riverbank. Yuk watched him go, a heavy feeling in the pit of his stomach. 'Come, Miriam. Let's get to the riverbank and find a good spot. My mistress tells me we may be in for a few surprises this year.'

The royal barge was halfway across the river when Meritaten raised a chubby hand and pointed. 'Look, there are the gods. Papa, why is the trumpeter swimming?'

As an embarrassed priest helped to pull the fallen trumpeter out of the water, Nefertiti gazed across the sacred water and took in the scene. Opet was a homecoming for the gods. Their effigies were carried in grand procession to the great temple of Karnak, to be reborn. She watched as the assembled priests jostled and pushed each other into a semblance of ritual order: a god, their priests, a god, their priests, on and on.

'Well, Moses, this should be interesting. Anen and Amun-Re; it's a match made in heaven.'

'Uncle Anen should be pleased. Amun-Re is a fine addition to his pantheon. A true father to his family of false gods.'

'I doubt he sees it that way. Every time he looks at the effigy of Amun-Re he will see your smiling face.'

Moses smiled on cue, and Nefertiti smiled with him.

Across the water, Anen looked on the assembled line of effigies. And he smiled.

The royal family were ushered from the barge which had brought them across the river to the east bank. Amid the fuss of exasperating priests Amenhotep noticed something amiss. He turned to Moses and gripped his arm. 'Brother, look at the effigies. What do you see? More importantly, what do you not see?'

A sharp intake of breath told him Moses had seen and understood. 'There's nothing we can do now; there are thousands watching. If we confront him now, there will be a riot. Let's play along and see what happens.'

'Very well, but I don't like it. Anen must have something up his sleeve to defy us so brazenly.'

Amun, Mut, and their son Khonsu, the royal family of the Theban gods, were borne aloft at the head of the procession. 'Behold the first family of the gods. See, they return. See, they are reborn. Sing praise, sing praise. Behold the family of the gods.' The priest intoning the ritual chant raised his sistrum and rattled it. The priests in the procession followed suit.

'It sounds as if a whole nest of vipers is here,' said Moses bitterly. 'And in truth, it seems appropriate today.'

As the ceremonial entourage approached the gates of the great temple, Moses saw a small statue of Amun-Re, on a wooden plinth. Another priest raised his voice.

'Behold Amun-Re. Behold the elder god. He rises to meet his family; he rises to greet his father, Amun.'

'I will have his head for this,' muttered Amenhotep.

The head in question appeared from the throng of priests. Anen sidled towards them, unable, or unwilling, to disguise the smirk that painted his features. 'Highness,' he crowed. 'See? Amun-Re is part of Opet after all. A small part, I admit, but he is here.'

'Explain, priest.' Amenhotep's voice was a rumble of suppressed thunder.

'Well, highness, there was a problem. A . . . textual problem.' he looked pointedly at Moses. 'Perhaps we can discuss this later. I must attend to my sacred duties now.' He turned in a swirl of ceremonial vestments and strode through the temple gates. Moses could have sworn the high priest was whistling.

'So, brother, do you still think our father was right?' Moses said. 'I am thinking we need to use a heavier hand in our dealings with the Thebans.'

'Perhaps you are right, brother. Perhaps you are right.' Amen-hotep wanted to spit in the dust at his feet. He was no fan of demagogues, but the time for diplomacy was over.

* * *

Yuk arrived at the wine house as the sun was setting. He walked past it at first, ambled to the next corner and looked around. He saw no one acting suspiciously and headed back to the inn; old habits die hard.

Simayuf was already there, nursing a cup in a shadowy corner. He waved Yuk over.

'I was half thinking you wouldn't turn up. I'd find it hard to leave that little woman of an evening.' Simayuf's lascivious wink made Yuk think he'd been in the inn for a while.

'Well, she's right, bless her. I should get out more.'

'So tell me, Yuk. You always know what's going on in the palace. What's all this fuss about who likes which god? I can't see why it's so important. I've always had a soft spot for my regiment's god, but then I'm a soldier, I would.'

'It's not really about which god,' Yuk replied. 'In this case, it's about one god usurping all the others. The pharaonic family, and a lot of their followers, believe Aten is the only god, and the others are just stories.'

145

'Well, I'm no priest, that's for sure, but I can see how that might upset a few of the bigwigs in Thebes.'

'Exactly, Simayuf, that's it in a nutshell. The bigwigs are upset at each other. And here's the thing; even if the argument is theological to start with, or looks that way, there's always politics behind it, power politics. And when power politics come into it, things tend to get a bit dirty. Moses and Amenhotep may be sincere in their beliefs; I know my mistress is. But in a situation like this, power is the real driver. You could leave the priests to argue a theological point for a century or two and nothing exciting would happen. But add in the royal family, and maybe the generals too, and then it's about power more than anything else.'

'So they're all plotting against each other, and the rest of us have to wait and see who wins.'

'Yes, but don't hold your breath; this could be a long argument, and the dirty stuff might affect more than just the priests and the pharaoh.' He set his cup down for a moment, and looked his old friend in the eye. 'You know, Simayuf, I'm not sure Manuba was killed by some random thief. I know he was doing something for Moses; then, a few days later … whoop, gone, killed by a thief in the night. Seems too convenient to me; why him?'

Simayuf's gaze was steady. 'I don't know. I need to look after my own job, and that's all I intend to do; not think about high-level machinations and random deaths. I just know that he was my mate and we both worked for the lord Moses, and the way people talk nowadays you never know who is doing what; it's all so muddled for a simple bloke like me.'

'Sure.'

'Well,' Simayuf smiled, 'Tell you what, let's bump old Anen off, and any other troublemakers too.' Simayuf's snort of laughter was brief. 'Then we could start again from fresh, and argue about something else.'

Yuk laughed. There was a pause. They drank, looked around the bar, thought of other things. Then Yuk seemed to surface. 'You know,' he said, 'I can't stop thinking of Manuba. You two were so close; you were his best friend and shared a room with him. How long had you known each other?'

'More than twenty years, you know. We were brought up in the same town, joined the palace servants when we were old enough and stuck together all these years in service. I miss the old bugger.'

Yuk thought he saw a tear in the guard's eye. A big, tough soldier close to tears.

'Maybe Manuba was just in the wrong place at the wrong time, maybe there were no assassins involved. If there were, my mistress would pay handsomely for any information or knowledge of the killer, or killers. Bear that in mind, my friend, should any information come your way.'

'I will, Yuk.' He took a large draft of beer. 'I tell you, the day Manuba and Moses seemed to be playing suspiciously with a scroll...' He was struggling with something, Yuf could see that. 'I am going to be honest with you now. I haven't told anyone this before...' he paused and looked around the bar as if expecting someone to be listening. 'So, keep it under your hat; it's not even for your mistresses' ears. I know it was an assassin.'

'Are you sure Simayuf? How do you know for sure?'

'How do I know?' Simayuf said. 'I know because...' He stopped in his tracks. He didn't want to say anything else. But then it all came out. 'You know what they did, the bastards? They cut off his hands and left them outside the door of our room; and I was the one who found them, me, his best friend, finding his severed hands outside the door of the room we shared. The bastards!'

Yuk was stunned. 'What did you do? Why you? This is all crazy.'

'I took them to lord Moses. Let him sort out the mess.' He stopped and took a huge swig of his beer. 'Hey,' he said, 'this is getting too serious. We are supposed to be having a drink, a catch up and some fun. Stop this talk.'

'Yes, you are right,' replied Yuk, 'Balls to life and death and politics. Let's get a good drink and talk of old times.'

Yuk's mind raced. Was the message of the severed hands for Moses, to tell him that they were after him? What had Manuba done to suffer such a fate?

His mistress would have to be told.

* * *

Moses wandered through the palace complex aimlessly. Poor Manuba. When his guard had come to Moses, ashen-faced, and shown him the severed hands, he knew this was a message for him. He was certain the priests were involved but he had no proof; he just had to get on with things, until he could find the bastard that had carried out the crime; that man would suffer.

He found himself in the corridor that marked the entrance to the harem. He smiled wistfully. He had meant to see her more often, but somehow the pace of events, and his guilt at his own feelings, had prevented him. He stopped, hesitantly, a few paces from the harem entrance. He didn't recognise the guards, but they obviously recognised him. They stood to attention, spears upright, and faced forwards, eyes fixed on some point in the distance. He stepped forward, and stepped back again, cursing himself for a coward.

Finally, he made up his mind. 'Guards,' he said, his voice querulous. 'I would speak to Kiye, thirty-fourth wife of the pharaoh. Fetch her for me.'

'Yes, lord. Just wait here for a moment.'

The eunuchs were called to the door and the guard whispered in their ears. The guard returned to Moses. 'Lord, please wait in the garden, this will not take long.'

Moses made his way through the archway to the garden and sat in the shade. A fountain sprayed refreshing water around a pool which reflected the sunlight emanating from his god. He was feeling much better.

Meanwhile the guards were in a quandary.

'I think we should tell someone.' The Nubian spearman was nervous. 'There is something going on here. This isn't the first time he has been here alone.'

'Don't be stupid,' his comrade said, 'it's nothing to worry about. You know what they say; old Moses there prefers his pleasures in another, erm, direction.'

His fellow guard made a rude gesture that made his friend giggle, but he was not entirely mollified.

'That's all very well, my friend, and you might be right, but really, he shouldn't be even talking to her.'

'They are family, so why not? They meet at family gatherings, don't they? Hell, it isn't up to us to tell the pharaoh's brother what to do.'

'Just in case, let's let one of the higher-ups know what's happening, kick it upstairs; that way the crap won't fall on our heads if something bad happens.'

'Well, that's up to you, but my advice is let sleeping dogs lie. The nobility have their own way of doing things, and it's not our place to interfere. We're more likely to get into trouble if we say something and Moses gets to hear of it.'

His compatriot leaned on his spear and thought about it. *He is probably right, but, on the other hand, Moses had asked him to escort Kiye to the temple cloister last week, a long way from the harem, and if someone found out there would be trouble.*

Kiye arrived and broke the spell. The guard pointed to the garden and she floated over towards Moses, who turned and smiled at her.

'My lady.' Moses needed the guards to understand that this meeting was proper. He winked at Kiye, who smiled back.

'My lord,' she said and curtsied.

'Walk with me,' Moses said.

Kiye followed until they were in a corner of the garden which was not visible from any other quarter. Moses looked around, then he threw his arms around Kiye and embraced her.

Moses looked deeply into her eyes.

'Follow me,' he said quietly, 'and let them see us for a while. Sate their appetite for intrigue. They cannot think for too long, they have a very short attention span. They will go back to their duties when they see there is nothing to interest them.'

The pair walked around the garden as if in deep conversation and eventually found a bench away from prying eyes. They sat, arms entwined, in a hidden bower.

When they had first started their secret affair, their conversations had begun with religion; Kiye was intrigued by Moses' faith, and wanted to learn about Aten. But over time, as they realised their feelings for each other, their talk had turned to more earthly matters.

Eventually, Moses was forced to face the fact; he was in love with her, and the feeling was not about to go away. She was the pharaoh's wife, and that was a serious matter. But Akhenaten had never lain with her, and had hardly noticed her since the day her father made a gift of her, like a living trinket.

In the end it was Kiye who moved things on. Her kiss had broken the dam of his misgivings and his feelings flooded through. Their lovemaking had been frantic, almost brutal. Afterwards, as he had lain beside her and looked at her slender, soft figure, Moses could not bring himself to feel guilty. *If this is wrong*, he had thought, *then I accept my sin. If my lord decides to punish me for it, then so be it.* He stroked the skin at the nape of her neck, and she stirred in her sleep, opening one eye.

'What, my lord? Are you ready again? I am your servant; your slave.' She stretched out an arm and brought his face close to her own. 'Don't fret, my love. This is right because it's right for us. It's our secret, and our life. And I would not change it for anyone or anything. But act quickly now; I must get back before the guards come looking for me.'

Now, in this garden open to the elements and perhaps the eyes of others, Moses could no longer hold back his feelings. He looked around, and, seeing no one, he pulled Kiye to the ground.

Moses strode into the royal chambers with a spring in his step. The world seemed lighter this morning; and the sunrise had been spectacular. He found Amenhotep slumped at his desk, muttering. 'Brother,' he called, 'What ails you?'

'I am ruminating on the best way to remove a priest's head from his shoulders,' he replied. 'I am entertained by my plans, but I fear they will not work. If I have Anen killed, his arrogant, bumptious son will take over. I will have replaced a viper with a jackal.'

'Think again, brother. There is more than one way to decapitate a viper.'

'You are peculiarly cheerful this morning, Moses. Is there something I should know?'

'Amenhotep, we are blessed. I am blessed. I have had a vision.'

A look of murderous envy creased Amenhotep's face for a second, before his features relaxed. 'A vision?'

'A vision of a city. And an omen, of great beauty, that showed me where to build it.'

'Moses, don't speak in riddles. I have soothsayers for that.'

'Sorry, brother, I'm not making much sense. But my heart is so full I don't know where to start.'

'Start soon, Moses; my patience is thin this morning.'

'Yes, yes, forgive me. When I travelled to Memphis recently, I passed a desolate piece of land on the eastern bank of the river. A shallow bowl of land, surrounded by low hills, and at the eastern end of the hills, a deep cleft.'

'You are more of a geographer than I am, Moses. I don't see the point of this story, but carry on.'

'As I looked out over this strange landscape, the most extraordinary thing happened. It can only be an omen. The moon hung over the cleft in the hills, about to begin its descent into the underworld. As I watched, there was a flash of light, a great flash of light. It obscured the moon for a few moments, and then it faded. But while the light flooded the valley, I saw a city, Amenhotep. A city devoted to Aten.'

'A nice dream, brother, but why are you so happy about it? And why are you telling me?'

'I want you to come with me, and look on this land. I think it is the answer to our prayers, and perhaps the solution to our problems with the Theban priests.'

A week later, in the grey pre-dawn light, two brothers stood at the prow of a gilded barge and looked to the east. They shivered, despite their fine cloaks. Moses stretched out his arm and pointed. 'See, brother, there at the eastern end of the valley. Can you see the cleft in the hills? Keep your eyes on that cleft. If I am right, Aten will deliver a message to us, and we will read it there.'

As Amenhotep watched, a tiny sliver of light tinged the point of the cleft with gold. Then, as his eyes widened with wonder, the sun's disc glided upwards through the cleft, flooding the valley floor with golden light. He breathed a fervent prayer, and turned to his brother, the fire of belief burning in his eyes.

'Moses, you were right. This is a sign from Aten. This is the place of his city. I can hear his voice; he is saying, "Here is my home in Egypt; here you will build my city, and here you will praise me, from now until the end of days."'

The brothers knelt, side by side on the gently undulating deck, and gave thanks to their god. Amenhotep rose and spread his arms wide, as if to encompass the whole valley.

'Moses, this is more than I had hoped for. We have witnessed a miracle; a miracle we can see every day when we live here. I will officially announce my change of name tomorrow, and then we will set about building a home for our lord. We will leave the Amun priests to rot in their ancient nest.'

On the thirteenth day of Mekhir, the Steward of Memphis wrote in the official record of the day:

Our Lord the Pharaoh, Amenhotep, lord of the two lands, lord of the many lands, on this auspicious day changed his name; henceforth, he will be known as Akhenaten.

'I wonder how long it will be before we receive a deputation from Thebes. Is it worth a wager, do you think?' Akhenaten raised his goblet. Moses and Nefertiti did likewise. 'I doubt we'll have time to set the stakes before they arrive at our gates.'

'Do you think Anen himself will come, breathing fire and holy water, or will he send the idiot boy to rail at us?' Moses took a sip of wine and giggled. He was seldom drunk; but tonight he was enjoying the unfamiliar sensation.

'The best thing about it all,' said Nefertiti, 'is that if they rush to berate us now they'll miss the real punchline. Anen will be furious when he hears the news.'

'I am quite sure he already knows, my love. His spies have been rushing back and forth for the last week. Perhaps he'll hold his fire until the next announcement, and then send the army.' They were all giggling now. Moses spilled some wine on his tunic and tried, clumsily, to wipe it off. It spread like a bloodstain on the fine white linen.

'That's not an omen, is it?' he mumbled. But the pharaoh and his wife were too busy giggling to hear him.

On the nineteenth day of Phamenat, a month after Amenhotep's decision to change his name to Akhenaten, the great Steward of Memphis recorded:

> *Today the king arrived at the site of his new city,*
> *which he has named Akhet-aten, which means 'on*
> *the horizon of Aten'. The Pharaoh is greatly pleased.*

'Behold, the pharaoh lays the foundation stone. Behold, the first stone of the city is laid.' The priest subsided, and Akhenaten laid aside his bronze trowel and signalled to the masons to begin their work. He stepped away and joined Nefertiti, Moses and the children.

'Well, there it is; the first stone. Our family temple will face the cleft in the hills. Every morning we will greet our lord as he rises.'

'Papa, why is it so dry and dusty here?' Meritaten shook her tunic in disgust. 'Ugh! And there are flies, everywhere.'

'Hush, child, don't fret. When the builders have done their work, and the landscapers have planted trees and cool ferns, you will find our new home to your liking.'

'Your mother is right, Meritaten. Soon this city will be an oasis of comfort. Let's go back to the barge and let the masons do their work.' Akhenaten gestured to their escort, and the royal family made their way back to the banks of the river. Behind them, the sun's disc rose above the hills and beat down, mercilessly, on the masons and labourers striving in the dust.

1344 BC

Thebes, Egypt. Year 7, in the reign of Amenhotep IV

Anen's office was a study in chaos. There was a queue of messengers waiting to get in, and a stream of them filing out. Anen read reports, gave orders, scolded and praised in equal measures. Slowly, order began to impose itself on the melee. Anen called for some food, and slumped into his seat, exhausted.

'If another outraged courtier sends me a message to tell me the pharaoh is building a new city I'll send him a mud brick for an answer. They'll all be going there soon enough; they might as well bring something to build their houses with.' He laughed bitterly.

'Holiness, we need to respond officially to this nonsense. Otherwise the people will think we approve.' Utzer, high priest of Mut, an ungainly man in ill-fitting robes, sat opposite Anen and waited for an answer. Anen studied him briefly and went back to his food. *I wonder if he knows he's chewing his own prayer beads.*

'Utzer, if there is anyone in Egypt who does not know the pharaoh is building a city to Aten, they are living in a cave in the side of a hill. And if there is anyone who thinks the priests of Thebes approve of the new city, we should take his wine jug away until he sobers up. No, Utzer, we do not need to make an official response. If anything, we would merely be making this mad monarch's follies official by doing so.'

'But, holiness,' said Joleb, high priest of Khonsu, a small man with the movements and features of a bewildered rodent. 'If we say and do nothing, we will look fatally weak.'

'And what could we say, Joleb, that would make any difference? That the pharaoh is a madman with a heretic for a brother? That two women with an unhealthy appetite for monotheism and idiots for husbands are running the empire? Leave him and his little band of fanatics to their city in the middle of nowhere. When they starve to death and the desert covers them, we'll go and dig them out and they can serve as a warning to the wise.'

'His holiness has the right of it.' Ijuju came into the chambers, supported by two young priests. The old man was nearly bedridden, but Anen did not think there was anyone else in the College he could trust as much. 'The royal family are entitled to build cities, and the pharaoh is entitled to change his name. If we were to say otherwise we would make fools of ourselves and, as the pharaoh and his vile brother have already made fools of us, I don't see what we can gain by adding to the mess.'

'I hate to say it, but the old man is right.' Aye had stood by the window, listening as the high priests went around in circles. He didn't like Ijuju much, not since that jibe about ears and mouths, but at least he spoke sense. 'If we should be planning anything now, it's in preparation for what comes next. Amenhotep—'

'Akhenaten, boy; let's give the fool his proper name.'

'Akhenaten will not stop here. He wants to wipe us out, or coerce us into officiating for Aten. We must be ready. If the pharaoh goes too far, our response must be radical, and swift.'

Utzer looked shocked. 'What are you suggesting, Aye? Are we to murder them in their beds?'

Aye smiled, but there was no warmth in the gesture. 'If it comes to it, we must be prepared to do it,' he said. 'They will have no compunction where we are concerned.'

'What Aye says is true. We must prepare for the worst. If the pharaoh's next move catches us unawares we are in real danger.' Joleb arched a brow and fixed Anen with a flinty stare. 'We were caught unawares by this, weren't we, holiness?'

Anen squirmed. He could have done without the interrogation. Best to face the bull than try to outrun it. 'There were warning signs, and our spies told us this was happening. But, as Ijuju says, none of this is illegal or heretical. The question is: what next? If the pharaoh goes any further, we must be ready to fight. And if that means doing as Aye suggests, we must be ready to spill blood. But I will not do this alone. I need unanimity among the College leaders. Do I have your support?'

Ijuju raised his trembling hand at once. Utzer waited a few seconds, and did the same. Only when all the other priests in the room had their hands in the air did Joleb raise his own.

'So, we are agreed. We wait, for now; we wait and plan. When they make their next move, we will be ready. Tend to your spies, gentlemen, and tell them to sharpen their blades. There is much to do, and it will not be clean work.'

* * *

'I can't believe we're living in a tent.' Aneksi fixed her husband with a steely glare. 'You never said we'd be living in a tent, Baufre.'

Baufre spread his arms and laughed. 'Look around you, Aneksi, dearest. Everyone is living in a tent. If the pharaoh himself was here, he'd be living in a tent; a bloody big one, most likely, but a tent nonetheless.'

Baufre had been among the first to follow the masons, surveyors and labourers to the new city. As he saw it, that many people all in one place would be needing some respite from the dust and the hard work, and a decent jug of wine was nature's way of saying this is your day off. But now he was here, he was having second thoughts. The city was little more than endless lines of rope and holes for foundations. So far, the only complete building was the royal temple of Aten, standing alone in a sea of mud bricks and mortar.

He wasn't the only one. His neighbour, a baker, had followed him a few days later. It had cost him an arm and a leg to bribe some masons to build him a brick oven; but he was doing a roaring trade now.

'I wish I owned a boat,' Baufre said, gazing out over the river. 'Those fellows are making a mint. I think every boat in Egypt is heading up the Nile to get a piece of the pie.'

'That's all very well,' said Aneksi. 'But how long before we get to live in a house, like decent folks?'

'Don't you worry, my precious; in a few months, we'll be in a nice, cool mud brick house, and living in the lap of luxury. I've made a little arrangement with one of the surveyors who likes his tipple; we're at the front of the queue. Well, after the priests and the toffs, obviously.'

It would be a year before Aneksi got her mud brick house. By then, the city had begun to take shape; first, temples, barracks and administrative buildings had gone up; then homes for the nobles, and their entourages; then dwelling for the tradespeople and builders. The pharaoh's palace compound was nearing completion. Akhenaten already spent most of his time there, watching the city of his dreams grow and thrive. Moses too, was a regular visitor; he had designed many of the temples, and took a keen interest in their progress.

He had laid out the grid that delineated the various quarters of the new capital, and introduced an innovative building technique to speed construction. Blocks of stone formed the corners of the buildings, and the spaces were filled in with mud brick. In this way, the bones of a city appeared in months rather than years. Some of his innovations had been harder to sell.

'Highness, you are a lot cleverer than me and much closer to god, but I still don't think you're right. A temple without a roof is like a man without a head.' A Hyksos mason with fists like hams and a blunt way of speaking, was in charge of temple construction. When Moses had explained his idea, he had actually laughed.

'I doubt many could match you for brains. As for your relationship with god, that's your own affair. The idea is that Aten can look down on his worshippers and shine his inestimable light on them. It's really not so outlandish.'

'And when it rains, highness?'

'So, how long have you worked here?'

'Just over a year, highness.'

'And how often has it rained?'

'Point taken, highness. I'll go and build some more walls, and leave the roofs to you and Aten.'

Ahnel, chief architect of the royal tombs, was not a priest, but he dressed and acted like one. He felt it suited the gravity of his calling, and the masons didn't know the difference. They treated him with the deference he felt he deserved.

But, as he made his way to the valley over the river from Thebes, where his team was working, he wondered if they would be quite so respectful when he gave them the bad news. He rounded an immense pile of newly quarried marble and stopped in his tracks. The masons were busy, but they weren't busy build-ing a tomb. They were packing their tools and equipment into panniers and satchels.

'Hoi, Rawer,' he shouted at the chief mason. 'What's going on?'

'Morning, my lord.' Rawer only came up to Ahnel's chin, but he was built like an Apis bull. 'I suppose you're coming to give us the bad news.'

'It seems I've made a wasted journey, Rawer.'

'Not entirely, my lord. I'm glad we get to say farewell. You've been a good master, as masters go, and you've treated me and the lads fairly. Now I'm going, I can tell you the priestly get up fooled no one, but all in all, I'd rather have worked with you than a lot of others.'

'So, you and your crew are off to Akhet-aten?'

'Yes, my lord. There will be work for years there, if what I hear is true. And I'm thinking the pharaoh won't be wanting this old tomb; what a waste. He's building a grand new tomb in his royal city, they say.'

'That's the truth of it, Rawer. This place will just sit here and moulder now. Shame, I quite liked it; for a tomb, it's not a bad house.'

Rawer laughed, and wiped sweat from his broad brow. 'And what will you do now, my lord? Are you following us to Akhet-aten?'

'No, Rawer. I'm too old for jaunts into the unknown and besides.' He leaned a little closer to his old friend. 'Just between you and me, I am not over-fond of this new god, Aten, and I don't like the way he's taking over. I can't see anything good coming from it.'

'There is truth in what you say, my lord. Just between us, you're not the only person who thinks that way. But working people must go where the work is, and if that means building roofless temples to the one god, then so be it.'

'Farewell, old friend. Take care downriver, and think of me when the next wall you build falls flat. I'll be here, drinking cool wine and laughing up my sleeve.' Ahnel clasped Rawer's hand. They locked eyes briefly, and then the mason turned and barked a few orders to his crew. 'Look lively, you lot. Let's get to the barges before they sail off without us.' He turned and waved, but Ahnel was already gone.

1343 BC

Simut, fourth prophet of Amun and overseer of building projects for the Karnak temple complex, was not renowned for his patience. 'Katu,' he hissed. 'I have explained the basic plan for the new courtyard in the temple of Ptah three times now. If you don't understand, then rest in your ignorance. I don't have time for this. Any more questions?'

Another priest raised a timorous hand. Simut sighed. 'Jemta?'

'Holiness, how will we do this without labour? Practically every manual labourer in the land is at work in —'

'I know there is a problem, Jemta, I'm not blind. Anyone whose skull is inhabited by a brain,' he looked pointedly at the questioner, 'knows there is a shortage of paid labour. That's why I have arranged for labour from the College prison. The high priest has approved the plan, and we have sufficient guards to control them. We still have four teams of masons.'

'Only four?'

Simut whipped his head round to see where the comment had come from, but no one owned up to it.

'Four teams of masons,' he repeated, sourly. 'And with the prison labour, the project should be feasible. As for finances . . .'

There was a commotion at the chamber doors. Simut strode over briskly and opened them. Outside, the guards held their spears across the chest of a perspiring servant, a man in a panic if he had ever seen one.

'What's going on here?'

'Holiness, this man claims he has to be admitted. Says he's a servant of the high priest.'

'And so he is, I recognise him. Let him through.'

Simut returned to the table at the centre of the room. 'Speak, Jahel. What is so urgent you must interrupt us?'

Jahel took a minute to get his breath back. 'Holiness, I come from the high priest's chambers. His holiness...' He choked back a sob. 'His holiness is dead.'

'Have you lost your wits?' A heavily jowled priest stepped forward. 'I saw Anen not three hours ago. He seemed in perfectly good health. We exchanged a few words, and he was in good spirits.'

'I assure you, holiness, he is dead. His Ka has left his body.'

Simut cut them both off. 'I will go at once and assess the situation. You,' he pointed at Aye, 'will come with me. Now.'

Aye took a step back, and then a step forward. He had been keeping a low profile in the meeting, and now he blinked as if a strong light had been shone on him. 'Yes. I mean, it's my father, of course, holiness, at once.'

Simut swept out of the chamber, accompanied by the distraught Jahel, practically dragging Aye along with him.

As soon as they had left, the room was alive with whispers. 'First Tinya, and now Anen. This can't be right.'

'But Tinya was poisoned. You don't think...?'

'It's the work of the pharaoh, or his zealot of a brother.'

'We don't know that yet. Anen was not young; the gods might have called him at any time.'

'Still, it makes you think. My cousin spies for the College in Akhet-aten. He says the city is alive with rumours.'

Jahel raced ahead down the final corridor to the high priest's chambers. Simut followed, still pulling Aye by the arm. His mind raced. If this was anything other than a natural death, the finger of suspicion could only point in two directions: at the monotheists in Akhet-aten, or at the man he was dragging along the corridor. If he were a betting man, which he most certainly wasn't, he would risk a few gold pieces on Aye.

Aye's mind raced too. The poisoner had told him the potion would work quickly and leave very little trace. If there was a risk of exposure, it was immediately after death. He peered after the servant sprinting ahead of them. *Did Jahel see anything? Perhaps we will need a little more of the potion.*

Jahel waited for them at the entrance, and when they caught up with him he flung the doors open. A shaft of light illuminated the figure of Anen, supine in his bed. In the light, he looked calm, even a little amused. But his lips were an odd colour.

'Jahel, send for a physician. We are probably too late, but it's best to be sure.' Simut held his hand to Anen's cheek. 'He is cold, and there is no sense of breath. We'll wait to see what the physician says, but I think there is no doubt.'

Aye knelt by the bed and took his father's hand in his, bowing his head. 'Oh father,' he cried, 'you are taken too soon. What will I do?'

Simut looked on impassively. This clumsy display of grief wasn't fooling anyone. It didn't prove Aye's involvement; he knew there was very little affection between Anen and his greedily ambitious son, but it didn't absolve him either.

Aye lifted his head from the cold hand, trying to hide an expression of mild disgust. Dead flesh was distinctly unappealing. He sensed Simut's suspicions — it would be hard not to — but he had paid off the high priest's physician and added a threat for good measure, so he was probably in the clear. *Still*, he though. *Now would be a good time to start rallying my supporters. I am the natural successor, but some people*, he glanced at Simut, *will not see it that way. And I need to speak to Ijuju at once.*

Akhet-Aten, Egypt

Akhenaten made a discreet gesture, and his chancellor tapped his staff on the floor of the royal dais. 'The pharaoh will rise; the audience is ended. Make obeisance to the living god, and depart. Behold, the pharaoh will rise.'

There was a flurry of robes as the people in the chamber bowed and turned to leave. There were a few whispers of discontent too, from those who had waited all morning and not had time to speak. They would have to queue up again the next morning and hope for better luck.

Akhenaten hardly noticed the fuss. His mind was already on the next part of his day, and the visit of the priestly deputation from Thebes. He was not looking forward to ratifying Aye as high priest; the man made his skin crawl; he was far more devious than his late father. If Akhenaten's spies were right, Aye had a hand in Anen's death. That could only mean he was plotting already.

On the other hand, the move to Akhet-aten, and the rise of the cult of Aten, had been a signal success. Thousands had flocked to the new capital, seeing revenue in the new religion, and the nobles had, without exception, followed the pharaoh. He knew they were not all happy; many had relatives and friends among the Theban priesthood, and some (so his spies informed him) still worshipped the old gods in secret. But the momentum was with Aten, and the mass of the people seemed happy with the new god, and the new rituals.

He left the audience chamber and walked to his private apartment. Moses was already there, standing on the balcony. Akhenaten joined him; in the distance, along the ramrod straight length of the Royal Road, which bisected the capital, he could see the cloud of dust that almost certainly announced the arrival of the deputation from the College.

'So, little Aye, the whinger, has come of age. Soon he'll be high priest, and it's cost him no more than his father's life.' Moses shaded his eyes with his hand, and watched as the procession slowly moved closer.

'A man who would poison his father for a step up in rank is not to be trusted. I will increase the number of spies in Thebes, and put a special team on our new high priest. If he looks to be causing trouble, we will act.'

'Perhaps you should find out who his herbalist is, and give him a dose of the medicine he gave Anen.'

'Let's see how things lie before we lower ourselves to the level of these scheming priests.' Akhenaten laid a placating hand on his brother's shoulder. 'I think we are in a very strong position, and I doubt that Aye has the cunning, or the brains, to undermine us.'

'I hope you are right, brother, but remember Opet. That kind of incident does not help us, and we should ensure the priests are in no position to repeat such a stunt.'

'And what would you do, Moses? How would you keep the priests in their place?'

Moses cupped his chin in his hand, and looked at the growing cloud of dust. 'I think we should impose the cult of Aten, make it the state religion. I know you find that hard to accept, but in the end we will have to.'

'Now is not the right time, Moses. First, as you say, we have the upper hand. The people have flocked to Akhet-aten, and the new rites are popular. Second, we have promised the people freedom of worship; we can't go back on our word without repercussions. The people have used that freedom of worship to come to us, and Lord Aten; taking it from them now would not be wise. It would make us look dishonest.'

'There are still huge numbers of people worshipping the old gods; that gives the College power, and as long as it has power, it will try and undermine us. I think we should act sooner rather than later.'

'And how would you deal with the army? They worship Montu, and as far as the generals are concerned, he is the army's own special god. Taking him away would likely lead to plots and dissent.'

'Perhaps you are right, brother. Let's worry about it another day. I am optimistic, on the whole.'

'Good, then let's go and greet our cousin and let him have his little moment of triumph. But not too much triumph.'

Ijuju was in the middle of a tense discussion with the chancellor. His plan to show the power of the College was being slowly strangled by the short, balding man in front of him. 'The pharaoh's retinue will precede you into the audience chamber, Ijuju. That is how it has always been; that is how it will be.'

Ijuju accepted defeat, but he couldn't resist a jibe. 'Who would have thought,' he sneered, 'that you monotheist upstarts would be such sticklers for tradition?'

The royal retinue formed up in front of the priests and began a slow march to the great doors of the audience chamber. Aye, seated on a litter in the middle of the column of priests, shifted under his veil. He was to remain covered until the pharaoh ratified his appointment; until then, he was invisible, a non-person.

The ceremony was usually a formality, but Aye was nervous. Rumours about Anen's death had spread far and wide; it was unlikely they had escaped the ears of the pharaoh. There was a possibility that his cousin would take the opportunity to undermine the College, and he didn't relish being the person responsible for that. *I need to pee*, he thought miserably. *If Akhenaten pulls any tricks, I'll probably wet myself in front of the great and the good.*

The chancellor tapped his staff on the doors. 'Behold, the priests of Thebes are here. The priests of Thebes plead audience with the living god. Will the living god admit them?'

After a brief pause that did nothing for Aye's bladder, the doors began to open, and the procession shuffled inside. The audience chamber was practically empty. Akhenaten sat on his golden throne, and Moses stood beside him on the dais. There was no sign of the rest of the royal family.

Behind the throne, a huge mural showed an image of Aten, his great round disc carved into it at its top, his life-giving rays arrayed across its surface. The sun's rays shone on images of Akhenaten and Nefertiti, seated with their children at its base; a sign that Aten would always give life to the pharaoh and his family, as the pharaoh would always give life to the people and the empire.

The chancellor stepped aside, and Ijuju stepped forward. He prostrated himself before the pharaoh and waited for the signal before he rose, stiffly and addressed him. 'Highness, first prophet of Amun, we beg your divine judgement. The second prophet of Amun is gone to the gods. We wish to appoint this man,' he pointed to the veiled figure in the litter, 'to be the second prophet of Amun. Will your highness give his permission?'

Akhenaten smiled at the old priest, and basked for a moment in the irony that he, the heretic king, was still the first prophet of a god he did not believe in. 'Ijuju, my old friend, it is good to see you, truly. I am sure that your choice for second prophet,' he raised a quizzical eyebrow at Aye, quivering under his veil, 'will be acceptable to me and to the gods. You have our permission. Unveil the man who would be second prophet.'

Two acolytes slid the veil from Aye, and he stood, doing his best to look powerful and pious, though he felt anything but.

'Aye, cousin, what a surprise.' Akhenaten's voice bubbled with condescension. 'This must be hard for you, Aye, so soon after the sudden death of your beloved father.'

'Highness,' said Aye, fashioning an awkward bow, 'it is as you say. But the decree of the gods cannot be refused.'

'Quite so, Aye, quite so. And I assume your first duty as second prophet will be to enquire into the strange circumstances of your father's death?'

'I, erm, but of course, highness. I would wish my father to rest in peace, not wander the earth as a shade seeking his killer.' *That was too much, you fool; now he'll expect you to come up with a guilty party.*

Akhenaten's smile was beatific. 'Go, Aye, attend to your duties. And relieve yourself, man; you look like you need to.'

1341 BC

Akhet-Aten, Egypt. Year 9, in the reign of Amenhotep IV

Henite applied a cool cloth to Kiye's forehead, and patted her reassuringly on the arm. 'You are nearly there, highness, a few more minutes, a few more pushes, and your child will be with us.'

Henite was impressed with the new royal mother. Since Aoh had died, and she had taken over as the royal midwife, she had helped dozens of noble women to give birth. But this slender creature was unique; she hadn't uttered so much as a cry through the whole of her labour. Now Henite could see the child's head emerging from the birth canal and still, Kiye struggled in silence, her face a mask of agony.

'It's a boy. Aten be praised, it's a boy. You are honoured above all the royal mothers, highness; you have given the pharaoh a son.'

Kiye lay back, exhausted, and cradled her son in her arms. Her joy in watching the infant suckle greedily at her breast was tempered by fear.

* * *

Aye had had enough of his fathers' peers. All talk and no action. None more so than Rebiu. He did not know if the general had treated his father the same way, or had a different relationship with him, but he never spoke about the pharaoh's religious plans to him. Every time Aye tried to talk about the need to usurp the Atenites and encourage Amun, the general brushed him aside. He knew that his father had had a relationship with him, and, together they had done things;, he was sure that they had somehow had old Amenhotep killed and his son deposed, so why wasn't he keen on a similar relationship with him? He was running out of time, impatience setting his teeth on edge. He had to make a decision, one way or another, to bring the general closer to his religious strategy or to find another more attuned with his wishes. Hence the party this evening. A small gathering, with gourmet food and the best wines; he would disarm people with hospitality and to listen to tongues loosened by drink and lack of judgement.

'Ah, general.' Aye greeted Rebiu as if they were the oldest of friends. The general was dressed in a simple robe; no military uniform tonight, this was an informal event. Aye, on the other hand, was fully made up. Red paint covered his face. Rings as big as lions' balls hung from his ears and the leopard skin hanging over his shoulder proclaimed his stature. He looked around the room: there were six others; two nobles and four more priests—he was the only military man present. *Well, it is a party; why ruin it with more than one military man?*

'Aye.' Rebiu stretched out his right arm and took the arm of Aye in its grip. 'You know, the older you get, the more like your father you become.'

Like hell, thought Aye. 'Come, general, sit with us. Now you are here the evening can begin.'

Servants brought a feast to the table: fish and fowl of all description, figs and vegetables.

'So, what do we do about Moses then, general?'

'Oh, he is no problem now, Aye; your father and I saw to that.' *Wrong answer.*

'And Aten, the one god religion?'

'Finished. Amenhotep is simply engaged with his family and nothing else. He humours his brother and keeps him out of the way.' *Wrong answer.*

'You have the pharaoh's ear so your judgement must be honest and true. There is no threat to Amun and the gods of the empire, then?'

'None whatsoever.' *Wrong answer.*

A hiccup moved the general forward and a belch followed on behind. Both men laughed.

'Excuse me, general. I need to relieve myself.' His decision had been made.

* * *

Akhenaten had been happy to hear that the thirty-fourth royal wife was with child; happy, and slightly puzzled. He was not an enthusiastic visitor to the royal harem; he loved his first wife too much. But he did his duty, and visited twice a month, usually fortified by a few glasses of wine, and a potion his physicians assured him gave him the reproductive powers of a bull.

He remembered Kiye from the audience at Memphis, when she was presented to him as a gift. A slender, regal woman with a shock of beautiful hair. He didn't remember her so well from the harem, though. Still, now he thought on it, he remembered very little of his conjugal visits; he suspected the wine was responsible for that. Now that she had delivered him a boy, a prince of the realm, he forgot his misgivings. He would name the child Thut-ankh-aten, after his brother, his love of life, and his god. *I must send Urhiya a gift to thank him for the bull potion,* he thought. *And gather the family for a celebration.*

Moses came wandering through a chamber full of sycophants wanting to be seen and heard by the pharaoh. 'Why don't you get rid of these fools, Akhenaten?' he asked.

'Oh, don't be silly, Moses. They are no threat. They simply massage my ego when I feel the need. It's good to be a celebrity now and then, you know. You should gather a retinue yourself. You surround yourself with your priests and ignore everyone else. There is a world out there, brother, full of people who want to enjoy their time in the overworld. You should free yourself now and again.'

Moses dropped his head. 'Yes.'

'Anyway, why are you here?'

'I heard you were appointing a new head of the army this afternoon so, I thought it would be wise for me to be here and give him Aten's blessing.'

'Today I will simply hand him the sword of office; nothing of any great importance. The full ceremonial will be organised by the grand chancellor in due course, probably for later in the month. You will be involved in that, I am sure. Aten must be part of any state rite.'

'So, who is this new general?' Moses asked, although he knew already; there were few secrets in the palace.

'Horemheb. You know him. He is second in command now. A great man with a brilliant future, they tell me.'

'Oh, I know him. I've heard a lot about him. What happened to Rebiu? Has anyone investigated his untimely demise?'

'It's a mystery. I was told that he was a good swimmer, but it seems that he went swimming near Thebes with a crowd and went missing. No one knows how or precisely where. The crocodiles must have taken him for Sobek. The gods take those they want, Moses. Strange, though; very strange.'

'You have made a good choice in Horemheb.'

'I make good choices all of the time, Moses,' Akhenaten said. 'Indeed, it seems I have made another great choice this morning.'

'This morning?'

'Yes, just been told I have another son. Not by Nefertiti, but by one of the harem concubines.'

'Oh, congratulations,' said Moses, 'which one blesses you with a son?'

'The princess from the north. Kiye.'

Moses drew a large breath and shuddered.

'What's up, brother? Did someone just walk over your grave? Laugh and celebrate with me; no sulking because you have no children.'

Amenhotep slapped Moses on the back. Moses didn't think his face showed his emotions. He hoped it did not.

1340 BC

*Palace of King Suppiluliumas, Hattusa, Kingdom
of the Hittites*

Year 10, reign of Akhenaten

'You lie to me!' Suppiluliumas shouted at the envoy. Even prostrate on the marble floor, the terrified man managed to tremble visibly.

'No, your highness, I do not lie; it is true. Akhenaten ignores the business of empire; he is so engrossed in his new city and his new religion, and—I hardly dare to say it my lord, it is so outrageous—he is obsessed by his wife and children. He spends all his time with them, or with his god, and leaves the running of the empire to others, to lesser men.'

'No true ruler considers his family before the needs of his country. Sentiment makes a king weak; he could lose his kingdom, or his head, while his back is turned. This is ridiculous. It cannot be so.'

Suppiluliumas turned to his chief general, who stood beside the throne, shifting his feet nervously.

'Have you heard similar stories from your spies? Is this madness real?'

'I have, your highness; it seems it is as this imbecile says.'

Suppiluliumas growled, his incredulity replaced by anger. He stretched out an arm heavy with gold bangles and seized the general by the throat; the bangles clattered and sang.

'You have heard this and you did not tell your king?' The bangles sang again, and the general spluttered. 'I should have your head for this.'

'Highness,' croaked the general, struggling to breathe. 'It was so ludicrous a story I did not think to trouble you with it. Who would believe it?'

'You seem to believe it now. What kind of fool do I give my army to?' The king let him go suddenly, and the general collapsed in a heap beside the throne.

'Tell me more,' he said to the envoy, quietly, as if his anger had never been.

'There was a royal audience for the ambassadors, highness, which I attended. I saw the Pharaoh before he entered the great hall, with his queen and their children in tow. My lord, he kissed the queen in public!' Suppiluliumas guffawed. No man did this, especially a king. 'I saw this, highness, with my own eyes. The ambassador from Amurru told me he had been refused an audience because he was encroaching on the pharaoh's family time.'

'This is no way for a pharaoh to behave; family included in royal business, walking with a king? Does Egypt allow this to happen?'

'Yes, your highness,' said the envoy, breathing a sigh of relief that clouded the mirrored surface of the floor.

'General, here is your chance to redeem yourself. I want you to go to the border with the Mitanni. Let us see if we can unsettle our neighbours, just a little, and test this loving pharaoh. Make a small incursion into their land and see what they do about it. A few miles, no more. Burn a few villages, bring me some slaves. Make a lot of noise.'

Suppiluliumas steepled his fingers and brought them to his lips. He had much to think about. If the pharaoh was as weak as he appeared, Egypt was uniquely vulnerable; not yet a fruit ripe for picking, but with time, who could tell?

'Let us see if the Egyptian king hurries to assist them or stays at home to play with his wife and children. You, envoy, go back to the pharaoh's shiny new city and report to me on what happens when Akhenaten hears the news. Now go, all of you, and you, Vizier, hurry off and bring me something fresh from the harem, something young; I think I need some family time!'

Suppiluliumas roared a great laugh, which reverberated around the room. His general, his envoy and the assembled nobles laughed with him; they always did.

* * *

The barge made good progress down the Nile. It was easy to navigate; the river ran south to north, so if you were travelling north you had the current to drive you, but the prevailing winds blew from north to south, so travelling against the current, the wind was your friend.

Aye had not enjoyed the journey. The truth was, he was deadly afraid of water, and always had been; he was a poor swimmer too. He hated being afraid of anything, which was unfortunate for a man who was scared of so much.

The sacred river was even busier than usual. Barges laden with goods made their way north to the new capital. Most numerous were the barges carrying stone and timber; it seemed to Aye that all the stone in the world was heading to Akhet-aten, and that did not make him happy. *When my feet are on dry land again; then I'll be happy.*

He disembarked at the edge of the new city, and his litter made its way through the district where the nobles had their residences. He had arranged the use of a house there; a favour from a man who, though he sensed the opportunity that the city offered, still worshipped the gods of Thebes. Aye had used his services before, to communicate with some of his spies in the royal household. This trip was for a different purpose, though; he had an appointment with General Horemheb. Now Rebiu was dead, Horemheb was the chief of the army. Aye neither liked nor trusted him; but he knew things about him, and that was enough.

They met in a garden cooled by the shade of bougainvillea and camellias. After a few minutes of tense small talk, Horemheb slapped a meaty palm on the table between them and said, 'Well, priest; you didn't arrange to see me so you could talk about the harvest. Out with it, man; what news?'

'General, there is grave news from Mitanni.' Aye stopped, puzzled; the general's head had sunk into his chest, and he appeared to be chuckling. 'General?'

'You mean that little piece of theatre on the borders? That's hardly grave, Aye.'

'I didn't think ...'

'You didn't think I'd know? I'm a soldier, Aye, a general; I'm actually paid to know these things. Unlike you.'

'And the pharaoh?'

'Oh yes, he knows. Apart from the fact I told him, my scouts told me they saw some of Thethi's men on the next hill; I suppose your chaps must have been on the hill after that. My scouts also said they could have sworn the Hittite general actually stopped and raised his hand to them, as if he was acknowledging his audience.'

'And what is the pharaoh doing about it?'

'He's doing the same as I am. Nothing, for now. If old Suppiluliumas turns out to be doing more than playing a game with us, he'll act, I suppose.'

'Suppiluliumas doesn't play games, general, unless they involve torturing people for his amusement. He is ambitious; and an ambitious king is a king who wants to be an emperor. I think we should take this more seriously.'

'There is some truth in what you say, Aye. And between you and me, I'm a little worried that the pharaoh may wait a little too long, and then we'll have a proper mess to clear up. Still, that's what the army is for, isn't it? Clearing up the mess made by kings.'

'And if the pharaoh doesn't act, what then?'

Horemheb looked away into the garden; he was afraid it would come to this. He shared Aye's misgivings about Akhenaten, and he was no lover of Aten, but he was loyal to Egypt, and that meant caution. 'You ask a difficult question, Aye. What's behind it?'

'Horemheb, we all know where this is going. The kings of the states around us sense weakness; they see Akhenaten devoting his time to his god and his family and they dream of conquest. We can't afford an invasion; the country is divided enough as it is. If the pharaoh fails to do the right thing, then we must.'

'And what does that mean?'

Aye seethed. Horemheb was virtually inviting him to speak treason. If he didn't know better, he'd think this was a trap.

'I'm not a man of action, like you, general, but it seems to me that our duty to the empire is to do something.'

'When and if that time comes, Aye, I might agree with you. But that time is not here, not yet. For the moment we must all play the waiting game, and see how far the Hittites are prepared to go. And Aye.'

'General?'

'You need to understand that the army is largely loyal to the throne. That may not always be the case, but it is now. If I find that you and your friends in the College are taking things into your own hands, I will have no choice but to stop you.'

'Then we are agreed, general. We wait and see, but if things get worse, we act.'

'Aye, you should return to your barge. I will watch what happens, and we may talk again. But beware. If I sense any machinations from you, you will find yourself in the Nile, swimming; and a little bird tells me you're not very good at that.'

* * *

'Gentlemen, I believe we are presented with an opportunity.' Suppululiumas smiled at his assembled generals.

There had been no response from the great Egyptian Pharaoh to his incursion into Mitanni lands, and the king, emboldened by his success, had applied himself to the task of settling accounts with old enemies. His treasury was bursting with plunder and tribute in equal measure.

After an abortive attempt to approach Syria by the conventional route, through the Taurus pass, Suppululiumas had attempted a more circumspect attack, bringing his army to bear by way of the Euphrates valley. Here was the one place for ambush, should the Egyptians or their allies decide to stop him, but they met with little resistance along the route. He was able to enter and sack the Mitannian capital, Wassukkani, gaining an immense amount of plunder.

To the west of the Euphrates, most of the North Syrian cities, seeing the rapid collapse of Mitanni power, hastened to offer tribute to Suppiluliumas. They felt they had little choice; the Egyptians had not come to help one of their greatest allies, so what chance was there of them coming to their aid? Akhenaten, no, Egypt, had let them down. Their messages to the Pharaoh, begging for help, had gone unanswered. They were left with no alternative; they must become vassals of Suppiluliumas, or let him kill them and take their lands, their wealth, and their women, away from them.

'So, gentlemen, do we stop now, and enjoy what we have? Or shall we do more? Shall we make our nation great, and hammer this Egyptian weakling into the dust where he belongs?'

The shout that went up was raucous and greedy. Flushed with victory after victory, they were ready to fulfil their king's ambitions.

* * *

Thethi slipped into the royal chambers unnoticed by the guards. He didn't need to sneak in like this, but it was good practice. Djau was already there, with two palace guards, holding the limp form of a beaten man between them.

Akhenaten looked startled when his chief spy appeared out of nowhere, but he soon went back to his cool appraisal of the miserable wretch before him.

'Why have you brought this man to me, Djau? Thethi, you are in on this too, I see.'

'Highness, this...creature has been spying for the Hittites.' Djau leaned between the guards and cuffed the man.

'Leave him be, Djau. If he is to answer my questions, he needs some breath in his body.'

'Highness.' Djau bristled, but stepped back.

'Speak, man. Is this true?'

The guards pushed the man into something resembling a standing pose, though he sagged between them. He looked up at the pharaoh from the ruins of a face. 'Mercy, highness,' he whispered through cracked lips.

'Mercy is mine to give, and yours to earn. Have you been spying for our enemies?'

'Highness, I have. The priests…'

'Priests? Why are we talking of priests now? I thought you said he was a Hittite spy?'

Thethi answered. 'Highness, we caught this man conferring with two priests from the College. They were handing him a letter for the Hittite king when we swooped.'

'High ranking priests?' For a moment, Akhenaten's eyes gleamed; this might be the opportunity he was looking for.

'No, highness, they were acolytes.'

'Were?'

'The priests didn't survive our encounter. We offered them to Sobek…we offered them to the sacred river so their bodies would not be found.'

Akhenaten let the spymaster's slip of the tongue go and turned again to the spy. 'And what did the priests ask of you?'

'They threatened my family, highness, said if I didn't do as they asked, it would go badly for all of us. They asked me to take a letter to a merchant who travels regularly in Hittite lands. They said he would know what to do. I didn't read the letter. I just thought of my family, and agreed to do as they asked.'

'This man is of no use to us. Take him away and execute him. But compensate his family for the loss.'

After the guards had dragged the sobbing spy out of the chamber, Akhenaten turned to Thethi and Djau. 'I know that you were acting out of loyalty to me, but if the priests are conspiring against me I need proof. Some wretch taking a letter from an acolyte is not enough.'

Djau almost snapped his reply. He was not blessed with tact, and that was why the pharaoh trusted him. 'If you had let the man talk more, you would have heard more. You're right, we don't have definitive proof that the College is colluding with our enemies, but we have enough to suspect them, and strongly.'

'Djau has the right of it, highness. We may need to act sooner rather than later.'

'Leave me, both of you. I need to think.'

Horemheb tried once more to get his message through. 'Highness, I think it is time to act. Suppululiumas has attacked several of our closest allies in the last months. But you know this; they have all written to you or sent envoys. If we don't crush this Hittite menace now, we will find ourselves in real trouble.'

'I have seen the letters, Horemheb, and I acknowledge that the Hittites are becoming increasingly aggressive. But we are not in danger yet. I still have a stream of allies coming to offer tribute and pledge loyalty. That tells me the empire is strong.'

'With respect, highness, those visitors could be interpreted rather differently. They may be coming here out of desperation, to try and move you to act. Highness?'

Akhenaten had slumped on his throne. He stared vacantly at something Horemheb couldn't see. A thin line of drool escaped his mouth. Horemheb was at a loss what to do. 'Highness, should I call for a physician?'

The pharaoh started back to alertness. 'Horemheb? What are you doing here? Oh yes, of course, the Hittites. We cannot let them abuse our power, Horemheb. I want you to take an army to the borders of Mitanni and crush this Hittite upstart's army. Show them the might of Egypt; teach them a lesson they will never forget.'

Horemheb was taken aback. There was a look in the pharaoh's eyes he couldn't fathom. Then he saw Akhenaten's face relax again. 'Highness, I will do as you order. We will stamp this cockroach into the dust where he belongs.'

'What? Oh, yes, general, that's it. Stamp him. That's it. Could you get me a glass of water?'

The cloud of dust that accompanied the army as they left Akhet-aten was visible for miles. Horemheb had taken the best part of the empire's forces with him, not just to ensure victory, but to show the kings of the allied nations that Egypt took the threat from Suppiluliumas seriously. He was determined to drag a triumph out of this mess; a personal triumph at least.

Six months later, he returned. His army hadn't fought a single battle worth the name. The Hittites, clearly in awe of the Egyptian army, had scattered whenever they came into sight. And then they had disappeared completely. Gone back to their braggart king to lick their wounds, no doubt, and salve their damaged pride.

His first audience with the pharaoh was a revelation.

'Horemheb, welcome back, I trust your journey was a pleasant one?'

'It was not quite what I expected, highness. The cowardly Hittites refused to give battle. In the end they simply upped sticks and disappeared.'

'Ah yes, they probably did. I sent an envoy to Suppiluliumas, and offered him a few parcels of land ... here and there. He won't bother us now.'

'But highness, you sent me to ...'

'I know, general, and I am sorry, truly I am, but Lord Aten teaches us to treat our enemies with respect, as people. I approached Suppiluliumas as an equal, and he saw sense. There's no more to be said.'

Horemheb bowed and backed out of the audience chamber. Outside the palace gates, he spat furiously in the dust and clenched his fists. 'This madman will make fools of us all,' he muttered. 'I will have to grit my teeth and talk to that devious priest again.'

1339 BC

Akhet-aten, Egypt. Year 11, in the reign of Amenhotep IV

Moses lay in bed, Kiye beside him.

'What troubles you, my love?' Kiye caressed his face and looked at him intently. She could sense his unease.

'It's nothing. Well, it should be nothing. I am worried about Akhenaten.'

'Does he suspect us?' Kiye was worried now. After Thutankhaten's birth, they had continued to see each other, though it was getting more difficult. She knew that if they were found out, she would be executed at once, royal mother or not; Moses would be banished, at the very least. They were playing a dangerous game, but they had no choice. They were lovers, and they couldn't be parted.

'No, Kiye, he doesn't suspect.' Moses chuckled and ran his fingers through her hair. 'Then why the worried face? You look as if you are carrying some weight on your shoulders.'

'It's . . . Oh, it's probably nothing. I just worry that, perhaps, something is ailing my brother.'

'Is he ill?'

'Not exactly. He is healthy enough in body; it's his mind that concerns me. Every so often he just…goes away. I'm speaking to him and then he's staring at something invisible, sometimes for minutes at a time. And he has sudden mood swings. One moment he is genial and happy, the next he curses like a mason and looks venomous. And he forgets what people have said, even as they say it.'

'It must be horribly stressful, being the ruler of an empire.'

'You're right, Kiye. That's probably all there is to it. But those blank episodes are becoming more frequent, and I'm not the only one who's noticed. I fear that Aye will hear of it and decide he can use it to his advantage.'

'You should persuade him to rest, Moses. You can look after affairs of state for a while. He knows that, and he trusts you with his life.'

'I'm not so sure. I suggested something of the sort and he blew up, accused me of plotting to take the throne from him. Then he changed tack completely and asked me if there was anything I needed. It was very strange.'

'And the physicians?'

'He refuses to see a physician. He says Lord Aten protects him, and no harm can come to him.'

'Perhaps he is right.'

'Maybe he is, Kiye. Aten cares for all his people, including my brother, but sometimes, just sometimes, I wonder what my brother really thinks of his position. Remember, he has been a god almost all his life. I sometimes get a feeling that he misses being a god.'

'Your religious affairs are too complex for me, Moses. Many gods, one god, gods here, spirits there; it is so confusing. I'm sure the pharaoh thinks deeply about these things.'

'Perhaps, Kiye. Moses reflected on recent times and Kiye's words. Were things going too fast for his brother to keep up with? 'Enough talk, woman.' He leaned over and placed a kiss on her lips. 'We have so little time together.'

Akhenaten paced the floor. 'You were right all along, Moses,' he said. 'We cannot trust the priests in Thebes. I need to do something.'

'What has happened, brother? Have you heard something?'

'We captured a spy. He was taking letters from a priest to the Hittite king. I didn't get the chance to question him properly, but I'm sure...'

'Brother, we know this; it happened moons ago. Why are you—'

'Don't question me, Moses; and don't call me brother. I am your Pharaoh, your emperor, your god.'

'Highness.' Moses thought about saying something to placate Akhenaten, but he was blank faced, staring into a world that only he could see. He waited, tensed for more trouble.

A few moments later, Akhenaten spoke. 'What was I saying? Ah yes, the spy. They have gone beyond the pale, Moses; they are conspiring with our enemies. We cannot let them betray the empire. We must curb their powers.'

'And how would we do that, highness?'

'Highness? I'm your brother, Moses. There's no need for formality.'

My brother is ill, Moses thought, I need to discover the cause. 'Do you have a plan?'

'Oh yes, I have a plan.' Akhenaten's smile was laced with venom. 'I have decided to make our one god religion, the Aten, the official religion of Egypt. What a wonderful irony, eh? The first prophet of Amun will tear down the temple of Amun and replace him with the disc of the sun. I wish I'd thought of it years ago.'

Moses walked to the balcony to clear his head; he was confused to the point of delirium. Akhenaten had refused to contemplate the idea of imposing Aten on the priests; now he was acting as if it was his own idea.

'You are right; this is a good plan.'

'Leave me, Moses. I need to work out the details of my plan. When I have need of you, I'll summon you.'

Moses bowed and retreated from the room. He needed to speak to Tiye, and soon.

* * *

'That was excellent, Miriam.' Yuk allowed himself a gentle belch and settled back in his chair.

'Eat more, husband, or I'll have to feed it to the chickens.'

'Oh no, my love. The queen mother shouldn't have to buy me a new set of robes just because you're a damn fine cook.'

Miriam giggled playfully and sat on his knee. 'So tell me, oh wise one, is it true what people are saying? Is the pharaoh going to make us all into Atenist's?'

'I fear so, my love, I fear so. I cannot see this ending well. Imposing a god might be reasonable; it's been done before. But imposing a god and saying he is the only god, that's asking for conflict. I can't see how the priests can just sit back and watch thousands of years of tradition dismissed with a royal gesture.

You know, it's a funny thing. I've talked to many priests over the years, and the more philosophical of them, when they talk about the gods, they tend to agree that, behind all the individual gods of the pantheon, there lies a greater power, an overarching divinity, if you like. They never put a name to this divinity, or give it a form. It's somehow abstract, if you like, a principle rather than a god in a form we would recognise.'

'I'm not sure I follow, Yuk. If the priests think there is some greater god, however abstract, surely they can't object to the pharaoh's belief in that one god?'

'Well, there's the problem, I think. So long as this great god remains an abstraction, it doesn't threaten the state religion, and it doesn't disrupt tradition. The various cults can keep their temples, and their believers, and their revenues. But to have that deity embodied in concrete form, as the disc of the sun, and then to have that form imposed on them? I don't think they will take kindly to that.

'And there's another thing: I was talking to a priest who is also a scribe in the royal archives. He has read everything on the subject of gods. He told me that, logically, making the sun into the one god isn't actually monotheism at all. The one great god created everything, including the sun. So he can't only be the sun; that doesn't make theological sense.

'Which means, if it comes down to a theological argument, the priests think they have the upper hand. But I doubt if it will come down to theology, sadly. This is a political conflict now; the people, and our beliefs and traditions, are irrelevant. This is about power; and arguments about power are arguments soaked in blood.'

'I can't say I understand all that you are saying, my love, but it brings fear to my heart.'

'As it probably should, Miriam. I am afraid we are set for difficult days.'

* * *

'You know, I can't be sure, but I think . . . wait; I can be sure, there's his mark.'

'Adudu, what are you wittering on about?'

'I'm not wittering, Tuta, I'm wondering. This bas relief was carved by my grandfather. There's his mark, just behind Amun's ear.'

Adudu and Tuta hung precariously on wooden seats, suspended on pulleys over the great gate of Karnak. Somewhere below them men worked the ropes to keep them steady, and watered the pulleys so the ropes would not fray.

Adudu worked his chisel fast and sure; this was not work he was used to, but he was determined to do it well. He chipped at the offending image on the pylon and it gradually gave way to the copper onslaught, losing first its crisp edges, and then its form.

'Imotep, how can you be sure someone won't have our heads for this? Or worse, that some angry god won't descend on us and punish us for blasphemy?'

'Adudu, the pharaoh, he's a god, right?'

'Yep, he's a god alright.'

'And the pharaoh told us to do this. I mean, he told the chancellor, and the chancellor told the clerk of works, and the clerk of works told me, but the principle's the same. If we're under orders from a god, we can't be damned or punished for it, can we?'

'I suppose not.' Adudu didn't sound too sure.

Tuta, his cradle swinging a little in the breeze, piped in. 'It's not the gods I'm worried about; it's the priests. They're not just going to sit back and let the pharaoh ruin their temples and replace Amun's name with Aten's.'

'I don't think the priests can go against the word of the pharaoh, do you?' Imotep sounded confident, but he looked over his shoulder nonetheless. When he didn't see a flock of vengeful priests charging the gates, he went back to his work.

'I don't think we have enough masons to carry out all of this, you know. It's a long way from the northern borders to the border with Nubia. Our pharaoh will need to use non-masonic labour if he wants the names of all the old gods defaced from every monument, and replaced with the name and image of Aten.'

'I know; good men like us are hard to find.'

* * *

In the palace at Akhet-aten Moses was not sure whether to laugh or cry. He was being given everything he ever wanted, but it didn't make sense. Akhenaten sequestered all temple revenues and redirected them to Akhet-aten. All sacrificial donations which normally went direct into the hands of Amun's priests were now the official funds of Aten. Money poured into the great Aten temple.

'I will have the country still administered by the Amun priests, but, in the name of Aten.' The pharaoh decreed that the majority of the priests from Thebes come to Akhet-aten, to be given new tasks devoted to the one god. Some went willingly, eager to pursue their careers and seek advancement under the new cult. Others went under duress, harbouring their old beliefs and waiting for the day when Amun and his family would reclaim their place in the pantheon, and the hearts of the Egyptian people.

Then, to the shock of the priests, the army, and every noble in Egypt, the pharaoh abruptly retired from the public sphere and devoted himself to the worship of Aten, and the company of his family; sightings of him were rare, counsels rarer.

1338 BC

Akhet-aten, Egypt. Year 12, in the reign of Amenhotep IV

'What you are saying is treason.' Horemheb was incensed.

'Technically, yes, but that is not overly important in the circumstances,' Aye replied. He avoided meeting the general's eyes. He was quite sure Horemheb would kill him on the spot if he thought it right.

'The changes have come too fast, and they are too many. The people are confused, Horemheb. Damn it, man, I'm confused; we all are.'

'I can't argue with that, priest. But to talk of opposing the pharaoh, even to think of it, that is treason.'

'Come now, general, are you telling me your men are content with all this chaos and singing the praises of the pharaoh? The pharaoh who has apparently abandoned us and left the country in the hands of his apostate brother, the man who started all this trouble?'

'There are murmurings of discontent, I can't deny it. My men are particularly upset about Montu; he has seen us through many battles, and they are not happy to part with his protection.'

'And how many of your men are willing to take orders from a woman?'

Horemheb scratched his head, bemused. 'There are no female generals, Aye.'

'Not yet, there aren't, but give it time. And in any case, the army's orders come, ultimately, from the pharaoh. And under the new law of succession, that could be, in fact definitely will be, a woman. Are you happy to take orders from a woman, general?' *Ah, that shot hit the mark.*

'Women know nothing of war!' Horemheb's face reddened with anger. 'Women shouldn't know anything of war. They bring life into the world, and we men take it out. That's the natural order of things.'

'So, what will you, or your successor, do when pharaoh Meritaten—do I mean pharaoh-ess Meritaten? I suppose someone will think of an appropriate title—tells you to march in completely the wrong direction and attack the wrong enemy?'

'That can't happen. Damn it, it won't happen!'

'And how do we stop it happening, general? Do you see? This rather brings us back to the point I was making. We have to do something about this before the empire falls to pieces and we end up as slaves on some Hittite mushroom farm.'

Aye had no trouble meeting Horemheb's eyes now. He knew he had the general where he wanted him. It was just a question of steering him through the next few paces.

'We have to start by agreeing that the problem lies in the palace.'

'Aye, I've told you. Any action against the pharaoh is treason. We could all lose our heads for this.'

'Who said anything about the pharaoh? I said the problem is in the palace. And so it is; the problem has a name too: Moses.'

'But he is still a god! We can't move against him; it would be sacrilege.'

'How can Moses be a god, Horemheb? There is only one god, remember? Moses is a man, no more than that, and less, if some of the rumours I hear are true. You are right, of course; we mere mortals cannot hope to prevail against a god. But against a man, we can have a damn good try.'

Horemheb walked away, to the edge of the garden, where he could hear the calming sound of the sacred waters; were they sacred any longer? He was confused. The devious bastard of a priest was right, and he probably had a spy somewhere in the garden writing down everything they said, so he would be as compromised as Aye if things went sour. It seemed that, whether he liked it or not, Horemheb had taken a side in the war of the gods.

Aye watched him struggle, smiling. He could practically see the thoughts welling up in the general's head. *They must be lonely in there, poor things.* A little more honey, a little more poison, and the old warhorse would be his.

Horemheb came back, his features still creased with doubt. Aye reassured him. 'Horemheb, we don't need to do anything right now. And when we do move, we will not move directly against the pharaoh; you have my word on that. But we do need to plan, and that we need to do soon, in the coming few days if possible, before things get so out of hand we can do nothing to change them. Are we agreed?'

The resignation on Horemheb's face looked for all the world like relief. 'Yes, Aye, we are agreed. I will wait to hear from you, and I will expect to hear from you soon.'

Horemheb left the garden slowly; age seemed to have caught up with him in the space of a single conversation. Aye noted the slump of his shoulders, and the way his head hung forward like a prisoner of war, and his heart soared.

* * *

In her dream Nefertiti could just make out the boatman, pulling his dinghy ashore, seeming to wade through the river mist that curled around his knees. *Oh to lie in that cool mist, just for a few minutes*, she thought. The night had been hot and sticky, and sleep had evaded her. Akhenaten had called for slaves to fan her with ostrich feathers, but that had simply moved the heat around. *That cool mist . . .*

It didn't help that she was heavily pregnant. It was impossible to find a comfortable position, and as soon as she settled, the heat made her shift again. It also didn't help that the royal midwife, Henite, had confidently told her the child would be a girl. Another girl. She loved her daughters, dearly; but the yearning for a son was like a void in her loins.

Suddenly she felt a chill in the still air. It was such a relief; she opened her arms to it, embracing the coolness. *I want more of this*, she thought. She left the cool mist of the boatman in her dream and slipped out of bed. A slave put slippers on her feet and placed a shawl of cool linen around her shoulders; she walked to the balcony, where the sun pierced the world with glittering light. The air suddenly was becoming cooler by the minute, but wait; the light was changing too. As she watched, birds and insects fluttered to earth, closing their wings, as if they were preparing for sleep.

She looked up. There, in the pale blue of the early morning sky, she could see the disc of the sun and, beside it, a pale disc of equal size. As she watched, the second disc seemed to bite into the sun. For a moment, fear caught in her throat. Then she remembered the lessons of the court astronomer in Mitanni. *An eclipse; perhaps a total eclipse. How beautiful!*

Now the world was silent and still; she followed the moon's progress as its shadow inched its way across the sun, careful not to look directly into the sun's intense light. *I hope Akhenaten is watching too,* she thought. Where was Akhenaten? Nefertiti had the sudden feeling that her husband should not be seeing this alone.

Akhenaten was not alone, but Nefertiti's fears were not unfounded. The pharaoh stood on the balcony of his office, Moses beside him. They had been discussing plans for further expansion of the royal city when the change in light had drawn them out to watch.

They looked to the east, where Aten had risen not an hour ago. The sun's disc was slowly disappearing behind the shadow of the moon. The eclipse was near total now, and a strange intimation of darkness had covered the world. As they watched, the moon's disc covered the sun completely. Only a ring of intense gold betrayed the presence of Aten. Three great teardrops, the colour of blood, appeared on the black disc of the moon; diamonds the size of planets sparkled along its edges.

Moses was awestruck; he had read about total eclipses, but he had never seen one before. It was more beautiful, and more ominous, than he had imagined it. He leaned over the balcony; below, in the fields close to the river, he saw farmers and labourers, on their knees, hands raised. *Such fear*, he thought. *Such fear grows out of ignorance.* A low moan sounded behind him; he turned to find Akhenaten on his knees, huddled, his arms wrapped around him.

'I am cold, lord; why am I so cold?'

'Brother, it will last only a few moments longer; the eclipse is already at its peak. Soon, the ...'

'Silence. I am talking to my god, and my god is talking to me.'

Moses stepped back into the room. He could still see the eclipse from there; the edge of Aten's disc was just emerging from the shadow of the moon. He decided to wait a while before he tried to talk to his brother again. He was in a quandary: perhaps Akhenaten was really talking to god; and perhaps this was another sign of his weakening mind. Either way, patience was prudent.

Nefertiti appeared in the doorway. 'Are you enjoying the dance of the planets, Moses? Isn't it beautiful? Is Akhenaten with you? I hope he hasn't missed the spectacle...'

Moses put a finger to his lips. He led her back out of the office and into the corridor. 'Nefertiti,' he asked. 'Has anything seemed to you amiss with Akhenaten in recent days?'

He could see the hesitation in her eyes. She didn't want to betray her husband's weakness, but Moses knew from her face that she was worried. 'I think things are difficult for him. He struggles to find a balance between affairs of state and his faith. And sometimes...'

'And sometimes?'

'I worry that everything is too much for him. He is not cut out to be an emperor; still less the emperor of a troubled empire.'

A wailing cry from the balcony stopped them in mid-conversation. 'Moses! Moses, brother, come, I need you.'

They found him squatting on the balcony, a cloak draped carelessly over his knees. He was smiling, but his eyes were manic. 'Nefertiti, you are here too, that's good.'

The smile faded and a look of wild suspicion took over his face. 'Have you two been talking about me? Deciding what's best for me? Well, have no worries on that score. My Lord Aten has spoken. He has spoken to me, personally.'

Nefertiti went to hug him but he waved her away. 'Hold, woman. I have things to say, truths to tell. You,' he said brusquely. 'Bring me a chair.'

Moses looked behind him, expecting to see a servant, but they were alone. He worried for a moment that his brother was having hallucinations, but Akhenaten pointed at him this time. 'You. Get me a chair. Must I, a god on earth, repeat myself?'

Moses went into the office and found a rattan chair; he brought it out onto the balcony, and he and Nefertiti helped Akhenaten into it. Where the pharaoh had sat, huddled, on the floor, there was a small puddle.

'Brother,' said Akhenaten, 'Why does the Lord Aten allow himself to be covered by the shadow of the moon? He is lord of all; why would debase himself so?'

'It is simply a natural phenomenon in the heavens, highness,' said Moses. He ignored the quizzical look from his brother. How he addressed a man barely in possession of his senses did not seem important at that moment. The planets move around us in varying cycles. Sometimes their paths cross; and from here on the ground, we see an eclipse.'

'Well, no doubt that is the opinion of learned men, brother; and you are a learned man, aren't you? But the Lord tells me a different truth. He covered himself from the world so that he could speak to me in private. There were things, secret things, sacred things, that he needed to say, and that only I was destined to hear. So, he hid himself behind the moon, and we spoke.'

'What did you talk about?' Nefertiti put a protective arm on Akhenaten's shoulder, but he brushed it away.

'What can mortals understand of the speech of gods? Lord Aten told me that I am his son, his only son; that I was born from his ribs; that I am his image on earth. I am his high priest on earth; I will relay his commands to my people, and I will relay their wishes to him. As for you,' he pointed at Moses, 'and you,' then at Nefertiti. 'You will obey me as you obey Lord Aten. I will sleep now.'

Akhenaten's head sank into his chest and in moments he was unconscious. Moses took Nefertiti by the arm and led her out of the office. 'He is not well, Nefertiti. We must do something to help him, to stop this madness before it consumes him.'

'I don't see what I can do, Moses. He is the pharaoh, and pharaohs are gods, aren't they? So if he proclaims he is a god, he's only saying what the royal family, and the priests, have said for centuries. He is my husband, and he is the pharaoh, and he is a god. I can only stand beside him, and do as he asks. I am sorry, Moses; I see your fear and I understand it. But it is not my place to call my husband mad.'

'But you saw ...'

'I saw something, yes; but I have never seen a person possessed by a god before. Perhaps it always resembles madness; divine madness. Who am I to tell a god he is mad?' Moses could see the lost look in her eyes, the fear; but he knew it was pointless arguing.

He turned and hurried down the corridor, not sure where he was going. He wished Hapya were still alive. He wished his mother had been more tolerant, less zealous. He wished he had not pressed his brother so hard to promote the cult of Aten. He wished it would all stop, before he joined his brother in madness.

'Well, it was worth waiting for. I have lived long, and I am no doubt close to death, but that sight was worth waiting a lifetime for.' Ijuju set down the woven sunscreen and took a sip of water.

'Worth waiting for indeed,' said Aye. 'It's not just a wonderful sight, Ijuju; it's a wonderful opportunity. Lord Aten, the god of the empire, has just been eclipsed by Amun. We must tell this story, while the event is fresh in people's minds. If Akhenaten's mental state is as fragile as our spies report, this may just tip him over the edge.'

'And are you so eager to be ruled by a mad pharaoh, Aye? A man who might take your head on a whim? I would be cautious how you use this omen.'

'And what would you suggest?'

'I think we should tell a story, but not such an obvious fable. Let's put it about that the eclipse proved that Amun and the old gods are still alive, still active. They have not usurped the usurper; not yet. But they are waiting, and they are watching.'

'You are far too clever, Ijuju. Why have you not had me poisoned and taken the high priest's mantle?' Aye laughed and offered his colleague a cup of wine. Ijuju chuckled.

'I have never been blessed, or for that matter cursed, with ambition. You, on the other hand; your ambition is boundless, Aye, and that may yet bring you into peril.' The old priest's eyes bored into Aye. *Does he suspect? No, unless the old goat is a mind-reader. I have never told anyone of my real ambition.*

'I will take your advice, Ijuju; and heed your warning, of course. We will send out the acolytes to tell our story. And we will tell them to repeat it every time a disaster occurs or misfortune falls on Egypt. If fortune shines on Akhenaten, it will do no harm. But if anything untoward occurs,' Aye paused, as if making a mental list. 'If anything bad happens, our story will look like an omen. And bad things always happen.'

* * *

Yuffu raised his ugly, scarred face to the sky and laughed uproariously. 'If you lot were any more ignorant, you'd end up in the army. Oh wait.'

Around him, on the Memphis training ground, his latest group of recruits were huddled together, looking up as the moon gradually slid away from the face of the sun.

'This is a natural thing; it's all to do with the procession of the stars and planets, or some such astronomical bull. Every so often the planets get in each other's way, and that's the end of it. Do you understand?'

The recruits nodded, but they didn't look reassured. Yuffu gave up.

'Don't stare at the sun, you idiots; you'll go blind. Now, pair off and get back to your sword drills. Oi, Mitry; are you sure you're old enough to be a soldier?'

'Why, sir?'

'Because, apart from the fact you don't have so much as a hair under your armpit, you've just wet yourself without noticing. Go and get cleaned up.'

Mitry trudged off, embarrassed, still casting the odd glance at the sky. 'When the wet one gets back, I'll explain properly what a solar eclipse is, and why it doesn't mean the end of the world. I don't expect you to believe me, because I doubt you've got a duck's skull full of brains between you. But ignorance offends me, even when it's right at home.'

Yuffu suddenly stood to attention, and the recruits made a ham-fisted attempt to follow suit. General Horemheb strode in front of the ragged line. 'Listen, men. I know you've had a bloody fright, but I'm here to assure you that it's not the end of the world. This ...'

'We know, sir.'

'Who spoke?'

A robust, but frightened, man stepped out from the rear rank, a farmer by his looks. 'I did, sir, begging your pardon.'

'And what did you mean?'

'Yuffu, sir. Yuffu told us not to be afraid, that it was some kind of natural thing, and the astronomers in the royal court are able to predict them.'

'Did he now? Yuffu?'

'Sir.'

'Come with me to the mess; some of my brother officers need to hear what you have to say. Carry on, you men.'

Horemheb turned on his heel with practised grace and strode off, Yuffu in tow.

'He can say what he likes, old clever boots there; I don't like it, and even if it's perfectly natural, I think it's an omen.' The farmer looked around him; most of the recruits were nodding their heads. 'And if you ask me,' he went on, 'it's not an omen our pharaoh is going to like too much. I think old Amun might have a few tricks up his sleeve.'

* * *

He sat crookedly on the throne, his legs crossed over his knee, and one foot wrapped around his calf. His head moved constantly, and he counted invisible things on his fingers. The list of new instructions was getting too long for the chalkboard Djau's young scribe held as he wrote.

The pharaoh's face was a procession of bewildering and conflicting expressions; smiles, twitches, grimaces and frowns followed each other like prancing animals in a circus. Djau was a loyal servant, and always had been. But the sight of his master, clearly out of his wits, was testing his resolve; and breaking his heart.

'You will advise the people that I am the son who came forth from one of Aten's ribs, yes, and inform them that I am the child of Aten by this action, yes, and that I am therefore the eternal son that came forth from Aten, yes, that is right, his only son that came forth from his holy body, the body of the one and only god. And carve these words very large, so all can see. Yes.'

'Highness, it will be as you say.'

'Yes, yes, make it so.' Akhenaten giggled. 'Make it so, Djau.'

As Djau left the chamber he met Moses in the corridor.

'What are his orders today?' Moses could see from Djau's face the news wasn't good.

'My lord, the Pharaoh has ordered stelae at all points in the empire pronouncing his new role as son of Aten.'

'Then you had better hurry and do what the pharaoh desires of you. Go.'

'Yes, lord.'

'And Djau?'

'Yes, lord.'

'We will get through this.'

'My lord.' Djau didn't look convinced as he moved away, his bewildered scribe in tow.

Moses entered the audience chamber apprehensively; which Akhenaten would greet him today?

'Good morning, brother.'

Akhenaten was reading letters from envoys. He looked up.

'Ah, Moses. Do you bring news?'

'News, brother?'

'News from our Lord Aten.'

'No, I don't bring news from Aten. Why...'

'There, you see. It is as I told you. Aten speaks only to me, only through me. You are just one of his little helpers.' Akhenaten cackled with laughter and dropped the letter.

'Akhenaten, we need to talk.'

'Talk? No, we don't need to talk, Moses. You need to listen. I brought you back from the dead! You would still be in the dungeons of Memphis had it not been for me. You owe me your life, *brother.*'

Moses bowed his head. 'Highness.' Then he left the chamber. He could hear Akhenaten's voice following him down the corridor. 'Brother, Aten's little helper. Oh yes. Oh yes.'

Tiye reclined against a pile of cushions, her eyes lidded. She looked so small, he thought. When Moses was a child, his mother was a towering presence; now she was folded up like a little, wingless bird. But her mind was still sharp and her wit acidic. Moses left small talk for another day.

'We have to do something for him, before we are forced to do something about him.'

Tiye raised herself, and her eyes opened fully, drilling into Moses. 'And what shall we do for him, Moses? Bring him some potion for his madness? Play him soothing music on the lyre? It's too late for that.'

'Mother, it's too late for jokes, too, and too serious. We have to do something, or the country will descend into civil war.'

'That may very well happen; you are right. Forgive me my cynical joke; I am at a loss. I've seen this kind of insane zealotry before, and it has no cure. Curse those Theban vipers.'

'The Thebans? Why? They didn't make him mad.'

'No, but they caused this situation, so they may as well have done.'

'I don't understand.'

'It was supposed to be you, Moses. You were destined to be the pharaoh, the harbinger of Aten. You would have known what to do; you would have been a great pharaoh, greater than your father. But they schemed and plotted, and eventually they pushed you out, and so poor Amenhotep had to take your place. He isn't suited to power, or the games that come with it. The responsibility, and the poison of power itself, together they have driven him mad. But the priests; the priests started it.'

Moses listened in silence. He realised, with a sinking heart, that his mother was just as deluded as his brother. He wondered if her relentless promotion of Aten was, at root, merely a stick to beat the priests with. Not that it mattered now.

'So, what shall we do? Wait for Aten to make the decision for us?'

'That is as good a strategy as any. Madmen do not last long on thrones. Let's pray that Aten removes him before someone else does.'

'I'll think on that. I'll leave you to rest, mother, you look weary.'

'So do you, Moses. Go to Kiye and find some comfort.'

Moses started. Tiye smiled a feline smile. 'Don't worry; your secret is safe with me, and has been for years. But step carefully; if Akhenaten finds out, while he's in this state, he will certainly kill you.'

When Moses had left, Yuk appeared from a curtained alcove.

'Well, my old friend, what do we do now?'

Yuk shrugged. 'Mistress, I don't see there is much we can do. Perhaps we can petition Aten to arrange another solar eclipse, and reverse the process.'

Tiye's laugh was brittle. 'Perhaps we can, Yuk; but I am not sure we can leave it to him alone. Bring me a quill and some papyrus, and then sit here and help me with the wording. I need to write a devious letter to my scheming nephew in Thebes.'

Akhenaten waved the letter at Moses, as if he could read it from a distance. 'Have you seen this? The king of Alashia. He's making wild excuses for not sending his tribute of copper.'

'What does he say?'

'He claims that Nergal, the god of pestilence, is abroad in the land. There is no one left alive to work the copper mines.' The pharaoh laughed abruptly. 'This is because I threatened him with the army. I told him Horemheb would come to Alashia and take the copper. It's my right. Isn't it?'

'As you say, brother.'

'Yes, well, what do we do now?'

'We could send an envoy to assess the situation. If the king is telling the truth, we will know. If he is lying, we can send the army.'

'An envoy, yes, that would work. You are good at this, brother. Perhaps you should have been pharaoh. Perhaps I should install you as pharaoh and concentrate on being god.'

'I am at your service, brother.'

'So you are.'

Akhenaten looked out of the window that overlooked the royal gardens. The day was cloudy and humid. Aten's disc was a perfect circle of yellow in a sea of grey. The pharaoh seemed to be listening to something. 'Yes. Yes, this is as it should be.' He turned to Moses. 'Lord Aten says things are well as they are. I will bear the burden of power a little longer yet. Go, Moses, and find me an envoy. We need that copper.'

The king of Alashia was not lying. Nergal stalked the land, winnowing his harvest of suffering and death. The plague spread quickly from Alashia. By the time Akhenaten read the king's letter, it had reached Byblos and Sumura and had devastated those lands.

Soon enough afterwards, it reached Akhet-aten, and the deaths began to mount.

1337 BC

The royal physician closed Tiye's eyes with a spatula; he had no desire to touch the body of a plague victim. 'Her majesty is gone to the god,' he intoned. 'I don't know if anyone is willing to . . .'

Yuk dismissed him with a look. 'I will prepare the queen's body,' he said. The physician nodded and left as quickly as was decent. Yuk looked on the body of the woman he had served for so long. Her face and limbs were bloated and pustulent; there was little left of the regal presence that had carried the royal family so far. *But I remember*, he thought, tears streaming. *You were a sight to behold, my mistress, and a presence in the world.*

He sent the other servants away—they were too terrified to be of any help—and took warm water and clean linen, and set to cleaning the body.

There would be no embalming, no seventy days of drying in natron. Tiye was buried in a tomb in the cleft of the mountain where Aten rose every day. She would be the first to greet him each morning, she would be the closest to the god she had helped to raise to power.

'Mother, you can't die, not now.' Akhenaten wept over her sarcophagus. He pulled a piece of papyrus from his tunic and cast it into the open grave. 'That damned letter!' He shook his fist, at what no one cared to ask. 'That damned letter carried the plague. I will die of it too. I will have his head.'

He turned to Horemheb, one of a small procession of reluctant mourners. 'You will send a team of assassins to Alashia. Bring me the king's head.'

Horemheb bowed. 'As your highness requests.' He would do no such thing; his spies had already told him that the king had died of the plague some weeks previously.

Moses took up the ceremonial trowel, the one Akhenaten had used to lay the first stone of the new city, and cast a little earth into his mother's grave. 'Aten keep you, mother; know that you were loved.'

He passed the trowel to his brother and walked away. He would grieve in private. Akhenaten's grief was anything but private, and it did not go unnoticed.

'No, I will not see him, or speak to him. I will only speak to you, Nefertiti; you and Lord Aten. No, no, I don't want to speak to Aten either. How could he let Nergal take my daughters?'

Nefertiti left the room and beckoned Moses. 'You heard what he said?'

'Yes, I expected as much. You must comfort him as you can.'

'That's not the most important issue now. I will do my best for my husband, but we have to do something for the country. It's not just the plague.'

'I know. I've just come from the royal counting office. It seems the economy is in chaos. It's my fault; we were in such a rush to replace the priests with new administrators I took on people who were not qualified to do the work.'

'We are all at fault, Moses. We have been so focused on Akhenaten, and on Aten, that we failed to see what was happening. I have a meeting with Aye in the afternoon.'

'Why? What can the Thebans do for us?'

'I wrote to him a few days ago, and invited him. We will meet outside the city, away from the plague zone. He has promised to consider helping bring some order to the economy; I have made it clear this is temporary, until the plague is gone and we can manage things again. He is no fool. He knows what I am really asking; that he looks after the economy until Akhenaten either recovers his mind or dies.'

'He will like that.'

'Not so much, I think.' She moved to the window and pointed out to the sacred river. 'The harvest will be poor this year, I'm told. I fear our troubles are just beginning.'

* * *

Horemheb met Aye at his barge, an hour before his meeting with the queen. The high priest looked inordinately pleased with himself. 'Well, general, you have survived the pestilence; so far,'

'You are too kind, Aye. You seem in good health.'

'The plague has not reached us in the south, nor will it. We are under the wing of lord Amun and we will be protected. You should join us, general; you and the army.'

'I think the army should remain neutral for now, priest. And I have no wish to initiate a civil war while half the population is suffering from this pestilence.'

'Well, think on it, general. The time for neutrality will soon be past. I'd like to feel that, when the time comes, you know where your loyalties lie.'

'My loyalty is to Egypt,' Horemheb said stiffly.

'Yes, well let's hope you still have an Egypt to be loyal to. These idiots have brought the richest country in the world to the brink of starvation, and our neighbours are watching closely.' He nodded briskly and stepped into his litter. 'Remember, Horemheb; when the time comes.'

* * *

Nefertiti returned to the palace compound in tears; the meeting had been tense, but it was the way Aye looked at her that upset her. Moses met her in Akhenaten's office. It was a good place for a private meeting; the pharaoh hadn't set foot in the place in months.

'Was it so awful?'

'Yes, and more. I held it together while I talked to the odious little man, but it was torture.'

'And what did you agree?' Moses took a quill and papyrus and prepared to write.

'Moses, what are you doing?'

'You returned without a written agreement. I think it's best if we write down everything now, so if Aye oversteps his powers, or lies, at least we have some record.'

'Yes, I suppose that's best. Though I'm sure Aye will lie his way out of any trouble we bring him. He is a most accomplished liar these days; he has learned on the job.'

They talked and wrote late into the night. Finally, Nefertiti stood up and yawned. 'I can't do any more, Moses. And I need to go and talk to Akhenaten. I will soften the blow, but he needs to be aware of what's happening.'

'I'll go with you and wait outside the chamber.'

They made their way to the royal apartment through corridors almost empty of people. The plague had killed so many in the city, there were few healthy enough to work, and those that were, were busy making bread and burying the dead.

Moses sat on a cushioned bench outside the royal apartment. He could hear the murmur of conversation inside. He settled himself for a long wait, and his thoughts turned to Kiye, and Thutankhaten. He marvelled, again, that his mother had known all along, and had kept their secret, carried it to the grave.

A change of tone in the royal rooms brought him back to alertness. Now there was only one voice speaking, Akhenaten. And his voice was rising to a shout. 'You have betrayed me. No, no, my love, don't turn away. I know it's not your fault. The priest has deceived you. It's his fault. No, not Aye; Moses. He has brought us to ruin; he would not obey me, he is envious of my special relationship with Lord Aten; he wants my throne. Well, he won't get it. Guards!'

The two guards at the door snapped to attention, and the door to the apartment was flung open. Akhenaten stood between the soldiers, and pointed at Moses. 'Seize him, and take him to the palace gate. See to it that he leaves, at once. I will not have him in the royal presence, or the royal household. Now!'

Moses stood, shrugged, and walked between the guards, away from Akhenaten, still waving a puny fist and shouting. Behind him, he could see Nefertiti in the apartment, in tears. He wondered if he would see either of them again.

* * *

Miriam wrapped the last strand of the winding sheet around Yuk's body. He had sickened so quickly, and died after less than a day. Perhaps he was lucky, she thought through her tears; the fever had killed him before the awful pustules could ruin his fine old face.

It was early evening; the birds sang farewell to the sun as it fell towards the rim of the world. Yuk had loved this time of day; his duties done, he would relax in the garden and tell her the names of the birds that sang around them. *Your duty is done now, my love*, she thought. *You gave the queen mother everything, including your life.*

She went outside. Yuffu had finished digging the grave; now he straightened up and wiped the sweat from his face. 'Are you all right, little lady?' The gruff old soldier laid a calloused hand on her shoulder. 'I suppose we should finish the thing, then.'

'Yuffu, I can't thank you enough for this. I don't know what I'd have done on my own.'

'He was my friend, Miriam, and he never refused to do anything for me. I'm not sure the old fellow refused anyone.'

They returned to the house and between them carried Yuk's body out to the garden. The grave was deep; Yuffu showed Miriam how to wrap the linen slings under the body as they lowered him down to rest.

Miriam had managed a semblance of composure, but now she wept as if her heart would burst from her breast. 'Oh, Yuk,' she cried. 'What will I do now? Who will teach me, and hold me?' She fell to her knees, and wept until Yuffu had filled in the grave, and set a stone at his old friend's head, with a simple inscription: *Yuk, loyal servant.*

* * *

Henenu leaned over the flood post and took the reading. 'Not good, Kewab; not good at all.' His assistant leaned over to have a look for himself. 'Step back, you fool; you'll end up as lunch for the crocodiles. Which would be fine, except I'll be in there with you.'

He took a last look, and stood up, arching his back. 'I'm getting too old for this nonsense. I'm not looking forward to reporting this to the chancellor, either.'

'It's two cubits below normal; write it down, Kewab, and let's be on our way. The harvest will be poor again, if there is a harvest. I've never seen the river so low for so long. It's as if the gods are thirstier than we are.'

'God.'

'What?'

'God, Henenu; there is only one god now.'

'Ah yes, that. I'm a simple man, and no doubt some priest could explain it to me. But I fail to see how there can be dozens of gods one week, and only one the next. I suppose the pharaoh knows what he's doing; I bloody hope so, or we are in very deep trouble.'

'If we're waiting for the pharaoh to get us out of this mess, we may be waiting a while. I have a cousin in the royal household, and she says he's as mad as a bag of frogs.'

'I don't need to hear that right now. Let's get on, and give the chancellor the bad news.'

* * *

Nefertiti's breath came in ragged gasps. Her handmaiden, Nofret, applied a cool, damp linen cloth to her brow. The queen sighed, and something like a smile softened her troubled features. Then a long, rattling breath escaped her, and her face relaxed. Nofret stepped back, distraught. 'Mistress? Majesty? Oh, gods, she's gone. What will we do now?'

She closed the queen's eyes and ran from the apartment. *Who do I tell?* In the corridor, she approached the first official she could find.

'Please, sir, may it please you ...'

'What is it, girl? I have duties to attend to.'

'The queen, sir. The queen ...'

Nofret sank to her knees and wailed. 'The queen is dead, sir. She's gone, sir. We are bereft.'

The official seemed to lose his footing for a moment. He composed himself and lifted Nofret to her feet. 'Go, girl; go to the physicians and tell them. And fetch some servants to clean her and prepare her. You are sure?'

'Yes, sir; I saw the Ka leave her body, I swear.'

'Someone will have to tell the pharaoh. I'll go to the chancellor and inform him. He can do it.'

Akhenaten's howl of grief sundered the air and filled the palace; it echoed along the silent corridors and escaped through every window. Djau recoiled from the feral noise; he knew he should try to comfort the pharaoh, but this creature huddled in a corner repelled him. 'Highness,' he said, 'I'll send for Meritaten and the other royal children. You should not be alone now.'

'What? Yes, send for them. Leave me, Djau; I need to think. I need to pray. I need ...'

Djau crept out without waiting for Akhenaten to finish.

Akhenaten struggled to his feet, unsteady. He went to the window and looked at the sun, slipping towards the western horizon. 'Ha, you are leaving me too. Or perhaps you left me long ago, and now I'm reaping the harvest. You have taken everything from me, Aten: my wife, my mother, my daughters. I have nothing left. My empire is on the verge of collapse and my brother, the only man I can trust, is an exile. I have been a fool. I have listened to you when I should have listened to him. Oh, Nefertiti, what will I do without you? How can I live when you don't?'

He sank to his knees on the balcony and rested his head against the cool stone. *I will be strong*, he thought. *I will rise, and take command, and Egypt will see a new Akhenaten. But not yet.*

'Highness, a messenger from Akhet-aten.' The acolyte bowed and backed out of the room. A few moments later he returned with the messenger. 'Thank you, erm,' *Damn it, what was the man's name?* 'You may go.'

Aye settled back in his chair, smiling. Another letter from the queen; she was becoming quite the pen pal. And that was just as well; in his long-term plan there was a wedding to a royal widow, a wedding that would cement his place as pharaoh.

But the messenger didn't produce a letter. He cleared his throat, and stood to attention. Just for a moment, Aye's heart soared. Could it be? Was the lunatic gone at last? 'Speak, man. Why are you here?'

'Holiness, I bring news from the capital …'

'I know that, you ass. Spit it out before I die of old age.'

'Holiness. The queen, Nefertiti …'

'Yes? What does she say?'

'She … She doesn't say anything, holiness.' The messenger looked as confused as Aye felt.

'What are you on about? What's the message?'

'The queen is dead, holiness.'

Aye recoiled as if he'd been stabbed. 'How dare she!' He recovered himself and waved at the messenger. 'Pay no heed; I am overcome with grief. Go to the kitchens and tell the servants I sent you. Be ready to ride again in one hour; I'll have a letter for you.'

Aye sat and fumed, watching his wedding plans dissolve like smoke before him. And not just the wedding; now he would have to deal with the lunatic pharaoh again, or worse, his fanatical brother. He knew Moses was ex-palacio, but now Akhenaten was alone, it would only be a matter of time before he recalled the only man who could actually help him.

'Setau!' he shouted. His assistant scurried into the room. 'Setau, we have much to do. Nefertiti is dead. Oh don't sob, man; she was a heretic too. Gather the prophets of Amun for a council. And get what's his name to write a letter of condolence; the usual nonsense. I'll sign it and send it back with the messenger. Now leave me; I need to think.'

* * *

Moses had taken a small house at the eastern end of the valley, the closest he could find to the magical cleft in the mountains. He often walked in the foothills, until he came to the base of the cleft. Here, he would stop and reflect on the events since his vision. If he was totally honest, he had rather gilded the story of his vision, to encourage Akhenaten to come with him. But that sunrise, the day they had arrived! That had been something divine. And yet, almost everything that had happened since their move to the new city had been a disaster. Now, as he looked up through the gap in the mountains, he wondered if that first little white lie had started an avalanche of dishonesty and delusion. He turned, and made his way back to the house. There was a royal messenger waiting for him.

He approached the man cautiously; there was no telling what his brother might have in store for him. 'You have a message for me?'

'Yes, my lord.' He handed over a short scroll. Then he turned on his heel.

'Wait,' said Moses. 'I may need to send a reply.'

'I doubt it, my lord.' The messenger walked away.

Moses turned the scroll over in his hands. It bore a royal seal, but not the personal seal of the pharaoh. He broke the seal, and read. The message was brief enough. 'Oh, Nefertiti,' he breathed, the scroll furled in his clenched fist. He looked up; the sun was a semi-circle on the western horizon. There was nothing for it. He went into the house, and sat down to wait.

The escarpment was littered with bones, and fragments of rusted armour. The man who waited, astride a black stallion, ignored the debris. He had been a part of this battle; it wasn't much of a fight, hardly enough to write a song about. The Egyptians had turned up in force and routed them. But that was nearly five years ago; now Egypt was a sick country run by a madman.

A clatter of scree told him his guest had arrived. The rider was a soldier, an officer, though not a senior officer. He goaded his roan mare up the stony slope, and came to a halt a few paces away. 'Rensiliu.' He offered a desultory salute.

Rensiliu returned the gesture with a wink. 'So, Irsu, what brings you to this desolate spot? You weren't at the battle, were you?'

'I was still training, a raw recruit. Those were the days.'

Rensiliu's face hardened. 'What do you have for me? The king is anxious to hear news from Egypt.'

'Then I think he'll like this.' Irsu handed him a scroll and a clay tablet. 'Here, it's in both languages, so your scribes won't have to work for a living.'

'What does it say?'

'It's bad news, if you're Akhenaten. Queen Nefertiti is dead.'

'Is she now? Shame. She was a most beautiful woman. Still, the worms aren't fussy.'

'Rensiliu, you have no soul.' Irsu chuckled.

'No, thank the gods. That's how I've survived all this.' He spat on the stones and bones at his feet. 'Well, I must bear this sorrowful missive to the king. I'm sure he'll be most upset.'

'Take care, Rensiliu. See you here in a moon's time?'

'Yes, let's do that.' He looked around at the mess of battle. 'Let's hope we don't have company.'

The message came sooner than Moses expected. This time, it was the chancellor who bore it. 'So, Djau, are we to work together again?'

'We are, my lord, and I for one am glad of it.'

'And how is the pharaoh?'

'You might be surprised, my lord. He has stepped back into the royal life with a vengeance. He actually looks and sounds like a pharaoh. There are moments,' Djau shifted uncomfortably, 'but on the whole, he is far better than one might expect.'

'And is he really ready to accept me back? I'm not sure I could stand to be exiled again.'

'He needs you, my lord; we all do.'

'Then I will come at once. Let's go, Djau; I'll come back for my belongings once I know where we stand.'

Djau had brought a spare horse, so they were back at the palace in a short time. Djau ushered Moses straight to the office of royal decrees. Akhenaten was standing at a table covered in maps and scrolls, giving instructions to Horemheb. His voice was different; there was a harsh edge to it, as if he were the soldier. 'And if it comes to battle, then so be it. I won't have our borders troubled by this scum any longer.'

'Yes, Highness.' Horemheb snapped a salute and turned to leave just as Moses entered the room. 'Lord Moses,' he said with a sardonic note in his voice. He bowed low. 'How good to see you back.'

'General.' Moses nodded in response to Horemheb's greeting. 'Where are you headed now?'

Horemheb glanced back at Akhenaten, who nodded. 'To the borders east of Sinai,' he said. 'There have been too many incursions of late. His highness has ordered us to clean them out and bring order to the marches. I am looking forward to it.' He swept out of the room, a retinue of junior officers running like puppies at his heels.

Akhenaten came forward and embraced his brother. 'Moses, Moses, I have missed you. I am sorry I sent you away; I was not in my senses. Will you work with me now, and put this empire back together again?'

'With pleasure, brother. I have never wanted anything else.'

'Splendid! Leave us,' he bellowed at the remaining officials, in a voice that sounded like it came from the training ground. 'I will speak alone with Lord Moses.'

When the room was empty, Akhenaten sank into a chair. 'I can't do it,' he sighed. 'I can pretend for a while, but I just can't. Without her, I'm nothing.'

'Brother, you must be strong. Egypt needs you.'

'Come closer, Moses.' Akhenaten beckoned with trembling hands. Moses crossed the room and stood before his brother. Akhenaten fished inside his tunic and produced an obsidian blade. Moses recoiled.

'No, brother, have no fear. The blade is for you to use.'

'And what need have I of a blade?'

Akhenaten pulled his tunic open. 'Kill me,' he said, calmly.

'Akhenaten, I can't ...'

'You must, Moses; you are the only one I trust to do it. Kill me, and take over. You'll make a better fist of it than I will. And I will be with her. It's best for everyone.'

'Brother, I will not do it. We will face things together. We are stronger that way.'

Akhenaten's mask of confidence faded, and he sobbed. 'There is nothing more I can do. No one trusts me, and the Theban priests are just waiting to strike. I've ruined everything.'

'There is plenty you can do. First things first; you need to take a royal wife. You cannot sit the throne alone.'

'And who will marry this pathetic madman?'

'Don't wallow in self-pity, brother. We don't have time for all that. I think you should marry, and quickly.'

'Marry who, brother?'

'Meritaten. That will seal the succession and stop the priests from acting, at least for now.'

Akhenaten bowed his head. 'You are right. I don't like it at all, but you are right. She will hate me for this.'

'Meritaten? Not at all; she knows her duty.'

'No, not Meritaten; Nefertiti. This is not how it was supposed to happen.'

'We will make it work, I promise you. Things will be well again.'

Moses looked out over the courtyard, alive with scurrying servants and officials. *It will work*, he thought. *It damn well has to.*

1336 BC

Thebes, Egypt. Year 14, in the reign of Amenhotep IV

Aye stood on the flat roof of the astronomer's tower, and beamed. It wasn't a total solar eclipse; that would be too much to hope for, and here in Thebes they were on the edge of the eclipse field. But it was an eclipse and, just as trusty old Khamet had predicted, it had arrived on the first wedding anniversary of Akhenaten and Meritaten. 'Well done, Khamet; well done.'

'Holiness, I accept your gratitude, and I'm always glad of praise. But I didn't actually arrange the eclipse; I just told you when it would happen.'

'Well, you've made me happy, Khamet, and that's a rare thing these days. And best of all, I am quite sure the folks in Akhetaten will be anything but happy.'

'I only wish I could have drummed up a total eclipse for you, holiness.'

'Actually, I think this may be even better. Setau!'

Setau, Aye's principle secretary, was standing at the parapet of the tower, looking down. He didn't look well. 'Yes, master.'

'Setau, come over there, in the centre of the platform; it's much more comfortable, and you will have a better view.'

'Holiness.'

'Setau, we need to send a message, to the priests in Akhet-aten who are still loyal, and to our spies. They are to spread a rumour that the eclipse is just the beginning. It's a sign of worse to come. Keep it vague; that way, if anything bad happens—and bad things always happen—we can link it to the eclipse; and, Setau, make sure that everyone knows it was a warning from Amun. Go to it, man.'

Akhet-aten

Horemheb came into the audience chamber like a man going to battle; his junior officers formed a phalanx around him, as if they were expecting opposition. Akhenaten stiffened when he saw the little squadron. Horemheb realised his mistake, hastily dismissed the officers and made his way to the throne alone.

'Highness, I came as quickly as I could.'

'So I see, general.'

The room was full of courtiers and nobility wishing for audience. Now that his general was here Akhenaten didn't want them around. 'Chancellor.'

'Yes highness.'

Akhenaten extended his arm and moved it sideways. The chancellor understood; he raised his wand and struck the marble floor three times. 'All leave,' he shouted.

The room cleared of all but the pharaoh, Horemheb and his detachment, the chancellor and Moses.

'Moses?'

Moses stepped from the dais and handed Horemheb a scroll. 'Byblos has fallen. We think it's an army of Hittites, but the dispatches were confused; the scouts were doing their best to get out alive.'

'We are to respond?' Horemheb asked.

'Oh yes, general; we are going to respond.' Akhenaten spoke in a quiet, menacing voice. 'You are going to take an army to Byblos and recapture the city. Then you will scour the surrounding countryside of any invaders. Find out if this is the Hittites, or an army of bandits. We need to know who we are facing, and we need to know soon.'

Horemheb felt the tang of battle and was happy. The pharaoh's voice brought him back to attention.

'Well, we could have lunch and discuss it, or you could be on your way. Now.'

'Highness.' Horemheb clicked his heels together and offered a smart salute. Then he turned and marched out of the chamber, already bellowing orders.

'That man worries me,' said Moses. 'He only really seems to enjoy taking orders from you when there's blood in the offing. And if Thethi's spies have it right, he seems to make rather too many excursions to Thebes.'

'He'll do his duty, Moses. But you're right; we need to watch him. Let's send for Thethi.'

* * *

Miriam took Yuffu's cloak and offered him a seat. 'So, old soldier, what news from the front? Have we taken Byblos back?'

Yuffu settled with a groan. 'I wish I could swap this back for a new one. Yes, Byblos is safe again, and old Horemheb is on his way back in triumph. So the news isn't all bad.'

'So what's the bad news?'

'I have an old mate, not as old as me, or he'd be beside me in a chair complaining about his back. Kagemni, his name is; he's a scout on the Hittite borders. Once in a while, Kagemni goes to visit a lady in a small town a few miles over the border; sneaks in at night and leaves before dawn.

'I saw him last night in the wine house. He told me he'd gone to visit his lady friend, and was about to head back when he heard horses; lots of them. He made himself scarce and had a look. A large body of Hittite cavalry—not an army, but a lot more than an average patrol—went thundering by, so Kagemni decided to follow them; they seemed to going in the same direction. They got to the border, and spread out. They didn't cross; he thought they were waiting for something, or someone, a signal perhaps.'

Miriam shivered, though the evening was warm. 'That doesn't sound good, Yuffu.'

'That it doesn't, my dear. I fear we are in for exciting times ahead; which is the last thing we need.'

Miriam brought him another cup of beer, and went to sit in the doorway. 'What are you doing over there?' asked Yuffu.

'Listening to the birds. Yuk used to do it every evening, and I can see why. It's very peaceful.' *But how long the peace will last,* she thought, *that's another matter.*

* * *

'Lord, you will not believe it.'

Aye was sitting at his desk engrossed in drawing trees, which he called 'help decision trees'. He was trying to create a pathway to victory but failing at almost every turn. Frustrated, he barked at the acolyte. 'What are you talking about?'

'The queen. The queen is in the temple complex. She is approaching the sacred way of Mut.'

Aye's ears pricked. His mind whirled. *What was Meritaten doing here?*

'Are you sure?'

'Yes, Sire, I have seen her myself.'

'Is the Pharaoh with her?' Aye put down his pen slowly. The acolyte stayed perfectly still.

'Take me to the place you saw her.'

The two of them left the room and headed to the inner temple. There, kneeling at the sacred altar of Mut, was Meritaten.

Aye motioned for his priest to go and held his forefinger to his lips. *Silently!* He tip-toed through the entrance to the shrine and stopped just behind the prostrate Meritaten.

'My Lady,' Aye whispered.

Meritaten drew the corner of her bright linen shawl to her eyes. *No one should see me like this.*

'Who is that?' she asked. 'How dare you interrupt your queen?'

Aye stretched out his arm in greeting. 'It is Aye, majesty. I heard you were here and wondered if you wished to see me.'

Meritaten sobbed and turned to collapse into his arms. The queen, wife of the heretic Pharaoh, was on her knees hugging him. What on earth was happening?

'My lady,' he said softly. He crossed his hands and placed them on her head as if to bless her. Then he realised what he had done and just as quickly removed them from her head. 'Forgive me, Madam, I should not have done such a thing. Your god Aten is to bless you.'

'Aten,' she shouted. 'He is to blame for all of this.' Aye could not believe his ears. Was this the queen talking? 'He has ruined our dynasty, he and Uncle Moses; Aten has made my father mad and my uncle has encouraged this, and now there is pestilence around the empire. My husband, my father, allows our enemies to run amok at our borders whilst he talks of love and peace and understanding. Oh, what a fool he is, he and Moses both.'

'My lady, you are depressed, suffering the grief of your family deaths. It is a hard thing to lose grandmother, mother and sisters in such a short period of time; and then having to marry your father and take on all of the stresses of the crown. You must be exhausted, majesty.'

'Oh, come on, Aye. Stop pussy footing. You are the arch enemy of Aten, you the thorn in the side of the royal family. You and your god Amun have never let go of your aims. You would get rid of my husband and his god in the blink of an eye.'

'Oh, my dear, I have tried to warn your family about the road they have taken. You must know this. But they have vilified me and my priests. Indeed, your father—sorry, husband—has had Amun's name struck from every monument in the empire. He cannot expect us to ignore this and become priests of Aten after thousands of years as servants of Amun. The recent catastrophes are the direct consequence of Aten's elevation above our lord. You, in your new understanding, must admit this.'

'I could, if it were in my interests and the interests of the state.'

'You know, highness, we would be on your side, if the state religion were returned to its rightful owner. I would personally press the council to make you pharaoh.'

'But a woman can't ...'

'If Amun were the state god the council would have to listen and do what we said. There is no reason why you should not then be pharaoh.'

'Are you sure?'

'My lady, I am certain. If Hatshepsut can be pharaoh then there is no reason why you can't.'

A spark ignited in the dark recesses of Meritaten's mind.

For a man flushed with recent victory, Horemheb looked distinctly nervous. The merchant's garden was familiar territory now, but the general looked around him as if he expected a spy or an assassin to leap out from behind a bush.

He jumped when Aye entered the garden. 'Peace, general, it's only me.'

'Aye, I was beginning to think you'd never get here.'

'I had to deal with something on the way. Priestly business; nothing to concern a soldier.' He sat and took a cup of beer. 'Well, now we're here, what shall we talk about?'

'Don't joke with me, Aye; you know what we will talk about. It doesn't make me feel good.'

'General, some years ago we made a kind of agreement. If things became so bad the country was in real peril from the fools in this city, we would do something about it.'

'We did, I remember.'

'So, what do you think, Horemheb? Have things come to that point?'

'I think they have, priest. I hate to say it, but the pharaoh seems set on losing the empire, and turning us all over to the Hittites.'

'Ah yes, the Hittite mushroom farms.'

'Quite.' Horemheb's face was sheened in sweat. He took a gulp of beer and tried to stop his hands shaking. 'Look, Aye, I have come to you honestly. I think we have to act before things get any worse. What we should do, however, I have no idea.'

'Well, one thing we must do is use opportunities as they come our way. A few days ago, one of the main towers in the great temple of Aten collapsed.'

'Yes, it did. My troops spent an unpleasant afternoon picking pieces of dead masons out of the rubble. How is that an opportunity?'

'I have been busy spreading rumours that the tower was sabotaged by the Hittites. And that our pharaoh knows this but is too afraid to retaliate. It's like when you send your skirmishers out in front of the lines to goad the enemy, Horemheb; I'm softening people up.'

'To what end?'

'So that, if anything bad should happen to the pharaoh . . .'

'Aye, I know we have to act. But killing the pharaoh; it's a huge step. So much could go wrong. And he's in good health, I hear, so it would be hard to hide.'

'There is, ah, something else I need to advise you of.'

Horemheb looked puzzled.

'The reason I was late today.' He paused, looked around, and put his hand to his mouth. 'I have met Meritaten and she is not happy.'

'Aye, have you let the royal family know that we are against them?'

'They know very well we are against them. And she came to me.'

Now Horemheb was baffled.

'Yes, she came to me. She is not happy with Aten, Moses or her husband. She wants to return to the old gods. So if anything were to happen to Akhenaten and she were made Pharaoh . . .'

Aye gave the general a few moments to ruminate on what he'd just said. In a few short months, Horemheb had gone from threatening to decapitate him every time he said something treasonous to musing over the practicalities of assassinating the pharaoh. That was progress. But now Aye had the ace. The next pharaoh would be on their side. The old systems would be restored. 'So, if anything should happen to the Pharaoh, the empire would be saved.'

'No, there are two brothers. Smenkhkare and Thutankhaten. They have a claim to the throne. The council would not allow a woman to reign.'

'That is easily solved. She is the only one of age. And if we could arrange a foreign prince to marry her—one of our choice, of course—then the council would have no argument about there being a woman on the throne; her husband would rule her.'

'I take the point but I'm still not convinced.'

'You will be. The Pharaoh must go, and Moses too; with them gone, Aten will fall. You are a soldier, Horemheb, and no doubt you're thinking that, if there's any killing to be done, you're the expert. And normally I would agree. You know far more about killing than I do, if you count heads. But this kind of killing is not work for soldiers. You don't have to worry yourself about this.'

'Are we to send assassins into the palace?'

'In a word, yes. But we need to do some groundwork first.'

'How so?'

'I will have my spies put it about that Moses and Akhenaten are having some kind of family spat. After all, it's not as if it hasn't happened before. We'll wait until the rumour has caught hold. Then I will have a word with my herbalist.'

'And you think this will work?'

'I think the gods—the real gods—will thank us for it; and so will generations of our people.'

'And what is my part in this?'

'There will be chaos, in the aftermath, and you will need to restore order. Make yourself look like a hero of the people. And you will initiate the hunt for Moses, the murderer. Moses the murderer; I rather like the sound of that.'

1335 BC

Akhet-aten, Egypt. Year 15, in the reign of Amenhotep IV.

In the dream, someone was tugging at him, trying to make him do something he didn't want to do. Moses shifted on his pallet and ignored the intrusion.

'Uncle Moses. Uncle Moses. Wake up!'

Moses opened his eyes.

'Thutankhaten. What are you doing here?'

'You must go, uncle. Run.'

'Nephew, you're not making any sense. What's going on?'

'Father is dead.'

His brother dead? Was he still dreaming?

'What happened?'

'We don't have time. You have to get out.' Thutankhaten held out a bundle of clothes; rough homespun, the kind that labourers wore.

Moses pushed the bundle to one side. 'I can see your urgency, nephew, but I need to know what's going on.' The boy took a deep breath and tried to compose himself. Moses grasped him by the shoulders, firmly but gently. 'Tell me.'

'Djau woke me, and told me my father was dead. He took me and Smenkhkare to him; he looked like he was asleep, but he was already cold. Then Djau told us he had been poisoned and, as we were the only sons, we need to be very careful, even as sons of second-rate wives. He told us he had suspected that there was something amiss. But the most important thing is this—while we were considering the position, we heard people running around, speaking loudly; they were saying that you killed father, and then there was commotion like you have never heard. Djau sent me straight to you. He says you must leave quickly. You must stay away until he discovers what has happened and... Uncle Moses, you have to go!'

'I killed him? But...'

'I know, I know, it's ridiculous, but there are people coming for you now.'

Moses rose hurriedly and started putting on the clothes. They smelled a little ripe; he clearly wasn't the first to wear them.

'Uncle, Djau has arranged for a stable boy to ready a horse. He did not advise the young man who it was for in case he has heard the rumours; say the word "Sobek" to him and he'll give you the horse. Here is a pouch of coins. Djau said, if he had time, he would go and put some more in your saddlebags, with some provisions. You have to go now, uncle, quickly, now.'

Moses hugged him. 'You've been very brave. I will return when all is well. It will not take long to prove my innocence.'

Thutankhaten placed his open hand on Moses' chest, directly above his heart. 'May Aten go with you.'

Moses almost wept. He grabbed the pouch and crept out of his room.

In the distance, he could hear people shouting orders; looking for him, no doubt. He hurried along the corridor and ducked into a passage used by servants, keeping close to the wall. It took a few minutes to get to the stables, but it felt like an eternity. He had to keep to the shadows all the way; small groups of soldiers and palace guards were everywhere, torches in hand, searching the palace.

There was a little light seeping out of the stables. Inside, he found the stable boy who, on seeing Moses, looked terrified. There was no time to reassure him. 'Sobek.'

'Take him, master, he's yours.'

'My thanks.'

'Aten go with you.'

The streets were far too crowded for the time of night. Moses got off the Royal Road as soon as he could and took a route through the winding lanes of the artisans' district. On all the main streets, people wandered in groups. Some simply talked about the pharaoh's assassination in loud voices—his name came up regularly—and some had more purpose, going from house to house and asking if anyone had seen the killer, Moses.

It was a relief to reach the city limits. He dismounted, and led the horse through some thick brush at the roadside. Just in time. A troop of cavalry thundered past, yelling; his horse almost bolted. When the road was clear, he remounted and rode on for a couple of miles, before turning off the road and heading north. He had no idea where he was going, but north seemed as good a direction as any.

He gave the horse its head, and it galloped happily for two hours. He stopped when he heard the babble of a stream, and led the horse to the water. It drank its fill and then munched lazily at the grass on the bank. Moses looked through the saddlebags; there was more gold, a lot of it, and provisions for five days or more. He mouthed a silent thanks to Djau.

Moonlight filtered into the clearing where he sat. He found his food and started to eat, and then found there was a scroll in the saddlebag.

'Your highness. My men have heard stories circulating for two weeks of a division between you and my lord Akhenaten and insinuating that you were engineering his downfall and death. I identified one of Aye's palace spies, Thethi, and had men follow him, but it seems we were too late. My lord is dead and I am sure he was poisoned. This leaves you in a very bad position. The mob is being stirred up and I have no resources to stop them.

Until I can put down the disturbance you must disappear. I will send for you when I feel the time is right.

May Aten be with you.'

* * *

The lamps around the walls of the chamber gave off just enough light; shadows flickered on every surface. Merkha didn't give them a thought. He had worked for so long in the underground mummification chambers it felt normal. 'Nebamun,' he said, 'bring me another sack of natron.'

His apprentice heaved the sack over and slit the top with a copper knife. 'That's it. Now take that scoop and pour some more of it into the body.'

Nebamun tipped the natron into the body cavity, spilling a little on the floor.

'Steady, lad; that stuff's expensive.'

'Sorry, Merkha, I'm a bit nervous; are you sure his Ka has left his body?'

'Of course; it left the moment he died. Probably glad to get out of this one. So yes, the Ka, and the Ba, and all the other souls have gone. They'll re-join the pharaoh when he's in his tomb, so they say.'

'What other souls, Merkha?' Nebamun looked around the chamber, as if he was expecting to see a lingering soul.

'Well, depending on which priest you ask, there are two, or five, or seven souls; they all have different names and they all have some sacred function or other. Course that doesn't matter here; as far as the Atenist's are concerned, there's only one of everything.' Merkha laughed at his own joke, his barrel chest heaving. Nebamun didn't join in.

They had been working on the pharaoh's body for fifty days now; the body was almost ready to be stuffed with linen and wrapped in layers of linen to form the mummy.

'I reckon the funeral will be in about twenty days, if you get a move on.'

Nebamun looked over at the canopic jars. 'So all his . . . bits are in there?'

'Not all of them. His heart is still in here.' He pointed at Akhenaten's chest. 'And we've thrown the brain away. As far as the physicians know, it's just for cooling the blood. The heart's the organ of thought and feeling.'

Nebamun examined the top of the dead pharaoh's head. 'How did you get the brain out? I don't see any cuts or holes here.'

'No, we use a couple of hooks for that; pull it down through the nose.'

Nebamun shivered. His new apprenticeship was going well, but he wasn't yet sure he was cut out to an embalmer. 'So tomorrow we start wrapping him?'

'That's it. Tomorrow we start to wrap him in layers of linen; first we have to seal all the cuts with wax, and test the skin to make sure he's dry enough.'

Merkha covered the pharaoh's body with a stained shroud, and started to pack his tools away. 'Sorry, highness,' he said. 'The next shroud will be a bit posher.'

Master and apprentice left the chamber, still lit by the lamps. Akhenaten lay in the last layer of natron, slowly desiccating.

The Aten priests continued with the ritual, chanting the death song for Akhenaten with their arms raised to the sun. Meritaten yawned. 'I'm bored,' she muttered.

Smenkhkare sneered. 'This is exactly why a woman shouldn't be pharaoh.'

Thutankhaten listened, keeping his council.

'Ah, brother, that old tune. Why am I not up to watching our father disappear very slowly into the afterlife?'

'You don't have the patience for it, you said so yourself.'

'And this from the man who fell asleep yesterday during the rituals?'

'That's not the point, and you know it. Everyone says it; it doesn't make sense for a woman to rule Egypt.'

'So you don't remember Hatshepsut, then? She seemed to do just fine, and in any case the priests of Amun are with me; they insist on my preferment.'

'Hatshepsut was an exception and Thebes is irrelevant. You would do well to remember who our god is and who you should respect.'

Smenkhkare huffed and turned away. The priests finished their chanting and backed away from the sarcophagus. A team of attendants took over and carried it back to the resting house, where it would stay until it was time for Akhenaten to be sealed in his tomb.

'Have a care, brother.' Meritaten's voice was sharp. 'Don't listen to tales; and don't try to undermine me; that would be a fatal mistake.'

1334 BC

The Egyptian desert. Year 1 in the reign of Meritaten

'I'll give you three gold pieces for the horse. You can keep the tackle and bags; they have, frankly, seen better days.'

'To be honest, so have I,' replied Moses. The horse trader laughed with the stranger, and they shook hands to close the transaction. Moses would be sorry to part with her; she had carried him a long way.

'Where are you headed?' The trader was curious. This stranger spoke like a noble, but he dressed like a beggar. And the horse was a fine animal; it could have graced the pharaoh's stables.

'Ah, I think I'll see where the road takes me.'

'All is well, stranger; I won't tell your secrets. Take care on the road.'

'I will and my thanks.'

Moses left the stables and headed for the market. The little town had plentiful produce, despite the poor harvests, and he laid in a good supply of provisions; he would need them.

Since escaping the palace, he had kept to his northerly tack, though he wasn't sure why. He knew no one in the north (which was perhaps as well) and had no idea what he would do when he got there. Sad as he was to give up his horse, he realised he was now even less visible. He had had a few close calls with strangers who had noticed his refined speech and his expensive horse and taken him for a noble refugee, or a fugitive.

For the next few days, he took advantage of anyone with a horse and cart who would help a man for the company of another human being, or some of his provisions from his bag. He slept in ditches and sometimes had the luxury of a barn, or enjoyed a moonlit night in a patch of cool reeds; he usually rested unnoticed. When his money, and then his provisions, ran out, he had to change plan. He was reluctant to steal food, but he was coming to the point when he might not have a choice. He decided to see if he could find some casual work in exchange for a little food.

Walking in the heat of the sun, hungry and often thirsty, was not easy, so, Moses tried to keep himself occupied by studying the wildlife around him or taking in the geography of the region he now passed through, but his stomach was a better teacher than his head.

There was a broad body of water up ahead. *Small Bitter Lake*, he thought. *We passed this place when I visited my family, all those years ago.* He went down to the lake shore, cupped his hands and drank. The coughing fit lasted a full minute. *Well*, he thought, his eyes streaming, *now I know how the lake got its name.*

The following day he rounded a hill and observed a small village on the higher reach of the lake shore; he could see the village square and the well. He was too thirsty to wait for night-fall; the lake water had seen to that. He walked cautiously into the roughly oval space at the centre of the village. The houses that stood around the space were modest, and some of them looked unkempt. *Good*, he thought. *I'm unlikely to meet anyone here who recognises me.*

He approached the well; there was a rope coiled on the lip of a low wall around the well, a small bucket tied to it. He grasped the rope and let it run between his fingers.

'Can I help you, sir?'

A young woman had appeared from one of the less dilapidated houses.

'Thank you, but I'm just going to take a drink, if I may, and then I'll be on my way.'

'You look weary, and, if you don't mind my saying, you look hungry too. Come to the house and I'll make you some food.' Moses noticed that her speech was not the rough demotic of a peasant; this young woman had had an education. He wasn't entirely sure he should trust her.

'My thanks, but I don't want to put you out.'

'It's no hardship. My father would scold me for turning someone away who so obviously needed help.'

'Then I accept. Thank you.'

She led him to the house and invited him to sit on a crude stool while she prepared food. The rich aroma of spices made his mouth water; he couldn't remember the last time he'd had a proper meal.

'Where is your father?'

'He is tending our sheep; he will be along presently.'

'So he is a shepherd?'

'Among other things.' She brought him a platter of food and he devoured it. 'Sir, I will have to talk to my father first, but I think you should rest for a few days and eat with us. We can find you some work to do to pay for your board. There is always plenty to do.'

'I'll think on it.'

The house door sighed on its leather hinges and slid open. The man who stood in the doorway was tall and broad, and had the weathered look of one who spent most of his time out in the sun. He looked at Moses with curiosity and a little suspicion. 'Stranger; what brings you to my house?'

'Your daughter, sir; she was kind enough to offer me some food.'

'She was right to; we don't let travellers go hungry if we can help it. My name is Jethro; and you?'

Moses was taken by surprise. It hadn't occurred to him that he might need an alias. 'Menkhaf,' he said, without thinking.

'We are well met, Menkhaf. And my daughter is called Mariam. But you have already met.' Jethro smiled. 'So, Menkhaf, what brings you to Small Bitter Lake? You sound like a noble, but you look like a tramp. There must be a story behind that.'

'Forgive me, Jethro, but I would prefer to keep my story to myself, for now.'

'As you wish, Menkhaf. And where are you heading?'

'To tell you the truth, Jethro, I don't really know.'

Jethro laughed. There was a warmth in his laughter that made Moses feel he could trust him.

'Father, can we talk?' Mariam gestured with a curled finger.

Outside Moses heard the hum of their voices but couldn't make out what they were saying. When they came back in, Mariam was smiling. 'Mariam tells me she has invited you to stay for a while, and perhaps do some work for us. She has a good heart. I am happy for you to stay, provided you pay for your keep with a little labour. Are we agreed?'

'We are agreed.' Moses felt a burden lift form his shoulders. For a few days, at least, he could relax and worry about small things.

'Let me show you where you will sleep.' Mariam led him to a little outhouse; there was a straw pallet and a wooden shelf in the tiny space. 'This is perfect,' said Moses. 'If you don't mind, I will rest now, for a while.'

Mariam left and closed the door. Moses sank onto the pallet and fell asleep instantly.

* * *

Akhet-aten

'Djau, I can't marry Smenkhkare. Apart from anything else, I hate him.' The new pharaoh perched like an intruder on the throne; Djau could sense her discomfort. However, the council of nobles was adamant; they would not accept her on the throne without a man at her side.

'There are other options, highness.'

'What would you suggest? Should I pick some condescending boy from one of the great families?'

'I think you should avoid marrying an Egyptian unless it's one of your family. How about Thutankhaten, if you don't like Smenkhkare?'

'He's too young, Djau. I think the sooner I produce an heir, the safer I will sit on this ridiculously uncomfortable throne.'

'Then a foreigner. Perhaps one of the minor Hittite princes.'

'That is worth thinking about. How do we do that without giving the Hittite king the impression we're offering him Egypt?'

'Well, that is an issue, highness. But if we are careful in our approach, we may find a formula to suit all parties.'

'That will make an interesting letter. Can you do it, Djau?'

'I think so, highness.'

'Then make it so.'

'You were supposed to make things happen. How can I restore the elder gods if I am not sole Pharaoh?' Meritaten was angry. 'You said this would be easy, but you are beholden to nobles and sages; they run rings around you. Oh, why did I trust you? I should have left you alone and organised everything myself.'

Aye was down but not beaten yet. 'Madam, majesty, we need some time to organise things; don't worry. Your father took five years to establish Akhet-aten, five whole years, while my father and others just let time slip by. We can't change everyone's mind in an instant. They have to be led; some of their decisions must be shown to be wrong first. Just give us time.' *This woman is a stupid as her father. She might be my relative but our ancestors must have ordered extra stupidity for her part of the family.*

'I don't have time you stupid man. They are trying to find a husband for me. They will make me marry that idiot brother of mine if they find no one else. Djau pretends that he is on my side but he was my fathers' man, a son of Aten, a friend of Moses; how can he help me get what I want? He is, even as we speak, sending envoys around the world to find a prince whom he thinks he can manipulate. Oh, how stupid that man is. If he thinks . . .'

Aye interrupted 'He is sending envoys? Where to?'

'Oh, everywhere.' Meritaten's smile was sardonic at best. 'They are even sending a letter to the Hittites, our sworn enemies. How do they think that will end?'

Aye felt the hairs on the back of his neck rise and stiffen.

The tablet lay on Aye's table. He looked down at it again, and raised his eyes to meet his spy's. 'You have done well, Nekure. This information is exactly what we need.' He turned to a shelf, stretched out his arm, and took a pouch of gold from it. He handed it to Nekure; the spy weighed the pouch in his fist and smiled.

'I have one more job for you, Nekure.'

'Holiness?'

'It's important that this letter gets to its destination. Now that I have seen its contents and understand what others are trying to do, the letter must carry on its journey to its intended recipient. The fellow you took it from ...'

'The messenger? Dead, holiness.'

'That's a little inconvenient. Kit out one of your men in his uniform and send him off with it.'

'Holiness.'

Aye rose and made his way around his desk. 'How long will it take to reach the Hittite king?'

'For us, no more than ten days, Great One.'

'Then you had better hurry.'

Nekure banged an arm across his chest in salute to the high priest and, turning, took the tablet and left.

Aye went in search of his secretary. 'Setau, we need to see general Horemheb, and soon. Find him for me, would you?'

'Holiness.'

Horemheb looked like a man in a hurry; a hurry to be somewhere else. He practically squirmed under Aye's gaze.

'General, you see the problem.'

'I see it, priest, but I don't see an easy solution.' Aye's smirk told him he was missing something.

'Do you remember, Horemheb, some while ago, when we met in my merchant friend's garden, we discussed the relative merits of soldiers and assassins?'

'I remember.'

'Well, I think we may need your expertise here.'

'What would you have me do?'

'Oh, I don't suggest this is something you need to attend to personally, general. I'm sure you have men you can trust, men who will do what is necessary and not ask questions.'

Horemheb had an uncomfortable feeling he knew where the conversation was leading. But he wanted the high priest to actually say the words. 'Yes, I have such men.'

'Then ready them, general. This Hittite prince will ride with an escort to meet his new bride, I think.'

'And?'

'Well, an assassin is very useful when you are killing one or two, but when there are more, I think it's a job for soldiers.'

'You're serious, Aye?'

'Oh yes, I'm serious. Your men will lie in wait for the prince's party and ambush them. Make it look like bandits. And make sure they are all dead; we don't need word of this getting back to either royal court.'

Prince Zananza rode with a small escort, ten men he trusted. When his father had received the letter from Egypt on behalf of Meritaten, he had called for Zananza at once. 'You, my boy, are about to mount the throne of Egypt. In a manner of speaking.' Zananza winced; his father's sense of humour would have graced a fish trader, but a king? 'You don't like my sense of humour, boy?'

'You spent a small fortune hiring tutors from Syria, Greece and Persia to educate me. They did well; I can speak and read four languages and I'm the finest swordsman in the country. Did you really expect I'd turn out to be a thug with a taste for toilet jokes?'

His father wasn't cowed by his well-educated son's sarcasm. 'Idiot,' he had said, 'it doesn't matter how situations are described, it's what we do that counts. The council are offering you the chance to bond our empires and create a great state which will rule the world. Your talents with words and swords are of no consequence. Get yourself to Egypt, and quickly. And marry her before they change their minds.'

His father's words rang his mind as they came close to the border; a few hours and he would meet his new wife, and taste the reins of power in an exotic land; and, he thought sourly, fulfil his father's wishes. In front of him his first cousin, Ramiliamus, crested a hill and then promptly disappeared. The escort looked on in amazement.

'That must be the hole where Egypt used to be.' The joke brought raucous laughter from the escort.

'Quiet,' the Prince's chancellor said.

The Prince ignored him. 'Let's go and fish our cousin out of whatever hole he's fallen into. If it's Egypt, so much the better. We must be close by now.'

They made their way forward at a slow trot.

As they crested the hill, they saw Ramiliamus lying face down in the dirt, an arrow protruding from his neck. The next arrow took Zananza, and then a full volley cut the party to pieces. The few who survived that onslaught turned to flee, only to see a party of horsemen on the road behind them. The hidden archers had finished the job before the cavalry arrived.

* * *

'After what happened to Zananza, I doubt any other king will send his son to be slaughtered.' Djau straightened his tunic and picked a date from the bowl on the table. 'I think we are left with little choice, highness.'

'You mean I am left with little choice, Djau.'

'In order to keep the throne, majesty, you will have to reign jointly with Smenkhkare; otherwise they will take the crown from you and give it to him to wear alone.'

'I will have to marry the upstart, eh? Smenkhkare will think he's going to be pharaoh, and I'm just his little lady. I shall have to disabuse him of that idea.'

Djau did not envy the prince. 'You need an heir, highness. You said so yourself.'

'Yes, but I'm not going to . . . not with him. I'll just have to get one of the stable lads to impregnate me and slit his throat afterwards. I'm joking, Djau; I think.'

1333 BC

The Egyptian desert. Year 1 in the reign of
Smenkhkare and Meritaten

'Will you come with us, Menkhaf? It is time we went to worship the lord Aten.' Jethro had a bundle of cloth under his arm. Moses thought he could make out the disc of the sun on one of the sleeves.

'Gladly, Jethro. It has been some time since I made the rites.'

They walked a few miles in the pre-dawn light. Up ahead, Moses saw a small, mud-brick chapel. 'This is the house of worship?'

'That's it. A plain building, but we are plain people.'

Mariam led Moses into the roofless chapel. Jethro disappeared around the side of the building.

A small group of worshippers had already assembled in the chapel: farmers, shepherds, women from the surrounding villages. They held prayer beads and muttered private incantations while they waited for the rites to begin.

Jethro reappeared at the chapel door. He was dressed in the vestments of an Aten priest. Moses stifled an involuntary gasp with his hand. 'Mariam,' he whispered, 'your father...'

'Yes, Menkhaf, he is a priest of the lord. What, is it such a shock to find a priest out here among the peasants?' Mariam's voice was teasing.

'No, it's just … It's just a wonderful surprise to find that Jethro is a servant of the lord. And it explains a lot.'

'Such as why a peasant girl and her father seem to have received an education?'

'Yes, among other things.' Moses could not hide his embarrassment, or his pleasure. He was beginning to enjoy Mariam's company; perhaps too much.

The first hint of the sun's disc filtered into the tiny chapel. Jethro began the ritual incantations. 'Behold, he rises. Lord Aten rises, the day brings life, the sun brings life.'

Moses joined the others in the ritual responses. It was like bathing in a cool, clear stream. Afterwards, he felt refreshed and somehow reaffirmed in his faith. Their conversation on the way home was intense, and joyful.

Jethro sipped beer from his ceramic cup, seated on a tree stump outside the house. The moon was full, and the village was bathed in pale, silvery light. 'I would feel better about you leaving, Menkhaf, if I thought you had somewhere—anywhere—to go.'

Moses sat on the ground, his back against the house wall, enveloped in shadow. 'I appreciate that, Jethro. But I've lived on your generosity for long enough.'

'That's simply not an issue. The real point is, since I know nothing about you, I cannot advise you, and that makes me feel bad. Tell me this, at least. Do you have enemies? People who wish you harm?'

'Yes.'

'That's it? "Yes"?'

'I'm sorry, Jethro, I can't tell you more. If I did, it might put you, and Mariam, in danger.'

'Now I'm really curious. If you don't tell me more, I shall make you marry my daughter.' Jethro chuckled, and reached for more beer.

'Mariam is a wonderful young woman, and she will make someone a fine wife. But it cannot be me.'

'Are you married, then?'

'No, but …' Moses thought of Kiye, wondered what she was doing at that moment. He missed her so much.

'Ah, I understand. Love is a complex puzzle.'

'That's the truth, Jethro.'

They sat in companionable silence for a while, listening to the song of the cicadas. When Jethro leaned forward, Moses sensed there was more to say. 'If it helps you, Menkhaf, I have friends in the royal city, priests like myself. We exchange letters now and again. I could make enquiries, so you can find out if the circumstances that forced you to flee are resolved.'

'Jethro, that is immensely kind of you. I fear those circumstances will never be resolved. But news from Akhet-aten would be welcome.'

'Then we are agreed. You will give up this foolish notion of going off with nowhere to go; I will give up on my foolish hopes for my daughter, and we will see what news comes from the royal city.' They lapsed into silence again. The cicadas filled the space with their fricative song, little priests of Amun rattling sistrums. The moon disappeared behind a cloud, and for a few minutes the world was truly dark. Then it re-emerged, and Moses gave silent thanks for the light. For the light, and the good fortune he had found by the shores of the bitter lake.

***

Moses watched the ball of light as it sped across the sky, leaving a glowing trail behind it. He had read many times of star-stones, and seen their tiny cousins at night, but this was the first time he had seen one so large, and in the daytime too. He was fascinated.

His sheep, on the other hand, were terrified. He cooed and hissed at them to calm them, but they skittered around him, scared as much by the loud hiss of the fireball as by the sight of it.

'Quiet, my friends, it's no danger to us. Well, I hope not.'

The fireball was quite low in the sky now, and he had the distinct impression it was heading straight for him. He readied himself to leap out of the meteor's way, as if he could do such a thing. The sheep would have to fend for themselves.

About fifty paces below him, under the brow of the hill, stood a lone acacia bush. As he watched, the celestial fireball made a keening, whistling sound and dived into the bush, which immediately erupted in flames. He stepped closer, cautious; the bush was completely ablaze now.

The burning bush, and the glowing ball in the midst of it, mesmerised him. He felt the world sway around him, and an irresistible compulsion to move closer. The fire crackled and spat. As he drew closer, his mind a virtual blank, he thought he could hear a voice; a harsh, crackling voice, emanating from the bush. He couldn't make out the words, but he was sure the fire was talking to him.

He sank to his knees, and prayed aloud. 'Lord Aten, if this is you, or a message from you, uncover your servant's ears, so he can hear and understand you.' The incendiary monologue continued for a few more seconds, and then the fire subsided. Moses felt as if he was being released from a dream.

He stood up, and went a little closer. There, under the star-stone, he saw a rivulet of metal, shaped like a knife. It was pointing south. The omen was too strong to ignore.

'Menkhaf! Are you all right? I saw the fireball and thought it was coming straight for you.'

Jethro strode up the hill, his dogs beside him. When they saw the sheep scattered across the hillside, they went to work, rounding them up and settling them into a small flock.

'It's just a star-stone, Jethro, though quite a large one. But look, it has offered me some star-metal.'

'Only a high priest of Amun carries star-metal; or a pharaoh.'

'It's not just a gift, Jethro; it's a message.'

His friend studied the remains of the bush, and the sliver of metal, and returned his gaze to Moses. 'So, now I think you will tell me more of your story.'

'My name is not Menkhaf.'

Jethro tipped his head back and laughed; the sound filled the little valley below them. 'I knew that the day we met. Is that the best tale you can offer?'

'My name is Moses.'

Jethro wasn't laughing now. His eyes widened, and he prostrated himself. 'Lord Moses!'

Moses stepped forward quickly and lifted Jethro to his feet. 'You are my friend; I will not have you on your face like this.' He grinned impishly. 'And anyway, you were facing downhill; that can't be good for you.'

'Lord . . . Moses. How can I serve you?'

'For now, by telling no one.' He saw Jethro's rueful expression and smiled. 'Well, perhaps you can tell your grandchildren.'

'I suppose that will have to do.'

'Jethro, this is an omen. The metal points south, to Akhet-aten. It is time that I returned. And the metal is a message too. I think there is danger ahead.'

'Then wait a couple of days. I'll take the metal to Menor, the smith, and he can shape it into a blade for you. When you are armed, and provisioned, you can go with my blessing.' He paused, embarrassed. 'Not that I should be blessing you.'

1332 BC

Akhet-aten. Year 2 in the reign of Smenkhkare and Meritaten

The palace gates were locked for the night. Paser cursed his luck; he'd pulled night duty for a week now, after falling foul of the chief of the guards. He hadn't meant to hurt the fool of an official; but when he insulted Paser's father, he couldn't help himself. It was only a slap, but he was a big man, bigger than his father had been. The official's nose had spread all over his face.

There was something about the figure approaching the gate. He didn't look like a royal messenger, or a soldier, but he carried himself with the bearing of a man of substance. 'Halt,' Paser called out. 'Who goes there?'

The man at the gate pulled back the cowl of his travelling cloak and, just for an instant, Paser's breath deserted him. 'Lord Moses!' Paser dropped to the ground and prostrated himself in front of the stranger. 'Lord, bless me. It is a long time since I had a blessing.' Moses removed Paser's hat and placed his hands on the guard's skull. It felt good to be home and felt better to be wanted again. 'May the Lord Aten bless you and keep you in eternal happiness.'

Paser rose, kissed Moses hand, smiled a huge smile and raced down the steps to the gatehouse. 'Setka, open the postern gate. It's Lord Moses.'

'Yeah, and I'm the ghost of Akhenaten.'

'Setka, you fool, I'm telling you the truth. Open the damn gate or I'll tell old frosty-chops what you were doing when I came in.'

Setka hastily put away the wine jug and struggled to his feet. 'You'd better not be playing a joke, Paser, or I'll have a few things to tell the captain myself.' He stepped out of the gatehouse, and slid back the bolts on the postern.

Moses stepped into the palace courtyard. Setka fell to his knees. 'Oh, my lord Moses,' he said. 'It's good to have you back, Lord.'

'Will you take me to an official? I must make my presence known, officially.'

'At once, lord.'

They crossed the palace yard and Setka knocked at the night door. 'Open up! Lord Moses is here.'

A scrabble of bolts, and the door opened onto a lamp-lit corridor.

'Hanef, take Lord Moses to the chancellor.'

Moses turned in the doorway. 'Wait. What is your name?'

'Setka, lord.'

'Setka, could you deliver a message for me?' Moses whispered in his ear.

'I understand, lord. I'll do it now.'

Djau had just finished his evening meal, and was contemplating a visit to a lady of his acquaintance, when the servant rushed into the room.

'What's the hurry, Hanef?'

'We have a visitor, lord, a very distinguished visitor.'

'What distinguished visitor chooses to arrive like a thief in the night?'

'I do, Djau. Will you throw me out?' Moses came from the shadows and shook the hand of his trusted lieutenant.

'Lord Moses. You are a sight for sore eyes.'

'Thank you, Djau; it's good to see you too. Now, tell me; what is the situation here? Will I be welcome?'

'Most certainly you will. I'll update you as we make our way to the royal apartments. Follow me.'

'The pharaoh's will be glad to see you, especially Smenkhkare; he has kept the empire and the royal dynasty together. Be careful of Meritaten though, she has not recovered from having to share the crown. She has acted totally out of character my lord; as a spoilt child rather than a great queen. We have tried for many moons now to find you; I thought you were dead, but here you are, my lord, back in the fold.'

Smenkhkare and Meritaten sat in silence at the dinner table. They had nothing to say to each other. Meritaten took a sip of wine, and stood up. 'I'm off to my bedchamber. You amuse yourself as you wish. That little chamber maid seems quite taken with you, heaven knows why.'

Smenkhkare was still working up to a suitable riposte when the guard rapped on the door. 'The lord Djau and another.'

'Enter,' said Meritaten, irritated by the interruption.

The doors slid open.

Meritaten's jaw dropped. 'Uncle Moses!'

Smenkhkare ran over to greet him, throwing his arms around him. 'Oh, my dear uncle, how wonderful!'

Moses felt good.

Smenkhkare allowed his uncle out of his arms. 'Come. Sit down. Eat. Tell us what has happened to you. We have been so worried about you. We have searched . . .'

Meritaten sat silently, a scowl on her face. 'Why have you not been arrested, Uncle?' she asked

'Why do you ask?'

'You are an outlaw. They say you killed our father . . .'

Moses ate and Djau remained silent and calm at the door; Smenkhkare talked incessantly about the state of the kingdom, the troubles on the borders, the constant bickering with Aye and his priests. His wife stayed silent and cast a cooling shadow on proceedings.

'Tomorrow you will resume your official position as high priest of Aten,' Smenkhkare announced without giving Meritaten a chance to object.

'Are you sure that's wise?' Meritaten said.

'Wise or not, that's what will be.'

'What will the people think?' asked Moses.

'The people know the lies. They still have you in their hearts. They will be pleased that you have returned safely.'

'And Aye?'

'Aye will be secretly pleased, uncle; it will give him something else to conspire about.'

'Meritaten?'

'I disagree, Uncle, but I have no choice. Your return to the high office will set the cat among the pigeons, and the Theban priests will once again attack the family. This is insane.'

'That's settled then,' said Smenkhkare. 'Djau, let's meet first thing tomorrow and make the necessary arrangements and announcements.'

'Highness.' Djau left the apartment, his head full of plans.

'Uncle, let's find you a room for the night. You can resettle in your own apartment tomorrow.'

1331 BC

Mycenae. Northern Mediterranean.

Year 3 in the reign of Smenkhkare and Meritaten

The sound came from the deep. It was the voice of a god, a rumbling, guttural voice. And the god was angry.

The shepherds who were tending their sheep near the coast heard it first. The sound came from the ocean and the land shuddered beneath their feet. They looked around in consternation; the ocean and the earth did not normally dance together.

When a second tremor shook the ground, the shepherds decided it was time to get back to the village. The animals had already made up their minds, and streamed ahead of them, bleating in fear. The men hurried to catch them up.

The rumblings became more persistent as they made their way home. The gods seemed to be angry with them; they needed to seek out the priest and ask him to pray to Poseidon, to placate him.

Arriving back at the village they found only confusion. People were out in the mud encrusted streets, running around like lost souls. There was nowhere to escape to, no safe haven. No one had experienced such a thing before.

There was a moment of stillness; silence, as if time had been suspended. It didn't last. The ground rumbled, and then it moved again, but, this time it lifted and, with a god-like heave, it split asunder.

On the island of Danaus, the family Telchine were working their ancient vineyards, which stretched down the side of the mountain. They had a beautiful view of the almost transparent turquoise waves which lapped along the shore.

Amongst those tending the vines an old man groaned and stood. His aching back needed stretching; if only he were young again. He looked outwards across the sea, and saw a small column of smoke begin to make its way toward the sky. It seemed insignificant but, as he knelt down to carry on his work, the plume grew. A few hours later, it was monstrous.

On the northern coast of Egypt, nothing out of the ordinary was happening, no rumbling voices from the sea, no sudden movement of the earth, no smoke rising like an omen in the distance, just some wispy strands of cloud frolicking along the horizon. Life went on as normal—for now.

* * *

Akhet-aten.

'I don't know where these rumours about the new Hittite king, Arnuwanda's, paternity came from.' Djau sighed. 'As far as I can see, he is every inch his father's son. The Hittites think every problem can be solved with a sword.' The chancellor looked up from the map he had been poring over. 'And he is no diplomat. We've offered generous terms to send him home, and he's refused.'

'So, what do you advise, Djau?' Moses paced the room. 'Do we go to war with the Hittites, again?'

'I fear we must, Moses. We can't have them threaten our northern borders like this. The Syrian kingdoms expect our protection, and they should have it.'

'Well this will cheer old Horemheb up, at least. He's never happy unless he's out on campaign.'

'And more to the point, it keeps him out of mischief.' Djau allowed himself a sly grin. 'If he and Aye spend any more time together we'll have to marry them off.'

'And a fine couple they make. I'll send for the general.'

'Talk to Smenkhkare too. He ought to review the troops before they set off.'

The officers were playing skittles in the barracks yard. Wagers were laid, and money changed hands. Horemheb sat on a stool, his mind wandering, while his aide-de-camp, Khuenre, threw and missed completely. 'Gods, Khuenre, if you throw a spear like that I don't give much for your chances in the field,' a voice from the behind him shouted.

Khuenre was one shot away from winning. He tried to hide his anger with a smile. 'Hey, Banefre, what a story to blurt out as I was aiming; you put me off my shot.' *Good excuse that.* 'Did they really say the sea was on fire?'

'I promise you, that's what they said.'

'And these were sailors?'

'Yes, Mycenaeans. They said they were afraid to return home.'

'What is all this nonsense?' Horemheb hadn't really been paying attention.

'Banefre here met some Mycenaean sailors, and they filled his ears with some poppycock about the sea catching fire.'

'Were they drunk, or were you? Next you'll be telling me there are frogs falling out of the sky.'

Banefre got no time to reply. A breathless messenger ran into the yard, and headed for the knot of officers. 'General, sir, a message from the palace.'

'Well, hand it over.'

'Sir.'

Horemheb read the scroll, and a smile spread over his features. 'Well, gentlemen, it seems we shall be playing a more interesting game than skittles. The Hittite king, what's his name ...'

'Arnuwanda, sir.'

'Thank you, Khuenre; it's good someone around here is awake. Yes, Arnuwanda is playing silly buggers on the Syrian borders again. The pharaoh has asked us to go and teach him a lesson.'

A ragged cheer went up from the officers. They had been idle for too long. Horemheb was happy too; he might be getting a bit old for soldiering, but at least going on campaign kept him out of that damned priest's clutches.

Smenkhkare stood on the royal dais and watched as the troops filed onto the field. They formed up into battalions, new recruits jostling for position with old hands. Horemheb rode ahead of them, and gave a signal to his battalion commanders. Slowly, the mass of soldiers wheeled into position, and marched past the royal dais. Smenkhkare saluted them, and reached for a glass of wine.

The darkness caught them all by surprise. The sun disappeared in a thick mass of clouds; the clouds piled up until the sky was as dark as night. Horemheb looked over to the edge of the parade ground; he could only just make out the pylons at the gate. The clouds seemed to be as thick at ground level as they were above.

'What on earth is that?'

'I don't know, sir, but the men don't like it. They are muttering about omens.'

'Well, get down there and make them see sense.'

'That would be easier, sir, if any of us had the remotest idea what's going on.'

'Oh, do your best, man. We don't have time to send for an astronomer. We should be on the march.'

'I think we should wait until this stuff lifts, or until we know what it is at least.'

Horemheb sighed, and gave the signal for the troops to return to barracks. The Hittites would have to wait for their game of skittles. He looked up at the sky, and shivered. Something about this was not right; not right at all.

In Akhet-aten rumours spread quickly. The world was on fire. The sea had collapsed. The sky was falling in.

* * *

Miriam hardly left the house; the gloom outside frightened her to her marrow. She couldn't imagine any natural event that would be so ominous. Her neighbours talked in whispers about gods and spirits; about war in the sky between the new god and the old gods of Thebes. She didn't join in; things were bad enough without supernatural rumours.

When the knock at the door came she hurried to open it, thinking it might be old Yuffu, coming to offer some common sense. But it turned out to be her cousin, Herit, a lady's hand maid for one of the noble families in the city.

'Miriam, thank the gods you're here. I was worried I'd lose my way. Can I wait with you for a bit until this clears up?'

'Of course, Herit, come in. Where were you?'

'It's my day off, so I thought I'd go down to the Nile, buy some treats from the pedlars, and dip my feet in the river. But the river . . . '

'What's wrong with it?'

'It's stopped, Miriam; it's not moving at all. There are dead fish all over the surface.'

'That sounds scary.'

'It is, trust me. This mist, or cloud, or whatever it is. It's making people cough, and my eyes were streaming. There's a strange grey dust over everything. I don't know, Miriam, I'm not a priest. But I don't remember it being like this before we all became Atenists. I think it's an omen, a bad one.'

'Nonsense, Herit, you see; in a few days this will all be forgotten. Sit down and eat some soup. I'll warm it up. Oh; the fire's gone out.'

The preacher stood on an upturned wine crate at the edge of the square. Here in the artisans' district there were always a few people doing nothing; a preacher was entertainment after a fashion. He pushed back the cowl of his cloak and one or two people looked up; this wasn't an Aten priest, or a mad itinerant prophet, it was a priest of Amun.

'What's he doing in Akhet-aten?' said Aneksi. 'If the palace guard catch him, he's for it.'

'He's just drumming up some business, I expect. That lot in Thebes must be stuck for something to do.' Baufre scratched his head and snitched a piece of fruit from a passing pedlar. 'Let's hear what he has to say, shall we? Should be good for a laugh.'

'Let's go a bit closer, then. This foggy stuff isn't just hard to see through; sound doesn't carry either.'

The crowd in front of the preacher was small; although the mysterious cloud had lifted a little that day, many people were still too frightened to leave their houses.

'People of the godless city,' intoned the preacher.

'Oi, steady, mate. We've got one god here for starters.' Pentu's jibe got a few laughs from the crowd. Baufre and Aneksi went to join him. 'So, he's the straight man and you're the comedian, eh?' Baufre gave him a playful slap.

'Think, people; remember. Before the heretic pharaoh brought you here, before this godless city was built, do you recall mysterious plagues and omens, darkness in the middle of the day, one poor harvest following on the heels of another? No, you don't; because such things never happened before. This is not a coincidence. This is a consequence.'

No one was heckling him now; he had their complete attention.

'Let me tell you something else. In Thebes, there was no plague. In Thebes, the skies are not covered over. In Thebes, the old gods reign, the true gods, and under their protection, we have seen none of these catastrophes. Think on that: your pharaoh brings you here, to the middle of nowhere, and gets you to build him a city. No sooner is the last brick in place but disaster strikes. Not just once, but again and again. How much proof do you need?'

The sermon was interrupted when a young boy ran into the square, shouting. 'Holiness, the palace guards are coming. There are dozens of them.'

The preacher pulled the cowl of his cloak down over his face and slipped away with the dissipating crowd.

By the time the guards arrived, the square was empty.

1330 BC

*Akhet-aten. Year 4 in the reign of Smenkhkare
and Meritaten*

'There, Herit, look; the sky is clear again. Whatever it was, it's gone.' Miriam stood in the garden. 'And listen; the birds are singing again. All's well, cousin.'

Herit came out hesitantly, looking in all directions. 'You're right, Miriam, it's gone. I'd better get back to the big house. They'll think I've run off with a soldier.'

Miriam gave Herit a hug and sent her on her way. She turned back into the house and started on the job of cleaning off the dust that seemed to have settled everywhere. It had a strange consistency, more like ash than dust. An hour later, the house was clean again and she had gathered a pile of dust in the corner of the garden; she had no idea what she would do with it.

The sun was shining; people came out of their houses and went about their normal business. There was a palpable sense of relief in the air. Miriam decided she would go to the market and get some fresh food; she was a little tired of cold soup.

In the market square, there was a small crowd around a man who looked like a priest of Amun. *What's he doing here?* she thought. *The palace guard will be here any minute.* She bought a few groceries and was about to head for home when she saw a commotion in the square. The palace guards were dragging the priest off. Most people laughed, but a few were struggling with the guards, trying to free the priest. 'Leave him alone; he's only speaking the truth.'

* * *

In the barracks yard the officers were playing skittles again. The Syrian campaign had been called off; scouts reported that the Hittites were just as scared of the dust cloud as everyone else. They had fled Syria and made their way home.

'Well done, Khuenre,' said a surprised officer. 'You got them all.'

'Thanks, now hand over the money. What's that?'

The officers looked up. A black cloud towered on the horizon. 'That looks like a thunderstorm from hell,' said a fresh-faced sergeant.

'It's moving pretty fast too.'

'Bloody fast; it's nearly here.' A hailstone the size of a fist crashed into the yard. 'Gods! What is that?'

A water pot broke into shards. The soldiers ran for cover. 'Wait!' shouted Khuenre. 'We need to make sure the horses are safe.'

A few brave souls headed for the stable yard. The horses were in a panic. Khuenre leaped over the corral rail and opened the stable doors; the horses streamed in, with the occasional panicked neigh as a hailstone hit. 'Right, let's get out of this mess and into the barracks.' He started off at a good rate of knots, then staggered and fell. The others rushed over to him. 'He's been hit; he's out cold.'

They picked him up between them and ran off clumsily towards the barracks. Inside, the medic checked him over. 'He'll live, but he has a lump on his head the size of a goose egg.'

An officer looked out the window at the hailstones that continued to fall. 'I doubt he's had the worst of it.'

It was nearly two days before the hail subsided.

Intef went out to look at his crops; here, right up against the banks of the Nile, the ground was rich and crops grew easily. He stopped in dismay, and surveyed his fields. The crops were smashed and flattened. Near the field boundary he saw a dead cow, its belly already beginning to bloat. 'Oh, no,' he cried. 'That corpse will poison what's left of my crop.'

He walked on; there seemed to be dead animals, small and large, everywhere. The hailstones that had caused the carnage had disappeared completely. He saw his neighbours, wandering as he was, trying to find something they could salvage from the disaster. *Good luck with that*, he thought. 'Dedi,' he called. Dedi, a stout man of Hyksos origin, turned and waved. 'Doesn't look good, does it?'

'It really doesn't. Here, Dedi, do you fancy bringing your handcart round to my lower field?'

'What for?'

'I need to move a dead cow.'

Using a thick rope and the help of a few neighbours, Intef and Dedi had managed to manhandle the cow onto the cart. Now they trudged slowly towards a fallow field on the rise above Intef's farm to dispose of it.

'Dedi, I'm sorry about that.'

'It's no bother, Intef, you'd do the same for me; if you were wise enough to get yourself a cart.'

'No, I don't mean that; I mean the cut on your arm.'

'I haven't cut myself. Oh.'

Dedi held out his arm; a stain of red spread into a blot on his forearm. As they looked, another one appeared, and then another. Intef looked up, and felt a drop hit his eye. Intef shuddered. 'Dedi, what is this? First hail the size of my head, now rain that looks like blood.'

'Sod it, I'm off. I need to get out of this horrible stuff. Let's leave the cow where she is; she won't mind the rain.'

They sprinted off together, splitting up at the crossroads that separated their farms. Intef got in to find his wife staring through the doorway, a look of resignation on her face. 'This will ruin us, Intef.'

'Not just us, love. I hate to think what this country will look like when the crops fail again.'

'Keep going, girl, keep going. Just another mile or two and we can stop.' Sabaf wasn't sure his horse could understand him, but it made him feel better to say something, and her foam-flecked flanks showed her exhaustion. Tanis was a blur on the horizon now; he was nearly there.

He felt the heat of the sun through the sweat-stained tunic and grimaced. *I should have brought a fresh cloak with me. I didn't have time to think of it.* He was at the outskirts of the city now, and people in the streets stared at the travel-stained rider careering along the main road.

The governor's mansion was right in the centre of the city, set behind high mud-brick walls and surrounded by a garden full of delicate, fragrant plants from all over the known world. Sabaf drew up outside the gates and leaped from his mare. A stable boy appeared and took her away for a drink and a much-needed brush down. *Well, at least you're getting what you need, old girl.*

He staggered up the steps to the entrance, where two burly guards blocked his way, their spears crossed. 'If you're looking to beg some food, you should go round the back to the kitchen; and to tell you the truth, I don't fancy your chances.'

'I need to speak to the governor. It's urgent.'

'I need to be two fingers taller, but it's not happening today. Governor's busy.'

'I'm not some vagabond on a stolen horse, man. Now, go and talk to someone with some rank, and a brain, and then let me in.'

'If you think I'm going to let you insult me...'

'Guard!'

'Sir.' Sabaf's pugnacious obstacle stepped back and his face turned from ferocious to sheepish.

'Sabaf, is that you?' The tall man who followed him up the steps had narrow features and a penetrating gaze. 'What happened? Have you been set upon by bandits?'

'There's no time, Sahrak. I have to see the governor; it's an emergency.'

Sahrak pushed the spears aside and led Sabaf into the cool interior. Fern fronds graced the entrance hall. 'You, boy,' he gestured to a servant. 'Tell the governor he has a visitor. 'And you,' he beckoned a young woman over. 'Find our guest some water to bathe in and a fresh tunic. He's had a hard ride.'

'My thanks, Sahrak, but I really ought to see the old man straightaway.'

'You know what he's like. If you're clean and neat he'll take more notice of you.'

Sabaf sighed in resignation and took the bowl of cool water the servant girl offered him. *I suppose a few minutes more won't make the disaster any more or less disastrous.* He had to admit he felt better after a quick wash and a change of tunic.

'So, what's the big emergency? Are we invaded?' Sahrak led him along the shady corridor to the governor's office.

'So, to speak. If you can call a mountain of dead fish an invasion.'

'Sounds intriguing, in a smelly sort of way. Mind if I stay and listen?'

'Be my guest; I'm yours.'

Sahrak rapped smartly on the door. 'Enter.'

No matter how often Sabaf came here, it never failed to surprise him. The governor's office contained more fragrant plants than the garden. The aroma was overpowering; Sahrak, after a glass of wine one evening, had described it as like the waiting room in a high-class brothel.

'Sabaf, what brings you here? We're not due a delivery for a week.'

'You may be waiting more than a week, sir. I've come straight from the coast. There are dead fish littering the shore for miles. I've got people salvaging what they can before rot sets in, but it doesn't look good.'

'So first the sea catches fire and then it throws all the fish out? Were they cooked?' The governor snorted a brief patrician laugh. 'Sorry, Sabaf, ignore me. Do you think it's a local problem?'

'No, sir. I spoke to some fishermen from the delta. Same thing happened there yesterday.'

'Gods! Damn it, what are we supposed to say now there's only one god?'

'I don't know if this has anything to do with gods, sir.'

'It has everything to do with gods, my friend, one way or another. I'll send a messenger to the capital and let the bigwigs know.' He frowned. 'Between this and the low Nile flood, I am thinking it's going to be a long year.'

* * *

Aye was pleased with events. Meritaten could sense it.

'And how does Amun propose we rid the world of my brother and uncle?'

'We will strive to make you pharaoh, highness; you alone.'

'Oh, you have been saying that for years now, old man. You have been beaten at every turn. I sit and wait but nothing happens. Smenkhkare keeps the crown and Moses the priesthood. The world could come to an end and they would still be there; the people are still with them Aye, not with you.'

'Every day brings more chaos to the country, every year the Nile shrinks and the harvest gets smaller. The people will get to a point where they must see the light, and the nobility will have no choice but to turn to Amun and the gods of old. Then, when that happens, we will urge them to denounce Smenkhkare and dispose of the heretic Moses. Just wait a little while longer and pray to Amun to hurry things along. All will be well, you wait and see.'

'Wait and see; that's all you ever have to say. It had better be sooner rather than later. My patience is running out.'

Meritaten turned and left the temple.

Aye presided over the assembled priests with a look of feline satisfaction painted across his face. 'Setau, would you be so kind as to inform us of the situation regarding food and provisions?'

'Holiness. The granaries are full, including the two spare buildings we've turned over to storage.'

'How?' The priest who spoke looked, Aye thought, like he'd visited the granaries a few times too often.

'For the last three years, we've been sending wagon caravans across the secret desert road to those weird farmer-astronomers by the great lake of Chad. They always have a surplus and we've bought several large consignments from them.'

'Why?' asked Patenemheb. 'Did we predict the famine?'

Ah, Patenemheb, still asking the wrong questions. Still an irritating son of a dog.

'It was a precaution at first; in case the Atenist's decided to go on the offensive and we found ourselves cut off or surrounded. Then the first low flood came and we bought more. We also have two hundred head of cattle from Nubia and two barns full of dried meat and fish.' Setau laid his clay tablet on the table and sat down. 'In short, we're not going to starve, not by a long way.'

'But surely the capital will call on us for help. They have spies here; they will know we have food.'

'They do indeed, and we want them to know. As for giving them any of our food, well, we'll certainly send a few wagons of grain and dried meat. But we'll retain the bulk of it; for our own use and to feed people outside the capital.' Aye sat back and steepled his fingers. 'I think we should be generous where we can; but the pharaoh's followers will have to ask Aten for help.'

Setau raised his hand from the table, a prearranged signal. 'Yes, Setau; there is more?'

'Holiness, I have a report from Akhet-aten on the activities of our missionaries. They are sowing the seeds of discontent, and their efforts are paying off.'

'Well, they are the only seeds thriving this year.' Aye nodded in appreciation of the polite laughter around the table. 'And have we lost any? Missionaries, I mean?'

'A few have been captured by the palace guard and thrown into the royal gaol, but if anything, that's only helping. The people don't like seeing priests imprisoned.'

'So, gentlemen, the situation puts us at a real advantage, perhaps for the first time in some years. I strongly recommend we use our advantage and press our attack on the monotheists. More missionaries, more rumours. Are we agreed?'

Hands rose around the table; even the surly Patenemheb raised his. The taste of impending victory lingered on every tongue. Aye closed the meeting and, after the prophets had left, called Setau over. 'Setau, I have a funny feeling one of our less trustworthy servants will be heading for the capital very soon; have him followed, would you?'

Setau's face was a question.

'No, don't have him killed. We want him to arrive safely.'

The rider made it to the palace gates as the sun was setting. In the courtyard he dragged himself from his weary horse—his fifth mount that day—and stretched painfully. *I need a bath. But Lord Moses won't thank me for being clean and late.*

Moses listened as patiently as he could; the spy had a lot to say. When he'd finished, Thethi dismissed him. 'Go and bathe, and find yourself a bed. You can rest here for a couple of days before you return south.'

'Sir.' The man wheeled dizzily and left the room.

'Are they really hoarding food in the midst of a famine?' Moses could barely believe what he'd heard. 'Aye's always been a devious bastard, but letting thousands of people die so he can win a theological argument is plumbing new depths, even for him.'

'I think it's actually worse than that. He is in a position to let a good number of us starve and then step in, like Min on that mural in On, handing out baskets of grain.'

'And this secret desert road; can we use it and buy grain from Chad?'

'Too late for this year; and those folk don't trust strangers. The priest has us over a barrel.'

'I'd like to put him in one, and nail the lid on.' Moses slammed his fist on the table.

'What would you like me to do?'

'Assassinate the high priest of Amun.' Moses laughed grimly. 'Actually, you could question a couple of those missionaries we've picked up. See if we can persuade one or two of them to tell all in public. So no visible injuries, Thethi.'

'Highness.'

Moses' anger grew as he hurried along the main corridor of the palace towards the royal apartments. Aye was planning to hold a starving nation to ransom; he had to be stopped. He swept into the apartment to find Smenkhkare reading letters from the chaotic pile on his desk.

'Uncle. What news?'

'Aye . . .' Moses clenched his fists. 'Aye is hoarding food, tons of it. He plans to keep it until we have starved and then hand it out to the people. Then he'll look like the saviour, and the Theban gods will be back in the ascendancy. I could kill him. In fact, I think we should kill him, now. Ah!'

He clasped his hands to his face and collapsed onto a divan. Meritaten chose that moment to enter the room. 'Uncle, are you well?'

'Where have you been, niece? The country is in a state of ruin and you're never here.'

Meritaten reddened. 'I was praying, Uncle,' she lied.

'Uncle Moses thinks we should assassinate Aye. What do you say, wife? Shall we kill him and start a war?'

'It doesn't have to be war.' Moses had calmed down, a little. 'He killed your father without one. We could do the same, if we're quick and clever.'

'I don't think it would serve us to be seen as the killers of the high priest; not when the country is in crisis. We are better than that, Uncle. If we do something so drastic now, we're more or less admitting what the missionaries are saying.'

'Nonsense; the missionaries are gadflies. No one listens to them.' Moses stood and paced the room.

'Actually, quite a lot of people are listening to them. We've discovered a couple of secret sanctuaries in the city. Some are worshipping the old gods again.'

'Then we'll kill them too!' Moses' voice had risen to a shrill falsetto. 'No, what am I saying?' He sat down again, his head in his hands. 'Sorry, sorry; I'm not in my right mind. You're right; we can't kill Aye. The missionaries are succeeding, and throwing them in prison is only making them look better. What do we do? Lord, what do we do?'

Meritaten turned to her uncle. 'You know, Uncle, if my thoughts were not those of a witless female, I would say that the country is in the middle of a plethora of plagues, the Amun priests are praying for these plagues and the old gods are giving them what they want.' She drifted onto the balcony; she didn't want the others to see the look of victory on her face. Moses was becoming increasingly erratic; was he succumbing to the same madness as her father? Was that the inevitable fate of Aten's prophets? *So much the better for me.*

* * *

Tener adjusted the strap on her basket and hacked at the rock. The child moaned again, an eerie sound. She lifted him out of the basket and comforted him, but the uncanny moan went on. *Not now, child, there's no time. If we don't work, we don't eat.* She settled to work again, gritting her teeth and trying to ignore the song of distress.

'Tener, take that young fellow home and find a physician. He's unsettling the crew.'

'I can't, Ani, I need the work. Please.'

The foreman loomed over her. 'Tener, you're in the way. Look, I'll pay you for today, but take the boy home. He needs help.'

'Thanks, Ani.' She set her tools down and headed for home. Her son's moans were rising into screams. People stared at her as she passed. *Quiet, Hepzefa. We'll be home in a minute. Quite, child, please.*

The physician was nonplussed. 'He has a fever, and he's dry to the touch. Let him rest, give him plenty of water, and let's see how it goes.' He put his instruments back in his satchel and headed for the door. 'Send for me if he gets worse.'

Hepzefa did get worse, and quickly, but Tener didn't send for the physician. By the time the pustules appeared on her son's face, she knew it was too late.

* * *

Meritaten was terrified. The son she had given birth to not two months previously was gravely ill. The lumps on his throat and his groin were growing as she watched; and now blood seeped from his penis. 'Is it the same pestilence?' she asked the physician.

'The same, or similar. I have heard accounts from all over the city. The illness looks like the pestilence that took your grandmother, and your sisters, but it is only affecting infants, and only in families where the infant is the first-born. If I didn't know better …'

'If you didn't know better, what?'

'I'd say it was the work of the gods.'

'That's heresy, Djedefhor.'

'That's as may be, highness, but this plague is not like others. Normally sickness doesn't choose its victims so carefully.'

'Can you do anything for him?' She looked down at the infant prince; he had slipped into unconsciousness.

'I fear not, highness. Now is the time for prayer.' Djedefhor bowed and backed out of the room. *Fool*, he thought. *She'll have you followed now, and you'll lead them to the secret chapel. Best make yourself scarce for a while.* He hurried to the palace gate, and from there to the nearest stables. 'I need a horse,' he said. 'Whatever it costs. I won't stay in this cursed city a moment longer.' He mounted and rode south, heading for safety.

He had to rein his horse in when he got to the main square. There was a large crowd, listening to one of those travelling Amun priests. The man was shouting, apparently unafraid of the palace guard. 'See, the pestilence is among you again. Who will save you? The one god who has caused all this? The unnatural pharaoh who lies with her brother? The apostate who abandons you and leaves whenever trouble raises its head? No, people of Akhet-aten, they will not save you. Look to yourselves. Look to the gods of old. Do it now, before it is too late.'

He rode on, leaving the clamour behind.

It took Meritaten two days to find her uncle. When the riots started, he had gone into hiding. Finally, she received a message from Kiye, saying she knew where he was. Now he stood on the balcony beside her and watched as the great temple of Aten succumbed to the mob. It wasn't the only building being attacked; Moses could see several noble houses burning, and wherever the crowds gathered, he could make out the travelling priests, urging the rioters on.

'Can't we send in the palace guard? If we make a show of force, the crowds will disperse and those damn priests will have no one to incite.'

'I think it's too late for that, uncle. We need to give them something now, before they tear the city to the ground. If only we had a stock of food to hand out.'

'This isn't about food, Meritaten; this is Theban work, and you know it.'

'It is about food: about food, and sickness, and strange weather. The priests are making it worse, of course. But they didn't bring plague and famine.'

'So what do you propose, highness?'

Meritaten looked sharply at her uncle; he only usually called her 'highness' in jest, or when he was being sarcastic. And this was not the time for jokes.

'I've discussed it with Smenkhkare. I'm going to reinstate freedom of religion. I don't understand why you took it away in the first place.'

'I didn't, Meritaten; that was your father's doing.'

'Well, whoever lit the torch, the house is burning. I think, if Aye sees we're ready to compromise, he'll finally release his stocks of food and relieve the famine.'

'He won't stop there and you know it. If you give him this, he'll want more.'

'And what would you have us do? Shall we stand here and relish our piety while the world burns around us? No, Moses; piety has got us nowhere. We've been so busy playing god we forgot to play politics. We need to start again, and soon; we are on the brink of losing the game.'

'Is this why Smenkhkare isn't here? Is he too ashamed of your capitulation?'

'No, he's a weakling, and you can play him too easily.'

'You have become hard, Meritaten. Power has changed you.'

'Do I have a choice? All the men in my family either go mad or run away when things get difficult.'

'That's not fair.'

'It's the truth, fair or not. And it's ironic too.'

'How so?'

'Because I'm about to suggest you run away again.'

Moses was stunned. Lost for words, he looked out over the city again. In the artisans' market square, he watched as the front of a wine shop collapsed outwards, trapping several of the rioters. *They are hurting and killing themselves when they really want to hurt me*, he thought. *And now Meritaten is exiling me.*

'Look well, uncle; what I'm suggesting is for your own good. If you stay, you will be killed; whether by an angry mob or a Theban assassin, it will happen. You need to leave, and you need to stay away; if and when some sort of order is restored, I will send someone to find you.'

But not to bring me back. Are you a threat to my life too, Meri?

'If I go, I'll take my supporters with me. That will be more people than you can afford to lose.'

'That would be a good idea. If they stay here, they will be vilified, or worse, and the mob will go for them; it would be chaos. Yes, best without all of you.'

'And what will you do, niece? Will you surrender to the priests?'

She almost spat her reply. 'What? Do you think I'm some sort of weak-kneed little girl? I'll find a compromise because the country requires it. Then I will rule, Moses, as a pharaoh should. I will lead Egypt back to greatness, and I will not sacrifice the good of our people for a theological whim. And Smenkhkare will be put back in his kennel, to dabble in books and pretty chamber maids, hidden away in a temple in Thebes. I will have no interference from anyone.'

'It's not...'

'Spare me, uncle. If you want to believe in a single god, that is your privilege and right. Your privilege, because you have the wealth and education to make the choice without constraint; your right, because you are a free man. But you do not have the right to bring down an empire, an empire that has stood against every challenge for two thousand years, because you think other people should believe as you do. There, I've said it. You can think what you will of me, Moses, but I will put Egypt first.'

'Then I have no choice, I will make ready to leave at once. If others wish to follow me, I'll do my best for them, as you will — as you must — for those who remain. I don't think we have any more to say.'

He turned and walked away. In the doorway, he looked over his shoulder, torn, wanting to make a proper farewell. But Meritaten was out on the balcony, watching another world and making plans.

* * *

Herit asked, 'So, are you going or staying?' Miriam had been thinking about it for a couple of days now. She looked wistfully into the garden; Yuk's grave was hardly noticeable now against the green sward, but the little headstone Yuffu had carved for him cast a sharp shadow against the sunlight. 'I can't, Herit. I can't leave him. I'm sorry.'

'Don't worry, cousin, I understand. But you take care of yourself; these are troubled times.' Herit embraced her and turned to go. 'And tell that old ruffian I will miss him.'

'Yuffu?'

'The very one. He'll have you all to himself now.'

'Pentu, I can't. If I up sticks and leave now, Aneksi will never forgive me. You know how she feels about living in a tent.' Baufre finished his wine and reached for the jug. 'To tell you the truth, I'm a bit surprised you decided to go. You've got a thriving business here.'

'Well, people need bread wherever they are. And I actually believe in Aten, which means my life might get a bit difficult if I stay.'

'Well, I'll miss you, my old mate. I shall have to find another partner to help me polish off the odd jug of wine.'

'Oh, there will be plenty in the queue for a free cup of wine.'

'Yeah, but they probably won't be as funny as you.'

'Well, if you two do change your minds, remember; paint a splodge of red on your door lintel. Then the followers will know to knock at your door.'

'Is that what you call yourselves then, the followers?'

'I'm not sure we have a name for ourselves; I expect there are plenty of people who do have names for us, but we probably wouldn't like them.'

'Give me a hug, Pentu, and take a jug of my finest with you. Raise a glass to me when you're on the road.'

Moses pulled his horse to a halt on the plain just to the east of the cleft in the mountains. She skittered a little and fretted at the bit. 'Shush, old girl, there's nothing to fear.' There was barely a sliver of moon, and the plain took on an eerie shade of grey. 'So, what do you think? Will we ride off, just the two of us, or will we have company?'

Two more horses, their saddlebags piled high with provisions, were tethered to the mare by ropes. He hadn't brought much with him, really; certainly not much to show for a lifetime in the service of his country and his god.

A small group of people made their way across the plain towards him. They had an ox cart with them, piled high with furniture and bundles of vague promise. *I told them to travel light,* he thought, annoyed. *Still, I can't start by telling them off; this will be hard enough as it is.*

'We are here, my lord.' The man who addressed him was unfamiliar. 'Oh, sorry, my lord, I should introduce myself. I'm Pentu, the baker. The oxcart has the makings of a bread oven in it, and some sacks of grain. Can't march on an empty stomach.'

'Well met, Pentu. I'm sure your oven will come in handy once we're on our way.'

'That's something I wanted to ask my lord; on our way where, exactly?'

'We have a destination, Pentu. If it's all right by you, I'll explain when everyone gets here. That is, if anyone else is coming.'

'I think you might be surprised, my lord,' said Pentu. 'I saw an uncommon amount of red paint over the last couple of days.'

Over the next hours, the little throng around him turned into a crowd several thousand strong. *Aten,* he thought. *How am I going to feed all these people?*

When it seemed the trickle of stragglers had dwindled to nothing, and as the light of dawn began to eat at the darkness, he addressed them. 'I want to thank you,' he began. 'To thank you from the bottom of my heart for your faith in Lord Aten, and in me.'

A ragged cheer went up. Moses raised his hand, and they subsided into silence.

'My good friend Pentu here has asked a good question. We know we're going, but where? Well, I can tell you; we have a place to go, a land to call our own. It is in Canaan.' The murmurs that greeted the news were not all positive. 'Smenkhkare granted us a large piece of land there, in a region that is almost uninhabited. It is a land without people, for a people without land.' This time the murmurs were more cheerful.

'Look to the eastern horizon. Our lord is preparing to greet us. So, let's get ready to greet him, and when we have prayed to him, we will be on our way.'

'Nine days walking, and I'm not sure we've got anywhere yet. I swear I can still smell my mum's cooking; unfortunately.' Paser wiped sweat off his face for the umpteenth time that day, and looked behind him. The untidy column seemed to stretch for miles.

'I'm still not sure why you joined us, Paser. I worry that I got you in trouble, passing you those messages.' Moses led his horse by the bridle; he tried to give her as much rest as possible, conscious of the many miles in front of them.

'Well, I've always wanted to see a bit of the world, and the army's not gone anywhere for a while, so I thought I'd take my chance.'

'I'm glad you're here. I need a few people with an idea how to march and make camp; it would be chaos otherwise.'

'Begging your pardon, my lord, but it is chaos. There are people out there carrying their houses on their backs.'

'They'll tire of it soon enough. The last village we passed by, I saw a lot of people bartering their furniture for provisions.' Moses had been surprised by the friendly reception they'd had in the villages. Most people were friendly and eager to help. Occasionally he'd preached about the one god, and some of the villagers had joined them on the march to their promised land.

'Keep an eye out to the fore, Paser. I'm going to ride down the column and try and hurry the stragglers.'

'As you command, my lord.'

As he rode back along the long line of carts, handcarts, and people struggling under the weight of their packs, he took stock of the people who had chosen to come with him. Only a minority were Egyptians; most seemed to be immigrants, Hyksos and Philistines, even a few Canaanites. This puzzled him. Why should these people, who had left their homeland to come to Egypt, choose to leave again?

A couple of hours later, while he sat at a small fire and ate a simple meal of dried meat and Pentu's fine bread, it came to him. These people came from regions and districts that had a single tutelary deity, a god of the place. They had never worshipped a pantheon of gods. So the idea of Aten had come naturally to them. And when their lives and faith were threatened, they had done what they had done before; gathered their belongings and set out on the road, looking for a new home, and a new life.

'I have made nomads of them,' he muttered.

'Mad? Who's mad? Apart from all of us, I mean?'

'Pentu, you should be running a travelling circus, not running away. I was just wondering why so many of the people who came with us are foreign born.'

'Egypt's not such a friendly country these days. I doubt they'd do worse by staying.'

'Perhaps you're right.'

Paser rode into their little camp. 'I rode back a few miles, and kept a good watch, my lord. No one is following us; or at least, nothing as big as an army is on our tail. I saw quite a few wild dogs, and the odd flock of pigeons, but no soldiers.'

'Thank you, Paser, you've set my mind at ease, for now at least.'

'Did you think we'd be followed? I thought they were glad to get rid of us.'

'I thought Aye and Horemheb might take the opportunity to kill me, to be honest.'

'They wouldn't need an army for that. They could just send an assassin posing as one of us, to slit your throat while you sleep.'

'Thanks, Pentu; you've made me feel a lot better.'

'I'm only here to serve. Now, I happen to have a jug of rather excellent wine among my belongings; what do you say we share it?'

* * *

Kiye wandered the palace corridors aimlessly. She'd tried to sleep, but it wouldn't come; every time her eyes closed, she saw him, riding at the head of a ragged column of refugees, beset by storms or bandits, lying dead in the desert. She had wanted to leave so badly it had torn her heart in two; but Thutankhaten needed to be here, and she couldn't abandon him.

She was startled by the lamplight; it was Meritaten. 'I've been looking for you, Kiye. Come to my chamber and have a glass of wine. I can't sleep either.'

The wine was a small mercy after her desperate wandering.

Meritaten got straight to the point. 'Kiye, I don't really have a right to ask this, but were you and uncle Moses lovers?'

'Why do you ask?'

'Because … because I've sent him away and I don't want him to be alone. If I thought he'd found some comfort with you, I'd sleep easier.'

'Then sleep, Meritaten; he was not always alone.'

* * *

Moses reined in his horse, and looked at the bend in the sacred river; around that bend was the city of On, the city of the oldest of the old gods. Now they were so close, he was having second thoughts. Would they be better to rest at On, or best to change course and push further to the east?

As he sat and considered his options, he saw a small deer a few paces away. It seemed to be following the course of the river, heading for the city. As it rounded the curve, a crocodile leaped out of the water and dragged the unfortunate creature into the water. The deer thrashed around for a few seconds, and went limp. The crocodile pulled its prey into the water, and only a small red stain on the water remained.

'Paser,' he called. The young soldier rode up and saluted.

'My lord?'

'We're changing our route, Paser. Get your fellows to ride down the column and let people know. We're heading east, around the Great Bitter Lake.'

Paser had persuaded a few of his comrades to join him on the great trek. They were practically the only armed men in the whole column, and among the few to own horses; they acted as a bodyguard for Moses, scouts, and when necessary, guards to chase off the bandits who occasionally harassed the followers of Aten.

A little while later, Paser reappeared, another of the soldiers in his wake. 'My lord,' he called out. 'You need to hear this.'

The second soldier drew up alongside him, a bluff young man with streaks of red in his hair. 'My lord, my family used to live on the shores of the Great Bitter Lake. There are a few things you should know.'

'Go on.'

'Well first of all, the area around the lake is mostly marshes; there are paths, but you need to know your way. I can guide the front of the column, but we should find out if there are others who know the area and have them stationed along the route, to keep people safe.'

'That's an excellent plan. Can I leave it to you to organise it? What's your name?'

'Of course, my lord. I'm Kenaten, my lord.'

'Paser, tell everyone to rest for an hour, and then we'll move off. Who is that?'

A rider was approaching, fast. 'Form up, lads,' shouted Paser, and Moses' bodyguard formed a cordon around him, swords out. The rider kept coming. Soon, they were able to see the royal insignia on his tunic.

'Who's sending a royal messenger?'

'Who indeed?' Moses felt for the comfort of the sky-metal blade at his side. 'Let's see what this man wants. Keep your eyes peeled, lads.'

They rode out to greet the messenger. He pulled to a halt and leaped from his horse, kneeling in the dust. 'My lord, I come with a message from the pharaoh.'

'Meritaten?'

'No, my lord, Smenkhkare.'

'And the message?'

'His highness follows, with a large squadron of charioteers. He wants to meet you and talk. See, my lord.' The messenger pointed to the south-west. A considerable cloud of dust billowed along the royal road towards them. 'His highness will be here soon.'

Paser was still gazing at the southern horizon. 'Well, the pharaoh coming explains *that* dust cloud,' he said, pointing, 'but what about the other one?'

Moses felt a tingle of apprehension. One army following him was a worry; but two?

Kenaten trotted up beside him. 'That dust cloud, that's no army.'

'Then what is it, Kenaten?'

'It's a local thing, my lord, and a nasty thing it is. Every so often a kind of sandstorm builds up; the wind keeps changing direction and it gets hard to see more than a few paces in front of you. We should warn his highness about it.'

'You're right, let's get to it.'

'Actually, my lord, it may be a bit late for that.' Paser gestured to the south. The dust cloud was close to the royal army; too close.

'Paser, take a couple of men and get down there. Do what you can to warn them.'

Paser and two companions rode off at a gallop. Moses kicked his horse into a trot and made for a scarce patch of high ground.

Smenkhkare struggled against the giant of a soldier who held him, but the man was simply too strong. The meaty hand clamped over his mouth made it hard to breathe, let alone shout for help.

'Keep still, boy; I'll release you when the time comes. Now, give me that crown.'

Smenkhkare felt his crown being ripped from his forehead. Ahead of him, he saw a figure don the crown and signal to the column of chariots, waving them forward. The sand storm whipped up around them and for a few moments he could see nothing. When the air cleared, he could not believe what he was seeing. The chariots were thundering past him at high speed, and the first of them had already tumbled into the marsh. The following vehicles were going too fast to stop or change course; they ploughed into the deep marsh after the lead chariot. Soon, the area in front of him was a sea of broken chariots, thrashing horses and struggling men.

Desperate, he bit the hairy paw that held him. The oversized soldier screamed in a high-pitched voice. 'You little bastard!'

Smenkhkare leaned forward to grab the reins of the chariot, but a sudden blow knocked him out of the vehicle and onto the ground. The world had tipped on its side; a cavorting mural of broken wheels, thrashing men and terrified horses performed for him. He giggled at the madness of it until the second blow brought the darkness.

Moses and his companions watched the tragedy unfold. From here, it appeared as if the pharaoh was ordering his men into the swamp. They were too shocked to speak. The tumult of chariots subsided, gradually, and the waters of the marsh appeared undisturbed, except for the occasional kick of a struggling horse or man.

Paser came galloping back towards them. 'My lord,' he shouted. 'Did you see what happened?'

'I think so. The pharaoh signalled the chariots to ride headlong into the marsh. It makes no sense, Paser.'

'It wasn't the pharaoh, my lord. We got close enough to see what was happening. The pharaoh was held captive while someone impersonated him. Then he tried to struggle free and someone . . .'

'Tell me, Paser. I need to know.'

'Someone came up behind him and struck him with a club, twice. Then they dragged his body into the marsh.' Paser was in tears.

'There's no time for grief, Paser. We have to get everyone as far from here as possible. Kenaten, get to the head of the column and guide them across. You,' He turned to the messenger. 'Ride south, like the wind. Make sure that Meritaten hears what happened. She must know the truth of this.'

'My lord.' The messenger saluted, and kicked his horse into a gallop. In moments, he was no more than a swirl of dust on the road.

The journey across the marshes was terrifying. Every time the wind changed—which seemed to happen every few minutes—giant waves careened across the marsh and flattened out with a world-shattering crash. People prayed aloud as they trudged through the sucking mud and black water.

'Aten, save us.'

Then the wind stopped. The waves that had danced around them formed a wall of water behind them. Kenaten took the chance, and hurried everyone across the expanse of marshes. When the last of the column had reached the other side, there was a deafening crash behind them. The strange wall of water thrashed back into the hollows of the marsh and the depths of the lake. The world became still.

They didn't halt until the marsh was far behind them. As darkness fell, they made camp as best they could. Moses' mind was in a whirl; he was just beginning to grasp what he had witnessed; his thoughts were the colour of blood.

With Smenkhkare dead, the vultures would circle around Meritaten; he couldn't see how she would survive this. Aye must be behind it. And that meant his next port of call would be Akhet-aten, to force Meritaten into a humiliating retreat. For a few moments, he considered going back, trying to help. But it was no use; by the time he got there, events would have run their course. Now, all he could do was press on, and get his people to the land they had been promised.

If they arrived and found that Smenkhkare's gift had been withdrawn, well, they would cross that marsh when they came to it.

1329 BC

'And then Moses, cursed be his name, raised his arms like this.' The preacher was an unusually tall man, slender and spindly as a reed; when he raised his arms, they disappeared into the awning of Baufre's wine shop. Aneksi came out, wiping her hands in her apron. 'You, preacher,' she said. 'Move off or you'll bring my awning down.'

The preacher threw her a baleful glare and stepped forwards, ensuring his arms would not interfere with her *beloved awning*. Once again, he raised his arms. 'Like this,' he said, 'and the waters parted, and the idolaters rushed through the gap. Then brave Smenkhkare and his charioteers followed them, but Moses lowered his arms,' he brought his unnaturally long arms down suddenly. 'And the waters crashed over them. They were dashed to pieces in the torrent.'

'Alas, poor Smenkhkare. Who will bind his body? Who will fill the canopic jars? Is he doomed to wander the afterworld forever, his rites unmade, his soul untethered? And all because,' the preacher raised a long arm and pointed at the sun. 'And all because Moses, the demon, the wizard, has fooled the world with his false god.' The preacher subsided, looking pleased with his work.

The preacher finished, and moved along the street to his next podium, looking for another crowd to persuade. The crowd that had gathered in front Baufre's shop dispersed, muttering and whispering as they left.

Yuffu, who had been passing with Miriam, took her arm and led her away. 'Moses the wizard, eh?' He chuckled grimly. 'And my granny built the great pyramid one night when she was bored.'

'The thing is,' Miriam said, 'it doesn't matter how outlandish the story is, people are beginning to believe it.'

'Well they don't know the half of it, I am sure of that. You know Miriam, I met a fellow in the wine house a few nights ago. He's a royal messenger; least he was—now he says he's keeping out of sight. He was there when all of this happened; he brought back news to Meritaten. He didn't want to talk too much about it but I got the impression that the story that spindly oaf was telling is a fairy story. I got the feeling that there was something fishy about the death of Smenkhkare but he wasn't about to tell me. However, he as good as nodded to me that there was foul play.'

Miriam shivered. 'Accident, murder, whatever, only Aten knows, but our lord Moses assisting in the death of his loved nephew? Never.' She walked on. 'You know,' she said quietly, 'my lady Kiye, is worried sick. I have never seen her this way since I became her maid after Tiye died. She wanted to go with Moses when he left, but she is pre-occupied with looking after her son; she is another old woman wondering around the palace now. Thutankhaten is the only man left in the family—but, he is so young and impressionable.'

'Whatever did happen out there Miriam, I think Aye had a hand in it. And there is something else I don't understand. That messenger I told you about, the one who brought back a message from the marshes for Meritaten, he doesn't seem to be around now; he was always in town, you could guarantee seeing him in the ale house every night.' They rounded the corner to the great Aten temple, looking up to admire the great entrance blocks.

'Isn't that marvellous?' Miriam said.

Yuffu was still thinking about the rumours. Thutankhaten, surely, is the only person fit to wear the crown, child or not. Your mistress has good reason to be concerned; recent pharaohs don't seem to last very long.'

'Let's get home quickly,' Miriam said.

* * *

'And the great sea parted, by the witchcraft of the apostate Moses; and the vermin who walk with him escaped through the gap in the waters. And when our lord Smenkhkare followed with his mighty army, the waters closed in over them.'

Setau paused for breath, and to allow the gathered nobles and priests to take in the full horror of his rhetorically enhanced version of events.

Meritaten yawned behind her hand, though she really didn't care if anyone noticed; she had heard Setau's bizarre tale a dozen times now, and it didn't get any more plausible with retelling. As the peculiar little man carried on with his grand narration, she recalled the visit from the messenger, a messenger sent by Moses, who told a rather different story.

She had been sceptical of him too. 'Are you sure?' she asked. 'My husband was assassinated?'

'Highness, I saw it with my own eyes. He was clubbed to death, and his army was fooled into crossing the marches, where they all drowned. Every last one of them. It was …' The messenger choked on his tears.

'And Moses sent you to tell me this?'

'He sent me to warn you, highness. The people who did this, they may come for you next. No one is safe.'

'Then I must thank you, and Lord Moses, for warning me. Wait here.' She slipped away into her chambers, took a small purse of gold coins from her desk, and brought it to the messenger. 'Here, take this; you deserve it.'

'Highness, no, I am doing my duty, no more.'

'I insist. Lord Moses would expect you to be paid for such a dangerous mission. And stay hidden for a few days. The people who did this will be looking for you. In fact, go to this house and ask for lodgings. They are my servants and you can trust them.' She passed him a slip of papyrus with an address scrawled on it.

'My thanks, highness. I will do as you say.' The messenger, clutching the laden purse, backed away, bowing, turned on his heel and disappeared.

Meritaten watched him for a few moments. Then she clicked her fingers, and a man appeared from the shadows in the corridor. 'You require me, highness?'

'Yes, Hafuet, I require your singular services, again. Follow him. When he gets to the safe house he will be a little confused; it has been abandoned for years. Befriend him and take him inside. Then you know what to do. Oh, and Hafuet; bring the purse back. I'd hate to think you were pilfering the royal treasury.'

'Highness.' Hafuet melded into the shadows, already about his business.

'And in the loving arms of Amun they will live forever, heroes to the last.' Setau had finally finished his lengthy rendition, and he sat, basking in the smug light of a bad job well done.

The muttered conversations that immediately broke out around the great hall surprised her. She wasn't, it seemed, the only sceptic in the room. She was more surprised when one of the nobles stepped forward and cleared his throat. *Apparently this one fancies himself as an orator too; gods save us from fine words.*

'The high priest's servant tells a fine tale. A terrible tale, and a tale of murder most foul. An epic tale, indeed, of heroes and evil villains. One might pause to wonder, though, if it is a true tale.' The noble's eyes flicked from Meritaten to Aye, who was too busy congratulating Setau to notice.

'Aye, what do you say to this?' Meritaten said. That got his attention. And, more to her liking, it shifted the suspicious gazes of the nobles from her to the high priest.

It took Aye a moment to realise that every eye in the room was turned on him. He blinked stupidly and then attempted to compose himself and summon the appropriate dignity. 'My lord may wonder,' he said haughtily, 'but the gods have the truth of it.'

'Your servant is a curious creature in many respects,' replied the noble, a few sniggers accompanying his arched eyebrow. 'But he is not even a priest, much less a god.'

'Quite so, my lord, quite so.' Aye was visibly struggling; Meritaten smiled to see his discomfort. 'But he speaks truth, and truth is the gift of the gods.'

'I presume you mean god, high priest?'

That made Aye angry. He drew himself up to his full height—*not a long job*, observed Meritaten drily—and faced his opponent. 'The elder gods have not dissolved into air because some apostate says so,' he fumed. 'Amun has not deserted us, nor will he.' He paused and scanned the ranks of nobles and priests. 'Which is more than one can say for the cursed Aten.'

That set the murmurs going again. Aye noted with some satisfaction that fingers were now pointing at the declared Atenist's in the chamber. He looked pointedly at Meritaten for support.

'I am sad to say that, in my experience, those that dedicate themselves to Aten often pay with their sanity. My father succumbed to it, and I fear that my uncle has followed the same tragic path. If Setau says he practises witchcraft now, I am saddened, but perhaps not surprised.'

'The pharaoh speaks as one who has lost a husband in this tragedy,' Aye said. 'We should heed her words.'

'Another husband lost; it's becoming something of an unfortunate habit.' Meritaten heard the words but couldn't see the speaker. She bridled at the insult but let it pass.

'And as pharaoh, I will ...' A delicate cough brought her to a halt. Djau stepped forward.

'The position of pharaoh,' he said, 'is something we need to discuss with some urgency.'

Meritaten spluttered in surprise and turned to Aye. The high priest didn't look shocked, and the glance he cast her wasn't exactly supportive. *The old bastard knew this would happen*, she realised, *and he's not on my side.*

'With the passing of Smenkhkare, there is indeed a power vacuum in the land.' Aye tried to look sympathetic, but the relish in his voice was obvious. 'It would perhaps be unseemly if the lady pharaoh were to marry another of her brothers, to legitimise her position.'

'Not to mention risky for the brother.' That hidden voice piped up again, and now the laughter was open.

Djau had seen and heard enough; a pivotal moment in the empire's affairs was threatening to descend into farce. 'Highness, gentlemen,' he said, loud and imperious. 'This is not the time for juvenile humour. We have a genuine problem here, one of law and lore, and we must attend to it at once. Highness,' he turned to Meritaten, and she could see his regret was sincere. 'The council will not accede to a female pharaoh ruling alone. These are perilous times, and we must act accordingly.'

Heads nodded in agreement around the chamber. Meritaten sighed in frustration; she had been outplayed, and there was nothing she could do about it. 'And what do you suggest, Djau? Or has this all been agreed and arranged in my absence?'

Djau inclined his head. Whether he was acknowledging the deceit, or merely being polite, she couldn't tell. 'It is the feeling of the council, and, I think, the nobles in general, that Thutankhaten is best placed to take the throne.'

'What?' Meritaten almost giggled. 'He is a stripling. How could he reign as pharaoh?'

'We will invest a council of regents; the new pharaoh will not without advice.'

I bet he won't, she thought bitterly. 'And who will serve on this council?'

'Well, it will take time to draw up a detailed plan,' said Djau, looking sideways at Aye. 'But I think it fair to assume that you, highness will have a place there.'

Aye took his cue. 'Yes, yes, of course. You highness will be a valuable mentor for the pharaoh.'

Meritaten brusquely removed the double crown from her head. *Bloody thing never fitted properly.* 'I see that I have no choice in the matter. Very well, do what you must, or rather, do what you want. I will serve the empire, and the gods, in whatever manner you see fit.'

Djau struck the floor with his staff. 'Call for the prince,' he announced. 'call for prince Thutankhaten.'

Almost immediately, the double doors at the end of the chamber opened, and Thutankhaten appeared. He looked nervous, but resolute; a child attempting to play a man's role. Meritaten stood up and stepped down from the royal dais, walked over and proffered the crown. 'Here, little brother, I believe this is yours.'

In the reign of Thutankhaten, Near the Great Salt Lake

Paser rubbed out the map he had drawn in the dust with his stick, and started again. 'We are here, and we're safe for a few days. There are animals to hunt, and a few farmers to buy grain from. The people can rest before we set out again.'

He sketched in a few details. 'To our north is the coastal path. This would be the easiest route, and the quickest. But we don't know if we are followed. If Aye, or whoever rules in Egypt now, sends a force after us, we'll be easy meat there, with our backs to the sea.'

'It's north or east, Paser.' Moses took the stick and drew two lines, to the south and west. 'We can't go back, and if we head west we are in the Delta.'

'The thing is, my lord, the east is ...'

'I know, Paser, the east is the desert. It won't be easy.'

'It may be impossible, my lord. Without a guide, we will be lost, and the desert tribes are not anxious to show strangers the secret roads through the wastes. They have precious few resources as it is; sharing them with a multitude like this,' he waved his arm at the sea of tents behind them. 'I don't think they'll agree to that.'

'So, we're back where we started,' said Kenaten. 'We have two choices, and they're both bad. That's a riddle I'm not equipped to solve.' He scratched his head, and peered at the map as if it might tell him something new.

'I think we must head east,' said Moses. 'I know the desert crossing will not be easy, but I don't think there is a better option. We must push on, and trust that the lord will show us the way.'

His companions nodded in assent; no one was happy with the prospect of crossing the inhospitable wastes of Sinai, but no one had come up with a better route. 'As you command, lord.' Paser stood and surveyed the city of tents. 'Let's give them two days to rest and eat, and then we'll head east and see what the lord has in store for us.'

Pentu was waiting in front of Moses' tent, a small loaf in his hand. 'Here, my lord; I've managed to rig up an oven of sorts. It's not my finest bread, but it's better than dust and dry meat.'

Moses took the bread gratefully, and sat down on a small boulder to eat it. He looked up, bread halfway to his mouth, when he heard the sound of weapons being drawn. 'Kenaten, what's the alarm?'

'This fellow says you want to see him, my lord.'

'And who is this fellow I want to see? Does he have a name? And does he remember why I sent for him?'

A pugnacious little bull of a man pushed his way past the bodyguards and strode purposefully towards Moses. Kenaten stretched out a long arm and grabbed him by the shoulder. 'Easy, my friend. You will approach Lord Moses slowly, and keep a respectful distance.' The stranger brushed Kenaten's hand away, but he slowed down. A few paces from Moses, he dropped to one knee, and smiled in greeting. 'Lord Moses, we are well met.'

'I suppose we are, stranger. Did I send for you?'

'Not exactly, my lord.'

'Then would you care to explain? And tell me your name, at least?'

The stranger dipped his head in a minimal display of deference. Squatting on his haunches, he looked even more bullish. 'I am named Jo-Shah, my lord. I am from the tribe of Levi, and part of the Hyksos nation.'

'Ah, the Hyksos. You people stole our northern lands from us and ruled over them for centuries, after we had been good to you and allowed you to settle and grow prosperous among us. It took my ancestor Ahmoses many years to regain it from you. Why should I trust any of you?'

'That was five hundred years ago my lord. I cannot speak for my ancestors, and I do not speak for the nation; I speak only for the tribe.'

'And what does the tribe of Levi have to say?'

'Ah, well, perhaps, in all honesty, I should speak for myself.'

'Jo-shah, you have a way of walking round the garden to get to the door. I am hungry, and my main ambition is to eat this bread while it's still warm. Can you get to the point?'

'Eat, lord, you won't offend me.'

'Then talk, Jo-shah, and you will offend me less.'

'My lord, in some respects you are well served with your companions.' He glanced over his shoulder; Paser and Kenaten were eying him intently. 'But I think you need something more. There are people here from many tribes and nations: Hyksos, Philistines, Canaanites, Nubians ...'

'And Egyptians.'

'As you say, my lord. Each of these groups needs a person to speak for them, and to convey your commands to their people. And, I believe, those people could serve as advisors too.'

'There is sense in what you say, Jo-shah, and I will think on it. I assume you are going to speak for the Hyksos?'

'If it please you, my lord. We have spoken together, and I have been chosen.'

'And what makes you the right person for this position, Jo-shah?'

'Let me tell you a little of my family history. My ancestor came to Egypt as a slave. His name was Jo-sef. He rose to prominence after he interpreted the dreams of the pharaoh, Sobek-hotep the fourth. When he found fortune, others of my family came to join him. That is how we settled in Egypt.'

Moses laughed; Jo-shah was bumptious, but he had a sense of humour. 'And will you interpret my dreams, Jo-shah?'

'No, my lord, I would not presume to do that.' *And you are no pharaoh; where's the reward?* 'But I will happily interpret your wishes, and convey them to my people.'

'Jo-shah, I am persuaded. We will ask each of the tribes to put forward a person to advise me and communicate with their people. When they are all chosen, we will meet and decide how we will work together. Does that satisfy you?'

Jo-shah nodded. 'It does, my lord.'

'Then let's be about it. I'll talk to the other tribes, and we'll meet here again in two nights from now.'

Jo-shah stood and walked away. It had not gone completely as he had planned, but it wasn't a bad start.

Moses beckoned Paser, and spoke quietly. 'Our new friend seems to know what he's doing, but I'm not entirely sure I trust him. Watch him, will you, and let me know if anything untoward happens.'

'My lord.'

1328 BC

Akhet-Aten. Year 2 in the reign of Thutankhaten

Thutankhaten bounced into the royal apartments, flushed with success. 'Ankhsenaten, where are you? I am back from the hunt.'

The new pharaoh's new wife, and half-sister, appeared from her chamber. 'And did your hunting go well, husband?'

'I've stocked the royal larder to bursting. We will feast for weeks!'

'Well, it's good that we are so well fortified,' she said, chuckling. 'You will need to be on your mettle. You have a visitor.'

The look on Ankhsenaten's face told Thutankhaten all he needed to know. 'I'm not going to enjoy this visit, am I?'

'I fear not, husband. Aye is waiting in your office.'

Thutankhaten sighed; Aye was the last person he wanted to see. 'Well, he can wait until I've bathed and dressed. I'm not ready for my day to be spoiled just yet.'

Aye's face was a picture of badly concealed rage. He had paced the ante-chamber to the royal office for forty-five minutes, and the pharaoh's belated entrance had done nothing to placate him.

'Aye, good morning. What can I do for you?'

'In truth, highness, it's good afternoon,' the priest replied testily.

'Quite so, Aye. Now we have successfully established the correct time of day, perhaps you would like to tell me the reason for your visit. I am sure a busy man like you hasn't just dropped in to exchange pleasantries, much as I enjoy your company.'

'Your highness is too kind,' the priest said through gritted teeth. 'I do indeed have an issue I need to raise with you, if this is a good time?'

'As good a time as any, Aye, though my stomach tells me that lunch is in the offing.'

'Then I will not take up too much of your highness' time. It has come to my attention that, every time I send an acolyte to the capital with a message, the message returns but not the priest. I am puzzled by this mystery.'

'There's no mystery, Aye. Now that we have restored freedom of religion, and reverted in so many respects to the old ways, we require priests here in Akhet-aten to administer the affairs of the empire. As new priests arrive, we assign them to vital tasks; we are grateful for the steady supply of qualified men to maintain the administration.'

'And we are of course only too pleased that our priests can serve the empire. But we are fast approaching a situation where we may not have enough priests to fulfil our theological and ceremonial duties.'

'Oh come now, Aye. The last time I was in Thebes I couldn't see the walls of the temple for white robes. Let's be frank with each other. We need priests for the administration, and you need spies in the court. As I see it, this situation is ideal for us all.'

'Your highness has the truth of it, I am sure.'

'I am sure too, Aye, and it's gracious of you to accept the point. Now leave us; I am too hungry to think.'

'Highness.' Aye managed a perfunctory bow and left the office. As he entered the ante-chamber, Djau arrived.

'Chancellor.'

'High priest.'

Aye left, scowling. Djau strode into the office. 'What did our Theban friend want?'

'Do you know, Djau, I'm not at all sure. He wittered on about a shortage of priests in Thebes. Hardly worth the trip.'

'He is fishing, highness; what for, who knows? But he's up so something.'

'He's always up to something. But unless he shows his hand, we must treat him with a modicum of respect and keep our eyes peeled.'

The governor of Khentit, on the Nubian border, was agitated. Thutankhaten could see that. 'Governor, what brings you so far in such haste?'

'I have trouble to report, highness. Trouble on our borders. The Nubians are testing our resolve. Their incursions are becoming more frequent, and bolder.'

'And how have we responded to these incursions?'

'With steel, highness, and arrows.' The governor spoke with pride. 'We do not suffer their games in silence.'

'I am glad to hear it. But you are still worried. Perhaps your forces are a little ... stretched?'

'It is as you say, highness. We have kept them at bay, but I fear they will become bolder, if we do not respond in a more forceful way.'

'You have done well, governor; well to keep them at bay, and well to apprise us of the situation. We will think on this problem, and let you know our decision. It will not be long in coming.'

The governor bowed, in relief as much as gratitude. When he had left the chamber, Thutankhaten gestured to a herald. 'Find general Horemheb and have him attend us here.'

'Highness.' The herald hurried off. A few minutes later, Horemheb appeared.

'General. How convenient that you were close by.'

Horemheb flushed a little. 'As you say, highness. I had business in the palace.'

Thutankhaten was well aware of the general's business; his spies had seen him conferring with Aye in the palace gardens.

'General, we have a problem on the Nubian border. I believe this calls for your expertise.'

'I am ready to serve, highness.'

'Excellent. Then I would ask you to prepare an expeditionary force and proceed with all speed to the border. I think our Nubian neighbours require a reminder of where power lies.'

'At once, highness.' Horemheb looked brighter already; the prospect of a fight always cheered him. He snapped a salute. 'If your highness permits, I will attend to the matter at once.'

'Do so, general. Teach these Nubian upstarts a lesson they won't forget too soon.'

Horemheb turned smartly on his heel and left the chamber. Thutankhaten turned to Djau and smiled. 'The thing I like best, and least, about Horemheb is his gullibility.'

Djau nodded. 'He is pliable enough, highness. Unfortunately, Aye sees this as well as we do.'

'Then best we keep those little lovebirds away from each other, eh? With Horemheb on the border, doing what he does best, Aye will have to scheme with someone else. As my father used to say, generals and priests are friends to the pharaoh when they are far apart. Talking of scheming, how fares my sister these days?'

'She is ensconced in Thebes, praying at the temple of Amun. Quite the devotee, I hear.'

'And quite close to Aye and his conspiring brood. Still, if she's down there plotting, she's not up here interfering.'

'Then all is well for now.' Djau's grin gave way to a frown. 'But we cannot afford to sleep too deeply while those three are active.'

'That's the truth, Djau. They are where we want them for now, but we can't let our guard down.'

* * *

'I know this land; I have been here before.' Moses looked out over the parched valleys before them. 'I have a good friend here, a priest of Aten, named Jethro; I think we will rest here, and consider our options. We can trade for mutton and wool, and perhaps some of the locals have useful knowledge of the desert routes.'

That evening Jethro and Mariam came to the camp. Jethro had hardly changed, while Mariam had matured into a very beautiful woman. Moses embraced them.

'So, Jethro, do you still serve our lord?'

'I do, lord, when the sheep will let me. I lost a very useful shepherd a couple of years ago, a man by the name of Moses. At the end of the day, though, he had a flock of his own to look after.'

The three of them laughed together.

'Well, as you can see Jethro, I have brought that different flock to meet you; I hope you like them. And you Mariam, are you not married yet?'

'Not yet, my lord. I still haven't found the right man.' The yearning in her eyes unsettled him, but it was a yearning he couldn't answer. *Kiye*, he thought. *I haven't thought of you for almost a whole day. I wonder what you are doing now?*

After the joy of their reunion, they got down to business. Jethro agreed to act as a point of contact between the villages scattered across the dry plateau and the travelling multitude.

'And what about a route through the desert? Moses asked. 'Do you know anyone who can guide us?'

'Sadly no, my lord. We don't venture that far, though we trade with those that do. You must find your guide elsewhere.'

Later, as night fell, Moses gathered his advisors and addressed the problem. 'We are determined to go the desert route,' he said. 'But until we find a guide, we are trusting to luck. And I don't like the idea of luck as a guide through such difficult terrain.'

'I may be able to help you there.' Jo-shah had the look of a cat that had found a rich source of cream.

'Jo-shah. How can you help?'

'There is an old man here, among the Levi. I met him just a day or two ago. It turns out we're related.'

'I'm glad you've found a long-lost relative, Jo-shah, but how does that help us?'

'Aron, my cousin, has some knowledge of the route through the desert. He crossed it many years ago, when he was a boy, and claims he can remember the way.'

'Let's talk to him.'

Jo-shah leapt to his feet. 'At once, my lord; I'll fetch him.'

He returned a few minutes later, leading an elderly man by the arm. 'My lord, this is Aron. He has much to tell us.'

'Well met, Aron. Sit with us, and tell us what you know.'

'It is a long tale, my lord; one best told over a cup of wine.' Aron crooked a finger at Paser, who looked at Moses with a quizzical expression.

Moses smiled. 'Pass him a cup of wine.'

The old man drank, licked his lips, and spoke. 'The wastes just to the east of us are called Paran by the people who live there. Paran is desert, but it's not impassable. We could cross it without too much trouble. But beyond it,' he paused for another drink. 'Beyond it is another waste, this one named Zin; it is a much tougher prospect. Still, we should be able to traverse it in relative safety.'

'Go on,' *said* Moses.

'At the eastern edge of Zin there is a huge oasis; the locals call it Kadesh. They are jealous of its riches, so we may need to negotiate, or fight, to get our share. But all things being equal we can rest there, and replenish our supplies. There is good grazing for sheep and goats there.'

'And you think the local people will just let us use the oasis for our needs?' Paser sounded dubious.

'As I said, young man, we will have to talk or fight to get what we want. But we are many, and the desert people are few. I believe we can manage it.'

Moses nodded at Paser to refill the old man's cup.

'Beyond the oasis there is a village called Kabrit. We should avoid the village; it is the home of thieves and bandits. But a little way east of it the mountains begin. We will need to traverse them. The pass at the western end of the range is called Mitla. It is a tricky climb, and we are likely to be harassed by bandits from Kabrit. I hope your young soldiers here are up for a fight.'

Paser smiled as if he'd like nothing better.

'When we are through the pass at Mitla we will find ourselves in a long valley with steep sides. There is some forage for ani-mals there, but not much. And there are leopards and wolves, so we will need to guard our flocks. The valley leads out to the north-eastern edge of the mountains, at a pass called Gid. It is not so hard a climb as at Mitla, but we will need our wits about us. The region is more populated, and we can't be sure how the local people will respond to such a multitude passing through their lands.

'From Gid, there is a broad track that leads out of the desert. When we come to the mountain they call Tarif, we will have completed our desert journey, and we will be a few months of travel from Canaan. I will do my best to guide you there. I am old, and it is many years since I passed through the mountains, but I am confident I will not falter along the route.'

'So, Aron,' said Moses, 'how long will we be travelling if we take the route you suggest?'

'Perhaps two years, my lord, certainly no less, and possibly a little longer.'

Moses looked around the advisors. 'What do you think? Can we take the risk of following this old fellow through the desert?'

The next hour saw an intense discussion. Some of the advisors clearly didn't trust Aron; this, Moses soon realised, was because of his connection to Jo-shah. The Hyksos were the most numerous group among them, and some of the smaller groups felt Jo-shah was trying to manoeuvre himself into a position of power on the back of their strength. At length, they came to an agreement; they would rest, and trade for stock and provision with Jethro's people. Then they would begin the great trek through the desert, trusting Aron to see them through.

An army, when it moves, moves like a giant insect, a series of scaled segments, one following another, weaving a single, devastating track through farmland or wilderness. A host of refugees has no such order; its segments move of their own accord, take off sideways at the next diversion, slither back to the main body just as another segment peels off and follows its own path at variance to the others.

Watching the heaving, scattered mass of people make their way through the pathless expanse of the desert, Moses felt a pang of pity, and of nostalgia. 'You know, Paser, I've spent many months on the road with a military column. There's a sense of belonging, as if you're part of one huge creature making its way through the world. But this; this is like a swarm of locusts. It's well there are no farms or villages here, or we would strip them of everything and leave dry husks behind us.'

'There's still a sense of belonging, though.' Paser shifted his saddlebags and patted his horse on the flank. 'Of course, I'm not sure how I feel about being part of a swarm.' He pointed to a knot of people towards the rear of the throng. 'And I'm not sure everyone has the same sense of belonging.'

Moses followed his gaze. There seemed to be a fight breaking out; but instead of taking place in one part of the crowd, it appeared to roll along the edge of the mass, peeling off every so often only to fold back into the main body of people.

Paser cursed, a soldier's curse. 'It's those bloody Hyksos again. I swear they would wager on the fall of a leaf, and fight over a deer turd, if they thought someone else wanted it.'

He remounted and kicked his horse into a smart trot.

Moses followed him, curious how his young soldier would deal with the belligerent Hyksos. He had his answer soon enough. Paser waded into the fighting men and laid about them with the flat of his sword. In a few minutes, something like order had been restored. Moses rode up to the now sullen little crowd. Jo-shah was among them, his right eye blackening nicely.

'So, advisor, are you having trouble keeping order among your tribe?'

Jo-shah smiled impishly. 'My lord, it's in our blood. We love to fight. If you had weapons enough, we'd make an army for you.'

'An army that would defeat itself daily, by the looks of it. I expect you to do better, Jo-shah; we can't keep up a good pace if half the people stop to fight, and the other half to watch them.'

Jo-shah had the good grace to look sheepish, for a moment at least. He bowed in a semblance of remorse. 'My lord, you are right. I will try to keep better order among my tribe.'

'You might start with yourself, Jo-shah; a man who lacks discipline rarely manages to instil it in others.'

'My lord.'

'You did well there, Paser. If we do have to fight, I'll rely on you.' They trotted up the flank of the mass of people, heading for the front. Moses wanted people to see him constantly, so they would be assured he was facing the same hardships they were.

'I'd prefer not to have to inflict such discipline on our people, my lord. I have the disquieting feeling, sometimes, that our Jo-shah is waiting for a chance; to do what, I'm not sure.'

'I think he will adapt to the discipline of the march in time; they all will. As for your feeling, I am beginning to share it. He seems to think he is special, and that the world will get around to acknowledging that, sooner or later.'

'They all do, my lord. I've heard them refer to themselves as chosen people. I asked one of the Levites what they meant by that, and he just shrugged; but he obviously believed it.'

* * *

The gates of Akhet-aten shone like marble in the spring sunshine; Horemheb sighed in relief at the sight. 'Home at last,' he muttered, 'but not as heroes.' He gestured to his aides. 'I'm off to find a warm bath and a cup of wine. Get the men into the barracks and then go and amuse yourselves; you deserve it.'

His second-in command, Rostauet, drew alongside him. 'The people are out to celebrate our victory, sir.'

'Ah, yes, victory. We did win, didn't we? I'm struggling to recall much of a fight.'

'You can only fight what the enemy fields against you, sir. And what they did send, we defeated. I'd say that's a victory.'

'No doubt you're right, Rostauet. I must be getting cynical in my old age.'

But he didn't feel any better about it. The campaign had been a success, if rounding up a few bandits and humiliating a weak client king counted as success. His encounter with the Nubian monarch had been almost as dispiriting as the tawdry excuse for a military expedition.

'So you know nothing about these bandits?' he'd asked, as the king pouted and ogled his table slave.

'Nothing, general. I would not send my own men to trouble your borders. I am a loyal servant of the pharaoh, though it can be awkward to remember just who is pharaoh these days.'

'You would do well to show some respect for the throne, highness. Act as if your life depends upon it; in fact, your life does depend upon it.' He caressed the hilt of his sword as he spoke, but there was no need. The king got the message.

'I am full of respect for the throne, general. Especially for a throne occupied by one so young. He is a remarkable boy, your pharaoh. It must be liberating to be ruled by one so ... fresh.'

'I am a patient man, highness, so I will not kill you for your mockery. But have a care; the next Egyptian you meet may not be so forbearing.'

'I mean no offence, general. The boy pharaoh is the wonder of the world; everyone says so. And not every king you meet will be as loyal as I.' The king's lascivious wink was almost enough to tip Horemheb into violence, but he held himself in check.

'I will carry your respects to the pharaoh. He will be pleased to hear you think so highly of him. And I will carry a few pounds of your gold and silver to persuade him your affection is genuine.' He smiled at the king's grimace. 'And perhaps I will carry something else to the pharaoh.'

His gaze settled on the young prince sitting at the king's right hand. 'Aniba, isn't it? How would you like to see the land of Egypt, Aniba, and meet the pharaoh? You will have lots to talk about; you are of a similar age, after all.'

The Nubian king spluttered, his wine soaking the silk of his robe. 'But you can't—'

'Oh but I can, highness. Prince Aniba will come with us to Egypt as a hostage; his life will depend on your behaviour. If you deal with these 'bandits' on the border, he will thrive, and even get a proper education. If, on the other hand, you fail to curb the avarice of your subjects, well, then I'm afraid...' He let the words hang for a few moments, enjoying the look of hatred mixed with fear on the king's face.

And that had been the height of his victory; that and a few skirmishes with lightly armed men who didn't seem very enthusiastic about warfare. Now he was home, and despite the cheers of the crowds, it didn't feel like very much at all.

The face that greeted him when he arrived at his villa, a generous compound sited under the cooling shadow of Aten's mountain, was not a welcome sight. Horemheb had hoped for a few days' respite before the irksome priest turned up. But here he was, at home in Horemheb's favourite chair, in his favourite spot in the garden.

'Well met, general. Your victories go before you.'

'Aye. What is so urgent you must set yourself between me and a very well deserved bath?'

'I am merely here to congratulate you, Horemheb, on a successful campaign.'

'You know as well as I, priest, that the 'campaign' was nothing more than a wild goose chase. If I were a betting man, I might wager you know more about that than I do.'

'Now, general, don't take on so. If I were a suspicious man I might infer that you don't trust me. And we need to trust each other, Horemheb; we have shared secrets that might destroy us both.'

The threat in Aye's words was obvious. Horemheb let out a frustrated sigh and settled himself in his second favourite chair, just on the edge of the comforting shade of the giant palm tree.

'Out with it, Aye. What are you plotting?'

'Oh, nothing specific. I'm simply looking after our interests; ours, and Egypt's.'

'And where, exactly, do those interests lie, currently?'

'Well, since you left to chase wild geese, things have moved on. Our new queen is with child.'

'That's good, isn't it? The succession will be settled, and we'll have some stability again.'

'There is stability, and there's the continuation of a bad situation. If Thutankhaten produces a male heir, we are stuck with the Atenist's for the foreseeable future.'

'Aye, you are surely not planning to kill a royal baby.'

'Well, young mothers are prone to losing children at birth, so it's possible providence will do our work for us; but yes, I was indeed contemplating such a thing.'

'I won't be part of it, Aye. It's not right.'

'You don't have to be part of it, general. But you know about it, and that puts you squarely in the frame.'

The damned priest was right. Just by knowing about a plot, Horemheb was implicated. This would not go well for him. 'Very well, Aye. What would you have me do?'

'About the child? Why, nothing, general. And it may not come to that. If the pharaoh dies before the child is born, there is no succession, technically. At least, that's a situation we can work with.'

'I don't understand. Are you simply deciding who to kill by lot?'

'I'm looking at all the angles, and considering what would be to our advantage. That's hardly treasonous, is it?'

'Practically everything you have said since I arrived is treasonous. I'm beginning to think you have taken leave of your wits.'

'Not at all. Not at all.' Aye smiled, a wolfish grin. 'Let's talk of more pleasant things. You are widowed, I believe?'

'As you well know.'

'But you are hardly an old man. Perhaps you should consider marrying again.'

'Where is this going, Aye?'

'Well, let's consider the whole situation. There is a heretic pharaoh on the throne, likely still guided by his even more heretic uncle, wherever he is. There is an ex-pharaoh languishing in the temple complex at Thebes, praying for her reinstatement by fair means or, well we know how her mind works, don't we?' Aye picked up the bell on the low table in front of him, rang it. A slave appeared instantly. 'Mint water, now; the general and his guest are thirsty.'

Horemheb was beginning to feel like an unwanted guest in his own home. He watched, irritation growing, as the slave served the priest fist, and then his master.

'Where was I? Oh yes, Meritaten. If she were to marry well, say to a famous general, flush from victory, then we would have an interesting situation, wouldn't we? If something unfortunate were to happen to the pharaoh, a hunting accident, say—our pharaoh is awfully fond of hunting—then the council of nobles might well look favourably on the general as a candidate for the throne. Our allies would be reassured, and our enemies would be cowed. And the pharaoh's wife is not an Atenist, at least, not any longer. All in all, that might be a very good outcome for the empire, for the people, for the gods; and above all, for you, Horemheb.'

Horemheb's mind was in a whirl. Aye's suggestion was ridiculous; wasn't it? And yet, something stirred in him, and he couldn't deny it. Some of it was lust; for all her careless loss of a succession of husbands, Meritaten was an enticing prospect. And some of it was something else, something he was loath to admit to himself; ambition.

Aye watched a series of expressions drift across the general's face, and smiled inwardly. *This is how the spider feels*, he thought, *when the web resonates with the weight of a fly.*

* * *

The edge of Sinai

The oasis was deserted. People spread out quickly and found grazing for their flocks around the green island in the sand. The first people to take a drink from one of several wells, however, were in for a nasty shock.

'This water is poisoned!' A portly woman reeled back from the well wall and threw up noisily in the grass. 'Someone has poisoned the water; who would do such a thing?'

Moses hurried to another of the wells and took a small sip of water; it was bitter. He shouted to the herders, 'Keep the animals away from the wells. We'll have to give them what's left in the panniers and gourds for now. And the rest of you, make sure no one drinks until we've worked out what the problem is.'

'And how, my lord, will we do that?'

'Jo-shah, if I didn't know better, I'd say you were enjoying this. But I don't suppose you want to die of thirst any more than I do.'

'That I don't, my lord. But I am very curious how you intend to solve this problem. I will watch and learn.'

While the people settled down under the shade of the palm trees, Moses paced the edge of the oasis. He couldn't quite dismiss the idea of sabotage from his mind. Perhaps the locals had seen them coming and decided this was the best way to drive them off. But surely they wouldn't poison their own water supply to do that?

'We have a visitor, my lord.' Paser pointed out to the south. 'One man, and a lot of sheep.'

He was right; the shepherd had a huge flock around him. Prancing dogs kept order, pulling the strays back and keeping a consistent shape to the bubbling mass of animals. Moses looked at the shepherd; there was something familiar about him, something he couldn't quite place.

The shepherd hesitated when he saw the great mass of people around the oasis. He turned to the dogs, and rapped out a series of orders. The dogs quickly herded the sheep into a rough circle and kept them stationary. The shepherd came to the edge of the oasis.

'Moses? What on earth are you doing here?'

'Lord Moses, stranger.' Paser laid his hand on the hilt of his sword.

'Lord Moses? So you're a lord now?'

'I'm sorry, stranger; should I know you?'

'Know me? Of course, you should…Oh wait, what am I saying? I was a boy back then. I'm Kiah, Jethro's nephew.'

'Kiah! I remember you now. You used to sneak up into the high pasture and use that weird whistle of yours to scare my sheep, you rascal.'

'That's it! I still have that whistle. I don't use it out here; it spooks the dogs.'

'That's a relief.'

'So, are you just out for a stroll with a few thousand friends?'

'You might say that.' Moses uttered a short, sharp laugh. 'My friends and I were hoping to find something to drink. But the water is not quite to everyone's taste.'

'No, well, it wouldn't be to your taste. Marah's famous for it.'

'This is the oasis of Marah?'

'Yes, it is. My tribe use it fairly regularly.'

'Your tribe? I thought you were from Small Bitter Lake.'

'No, I'm related to Jethro on my mother's side. I used to spend time with him when I was a boy. Now I'm back permanently with the tribe.'

'Kiah, is there anywhere else we can find water?'

'No, not for another fifty miles or so.' Kiah smiled; the lack of water didn't seem to bother him, despite the size of his flock.

'So how are you going to water your sheep?' Moses was glad to see his old friend, but was beginning to feel the first pangs of irritation at his blithe reaction to the disaster.

'I'll water them here, of course.'

Moses strode over and grasped him by the shoulders. 'Kiah, please explain how you are going to have sheep drink from poisoned wells?'

'Ah; it's not poisoned, it's just bitter. And there is a way to sweeten it, for a while at least. Come with me.' Kiah and Moses, with a following in tow, marched to the northern boundary of the oasis and pulled a couple of branches from a peculiar palm tree. 'See this tree? It looks like a date palm but it never fruits. But it does have one grace.' He took the branches and threw them into the nearest well. 'Wait a couple of minutes, and then have a taste.'

They waited a while with puzzled faces.

'Now,' the young shepherd said, 'taste that.'

Moses reached down to taste but Paser stopped him. 'Let me, my lord,' he said and bent over and tasted the water. He smiled. 'It is good, lord. Moses directed people to take branches from similar trees and throw them into the other ponds and wells. Within ten minutes, they were all drinking clear, sweet water and filling gourds, pots and barrels.

Later, as night approached, Kiah spoke with Moses. 'So, now you are all watered, tell me, Moses, how come you're a lord? And what are you doing in the middle of the desert with half the population of Egypt?'

'That is a long story, Kiah. We are heading for Canaan. The pharaoh has granted us some land there.'

'Who, Thutankhaten?' *Well*, thought Moses. *That's one question answered.*

'Actually, it was Smenkhkare.'

'Ah. There are some odd stories about him. Your name is sometimes mentioned.'

'I'd like to hear those stories, Kiah. Though I don't suppose I will enjoy them.'

'I don't think you will. So, if you're heading for Canaan, why aren't you travelling the coast road? It's got to be easier than tramping through the desert.'

'We couldn't take the coast road; we might have found ourselves followed by an army; one that didn't have our best interests at heart.'

'Well, that would explain the stories. Listen, my tribe are generous enough to strangers, but we can't afford for people to drink our wells dry. It would probably be best if you got going in the morning. I don't mean to be rude, but ...'

'That's fine, Kiah; we need to get going soon. Please convey our gratitude to the tribe, and tell them we won't be back. By the way, you called the oasis Marah. You are sure of that? This isn't Kadesh?'

'Kadesh? No, this is Marah. Kadesh is a good fifty leagues east of here.'

Moses turned to his lieutenant. 'Paser, go and find Aron. I need to have a word with him.'

1327 *BC*

Akhet-aten. Year 3 in the reign of Thutankhaten

'Am I in the underworld?'

Thutankhaten' s eyes were heavy and painful. And it hurt to breathe.

'No, highness, you are here with us.' Djau smiled down at the bruised body of his young lord.

'What happened?'

'You had an accident, highness, on the hunt. One of the archers saw a big cat and thought it was about to pounce on you. He shot at it and missed, caught you in the leg. You were dragged along behind your chariot for some way.'

Thutankhaten had a vague memory of being out hunting, of seeing a big cat. After that everything was hazy; hazy and painful.

'Is he all right?' he asked.

'The cat? No, highness, it was killed by a couple of spearmen.'

'No, the archer, you old fool.' Thutankhaten laughed and quickly thought better of it; his ribs threatened to invade his lungs. 'He must feel terrible, poor man.'

'He might, I suppose.'

'Djau, what do you mean?'

'He has gone missing, highness. My men have searched high
and low for him, but as yet there's no sign.'

'So it wasn't an accident?'

'I fear not, highness. But unless and until we find the archer,
we cannot say who is behind it.'

'That's hardly a mystery, Djau. Find Aye and frisk him for
feathers.'

Now it was Djau's turn to laugh. 'I think you are recovering
rather well, highness. But it will be a few weeks before you are
up and about again. Your leg was broken, and a couple of ribs.
You need to rest and gather your strength.'

'Yes, of course, but I want to see Ankhsenaten. Has she had
the baby yet?'

Djau looked away. This did not feel like a good time to tell
the pharaoh his child had been still-born. But it would be hard
to hide it from him. 'I am afraid, highness, the birth did not go
well. the child was still-born.'

Thutankhaten' s face fell, crumpled into tears. 'Oh, poor
Ankhsenaten. Is she . . . Is she well?'

'As well as one might expect, highness. This has been quite
an ordeal for her; particularly as you were indisposed.'

'Wait, how long have I been here, unconscious?'

'Ten days, highness.'

'Ten days? They must have come very close to succeeding,
the assassins.'

'Too close for comfort. I will send for the queen, and your
mother. They will be overjoyed to hear you are awake and well.'

Kiye and Ankhsenaten were overjoyed to see him; but the pain
of the stillbirth was etched on his wife's face, his mother's too.

'Look, husband, I've brought you a toy. Mama tells me you were obsessed with this puppet when you were a child.'

'So, I was; and I'm still a child.' He held the simple wooden effigy up in front of him and manipulated it in a clumsy dance. 'This is me,' he said, glumly. 'A puppet; no moving parts, no will of its own. Whoever holds the string controls the puppet. And whoever controls the puppet rules the world.'

'Don't talk like that,' said Kiye sharply. 'The game is not lost, not yet. As you get older, the nobles will come to trust you more.'

'If I get older. The Thebans won't stop now. I'll suffer another 'accident' soon enough, if they have their way.'

'Have faith, son. We will find a way.'

'I would find it easier to have faith if Uncle Moses were here to advise me. But I suppose he's gone for good now; off to settle the promised land with his followers. Gods, I miss him.'

'So, do we all,' Kiye sighed.

'So why don't we just get him back?' Thutankhaten and Kiye looked at Ankhsenaten, astonished.

'But we can't, my love. Moses is an enemy of the powerful now and in any case, no one knows where he is.'

Kiye stood abruptly and paced the room. Her expression changed from dark to light, to dark again, Finally, she stopped and looked at her son. 'Perhaps you are right; perhaps we are lost, after all.'

'Actually, there may be something we can do. Do you remember that cavalry captain? The Nubian fellow with those odd green eyes?'

'You mean Ramose?' Kiye didn't see where this was going.

'Is he still in the palace? He's not on campaign with Horemheb is he?'

'He's here, in Akhet-aten.'

'Can we trust him, do you think?'

'I think so. What do you have in mind?'

'I think we should send someone after Uncle Moses.'

Kiye's face was a mask. 'But Moses has disappeared. There's no sign of him.'

'Mama, you can't disappear with five thousand people hanging onto your cloak. There must be some sign of him.'

'So, what are you suggesting? We ask Ramose to go on a wild goose chase looking for a man who doesn't want to be found?'

'Yes, in a word. Ramose is a skilled tracker. Remember when he found that leopard that had been taking children from the village at the Elephantine Lake? And we know Moses went north and then east. I won't beg him to come home. But if we could have some channel of communication, I'd feel less alone. And, if he did choose to return ...'

'If he has gone east he is heading into the desert. Who will be able to track him there?'

'A Nubian might.'

Ramose looked distinctly uncomfortable in dress uniform. He was more suited to the outdoors. He stood to attention in the royal apartment, and stayed that way even when Thutankhaten invited him to sit.

'Highness, how may I be of service to you?'

Thutankhaten glanced at Kiye; she nodded. 'I want you to find someone for me, Ramose. Someone very important. But this must stay a secret between the three of us. If anyone finds out, we are all likely to be in danger.' He saw the soldier bristle at the idea that he was bothered by a threat. 'Including my mother.'

'It shall be as your highness commands. I would rather cut off my sword arm than bring peril to you, my lord, or the lady Kiye. Who am I to find?'

'My uncle Moses.' Thutankhaten studied Ramose's reaction. *He thinks I'm mad. And if he doesn't, he should.*

But Ramose took the order stoically.

'I will need to take a couple of men with me; men skilled in tracking, and who speak the languages and dialects of the borders. Rumour has it Lord Moses is attempting to cross the eastern desert. We could begin there.'

'Excellent. You will find us grateful, Ramose, if you can find him.'

* * *

'You imbecile! I get back from a murderous little sojourn in the Syrian hills to find our pharaoh has had an accident. Except every old woman in the market knows it was no accident, and every drunk in the city is discussing what you will try next.'

'It wasn't meant to be like this.' Aye wasn't used to being the one to be scolded; he didn't like it one bit. Horemheb was beside himself.

'And how was it meant to be? Half the population wants your head, Aye. Perhaps I should give them it.' He made to draw his sword.

Aye shrank into his shoulders and began to pray silently to Amun.

'Don't worry, little priest. I am not going to hurt you; not yet, anyway. Tell me how you are going to fix this.'

Aye rose and drew his shawl around himself. 'Horemheb, sometimes mistakes are made when you rely too much on other people.'

'Then don't rely on others again. Do what you have to do, and do it yourself.'

Aye pulled at his shawl, trying to make himself look like the high priest instead of a snivelling coward. 'There is only one way to fix this. We finish the job we started.'

* * *

Moses looked up, shading his eyes with his hand. 'That eagle owl has been following us for days.' The magnificent bird hovered over them; then, in a flash of outspread wings, it flew off to the north-east. 'I think he's trying to tell us something.'

'Well, if a bird of prey is out here, there must be something to eat.' Paser watched the bird until it was out of sight.

'We can't feed this lot on desert mice.' Kenaten twitched the reins and kicked his horse forward. 'I think we'll have to rely on ourselves for that.'

The last few days had been the hardest part of the trek. The valley slopes were shallow here, and there was little shade from the relentless sun. The murmurs of discontent had grown louder. Some people had chosen to leave the camp and head back; few of them survived for long.

A scout galloped towards them. 'My lord, the oasis; we're nearly there.'

'Thank the lord. We can rest and replenish our supplies.'

In less than an hour, the front of the column was in the oasis. The sense of relief was palpable. As the last stragglers made it into the shade of the palm trees, Moses climbed onto a boulder at the edge of the cool grass. The boulder didn't seem to be the same type of rock as the low mountains around them; it was as if it had landed there from the sky. He waved his arms to attract the attention of the crowd.

'People, the lord has provided for us again. See how he protects his chosen ones. Have no fear, pray to Aten and all will be well.' He scanned the crowd; most of them seemed happy and relieved. At the back of the throng, he noticed the Levi elders gathered around Jo-shah, deep in conversation.

He jumped down and took Paser to one side. 'Paser, our Hyksos friends seem to be planning something. I think we should try and find out what it is. I am beginning to think elevating Jo-shah to advisor may not have been the wisest decision.'

'My lord.' Paser was only too happy to spy on Jo-shah and his allies; he hadn't trusted him from the start.

A young woman approached them. 'My lord,' she said, 'I've found some kind of inscription on a rock at the main well.'

'Let's go and take a look. It may have some useful information for us. What is your name, lady?'

'Herit, my lord.'

'Herit, you have done well.'

The inscription was a single row of demotic characters scratched roughly into the rock. 'I think it's the name of the oasis,' Moses said. 'It's basically a single word stretched out a little. Elim. No doubt that's a fine name for an oasis, but shouldn't it be Gid?'

'If this is Gid, then we should soon see the pass.' Paser looked out to the east. 'I'll send a scout.'

The scout returned a few hours later. He hadn't found the pass; in front of them there was only the long, monotonous reach of the valley, the oppressive mountains looming over them from either side. Moses didn't want to use the word 'lost' but they were clearly off course. And Aron seemed to have disappeared.

* * *

'You are a little ripe, priest. Couldn't you have washed before your visit?' Meritaten eyed the sweat stains on Aye's tunic with disgust.

'Priests wash five times a day, highness, but you message said the matter was urgent. I came immediately.'

'I would have been happy to wait a few minutes. Stand near the window; you are just about bearable there.'

Aye did as he was told, chafing at the indignity of it. The ex-pharaoh was truly unbearable at times. *One day*, he thought, *I will repay you for the insults.* 'And what is so important that it could not wait?'

'I have news from the palace.' Meritaten resented being in Akhet-aten most of the time, but it meant she was closer to her spies. And in Thebes it was harvest time; dust from wheat and barley contaminated everything, even the air one breathed. So all in all, she was better off here, apart from the stench of rank priest.

'There is news, from Ramose. He managed to find Moses. From his dispatch, it seems he simply followed a trail of corpses to find him.'

'So, the apostate still lives?'

'My uncle still lives, Aye, yes. Ramose apparently thinks most of the dead were people who abandoned the march and tried to turn for home. They starved or died of thirst.'

'How do you know this? Is Ramose working for you?'

'No, but I saw the dispatch before Djau did. My spies are lighter on their feet than his; or yours, for that matter.'

Aye swallowed the insult and managed a stiff smile. 'So, Moses' 'chosen people' are starving; eh will not last long before one of them slits his throat, I am thinking.'

'It's funny you should say that. Among the dead, Ramose apparently noted one old man, Hyksos by the look of him. His throat was slit from ear to ear.'

'Ah, so the infighting has already started. This bodes well for us.'

'Perhaps. It's just as likely he had a few coins about him and was killed by bandits. Not that it matters—oh, what is it now?' The knock at the chamber door had been sharp and urgent.

'Messenger, highness, from the palace.'

Meritaten shooed Aye towards a tapestry in the corner of the room. 'Go, hide. I don't need rumours about smelly priests in my chamber to circulate. Enough people hate me as it is.'

The messenger hustled into the chamber and bowed briefly. 'Highness,' he said, and stopped. His nose twitched, and he turned his head towards the tapestry. 'I bring further news on Ramose.'

'Well, out with it, man.'

'It seems he remained at the palace only long enough to eat and change horses. Then he rode off again, with a small troop of soldiers; and he had a female companion.'

'And do we know the identity of this companion?'

'Yes, highness. It was the lady Kiye.'

Meritaten dismissed the messenger with a casual wave of her hand. Then she crossed the room and lifted the tapestry away from the wall, holding her nose. 'Did you hear that, priest?'

'Well, we can be sure that he found Moses. Presumably Kiye is keen to be reacquainted with her erstwhile lover.'

Meritaten was taken aback; she was sure no one else knew about the affair. Aye saw the look on her face and smiled officiously. 'Your spies are good, highness, but mine have their uses too.'

'So, what do we do now? Send an army after him?'

'I don't think it requires an army. And I don't think the pharaoh would thank us for that.' Aye loved the way Meritaten grimaced every time he uttered the word 'pharaoh'.

'Perhaps we need do nothing but wait. If my uncle's people are starving, he will be too. You know how he loves to share their suffering. Poor Kiye is in for an unpleasant surprise, I fear.'

'You may be right, highness. But I think we should put someone in place, just in case. The last thing we need is Moses returning in triumph again.'

'That someone being an assassin, I assume.'

'Quite so, highness.'

Meritaten sighed. 'So be it; we must do what needs doing. I feel a little sorry for Kiye, though. She is an innocent in all of this.'

'When elephants fight, the grass suffers too. Kiye has made her choice, and she must live or die with it.'

* * *

There was still no sign of the pass. And the going wasn't any easier. Moses continued to send out scouts, but he had the distinct feeling he was being deliberately led in this direction; whether by Aten, or by the Hyksos, he wasn't sure.

A commotion at the front of the column drew his attention, and he rode forwards to find people pointing and shouting. There, in the distance, a more or less vertical column of smoke rose into the air. It didn't drift in the breeze, but held its shape, as if it were made of something more solid than smoke.

'Whatever that is, I don't like it.' Kenaten drew up beside him. 'It looks like a fire mountain; I don't think we should venture too near it.'

'I hear you, Kenaten, but it lies in the right direction. I think we could use it as a guide for a few days.'

'You'll have trouble convincing everyone of that. Some are leaving already.'

'They'll be back, Kenaten; they have nowhere to go.'

'I'm not so sure, my lord. I think some of them are at the end of their tether. They probably feel they might as well take their chances on their own as head into uncertainty with a crowd too big to feed.'

Kenaten was right; by the end of the second day trekking towards the strange pillar of smoke, close to half the column had disappeared. At night, fire could be seen at the base of the pillar; its red luminescence was unsettling. Moses' captains had done their best to calm people; now all they could do was hope and pray.

When they were near enough to the pillar to see the flames in the daylight, Moses called a halt. 'I am going to ride down to that thing and see what it is. If it's a sign from Aten, maybe I will find some evidence there, or a message to tell us what to do next. But first,' he beckoned Paser over, 'find me Jo-shah. I need to talk to him.'

The Levite was not happy to be summoned. 'I'm trying to keep my tribe together,' he complained. 'People are leaving all the time. This,' he waved vaguely at the tent walls, 'is a waste of time.'

'Perhaps.' Moses was not in the mood for Jo-shah's petulance. 'But fewer of your people have left than any of the other groups.'

'They have faith, my lord, in you and in the land we are promised.' Jo-shah's words didn't quite match the expression on his face. *He's hiding something.*

'And what of Aron; has he left?'

'I haven't seen him for a few days.' Jo-shah shifted from foot to foot.

'So, does that mean he has left?'

'Possibly. Probably. I don't know, to be honest.'

'So, our guide has disappeared and we are not sure of our course.'

'I suppose so. I don't see I can do anything about that.'

'You can stop lying to me, Jo-shah. That would help.'

'Why would I lie to you, my lord? What secrets can a man keep out here in the wilderness?'

'I am beginning to wonder about that. Leave me, Jo-shah, I have a hard ride ahead of me. We will talk more when I return.'

The house of Imbubu, Akhet-aten

'I don't understand, highness. Surely Moses doesn't want to return. Isn't that the whole point? He took his followers with him.' Horemheb's face was a mask of confusion. He didn't know why he'd been called to this meeting, and now he was here, the things he was hearing didn't make sense.

'Think, general.' Meritaten's voice was honeyed but her eyes were glacial. 'Lady Kiye is not about to run off to Canaan and abandon her son, the pharaoh. The only reason she has for going to see him is to persuade him to return.' *Well, not the only reason, but the details needn't concern a stupid soldier.*

'I still don't see it. Moses must know his life is at risk if he comes back to Egypt. Unless he skulks in the shadows, he is a marked man.'

Aye leaned forward in his chair, and steepled his hands under his chin. 'General, even if the situation is not yet certain, we can't afford to wait and see what happens. We've done that before and it didn't end well.'

'So, what do you propose I do? Send an army off into the desert wastes to search for a missing man we'd rather not find in the first place?'

'You, general, don't need to do anything. Well, nothing that involves armies.' Aye fidgeted with a sweetmeat from the over-laden table but didn't make to eat it. 'We do need a competent scout, though. Is there someone you can trust to be discreet?'

'Scouting is a discreet business, Aye. But yes, I have men I can trust. Will this scout be guiding an assassin or two?'

'Likely yes,' said Meritaten, but Aye immediately raised his hand.

'Actually, that may not be necessary.'

'How so, Aye? Are you thinking his people are so desperate they will turn on him?'

'In a manner of speaking. I learned only yesterday that a man called Jo-shah is among the followers. He's Hyksos, a trouble-maker. We have used his services in the past, and he's certainly not averse to killing.'

Horemheb scratched at his brow under the rim of his cap. 'And how does that help us, exactly?'

'If Jo-shah is with Moses it isn't for theological reasons. He's an opportunist; though quite what the opportunity is I can't fathom.'

'Can we use him now? A sufficiently large bribe, perhaps? It would be easier on all of us if my uncle were killed by one of his own.'

'I believe we can, highness. I'm thinking Jo-shah must have realised by now that the great trek is a fool's errand. A little incentive from us, and the resentment he is likely feeling already; I believe I can smell blood.' Aye's smile was reptilian. 'So, general, if your trusted man can find the Hyksos contingent, break bread with them, offer a healthy amount of gold, I think we can just sit back and wait for the bad news.'

Meritaten clapped slowly. 'I have to allow, priest, that you are the most devious among us. I think this will work.'

Horemheb wasn't fully convinced. 'How far ahead of us are Ramose and Kiye? If they get there first they could scupper our plans before they hatch.'

'A couple of days, no more. Kiye will slow Ramose down, too, so your man should easily catch them up; and pass them. If the trail of corpses is as obvious as Ramose's report indicated, then he won't need to follow a couple of runaways. He can just use his nose.'

'Very well, I'll put a man on it at once. Now, if there is nothing else ...'

'Ah, but there is, general.' Aye rubbed pastry crumbs from his hands. 'We have unfinished business here.'

'You mean—'

'He means my brother, general.' Meritaten glittered with righteous anger. 'Having made a mess of his first attempt, our friend here rather needs to finish the job before too many questions are asked, or someone finds that missing archer.'

Aye drew a finger across his throat. 'That's unlikely, highness. But I take your point; we should make haste to rid ourselves of the heretic child on the throne. If we leave it too long, there will be an heir, and that's a situation none of us want to see.'

Horemheb chuckled grimly. 'So, do I need to find another disposable archer for you, priest?'

'That would be most kind, general. Most kind.'

* * *

Moses returned to camp the following evening. As he had suspected, the pillar of fire was a fissure from an otherwise dormant volcano. He had never seen such a thing before, but he had read about them in the library at Memphis. He spent some hours exploring, going as close as he dared to the column of fire. It emitted a low sound, a rumble and crackle that reminded him of the bush that had burnt under the impact of the sky-stone.

He sat and listened to the inchoate voice of the pillar of fire, and as he listened, he drifted through memories: the burning bush; Kiye, and that first kiss; Akhenaten after the eclipse. Everything seemed so chaotic, but it was part of Aten's plan, he was sure of it.

'Chaos,' he mused. 'Chaos must give way to order in the end.' His mind made up, he gathered what he needed and prepared to return to his people.

'People of Aten! I have been to the mountain of fire. Beyond the fire, there is good grazing for our flocks, fresh water, everything we need. We can be there in a matter of hours. But first,' Moses looked over his people from the rocky promontory he stood on. 'First, I must deliver a message from the lord.'

He held up two pieces of flat volcanic tuff. On the faces of the stones, there were scratches, a squiggle of lines and curves that resembled writing. Those at the front of the crowd craned forward, trying to make sense of the script. Those behind asked what was happening.

'These stones are a gift from Lord Aten. They are the tablets of the law. His commandments are few, and simple. But if we do not obey them, we will be lost.'

He held the tablets aloft, so as many people as possible could see them. Then he lowered his arms, and began to read.

'There is only one god, and he is Aten. You will have no other god.'

There was a murmur of approval in the crowd. This was why they had left Egypt; to follow the only god.

'You will make no images of our god.'

He could see the puzzled faces of the people at the front. Why did it matter?

'Many of you,' he went on, 'carry talismans, images of the old gods, or spirits, to ward off evil, or to bring you luck. Lord Aten commands that you throw these images away. You have no need for them. And you have no need for images of the lord. He is with you every day, in the great expanse of the sky.'

Paser and the captains, at his discreet signal, began to circulate, encouraging people to take the talismans from their belongings and throw them away. The trickle of discarded images became a stream, and then a torrent.

'Say his name!'

'Aten!'

Say his name!'

'Aten!'

'This is how you say the lord's name; in praise, in worship. Do not use his name as a curse, or you will bring the curse of the lord on your head.'

He waited until the shouts had died down.

'Remember the oasis, where the lord sweetened the water for us? Remember how we rested there, free of our labours, in praise of Aten? The lord commands that one day in seven, we will rest from our labours. That will be his day, a holy day. And we will keep this day holy from today, until the end of time.'

Pentu winked at Herit. 'A day off, on the lord's say so,' he whispered. 'I like the sound of that.'

'We all come, originally, from Lord Aten, who created everything. But your seed, the seed that formed you, is from your mother and father. Honour them, for without them you are nothing.'

'Do not kill. Life is Aten's to give, and only his to take.'

'Do not lay eyes on another man's wife, and do not commit adultery. This is an abomination to the lord.'

Kiye, I'm sorry. What we did was wrong. But I would not change anything for the world and all its riches.

'Do not steal. The lord has provided everything you need. Don't take what another person needs to satisfy your greed.'

'Do not lie. If anyone asks you to be a witness in a dispute, don't give false testimony. The lord is honest with you; you must be honest in turn.'

'That is all. A few simple commandments. If you can keep these commandments, the lord will look on you with pleasure. If you cannot, he will abandon you. Think on these laws, my people, and remember them in your hearts. These laws are what mark us out as a chosen people, chosen of Aten; there is no other people on earth like us. When we arrive in the land we have been promised, these laws will provide order and safety in our new home. Soon we will march again; and soon we will arrive at our destination. The lord has spoken. Now rest, and prepare yourselves.'

He was exhausted now. The heat of the sun, and the effort of keeping the attention of so many people, had drained him. He hadn't had time to explain how they would enforce the commandments; how he would appoint judges from each of the tribes. He hadn't really explained the rules for those who were puzzled by them. He had seen Paser's face when he had said 'do not kill'. How could a soldier interpret that?

He stumbled towards his tent, oblivious to the people around him.

The details could wait for another day.

1326 BC

Sinai. Year 4 in the reign of Thutankhaten.

Ramose and his men broke camp, while Kiye washed her face and hands in the little stream that had kept her awake all night, babbling an incoherent message she kept trying to understand. What she would give for a warm bath. She walked back to the camp; Ramose was deep in conversation with Henuef, his chief scout.

'Good news, highness. Henuef rode ahead before dawn. He says there is a large body of people, heading towards the plateau in a ring of small mountains the local people call Pisgah. It can only be Lord Moses and his followers.'

Her heart raced. Her mission was to persuade Moses to come back to Egypt, re-establish the rule of Aten, and help her son, but now they were close, she could only think of seeing him again, of holding him in her arms.

Ramose interrupted her thoughts. 'If we make good speed, we will be with them by late afternoon. We have saved many days by using the coast road. I am still puzzled why Lord Moses chose to take the desert route.'

'He could not be sure of his safety, Ramose. For all he knew, there might be an army at his back.'

'Perhaps, highness. But it's no matter now. We are nearly there.'

Kiye laid her hand on his arm. 'Thank you, Ramose. I will not forget your help.'

'I am yours to command, highness.'

She watched him walk away, a tinge of regret weighing in her heart.

Oh, Moses; I hope, when we meet again, it will turn out to be worth it.

* * *

The foothills below the mountain of god were carpeted in lush grass and herbs. Flocks of emaciated sheep and goats fed happily on the slopes. The people of Aten had spread out over the plateau, gathering vegetation and herbs. They had arrived at the mountain a few days earlier after many, many moons of toil.

One late afternoon, as the day was cooling, Moses and a few well-chosen men rode to investigate a fissure where smoke had had left the earth in huge quantities. It was not a pillar of smoke like Aten's mountain but a long slither of ruined rock and blistered soil. When they reached the site the smoke appeared to be returning through a jagged crack in the ground. Paser looked at the strange sight. 'Is it an omen, my lord?'

'It is Paser. It is time to move on. We are in the final stage of our journey. As he turned his horse he noticed an eagle owl hovering above him; again. 'If we had eyes as good as our friend up there,' he said, pointing to the eagle, 'we would be able to see Canaan.' He laughed, dug his heels into his horse's flanks and yelled as it sped off back toward the camp.

He was almost at the encampment when a young acolyte ran towards him, a look of consternation on his face. 'My lord, I think you should see what is happening in the camp.'

'I should see what?'

'The Hyksos, lord. They have golden images which are not of Aten.'

'Images of pagan gods?'

'Yes lord.'

They headed for the plateau at a gallop.

A large crowd had gathered in the centre of the encampment. They were singing, dancing, and drinking.

Paser said, 'It's alright lord, they are simply thanking the lord for their safe arrival. I don't think we need to interrupt.'

The acolyte disagreed. 'No, lord. Look on the rock in the middle of the crowd, that gold statuette glistening in the light of the fires.'

'Wait, that's a statue of Hathor. What on earth is going on?'

They party rode down the track towards the golden idol, scattering people as they went. The people nearest the idol didn't notice them at all.

'Stop this,' Moses shouted. Nothing happened.

'Sound the gong.'

The gong brought a few of the revellers to their senses. They saw Moses on his horse, incandescent with anger. He looked like a god.

'What's going on here?'

An old man was pushed forwards; he didn't look too keen to be the spokesman. 'We are celebrating the day of Hathor, lord.'

'Have you forgotten so quickly? You will have no other god but Aten. Not Amun or Re or Horus or Seth and not...' He took a sword from Paser and struck the golden statue. 'Not this piece of metal.'

The crowd were still now. No one felt like celebrating.

'You.' He pointed at the elders. 'You take your families and all these idolaters and leave. Now.'

Moses turned his horse and rode away. From the margins of the crowd, Jo-shah watched him go.

Akhet-aten

Henu sighed. It didn't matter how many times he looked at the flood marker; the news was still bad. 'Kewab,' he called. 'Make a note. It's actually lower than two years ago, and that was a disaster. It seems last year was just a temporary reprieve; that or a gift from Amun.

Kewab's eyes widened.

'Oh, don't be so alarmed, man. There's no one here to hear us, and if there was, I doubt they'd raise an eyebrow.'

'But the god, Henu.'

'The days of the one god are numbered, I think. And these numbers,' he pointed to the flood marker, 'are the ones that will count him out.'

Djau held the flood tallies in his hand. 'I'm afraid, highness, it's bad news. Very bad news.'

Thutankhaten scowled. His sister, Neferneuaten, looked at the chancellor blankly. *She is already drunk*, the old man thought, *and the day has hardly started*.

Djau continued. 'That's six years out of the past seven that the Nile has been low. The only good tide had to come in the year of the great festival of Amun, of course. It's as if we are being mocked by heaven.'

Thutankhaten couldn't argue. The granaries were practically empty; this year's harvest was not going to fill them. 'I would pray for guidance, Djau, but to be honest with you, I don't find I have much enthusiasm for prayer these days. It doesn't seem to make much difference.'

'Have faith, highness. Things will turn around, in time.'

'Well, that's one thing we don't have. I imagine Aye is laughing at us in Thebes.'

'Actually, the laughter is rather closer than that. Aye and Horemheb are both here in the city.'

Thutankhaten sighed. 'Then we are close to the final act, I think. Aye will be eager to blame us for the poor harvest; and I'm sure he has another archer waiting for me. This time, I may not be so lucky.'

Djau looked at his young protégé, pityingly. *You are right, majesty. I doubt you will see too many more years. And neither will I, I fear.*

'I wish . . .'

'You wish what, brother?' Neferneuaten made to rise from her seat, but decide it was too much effort. 'That the river would grow overnight?'

'Well, that's a thought.' Thutankhaten laughed bitterly. 'I wish Uncle Moses were here. I don't suppose he could raise the river by himself, whatever the tales the priests tell about him, but I would feel better to have his counsel.'

'Do you want Aye and his henchmen to kill us all?' Neferneuaten found the energy to leap from her chair. 'If Moses was here, do you think the priests of Amun would sit idly by? The army? Moses is a torch in a room full of lamp oil, brother.'

'You never believed in him, did you, sister?'

'It's not him we were supposed to believe in, brother. Uncle Moses is just a man; a man who stupidly believed in a god that doesn't exist. Anyway, who knows if he still lives?'

'My mother does. She has gone to see him, to persuade him to return.'

'Why did you let her go on such a fool's errand?'

'I couldn't stop her.'

'And if she succeeds? If she brings him back now, with Aye and Horemheb here, and the harvest a disaster? How will he survive that? How will any of us survive that?' Neferneuaten turned to leave. 'You enjoy the bad news. I don't think you need advice.' She flounced out of the chamber, staggering and swaying.

Thutankhaten gave Djau a rueful smile. 'Well, my old friend, it seems we are on our own.'

'Perhaps, highness. If Moses is alive, and your mother is with him, she will bring him back. But I fear your sister has the right of it. That won't be the end of our troubles.'

'No, it won't. What shall we do, Djau?'

'I am old, highness. I will die soon enough. I would prefer to die here, where my ancestors lived in the true light of Aten.'

'Then we will wait and see what the day brings. And I'll have a word with Thethi, ask him to keep an eye on Neferneuaten. We hardly need another enemy in the family.' *Or maybe I should have the old witch brought here again, sacrilege I know, but, I am losing faith in everything. Maybe she might have some good news for me?*

* * *

The guard popped his head around the flapping doorway of the tent.

'What is it?'

'A lookout from the southern edge of the camp, my lord.'

'Let him in.'

The lookout, a small man with no teeth, entered the tent.

Moses rose to his feet. 'What news do you bring?'

'My lord, there are people approaching the camp. They have Egyptian insignia and they have a carriage with them. Where they would be going in this god forsaken part of the world I don't know. But, they are currently heading in our direction.'

Moses patted the man on the back and sent him off, back to the edge of the camp. He turned to Paser. 'They shouldn't be in these parts if they value their lives,' he said. 'Let's go and see what they want.'

Paser and Moses rode through the camp. 'Kenaten,' Moses shouted over his shoulder. His aide quickly mounted and joined them and they made their way to the southern end of the encampment.

Moses sent Paser to greet the visitors.

'Fifteen, maybe sixteen people; hardly an army,' Kenaten said. 'I think you are safe enough, my lord.'

Paser, with visitors in tow, rode up the side of the hill. They reached the centre of the camp as the sun was setting; fifteen mounted men, and a small carriage. Moses didn't recognise the soldiers, though the big Nubian looked vaguely familiar.

'You are welcome,' he said to the officer was obviously in command. 'Come inside. What brings you here? What news from Egypt?'

'Many questions lord, but do you not know me?'

'No,' said Moses, 'but I seem to have your face engrained in my mind.'

'I am Ramose, of the pharaoh's guard.'

'Of course.'

'And I am Kiye, of the pharaoh's family.'

Moses' heart lurched.

Kiye stepped out of the carriage. Their eyes met and their hearts stopped. Moses marvelled at how she looked; he thought of that day, the first time he had seen her. She hardly seemed to have changed. And in some ways, neither had he; if this was the first time he had seen her, he would have fallen in love all over again.

She whispered his name, as if it was a secret. He half turned and indicated the entrance to his tent. She dipped her head and stepped inside. The tall Nubian followed her. Paser placed a hand over the chest of Kenaten and whispered, 'You see to the party, give them water to wash and good food and drink. Look after them. I will see you later.' Kenaten winked and turned.

Moses took Kiye's hand; they sat on cushions, in a circle, Paser and Ramose opposite the lord and lady.

'Now I remember you properly,' Moses said. 'You tracked and killed that leopard at the Elephantine. I am so glad you are here. But whatever brings you to this forsaken place?'

'I have some documents for you, Lord Moses. From the pharaoh.'

'Meritaten?' Moses said despondently.

'No, lord, Thutankhaten.'

The shock on Moses' face made Kiye laugh.

Ramose spoke again. 'I will leave them with you, highness. If I don't hear anything by tomorrow evening, we'll make our way back to Akhet-aten. These are my orders.' He stood, his broad frame shadowing the entrance for a second, and then he was gone. Moses nodded to Paser, who followed him.

Now they were alone, he had so many questions. 'So Thutankhaten is pharaoh, poor boy; he's far too young. Who advises him?'

'Djau, and sometimes I try to help. He is married to your niece Ankhsenaten, who is far too young to be of any help; and then of course there is Aye and Horemheb hovering like a pair of vultures; and Meritaten doesn't help.'

'That has the sound of a deadly tug of war.'

'That's the truth of it; he's being torn apart for the sake of the kingdom. He needs you, Moses.'

'What good would I be? Every time I've tried to do things for Egypt I've engendered a disaster.'

'If someone doesn't help him; if you don't help him, they will kill him. They have already tried once. I can only hope to find him alive if and when I return.'

'If?'

'I have had enough of being alone, Moses. If you return, I'll return with you. If you choose to stay here, I will stay with you. It tears my heart to leave him, but I am destined to be with you, whether we live or die.'

'I must take the people to Canaan; then we will see what happens.'

* * *

Three men in Bedouin clothing arrived at the camp edge. They had waited until dark before approaching the edge of the camp and had in like birds on the wind. In a clearing on the northern edge they found who they wanted.

'What brings you to us?' asked a Hyksos guard.

'I have a message for your elders.'

'Who from?'

'Important people in Egypt.'

'I know nothing about that. Our tribe elders make the decisions.'

'Then take us to them.'

'Why should I do that?'

'Look old man, I don't have time to mess about. Either take us to your elders or we will have to find another route; without you.'

'You threatenin' me?'

'Yes.'

The old man crumpled to the floor.

'What do we do now?

'Ask someone else.'

'What do we do with him?'

'Don't you worry. With an uneducated mob as big as this there will be a new body found every night.'

'You looking for the Hyksos elders?'

Aye's mans hand drew his knife again, swiftly.

'No need for that, my friend. I seen what you done. Follow me. I will take you to where you want to be.'

A short walk and they were asked to stand outside a tent; big, but dirty.

'Prove who you are.' The voice came from inside the tent, and it carried menace.

Aye's man took out a roll of papyrus from within his cloak. 'Do you see the seal on this parchment?'

'I don't recognise it. Could be any old seal.'

'Look more closely, at the centre, the image there.'

'That's Amun; you're not supposed to have him here. You're from where again?'

'Egypt. Thebes. Temple of Amun.'

'Wait here.'

Aye's man waited. After a few minutes, the tent flap opened.

'Come with me,' a bearded man said. Aye's men entered the tent; ten faces peered at them, most old and tired, a couple old but fresh, and two young ones. One of the young ones came forward to greet him. 'Well, what are you doing here?'

'The high priest of Amun asked me to deliver this.' He took out the scroll from inside his cloak again. 'To the chief of the Hyksos. These are my orders. Now, who shall I give this to?'

'Me,' the young one said, holding out his hand and flexing his fingers.

'I doubt it.'

'Me.' Jo-shah was clean cut and obviously in charge. 'I will take your message and I will discuss it with our council. Do you require a reply?'

'My master has asked that I take your response back to Thebes. It doesn't do to disappoint him.'

'We will not,' replied Jo-shah. 'Please wait outside, all three of you. We may be a while.' He turned to a guard. 'Make these men comfortable, give them good food and drink. Ensure that they do not come to any harm.' He turned back to the one who had brought the scroll. 'We will give your message our attention and give you our response. I will call you when we are ready.'

'Read it, Jo-shah.'

Greetings,

My servants here in Thebes have been considering the happenings in the court at Akhet-ten. We are greatly displeased with what we hear. It has come to our attention that a company of the royal guard together with the queen mother Kiye, have been sent to find your community. They are there specifically to persuade Moses to return to Egypt and bring all of the community back with him. Our friends in the palace advise us that there is no doubt that Moses will return and no one will carry on to Canaan. This will not be any good for Egypt, and, we are sure, will not be any good for your tribe either. I thought it best therefore to let you know of the intentions of your current leader, Moses, and his officers. We leave you to decide what will benefit your nation, Hyksos. We would prefer

> *your community not to return to Egypt but to carry*
> *on to the land promised to you where you no doubt*
> *will build a nation to be proud of.*
> *I leave you the blessings of Amun and all the gods and*
> *hope that you do what is necessary*
> *Aye*
> *High Priest of Amun — Grand Vizier to the Pharaoh*

'I told you this would happen.' Jo-shah's expression was a mix of venom and triumph. 'And, as much as I trust the Thebans as far as could spit them, this letter rings true. Now, gentlemen, what are we to do about it?'

There was only one thing they could do. Jo-shah asked the question and every hand rose.

* * *

'They should have returned by now.' Aye was fretting. 'If Moses or his friends have found them out ...'

'Calm yourself, priest. They will be here.' Horemheb busied himself sharpening a dagger with a stone; the sound irritated Meritaten but she tried to ignore it.

'I hope you are right. I am bored of waiting and doing nothing.'

'It won't be long now, highness.' Aye said. 'Your coronation will be before the end of the year; I promise you.'

'I will believe that when the crown rests upon my head; as sole ruler.' Aye cast a glance at Horemheb. *Not now.*

There was a knock on the door.

'Enter.'

'Lord,' a servant entered the room, 'there is a messenger.'

'Send him in.'

Aye went to greet his man and drew him into the room. 'What do you have to tell us?'

'I delivered the scroll as you requested, lord.'

'And?'

'And the response is here.' He handed a parchment to Aye.

'Open it!' Meritaten's boredom had evaporated

'Read it.' Horemheb looked at the messenger, who still stood close to Aye. 'Rather, read it when . . .'

Aye dismissed the messenger. 'You will be rewarded well. Now leave us.'

> *Lord of Amun, Greetings*
> *We thank you for your message. We have taken note*
> *of it. We understand the position you find yourself in.*
> *Moses is, however, crucial to our needs.*

'Oh hell,' Meritaten said. 'That's not a good start.'

'No,' mumbled Aye.

'Be quiet, both of you and read it through. You should never try to understand a position simply from the first move.'

> *If what you say is true then it will put us in a very*
> *bad position and we will have to act.*
> *If Moses stays on course we will be with him all of*
> *the way to Canaan. However, if he should decide*
> *to return to Egypt, alters the situation. Under those*
> *circumstances we would have no alternative but to*
> *prevent such a turn.*
> *We hope this has answered your query.*
> *We send the blessings of the one and only god to you.*
> *The council of the tribes of Hyksos.*

'Well, there we have it,' said Aye. his heart hammered in his chest; victory was so close he could smell it, and it smelled of blood.

1325 BC

Sinai. Year 5 in the reign of Thutankhaten

'I have made a decision.' Moses stroked Kiye's hair. 'Aten has spoken. We will return to Akhet-aten Kiye and help Thutankhaten. We will rid the empire of Aye once and for all. The country will be great again.'

'And when do we return, my love?' Kiye was already packing things into a bag.

I must let my officers and the tribe elders know. I don't think that will be an easy conversation. People have suffered so much to get here. But I must do what my lord commands, even if it makes me yet more enemies. What is it about my life? Every time I make a decision, I hear a blade being sharpened.'

'Oh, Moses, that will change. When all is settled in Egypt, you will be safe.'

'I hope so, but I won't wager on it yet.' Moses called for Paser.

'Paser, we need to bring the officers and the elders together.'

'For what purpose, highness?' Paser asked. The expression on Moses' face puzzled him.

'For the purpose of returning to Egypt.'

Paser froze. 'Pardon, lord?'

'You heard correctly, Paser. We are going home. Now bring the officers and elders.'

'Yes, lord.' Paser turned and made his way from Moses' tent. He could feel snakes coiling in the pit of his stomach.

* * *

Rumours were spreading like wildfire within the camp. Within minutes of the meeting Moses had had with the elders, almost everyone knew what he had said. Their confusion, and their innate faith in their leader, was in stark contrast to the discussions in the Hyksos elders' tent.

'The woman is a complication.'

'Of that there is no doubt,' said Jo-shah. 'But if we are to do as we've agreed, she cannot return to Egypt. We would have an army at our backs before we had time to strike camp.'

'So, we cannot let her go back to Egypt.' The wizened elder stroked the stubble on his chin.

'So, we are agreed; we must kill her along with him.'

'It's not what we want,' said a bearded man with hands like hams, 'but what circumstances bring to us. He must die, there is no question. Her being here makes things a little messy, but it's just another body, when all is said and done.'

The wizened man cackled grimly. 'More than one; the soldiers cannot be allowed to escape. It doesn't matter who the messenger is if bad news is carried.'

Jo-shah stood. 'Leave it to me,' he said, 'I will ensure all is taken care of. It is best that none of you know what is to happen; safer for you if anything goes wrong. Caleb, Jedediah, come with me.'

'Wait a moment,' Jo-shah said to his two companions. 'I have a letter to write.' He slipped into his tent.

My dear friends,
I have seen how you reacted to my decision to return
to Egypt. It hurts me to see that many of you are
against it. The lady Kiye and I have therefore decided
to leave you all and allow you to go on. I will watch
you enter the promised land from the top of the moun-
tain of Pisgah. We will then return to Egypt together.
We wish you all life and grace with our lord Aten.
Have faith in him and he will return that faith a
thousand times. With the blessings of Aten I leave
you. Go in peace.
Moses

He returned five minutes later. Caleb looked worried.

'I don't like this. Killing a woman is bad but killing a woman who is a god?'

'She is not a god.'

'She is a member of the royal family; she is a god.'

'There is only one god.'

'But . . .'

'But nothing. Stop fretting and get on with the job. I know some people who care not who they kill; as long as there is money involved.'

In a clearing at the side of the encampment Jo-shah found who he was looking for.

'Are you still available for the work?' Jo-shah asked the man.

'Are you still able to pay?'

'Here.' Jo-shah passed a small bag to the man. He smiled and reached out to take it.

'Not yet. Not so quick.'

The man looked daggers at Jo-shah.

'Half now, and half when the job is complete.'

'Three-quarters now.'

'Half.'

'You had better come up with the other half or you will be joining them in the underworld.' Jo-shah ignored the threat, though he had no doubt it was serious.

'You will suffocate both Moses and Kiye and get rid of their bodies. You will leave this papyrus in a prominent place.' Jo-shah fetched a roll of papyrus from his cloak and handed it to the man. 'Understood?'

The assassin smoothed his beard with a curiously cultured hand. 'I will have to engage an accomplice.'

'The more eyes, the more mouths. I don't like it.'

'They are royalty and so will not sleep in the same bed. That will make it more difficult. We will have to kill two at the same moment. So, two souls needed to kill two souls.' He looked into Jo-shah's eyes. Could he force more gold from the man for the extra death? The resolute look he received in return told him the answer was no.

'If you think you are not up to the job, tell me now. You are not the only killer in the desert. I am paying you enough to sort out any complications. If you have to use another it is at your cost, financially and physically; fail me one or the other and you will die.'

'Do not concern yourself. I know a man with no tongue; he and I will do the work.'   'Make sure they disappear so no one will ever find them; and, no blood, understand me? There should be no evidence of any struggle. It should look as if they have deserted the people and gone off together.'

'It will be as you ask.'

'Good. Now go, and quietly. It is best if no one sees us together.' The assassin made to leave. Jo-shah grabbed him by the arm. 'And don't forget to leave the papyrus in a prominent position.' The assassin nodded and lifted the scroll for Jo-shah to see, and slipped out of the tent into the shadows.

Jo-shah beckoned to Jedediah. 'Take two men with you. Go quietly. Follow him and his accomplice. When they have done their work...' He slid a finger across his throat. Jedediah smiled and left. He sighed. 'Ah, Moses, we could have done some things together, you and I. But you cannot tear yourself away from Egypt, and that will be the death of you. No matter. The chosen people will find their way without you; after all, they have me.'

Through the ropes and debris, moving with infinite patience, the two men threaded their way, focused minds, eyes like eagles, men on a mission. The quality of the light changed, just for a second, and they stopped, instantly alert. Among the soft shadows of the tents, something sharper, deeper, moved. A line of black creased the moon's crescent, then folded and fell from view. The tall man focused his very being on to the dark sky with the barely visible curl of white light. Moments later, the black shape rose into sight again, some unfortunate small creature struggling in its talons as it once more cut through the shining moon. He let out a slow breath, only now realising he had been holding the air in his lungs; an eagle owl, and he has made his kill; a good omen, he was satisfied. He tapped his colleague on the shoulder, three times; all clear. The assassins moved on, slowly, carefully, until their target loomed in front of them.

They covered the last few steps at a snail's pace, stopping by the wall of the tent they knew was their goal. The tall man took a small, lethally sharp knife from his belt and crouched. He looked around, once, twice; he whispered into his friends' vacant ear. Are you ready? Is this all clear for you? As his friend nodded his affirmative readiness the man gently slit the jute fabric until the gap was just big enough for him to crawl through.

He put the knife back in its sheath; this mission called for subtler methods than the blade. One last look around, one last consideration of agreement from his colleague and they were gone; moving swiftly and silently into the tent.

The eagle owl hovered over the plateau, no more the wriggling outline in its talons, it was a still silhouette against the stars.

1322 BC

The hills at the far side of the valley of death.

Year 8 in the reign of Thutankhaten

She knew death was near; it whispered to her on the wind. As for the boy—his light would shine again, but it would take a very, very long time. Gold would be his legacy to the world, not his brief career as pharaoh. Should she stop it? She had the power to do so. No, it was fate; what had to be, had to be.

She could hear the man climbing down the cliff face. She could see him too in her mind; he did not look like an assassin, but whoever did? Did he realise that he would rot in the underworld, burn endlessly? Perhaps; or maybe someone had lied to him, given him a false sense of righteousness.

It bothered him. Killing the witch was not a good thing to do. She was a priestess of Heka, and it could be that he may be damning his soul for eternity at the vengeance of the goddess. But Aye had informed him personally, Amun would protect him, Amun, the greatest god of all. No, no need for concern, his soul was protected by the greatest of gods.

He slipped on a patch of scree. 'Shite!' It came out as a loud whisper but even so he placed a hand upon his mouth. No need for her to know he was approaching.

She was waiting for him at the entrance.

'Come in.'

Did she know he was coming? Ah, no; the witch had sensed his approach, that was it. Her mind was cued into all around her.

'Welcome.'

She led him into her cave and as he followed her along a coarse trail as she spoke. 'All is well.' She said. 'You must do what your masters have ordered. The gods are at ease with your quest.'

He blinked. Every time he'd met the witch she had surprised him with her knowledge. *I suppose now is no different.*

At the back of the cave, on a shelf of stone which jutted out from the wall, a phial waited. 'Here is your potion,' she said. 'It is the last I shall ever make, so your master should use it well. If he falters in my instructions he will fail.' She took the phial from the shelf and passed it to him.

He took the weird jar, made a of a substance he had never seen before. 'Thank you.' He said.

The witch led him to the centre of her cave. A small table stood there with three stools equidistant; remnants of a fire laid in the centre, a small pan filled with some dark liquid waited in the embers. 'Come now. Have some tea before we go to the last stage of our journey together.'

They sat.

She smiled.

She talked, gibbering to the third stool.

He started to sweat profusely.

She poured the thick, dark liquid from the pan adjacent to the dying fire. 'Here.' She held out the beaker for him.

Should he drink?

His sweating increased.

He started to shake.

He had no choice.

He took a small sip of the viscous liquid and set the cup down. Now was the time.

He slowly and deliberately took out the knife he had hidden in the pocket of his cloak and did what he had been paid to do.

The dying witch stared at him as blood left the hole which now crossed her belly. He felt terminal shivers edging down his spine.

'Aye lied to you,' she said through the blood that emerged from her mouth and stained her soiled tunic. 'You are cursed. You will burn forever in the outer reaches of the underworld.'

He screamed.

EPILOGUE

Miriam stood in the garden, at the foot of Yuk's grave. The inscription Yuffu had carved for his old friend was already starting to fade; she could read 'servant' well enough but 'loyal' had almost disappeared.

The news of Thutankhaten's death had surprised no one. The proclamation that followed had caught everyone off guard, though. Aye had married Ankhsenaten, who was renamed Ankhsenamun; Aye was now Pharaoh. He was burying Thutankhaten as Tutankhamun, to prove that the pharaoh really was a follower of Amun and not the anti-god Aten. The young pharaoh would be buried not in Akhet-aten where his tomb had already been commenced, but in the death valley in Thebes. Stelae had been placed around the edges of the empire attempting to show that Thutankhaten had apostatized and changed his name of his own accord, taking the capital back to Thebes, and re-establishing the old gods; but she doubted this, more propaganda from Aye.

She was in the artisans' market, chatting to Aneksi, when the herald had marched into the square, accompanied by a squad of palace guards. 'Behold, the new pharaoh rises. Behold, he ascends. Praise be to Aye, beloved of Amun and his queen Ankhsenamun.'

'Well, that didn't take him long,' said Aneksi. 'First he kills that poor boy, then he jumps into the wife's bed, and now he's grabbed the crowns. Fast work for an old priest. Wonder what Horemheb thinks of all this happening while he is half a world away fighting in Syria?'

Miriam looked again at the headstone. 'You'd have worked it out, wouldn't you, my love?' She pulled up a couple of weeds from the grave mound. 'Nothing the elite did ever surprised you. Well, they are all gone now. In a few years, no one will remember Moses, or Akhenaten, and who will think of poor Tutankhamun? As for Aten, who will believe that a single god could ever rule the world? No, there will be a multitude of gods forever.'

She turned away from the grave, and looked out to the west, beyond the bounds of the city. The sun was barely a crescent of gold above the horizon; and then darkness fell.

AUTHOR'S NOTE

On a sunny afternoon in early August nineteen-seventy-six, my wife and I visited a junk stall at a market in Skegness, Lincolnshire, England. There, lying on the floor was a solid brass copy of the death mask of Tutankhamun. Tut had always been a fascination with me from early childhood, when I would tell my fourth-grade class that I had visited Egypt and seen the treasures of his tomb—all in my mind, you understand! I had, and still have, a vivid imagination, or some may say a strange and weird foresight, for one day I did make that journey to Egypt, and made that dream real. However, at that stage, in a sink school in a north-east England mining village, it was totally unrealistic for me to imagine that I, or my family, would ever be able to leave the village, never mind make that visit.

Then there was my fascination with Moses. A strict church upbringing had introduced him to me at a very early age and a desire to know him more had my young mind spinning. Consequently, another unrealistic dream saw me taking the Exodus alongside him, and writing dramas about our adventures for school consumption. 'Has great dramatic ability,' the teacher would write on my report, ' …a wonderful imagination.'

So, as the years went by, and I grew and escaped the slums—becoming what some may call an 'educated' person—my mind played with my two heroes. It interlocked them into a particular period of history, and I studied them more deeply to find a connection. And then I came upon Akhenaten, and I was completely blown over.

Here was the link to Moses; here was the link to Tutankhamun; here was what I had always known was there—a man of great stature, a man who changed the world, a man linked to another great, Moses. And all in the same time frame. I had opened the door. I had seen the light!

My thoughts became my research, subjectivity taking the back seat to objectivity, discovery before imagination. I spent years trying to get to the bottom of these three lives and how they interplayed. I found that Akhenaten had started monotheism, that Moses had developed it, and that Tutankhamun, under great pressure from religious and military leaders, stopped it in Egypt, allowing Moses followers to expand it in Canaan.

I found what I believe is the true story of the beginnings of Judaism, Christianity and Islam. I found on the banks of the Nile the one true God. I found Moses, a real Egyptian Prince; not a foundling in bulrushes but a prince born into the royal household and given the name of Thutmoses, brother of Akhenaten. He was not Hebrew; indeed, there is no contemporary evidence of any such people at that time, in Egypt or anywhere else, he was an Egyptian.

So, this is my story. The story of two brothers who changed the world and a son whose tomb discovery rocked the world. Akhenaten, the focused pharaoh who suddenly and uniquely changed the religious practises of an Empire, and died for it; obliterated from history by his successors. Moses, his fanatical brother who forced forward those changes and died for them;

elated to the highest of high in a monotheistic movement. And a son Pharaoh Tutankhamun who died inexplicably early perhaps by the hand of those who killed his father and ended the life of his 'uncle', Moses. And of a priest, Aye, who succeeded Tutankhamun to the throne, and, by sheer perseverance, engineered much of these events.

Aye married Ankhsenamun, Tutankhamun's wife, immediately after Tutankhamun's death, thus giving himself rights to become Pharaoh, manoeuvring around his lack of legitimacy for the crown. As Amun High Priest, Commander of Chariotry and Fan-bearer at the King's Right Hand, he also had the power to use his own contacts to ensure his claim.

Aye then ruled Egypt for three years and instituted a programme of return to orthodox religious practices. He died without an heir, so leaving a vacuum at the highest level into which Horemheb was quick to pounce and take the throne. To legitimate his claim, he married Mutnedjmet, the last surviving female member of the royal family of the 18th Dynasty, sister of Nefertiti; he was not of royal blood, he too needed legitimacy for his reign.

As a result of his hatred of Akhenaten and the curse of Aten, Horemheb attempted to destroy all public records and monuments erected by Akhenaten, and to erase the memories of Moses, Tutankhamun, Smenkhkare and, of course, Aye. He would rule Egypt for the next twenty-seven years, and, in that time, Egypt returned to its former status as a great power.

Was Tutankhamun's plan to bring Moses back discovered by the wrong people? Was Tutankhamun murdered to stop the return of his father's religion? Was this the secret found in Carter's scrolls which so easily disappeared? It may well be that they, or another manuscript, may be found at a later date, written by the same scribe who secreted the scroll within Tutankhamun's tomb. We may never know the objective truth.

However, there are three facts that we can rely upon to question the status quo. The first concerns Thutmoses' (Moses) whip and personal dagger, both found in Tutankhamun's burial chamber, which begs the question, why? If his uncle had died many years before his birth, would his, Thutmoses, personal possessions to be buried with Tutankhamun? Second, the dagger is made of an element not found anywhere on earth. It could only be made from something extra-terrestrial, a meteorite landing in ancient times, which, when landing, could have ignited a bush, hence the burning bush story. And third, why is Aten's symbol the only symbol shown on Tutankhamun's golden throne? If he had restored the kingdom to Amun, why not Amun with him in life and death; why Aten? And this tomb, so small for such an important man. Was this the tomb his father had begun as Pharaoh Amenhotep whilst still in Thebes, only to be abandoned when he moved to Akhet-aten? One must have been started before he changed the capital, and thereby his burial chamber. It would still have been there in the Valley of the Kings, an empty structure with a few chambers unfinished.

Tutankhamun's tomb was buried by the sands and his name forgotten until Howard Carter discovered the site in 1922; together with those mysterious scrolls.

Questions also remain about the official story of Uncle Moses — he who would not enter the promised land when he had striven all his life for his god and its place in the world? Why would someone who had done so much for his cause suddenly decide not to partake in the final act of establishing Aten supreme and omnipotent? Why would he decide when seeing the promised land not to set foot in it? Death, by Hyksos murderers, was why he never reached the promised land, choosing to return to help his Thutankhaten in Egypt rather than go on to it, upsetting the new status-quo.

During my research, I read Sigmund Freud's rare book on the period. Freud considered that Moses must have been involved in this period and developed a psychological observation of the development of Judaism through Atenism. We have this in common.

As an afterthought, it is worthwhile reading a stele from Tutankhamun's reign called the 'Restoration Decree of Tutankhamun'. It describes a country in chaos at the death of Akhenaten; a position Aye needed to portray. It tells us that the cults of the gods had been abolished by Akhenaten, that their temples had been abandoned and that, as a result, they no longer heard the prayers of the people. Then it advises that Tutankhamun carried out repairs to the derelict temples and restored the old gods' religion, righted things to Aye's required right, and removed the god Aten from prime position. However, Tutankhamun was too young to direct and write this—was it written and exhibited by Aye to help him move easily into his role? These words, exhibited in the appropriate place, would prove that he had been right all the time, and confirm his right to take the throne as Pharaoh!

There are few remaining relics which help us understand what really happened during that period in Egyptian history, so we are left with differing views of the Moses legend (I use that word as there is no contemporary evidence for his existence) from holy books, written hundreds of years after the event to revitalise the monotheistic movement. These start with the plagues which no doubt did rock Egypt at the time. The Jewish Bible and the Islamic Koran agree that plagues occurred, but they differ on the manner of that occurrence, and this difference is very important to your understanding of Moses actions.

In the Bible the plagues are consecutive as follows:

Water into blood: Exodus. 7:14—24
Frogs: Exodus. 7:25—8:15
Lice: Exodus. 8:16—19
Flies or wild animals: Exodus. 8:20—32
Diseased livestock: Exodus. 9:1—7
Boils: Exodus. 9:8—12
Thunderstorm of hail and fire: Exodus. 9:13—35
Locusts: Exodus. 10:1—20
Darkness for three days: Exodus. 10:21—29
Death of firstborn: Exodus. 11:1—12:36

The Book of Deuteronomy mentions the "diseases of Egypt" (Deuteronomy 7:15 and 28:60), but this was something that afflicted the Israelites, not the Egyptians; in fact, it never mentions the plagues at all which can only be found in the book of Exodus.

In the view of Islam, the plagues happened simultaneously, as one event instead of ten separate events. (*Surah Al-A'raf verse 133*)

The Quran further relates that the plagues included a mighty blast, showers of stones and earthquakes (*Ali, Notes 3462-3464 to S. XXIX.40*), which is very close to the eruption of a volcano as used in this book. This event is also described in many contemporary ancient texts.

Consideration should also be given to the parting of the Dead Sea, which event is attached to the plagues. The parting of the waters need not have been a sea parting. It is known that there were marshes at the site of the Great Salt Lake, which were treacherous and could easily have been the site of the death of the Egyptian Pharaoh, as shown in my book. An entry on the Palermo Stone reporting King Den's visit to the sacred lake of Heryshef at Nenj-neswt, the ancient name of the city, suggests that it was already in existence by the mid First Dynasty, and close to the small 'sea'; was this the 'sea' which parted; a marsh of shifting waters?

Finally, the names of the Jewish and Muslim God are an interesting point to consider in our search for the connection between western religion and Atenism. Adon is the first name given to the Jewish God. It is a mispronunciation of Aten. Adonai 'My Lords' is the plural form of Adon, which is translated as lord. In the Hebrew Bible, it is only used to refer to God. In Jewish culture, it is forbidden to pronounce God's name the way that it is spelled, so, in prayers it is pronounced Adonai; my Aten? Allah is the name given to the Muslim god which again has uncanny tone references to Aten and Adon.

To remain true to the original principles and the Land of Egypt the book tends to use some contemporary names and parts of the Ancient-Egyptian calendar to place events, although in certain places I have found it necessary to use the Gregorian calendar simply to assist the reader. The Egyptian calendar was split into eras of Pharaohs' reigns, each year being given a chronological number. Hence the year a Pharaoh commenced his reign would be Year one, the next year, Year two, and so on. Each year consisted of 365 days, split into three seasons of 120 days. The first season (June to September), the flooding season, was known as Akhet; the second (October to February), the growing season, Peret, with Shemu (February to June), the harvesting season, completing the agricultural year. A period of five epagomenic days (leap days) ensured a full year. A copy of a letter from the Steward of Memphis referring to Amenhotep IV (Akhenaten), advised that on Day 13, Month 8, in the fifth year of his reign, the king arrived at the site of the new city Akhetaten. So, we know that Akhenaten visited his new capital on 13 January 1348 BC.

The table below shows the Egyptian calendar vis-à-vis Gregorian calendar.

Gregorian Calendar	Egyptian Calendar	Egyptian Name	Season
June	Month 1	Thoth	Flood
July	Month 2	Paophi	Flood
August	Month 3	Athyr	Flood
September	Month 4	Khoyak	Flood
October	Month 5	Tybi	Growing
November	Month 6	Mekhir	Growing
December	Month 7	Phamenat	Growing
January	Month 8	Pharmuti	Growing
February	Month 9	Pakhons	Harvest
March	Month 10	Payni	Harvest
April	Month 11	Epiphi	Harvest
May	Month 12	Mesore	Harvest

To assist with length and weight to help the reader understand more of the era I have occasionally used Ancient Egyptian measures. These are:

Teba approximately 2 cm

Mahi is just over 50 centimetres.

Khet around 50 metres

Ater just over 10 KM

Deben — around 100 grams

Finally, thanks need to be given to the many people without whom this book could not have been written, especially Juno my editor and Chris of Writers Services; their help has been phenomenal. My thanks also to my many 'readers', especially Margaret Terry, who must have been bored out of her mind with all of the edits.

Most of all though, I dedicate this book to my ever-loving wife and soul-mate Hazel. Her perseverance and encouragement were boundless.